C000279786

ELIMINATION

MARK SEXTON

ArrowGate

Published by Arrow Gate Publishing Ltd 2020

14 13 12 11 10 9 8 7 6 5

Copyright © Mark Sexton 2020

This novel is entirely a work of fiction. The names, characters, and incidents portrayed in it are the work of the author's imagination. Any resemblance to actual persons, living or dead, events or localities is entirely coincidental.

The right of Mark Sexton to be identified as the author of this work has been asserted by him in accordance with the Copyright, and Designs Patent Act 1988.

All rights reserved. No part of this publication may be reproduced, stored in or introduced into a retrieval system, or transmitted, in any form or by any means (electronic, mechanical, photocopying, recording or otherwise) without the prior written permission of the publisher. Any person who does any unauthorised act in relation to this publication may be liable to criminal prosecution and civil claim for damages.

A CIP catalogue record for this book is available from the British Library.
ISBN 978-1-913142-12-4

Arrow Gate Publishing 85, Great Portland Street, London W1W 7LT

Book cover design and images conceived by Natalie Sexton

This book is sold subject to the condition that it shall not, by way of trade or otherwise, be lent, re-sold, hired out, or otherwise circulated without the publisher's prior consent in any form of binding or cover other than that in which it is published and without a similar condition including this condition being imposed on the subsequent purchaser
Visit **www.arrowgatepublishing.com** to read more about our books and to buy them. You will also find articles, author inter-views, writing tips and news of any author events, and you sign up for our e-newsletters so that you're always first to read about our new releases.

Acknowledgements

To my beautiful daughters Natalie and Charlotte, now you know anything, and everything is possible.

To Spencer Honnibal, writer, editor and ghost writer. Thank you for your help, advice, support and professionalism. You went above and beyond what I expected, and I will always be eternally grateful. Without you, this book would never have been possible.

To Sandra David and all your team at Arrow Gate Publishing, thank you from the bottom of my heart, thank you for believing in me and bringing my book to life.

11 OCLOCK AT NIGHT and the sound of sirens echoed around the houses, blue strobe lights illuminating the darkened streets. A police car pulled up outside 24 Birch Close, PC Patrick's muscular, twelve stone frame climbed out of the driver's seat, closely followed by PC Arnold. 26-years-old and with a face that was far too pretty for a job in the force, Kate was the daughter of a recently-retired police officer who had a brother in the job also.

"Let's do this," Pat told her.

They approached the well-to-do, detached house, whose windows glowed from the lights on both floors. PC Patrick knocked and, almost straight away, a tearful female in her forties opened the door. She'd been punched at least twice in her face – her left eye was badly swollen, and there was a small cut under her eyelid that was bleeding profusely. She dabbed the laceration with a tea towel, but blood continued to flow, saturating the towel. Her mouth was also swollen, her top lip cut, but not bleeding.

"You'd better come in," she said, a grim expression on her heavily-furrowed face.

"Thank you, Mrs Cleverly," said Pat.

She walked them into her lounge, sitting on what looked like a stupidly expensive corner settee. Pat looked around the rest of the room, which was very tastefully decorated and clear evidence of money in the family. He shook his head as he stared at the woman's battered face.

"Can you tell me who did that to your face?"

"My husband, Derek," Mrs Cleverley responded in a quiet, shaky voice. "He's upstairs and said he'll kick off with the Old Bill when they arrive."

"Okay, well we'll worry about that in a minute. You're going to need to see a doctor, as that's likely to need stitches. Perhaps you can talk me through what happened today?"

"Today? This has been going on for over twenty years, and today is the first time I've called the police! My eyes have been black and blue more times than I can remember, and he's even broken my ribs. But enough is enough, officer – I can't do this anymore!" Mrs Cleverly started to cry, hiding her face in the blood-soaked towel.

PC Patrick spoke into his radio: "Calling Control from Tango Alpha One. Can we have an ambulance to twenty-four Birch Close? Female with an eye wound that's bleeding heavily." He turned to face the latest victim of a rapidly disintegrating society. "Mrs Cleverly, will you support a prosecution at court? Are there any children here?"

"No, no kids. They're grown up, and the youngest is at university. They saw this all the time. My eldest son left home because he was always fighting with his father, every time Derek had a go at me. Yes, I'll go to court. I'm forty-six-years-old, and I'm not going to be his punchbag anymore – it's over! It's over! This is it for me – lock him up and throw away the key!"

Pat was shocked to discover she'd been on planet earth 46 years. She was attractive, had a good figure and was slim, with glossy blonde, shoulder-length hair. And though her eyes were sunken, with black circles around them, and her cheekbones were protruding, she didn't look a day over 40, despite the years of abuse she'd endured at the hands of her husband. Heading towards the stairs, Pat gestured at PC Arnold to accompany him.

"Watch yourself," said Mrs Cleverley, her hand trembling. "He's a big chap with a rotten temper."

"Don't you worry about me," said PC Patrick as he climbed the stairs, trailed by PC Arnold. At the top of the stairs, he called out: "You up here, Derek? It's the police. We need to talk to you."

"GET THE FUCK OUT OF MY HOUSE! COME IN HERE, AND I SWEAR I'LL KICK OFF!" Barked a voice from a room at the end of the hallway.

PC Patrick walked to the bedroom door, opened it, and stood there looking at Derek, a well-built man in his mid-forties, sat on the edge of a massive bed in a spacious bedroom. Standing, he was a good six foot two and around sixteen stone, with broad shoulders and a slight belly visible under his shirt. Bristling with rage, he eyeballed Pat.

"I fucking told you to get out of my house! I'll kick off, so get out now!"

As Derek started to walk towards the officers, PC Patrick rushed over and, with both hands, shoved him in the chest, knocking him onto the bed. In a flash, Pat grabbed his handcuffs and snapped them shut around Derek's left wrist. Dragging him onto the floor, Pat pulled him onto his stomach and forced his handcuffed arm behind his back.

"Put your other arm behind your back, or I'll break your fucking wrist!"

"Okay, okay! Ease off, for fuck's sake!"

Derek put his other arm behind his back, and Pat handcuffed him with his hands back-to-back.

"You are under arrest for beating up your wife. For being a cowardly woman beater. For the twenty-six years of abuse that poor woman has had to suffer, you're a disgrace!"

Derek snarled as he was cautioned, while PC Arnold stood at the ready, right behind. As PC Patrick walked Derek down the stairs, Kate followed, before heading into the lounge to advise Mrs Cleverley. The flashing lights outside heralded the arrival of an ambulance, paramedics were streaming out of it while PC Patrick quite literally threw Derek into the back of his police car. When Kate climbed into the back of the car, next to Derek, Pat went back into the house to address Mrs Cleverley.

"Don't worry. We'll take Derek to the cells. Now, get yourself to the hospital, and we'll catch up with you there in about thirty minutes. I can assure you he won't be going anywhere until at least midday tomorrow afternoon."

"Thank you, officer," said Mrs Cleverley, smiling frailly.

Climbing behind the wheel, PC Patrick drove towards the local nick, about ten minutes away. To his considerable surprise, Derek remained silent throughout the duration, his snarling belligerence of minutes before nowhere to be seen. In a rare occurrence for a patrol car, nobody breathed a word during the drive.

When they reached the police station, PC Patrick took hold of Derek and marched him inside, PC Arnold a step or two behind. At the cell block, the Custody Sergeant awaited. A touch effeminate in appearance, he was in his late thirties and clean-shaven with perfectly set hair, a flawless complexion and sky-blue eyes that had an almost otherworldly feel to them; framed in a pair of thick-rimmed glasses.

"Sergeant, this is Derek Cleverley. He's been arrested for assaulting his wife, who's been left with a nasty bruised and cut eye, and a split lip."

Starting to enter the relevant information onto the station's computer, the Custody Sergeant looked up over his glasses.

"Why's he been handcuffed?"

"He made the mistake of thinking he could intimidate and bully me the way he does his wife. He failed, Sarge."

"He's not the first, and I'm sure he won't be the last, Pat," smiled the Custody Sergeant.

PCs Patrick and Arnold left the custody block and went to the officers' paperwork room, in which a handful of other officers were present, along with the Shift Sergeant, Dave Rose, a tough nut with a sprinkling of scars dotted over his arms and face.

"How bad are her injuries?" he asked, tucking a biro behind an ear.

"Nasty, Sarge. He'll go down for this. She's at the hospital, but we'll need photographs of her injuries and from inside the house – there's blood everywhere. Kate can go to the house. I'll go to the hospital and make a start on her statement, while she still wants to make a complaint against him."

"Okay, well done, Pat."

While Pat left the room to head to the hospital, Kate picked up a camera with which to photograph Mrs Cleverley's injuries.

"He just knows what to do every time," said Kate, flicking her head at Pat. "Cleverley's a bloody big bloke, and Pat just totally demoralised him. He makes me feel useless! I just stand and watch, Sarge."

"Don't flatter him, PC Arnold. I can see that noggin of his swelling by the second."

"Seeing's believing," smirked Pat, who winked at the Sergeant.

En route to the hospital shortly afterwards, a call came in over the radio:

"Any unit, immediate response please to flat twenty-three Lime Court. Marie Jones is on the phone – there are people at the door trying to break in."

"For god's sake, not again!" sighed Pat.

He hoped somebody else would take the call. So, he waited. Nobody did. Around 20 seconds' silence. Then:

"This is a second call. Please, any unit to twenty-three Lime Court."

"Tango Alpha One, I'm just around the corner," Pat said, more out of duty than desire. "I'll go."

"Thanks, Pat. I'm sure you know Marie. She sounds in drink, and I could hear lots of shouting and banging in the background."

Arriving at the block of flats that housed Marie, Pat parked up and got out of the police car. Stepping past piles of torn, bulging bin bags that spewed leftovers, dirty tampons and spent bottles of alcohol, he entered the block, the familiar sight of graffitied walls greeting him, accompanied by the stench of rotting urine as he scaled its stairwell. This was a building where the no-hopers and scroungers ended up. And, as a consequence, one where the local police tended to spend far too much of their valuable, increasingly scarce time.

Pat walked up the stairs to the fourth floor. It was quiet on his arrival and, as he reached Marie's flat, he clocked a newly-fitted door littered with boot marks. If past form were anything to go by, she'd be needing another soon enough.

He knocked on the door and shouted: "Marie, it's Pat!"

A few seconds later, Marie opened the door. Drunk, and very possibly high too, she smiled at Pat.

"Hey, Patty, I'm glad it's you. The others never do anything. They just, well … you know. You know what I mean."

"What do they want this time, Marie?"

Marie and Pat had known each other for years. They were brought up in the same neighbourhood, went to the same schools, and were in the same classes between the ages of 4 and 16. They even had a sort of boyfriend/girlfriend relationship, but it didn't last long, and they remained friends. Jones was a school dancing champion who went onto bigger and better things after leaving school. Aged 20, she went on a dancing tour, where she met and married Darren Jones, a fellow dancer on the tour.

Pat remembered how happy they'd been on their wedding day; wondering what kind of path lay ahead for them both and now he knew. Darren became a successful talent agent, while Marie stayed at home to look after their twin boys, Alistair and Raymond. The perfect life they had ended abruptly in the winter of 2003. Marie was at home on a cold, snowy Sunday night when two police officers knocked at her door. They were invited in, and Marie's life, as she knew it, ended with the words that continued to haunt her every drink and the drug-fuelled day thereafter:

"Mrs Jones, I'm afraid we have some bad news. There's been an accident. A truck lost control veered across a carriageway and crashed head-on with two oncoming vehicles. One of those vehicles was a blue BMW, registration number D4 REN. I'm sorry, Mrs Jones, but the occupants had no chance. Paramedics did everything they could, but the three people in the car were dead at the scene."

Just like that, her husband and 10-year-old twin boys were gone. Marie never recovered, turning to alcohol, prescription drugs and, finally, smack and other, far more corrosive substances that stole so much of who she was. Her lavish lifestyle disappeared. She became bankrupt, homeless, and lost her family and friends along the way.

Pat lost touch with Marie soon after the funeral. Their paths crossed again two years ago when he responded to a disturbance at the same flat. On that foggy, shitty day, he was stunned to see her at the flat. It had been at least 7/8 years since their paths had last crossed, and time hadn't been kind to her.

Once a beautiful, elegant woman, he found himself looking at a red-faced, haggard, skinny mess. Her heavily bagged eyes bore no resemblance to their vibrant counterparts of old, her greying hair was matted and dirty, her once sparkling white teeth a nicotine yellow; heavily entrenched lines that made her once beautiful face look like a roadmap of wrinkles, and fading, flaking nail varnish that looked weeks old. In fact, she was so far removed from the woman he knew that he didn't recognise her until she hugged him and told him who she was.

Pat tried to help her over the couple of years that had passed since, but she was too far gone. Police were now regulars at her flat, and she had become a constant drain on time and resources, forever calling the emergency services to get rid of the other drunks who would often spend two to three days at a time getting paralytic with her ... helping her to forget; until those soul-sapping moments of post-obliteration clarity shook her to the core, bringing it all back, after that the process would begin all over again.

Nobody else knew about their acquaintanceship. Marie respected Pat too much to ever let it be known that they had a past, with enough awareness of male 'banter' to realise his colleagues would slaughter him for their association, however loose. And so, it remained just between them; their awkward, but perfectly harmless alliance.

"They kept kicking my door and screaming through the letterbox. It's payday, see, and they know I've been to get some supplies." She pointed at the corner of the room, where a plastic bag bulged with cheap cider and vodka.

"Okay, I'll have a look around. I suppose it's the usual suspects. Lock the door and don't open it. Marie, are you listening to me?"

She nodded her head, stood up and shook PC Patrick's hand, holding onto it as she saw him to the door.

"Thanks again, Pat," she smiled weakly, releasing her grip, Pat removing his hand and involuntarily wiping it on his trousers. "You're a good man. It's the anniversary next week – ten years. It only seems like yesterday. Ten years, Pat."

Marie started to cry, and Pat very gently touched her cheek, the hostility he was so used to using as a defence crumbling as he saw the pain in her eye. There was a crushed, broken-hearted expression on her tired, worn-out face.

"I know, I know. I'll pop in next week. Make sure you have enough money for food, and not of the liquid kind. Okay?"

"Okay," Marie nodded, looking anything but convincing.

PC Patrick left the flat, hearing Marie lock her door as he walked to the stairs. He checked the stairwells, but nobody was around.

"Tango Alpha One to Control. There's nobody around now. Jones has been checked. She's high and drunk but has locked her door. No offences here, so can you close that incident please."

Driving to City Hospital, in Dudley Road, Pat found the ward Mrs Cleverley was in. Her bruising was even more pronounced, and, to his surprise, she provided a statement of complaint against her husband. So many didn't, perpetuating a perpetual cycle of abuse. His job had induced in him a particular dislike of bullies, especially the knuckle-dragging Neanderthals who got a kick out of hurting women. Social scroungers and dossers were ever-presents on his shit list, but misogynistic aggressors were right up there with nonces and those who preyed on the most vulnerable in society's sewer of shame.

After leaving the hospital, Pat drove home, sitting in front of the box. He sunk into a sofa, in the opening rounds of what would be a long battle with age. Unable to settle, he paid little attention to the crap on TV, disappearing into his thoughts until flashing back into the present, the following day already tainted by the certainty of having it stolen away by fucking idiots with nothing better to do than indulge themselves at the expense of others. Switching the box off, he traipsed upstairs and called it a night, folding his hands over his quilt.

CHAPTER 2

RISING AT 5 AM for a 7 am shift, Pat showered, washed a slice of heavily-buttered toast down with a strong coffee, then made his way into work. Always first in, despite being the senior shift member, he would have the morning cuppa ready for the shift and the Sergeant's briefing. The briefing room was spacious enough to comfortably accommodate a trio of large tables jammed together, around which a dozen or so chairs were stationed. Its walls stained by reminders of the crème de la crème of contemporary society – a multiplicity of local crooks peering down at them, none of whom would win any beauty pageants; their ugly mugshots silently sneering.

The early shift's staff rolled in one by one, but on this occasion, it featured a new face: a male officer, who sat quietly, working on some paperwork while the rest of the shift chatted away. The three female officers on the shift stared as if transfixed, at this handsome new officer. Six-foot-tall with thick dark hair, neatly trimmed goatee beard and pearly white teeth, he had the kind of physique that suggested some serious training, his muscular trunk impossible to hide in his police regulation shirt. Around the mid-thirties mark, he looked like something more befitting the catwalk than the police force.

Sergeant Rose was a straight-talking, but well-liked and capable member of the force. In his late forties and standing at around 5ft 7in, he had short dark hair, the hint of a middle-aged spread and radiated a musky aftershave that left its trace whenever he went – not to everyone's tastes. Straight-backed, he strode into the briefing room, carrying a large bundle of crimes and incident sheets, sitting next to the new officer.

"Morning, you lot. First things first, this is our new shift member. It's his first day today, fresh out of the box. I'm sure he won't mind me introducing him. This is Kyle Aston, a transferee from the Met Police, with five years' experience. He's come here, not to take over from Pat, making the tea, but because we're one down, with Lucy on maternity leave. I'm sure you'll all make him very welcome. Pat, for the first week or so, can you show him around and introduce him to the lovely lowlifes, drunks, druggies, homeless, battered wives and, of course, the wonderful residents from our favourite block of flats."

PC Patrick nodded and smiled at Kyle.

"Err, ladies, put it back in your pants, please. Kyle, watch yourself around those three, either on their own or as a collective. You have been warned!"

"Thanks for the tip, Sarge," smiled Kyle, speaking in a refined English accent with a hint of cockney twang.

There was a collective chuckle from the ten-strong shift. Sergeant Rose wagged a finger at Pat.

"Pat, mister wife-beater was remanded and in court first thing the next morning. He admitted hitting her – he says in self-defense! What a complete tosser ... oh, and he's making a complaint against the arresting officer for nearly breaking his arm!"

A loud cheer from the entire shift. A smattering of applause. Every week, without fail, somebody somewhere complained about Pat, which he took as a source of pride, considering the kind of people reporting them.

"Kyle, please don't be put off," smiled Sergeant Rose. "He's a pussy cat."

"More like a Rottweiler, Sergeant," said Martin, or Squirrel as he was more commonly known, on account of his puffy cheeks, and teeth that leant forward where they met his mouth.

"Right, Pat, can you and Kyle go to St Mary's. Carl Baker has gone walkabout again and is said to have a knife. He was heading towards the park and is adamant he's going to end it all this time. Don't rush, the call came in at four in the morning and the night shift were too busy to take a look. If he's already done it, there's nothing we can do."

"Yes, Sarge," said PC Patrick. "Can I request that for the rest of the tour, I actually get to deal with real crimes and real criminals, instead of all these wasters? When I find Baker, I'll be arresting him."

"Arresting him? Are you nuts? He'll be a constant watch. Just take him back to St Mary's," sniffed Rose.

"Nope, he'll be arrested. You wait and see."

"Oooooohhhh!"

They liked that one. Pat, less so. He stared at the desk and shook his head, sick of the repetitive behaviour of the tossers wasting his and other officers' time. If more of them were banged-up, even temporarily, it gave the communities they terrorised a breather; and people like him the vague hope of catching far more serious criminals, doing what he was paid to do.

Once the briefing had finished, and each officer, in turn, introduced themselves to PC Aston, Pat picked up a set of keys and went out to the car park to check his police vehicle, PC Arnold hurrying towards him, a goofy smile splashed across her face.

"Pat, I want to know everything about him! I so need to know if he's single. He's very cute, and I expect a report on my desk by midday."

PC Patrick smiled as Kate skipped away, like a little schoolgirl with her first crush. After finishing giving his vehicle the once over, he headed back into the office, sitting next to PC Aston.

"For the first couple of days, just follow my lead. The paperwork is horrific here, as I'm sure it was down the old smoke. It won't take you too long to find your feet. Don't forget to get all your computer passwords as soon as possible. When you have them, I'll show you the force website." Pat stood up. "Right, grab your stuff. Let's go and get this fucking waster before he does something stupid."

The three female officers were all stood together, whispering and giggling. It couldn't have been more obvious that they were discussing PC Aston.

"For god's sake, you lot, get a life. Come on, Kyle, before they pounce."

PCs Patrick and Aston picked up their kit bags and went downstairs to the police car, where Pat handed his new colleague its keys.

"Are you okay to drive?"

"No problem."

Jumping behind the wheel, Kyle drove out of the car park and headed towards St Mary's mental hospital, a regular haunt a fifteen-minute drive away.

"This fucking hospital is useless," Pat began. "Almost daily, we get society's finest escaping or running off, and then we have to go and find them. Most of them in there are faking it, and just do it to have a warm bed and some hot food. Get used to coming here – it's a routine pit stop."

"Sounds interesting. How long you been in the job?"

"Too bloody long – over eighteen years now. So, you've done five in the Met … were you reactive?"

"Yeah, reactive."

"So, the million-dollar question is: what brought you up here?"

"I just needed a change."

"From what?"

"From, well … you know … just a change."

"Let me guess: women."

"What else, Pat?"

Other than uneasy small talk, PC Aston said nothing else on the way to St Mary's, but Pat figured it was his first day and that he'd open up as the week went on. Very few new recruits shot out of their shells, emerging much more slowly once they'd wedged their feet under the table. That didn't tend to take long, the intensity of the job tossing them into a world that made old friends of nightmares.

After arriving at the mental hospital, Pat pressed the buzzer to the side of the entrance and announced himself. Stepping inside, the receptionist rolled her eyes at him.

"Sorry, but he's run off again. It was hours ago. He said he was off to the park to kill himself. That he's got a knife ... but we doubt it. You must be sick of us, and Carl. I know you must have more important things to do. I'm so sorry."

There was a genuine embarrassment in her expression, which became even more awkward with every additional visit. The police had issued guidance to make the premises more secure, but the hospital hadn't acted, and so the hospital's so-called residents saw it as a recurrent invitation to take flight.

"Okay, no problem. We'll go and have a look for him. It's breakfast time, so if he returns, give us a call, and we'll come back. He won't be too happy to see me – I told him the last time he did this that if he played up again, I was going to arrest him for wasting police time."

"When was that, Pat?" asked PC Aston.

"Two days ago, twice last week, and two or three times the week before. Do you get the picture, Kyle?"

He looked at Pat in disbelief as they walked back to the car, driving to the nearby park. They got out on foot and entered the expansive parklands, containing a small forest area, lake, children's play area, tennis courts, football pitches and cricket pavilion.

"He'll be hanging around the pavilion. There's a bench in the open porch. This cocky little prick is a total waster. He pisses me off so much – never worked, uses the police as his private taxi firm, hangs around the hospital, and scrounges free tea and food. Society owes him, and he knows his rights … blah blah blah. We always hope that one day he actually carries out his threat to top himself … but I'm not holding out any hope. He takes up so much of ours, the hospital's and social services' time. He's a fucking drain, Kyle."

Pat took a breath. He realised he was ranting, but it was so ingrained in him that it had become an integral part of his personality; his politics. Decent society was collapsing and, with it, his and his fellow officers' morale.

"I'm sorry for going on, Kyle, but this lot really piss me off. Get used to it, pal. It's all we seem to be dealing with these days – mental health, druggies, alcoholics, missing persons who are never missing, and wife beaters. I can't remember the last time I had a good foot chase after a car thief or burglar.

"The shit of society, mate. One per cent of the population scrounging and demanding they use the police, ambulances and hospitals while getting extra money because they're alcoholics, free prescriptions because they're druggies, council houses rent-free, and they don't pay council tax or any other form of tax. Yet the other ninety-nine per cent, who work and pay their way, rarely use the police or hospitals – they just keep the scum of society comfortable in their free, piss-taking lives."

Silence for a few moments as they closed on the cricket pavilion.

"I've no doubt this is how it is down the smoke, but tenfold. I promise I'll cheer up as the day goes on. It's your first day, and I'm supposed to be setting an example. Rosey will be livid if he finds out I've gone off on one like this. Mind you; he's even worse than me."

Kyle chuckled.

"Pat, I get it. Eighteen years of this must drag you down. If I last that long, I'll probably feel the same."

Sure enough, as they reached the pavilion, there he was, sitting on a bench, in all his glory: one Carl fucking Baker.

"Alright, Pat!" he smirked. "Have you come to take me for breakfast? Pissed me off last night, they did. I only wanted a fag. Not a lot to ask, is it – one bloody fag?"

Carl Baker was 30-years-old, skinny, around six-foot-tall, with greasy black hair that looked as if it hadn't been washed in months. He had dirty yellow teeth, a beard that wasn't so much hipster as couldn't be arsed, and had the same filthy, pungent clothes on that he wore when Pat last saw him a couple of weeks before.

An alcoholic, Baker was also dependent on heroin and happy to abuse any other drug he could get his hands on. A thorn in the side of the police force, and the entire community in which he operated, he routinely stole from shops and residents alike to fund his habits, while claiming to have mental health issues. Another of society's finest, this one had the lot. Whenever he was arrested and brought into custody, he had to be continually watched by a police officer posted outside his cell door, until he was released – another complete waste of time and money.

"Do you remember a few days ago?" Pat began. "I said that if I had to come looking for you again, I was going to nick you and put you before the court for wasting police time. Well, guess what – you're nicked, Baker."

PC Patrick grabbed Baker by the scruff of the neck and quite literally dragged him to the police car.

"Oh, fuck off, Pat! You'll only get a bollocking for wasting your precious resources. You know as well as I do that I'll be out, back on it, in no time."

He was right. But amid the cockiness was a trace of doubt. The little twat knew that if he were locked up all day, he wouldn't get his medication, drugs, alcohol, free food and a warm bed from St Mary's. Wishing that another spell inside would give Baker the kick up the arse he needed, but knowing different, Pat slung him onto the car's back seat.

"Shut the fuck up, Baker! I'm sick to death of you and your bullshit. I'm not playing your games anymore. You're in all day because it'll take me all fucking day to write my statement. And that means you'll be in all night and put before the court in the morning."

"C'mon," said Baker, the trace of doubt morphing into full-blown terror, the deepening realisation of his predicament forcing a change in tact. "Let me go, and I promise I won't fuck up again.

One more chance. Take me back to St Mary's and I'll keep me trap shut."

Ignoring Baker, Pat spoke into his radio: "Tango Alpha One to Control. Just to let you know, the delightful Mr Baker has been located. We have him in the back of the car, so can you let Custody know we have one coming in, travelling time from St Mary's park."

"Tango Alpha One from Tango Alpha Five Zero," came Sergeant Rose's voice across the police radio.

"Go ahead, Sarge."

"What's he been arrested for? Has he got a knife on him?"

"No, Sarge – no knife. I've arrested him for theft of oxygen." There was silence over the air, Pat picturing officers and Control staff chortling at his irreverent brand of humour. "Wasting police time, Sarge. He was warned two days ago."

"Pat, can you call me on my office extension."

Using his police radio, PC Patrick dialled Sergeant Rose's number.

"Pat, what on earth? He'll be a constant watch, and we're too busy to babysit him. Custody won't be pleased either. Take him to St Mary's, then come back in. Kyle needs to sort his passwords for the computers."

"Okay, if I must. He gave it his usual cocky bollocks routine, to begin with, but bricked it when he knew I was serious. It was worth it just for that, Rosey. We'll drop him off. See you in a bit."

"Good man. Hurry up, Pat – I need another cuppa. And bring some biscuits."

"Right, you time-wasting little shit, it's your lucky day," said Pat after hanging up. "We've been ordered to take you back to St Mary's."

"Thanks, Pat, you're a proper top bloke. I promise you won't hear a peep out of me again."

"Shut up, Baker. You're boring, and you're a liar. Don't say another word, or I'll change my mind."

PC Aston didn't speak at all. He watched, listened and took it all in. When they arrived at St Mary's, Baker was pulled out of the rear of the car and frogmarched into the reception.

"Carl, Doctor Faraz has said there's nothing wrong with you, so you can go home," said the receptionist by way of a greeting.

"Oh, come on, Liz, that's bull, and you know it. Have I missed breakfast?"

"Carl, you're not coming in here today, and you need to stop coming here full stop. Alcohol and drugs are your problems. This is a secure mental health institute, not a dosshouse. Doctor Faraz has given all staff strict instructions that you are not to be admitted here anymore. Sorry, Carl, doctor's orders." Liz seemed very pleased with herself as she glanced at Pat. "I bet you've been waiting a long time to hear that from this place?"

"That's it, then, Carl," said Pat, struggling to restrain a smugness he wanted to unleash. "Plan B methinks. Come on, back to your taxi. Chop chop – places to go, people to see and all that."

Baker was speechless. No bullshit promises were offered up. He looked like his entire world had collapsed there and then – no more free food, cups of tea and, most importantly, a warm bed in winter. PC Patrick walked him back to the car, followed by a bemused PC Aston.

"Right, Carl, where are we taking you? I'm not having you running around all day, phoning us and wasting our time. Somewhere I know you'll be safe, fed and watered. Where is that place?"

"Better take me to our Michelle's, then," groaned Baker. "She should be still up. You know where she lives."

"Great, Michelle's it is, then." Pat looked at Kyle. "Michelle's his older sister. She works, pays bills, and has never been in trouble with the police. The total opposite of what's behind us."

"Right. But will Michelle be okay with us turning up there? I mean… well, you know… he's not very …?"

"Clean, decent, respectable, nice to look at, and baring gifts?" Pat interjected.

"Yeah. If he turned up on my doorstep, I'd be very politely telling you where to go."

"Leave it to me. I'll use my charm, wit and, if all else fails, I'll faint and get the sympathy vote. We must get him in there. Otherwise, he'll give us hell for the rest of the shift."

The car drew to a halt outside 15 The Avenue, a small but tidy two up/two down with clean curtains, flowers in a pretty front garden, a hardwood door wearing a well-painted coat of royal blue and a brand new, gleaming red Ford Fiesta parked outside.

"Not what I was expecting, Pat," said Kyle. "Very nice."

"Wait here with brother 'IT', while I see what kind of mood she's in."

PC Patrick knocked on the door, which was almost immediately opened by Michelle, standing in a dressing gown. 36-years-old, with shoulder-length blonde hair, her largely unlined face wore the expression of somebody who knew what was coming next. Behind them, PC Aston had to open the car door to get some fresh air – Baker needed a wash and a change of clothes, and he could hear the conversation between PC Patrick and Michelle.

"That was quick, Michelle. How are you? I love your new car."

"I saw you pull up just as I was closing my curtains to go to bed. As you know, I work shifts. In fact, I've only just finished a twelve-hour night shift at the care home. I'm tired, irritable and not very pleased to see you. Why would that be? Hmmm, let me think. You have that thing in the back of your car, who some say is my brother. Well, I want a DNA test. Who's kicked him out this time? The tramps down the park?"

"Look, he told us to bring him here. He needs a shower, his clothes washing, a shave and a couple of toothbrushes, please. Speaking frankly, it's here or the cells, and I don't have the time today, Michelle."

Michelle walked over to the police car, staring at her brother. "I'm ashamed of you, Carl, but you know that? Mom was ashamed of you, and you knew that too. This is the last time you'll be coming to my door unless you sort your shit out. I'll disown you, and then you'll have no one. No one! Are you listening?"

Michelle gestured with her thumb for Carl to get into the house. Climbing out of the car, he sheepishly walked up to her drive, accompanied by Kyle, before entering her home.

"This is the last time, Pat. Seriously, look at him – he'll stink my bloody house out! I've only just recovered from his last visit, courtesy of your lot. I had to fumigate the damn place! I'm on nights tonight, but I'll try and make sure he stays home while I'm at work. But I can't have him here long-term. It's one night, then he's out. And you owe me, big time, mister."

"Thanks, you're a diamond. I promise I'll never darken your door again."

"Well, you can, but only if you bring him along. He's cute." She offered Kyle a lopsided grin. "What's your name, PC Cute?"

"Oh hello, I'm PC Aston. The new kid on the block. Nice to meet you, Michelle."

After flashing Kyle another grin, Michelle went back into the house and, despite closing the door, shouted loudly enough to be heard outside: "You fucking stink! Get in that bathroom now!"

Pat and Kyle got back into the car, laughing as Pat took his turn at the wheel, driving off.

"Fuck me – that was close. Michelle doesn't deserve a wanker of a brother like him. Thank god it's not our problem now."

"You're a right little charmer, aren't you, Pat! You had her eating out of your hand. Pure class, mate!"

"Why thank you, PC Cutey Pie."

Back at the station, Sergeant Rose met them as they were about to enter the officers' room: "Well, where is he?"

"He's safe and well. Not at St Mary's – they told him never to come back. It was priceless, seeing his face drop when they finally grew some balls and let him have it. We took him to his sister's. Michelle helped us out big time, Sarge. She'll be home all day as she's on nights, but promised he'll stay there until tomorrow … then he's out."

"Good news – twenty-four hours' peace! I'll make sure the Inspector knows, as he was starting to get aerated. Kyle, we need to go through your computer passwords, so you can access the force sites. Pat, get that bloody kettle on."

THE REMAINDER OF THE shift went off without incident. There was just one more early to go before the fun started over the weekend and Pat, back on the night shift, would get to see the worst of it.

The first of his shift in again, at 6.30 am sharp, he washed all the cups, then made everybody's tea, ready for the morning briefing. The rest of them arrived a few minutes apart and, finally, Sergeant Rose entered the briefing room to find a variety of faces staring back at him. Some – typically the younger, greener coppers – were wide-eyed and keen to impress, while the older, more cynical members of the team, with their drained, weary expressions, looked like an apocalypse was about to strike.

"Morning, team. One more early, then the weekend madness. Kyle, nights here at the weekend are not for the faint-hearted! Anyway, you all know your call signs – the same as yesterday, please. Rob and Tony, can you two have a look at this, please. We've had a complaint from the coffee shop on the high street.

The local drunks are starting to gather outside and are harassing customers. Make sure you do this one right, as it's come from the Inspector. Ian and Faye, a domestic from last night – the husband is locked up for a nasty assault, and the complainant is still in the hospital. Can you go and relieve the night shift and get a statement from her?

"Kate, can you go down to the cell block. We have a constant watch – the wonderful Jimmy Collins was arrested on warrant last night. Someone from the night shift is down there, so straight away, please. And while you're all here, the coroner's inquest for the Butler boys' hearing has been set for next week. Myself, Pat, Tony, Kate and Rob have been asked to attend. It's at ten am, at the courthouse. Shoes shined, and shirts ironed. Boys, clean-shaven, please. Ladies, no nail polish and hair up. Yes, Kate – hair up. Pat, can you and Kyle have a look at the open incident for the bail hostel. Simon Walters kicked off last night. I'm not sure if he's to be arrested, so be careful – especially if he knows he's being recalled to prison. He will kick off. That's it – get out."

While the officers went about their business, Sergeant Rose gestured at Pat to follow him into his office: "Pat, can I have a word before you go?"

"Sure." Pat stepped inside. Stood on the spot, waiting for Rosey to overtake.

"Shut the door, Pat."

Closing the door, PC Patrick sat down. "What's up, Sarge?"

"I just wondered how you were getting on with the pin-up. What's he like?"

"Nice enough," said Pat. "Quiet. A bit too polite, but I've no doubt that'll change in the weeks to come. I went through the paperwork with him yesterday, and he can log onto the computer and view the incident lists. It's early doors yet, though, Sarge. Ask me after the weekend."

Sergeant Rose opened his mouth to speak, only for the police radio to crackle into life: "Any unit, please. An immediate response. Hysterical female calling from fifteen The Avenue, saying there's been a hanging. Any unit please."

"You know who that is, Sarge," said Pat. "That twat, Baker. That's his sister's address. We left him there yesterday if you remember. She will be kicking him out, and he's acting the gimp."

"Oh, yes, of course. Respond to that, then, on your way to the hostel."

"I thought you'd say that." Pat spoke into his police radio: "Tango Alpha One, we'll take that one. It'll be the lovely Carl Baker being kicked out by his sister."

"Roger Tango Alpha One, the female was hysterical, and we've had a call from ambo, saying they're also responding."

Pat looked at Rosey. "On my way, Sarge."

Within minutes, blue lights flashing and sirens wailing, PCs Patrick and Aston were flying along in the police car, heading for 15 The Avenue.

"This'll be a load of bollocks, Kyle. She's kicking him out today, and he'll be playing mind games, threatening to top himself as usual. I can't wait to deal with this twat again."

PC Aston sat back, not breathing a word while Pat raced to the address. On their arrival, the front door was wide open, both officers rushing inside to find Michelle sitting, slumped, in her nurse's uniform, her back against the wall, sobbing.

"Michelle, what's he done this time?" asked Pat.

Unable to speak, Michelle pointed in the direction of the stairs. Her broken expression told Pat that this was more serious than he'd assumed. And as he and Kyle walked upstairs, they saw why. At the top of the stairs, a rope around his neck, a stool kicked away, Carl Baker's lifeless body hung like a rag doll. His eyes were wide open, his face purple and puffed out at the cheeks.

"Fuck me, he finally did it," said Pat. "I'm surprised he did it here, Kyle, but he finally fucking did it. Shit." He spoke into his police radio: "Tango Alpha One, we have a deceased male here, as a result of hanging. Can we have the Duty Sergeant and Scenes of Crime here, please? I can identify the deceased as Carl Baker. Next of kin is on scene."

"Roger, Tango Alpha One, received."

PC Patrick stood there, transfixed, looking at Baker's hanging body. All the hassle he'd caused over so many years, and now, here he was, a rotting hunk of flesh and bone. Pat must have been standing there a good few minutes before turning to speak to PC Aston, only to find he wasn't there. Heading back downstairs, Pat entered the kitchen, where Kyle was making a cup of tea for Michelle.

"Michelle, I don't know what to say. I mean, well ... you know, it's just ... you don't deserve this. This may be a stupid question, but are you up to giving a statement? The coroner will want one for the inquest, as you're next of kin and found him."

"I had a right go at him before I went to work last night, Pat," said Michelle, her voice trembling, her arms locked around her knees. "It's my fault, not yours. I really gave it to him both barrels, and he sat there and took it all, just like he always did. He made me all sorts of promises, just like he always did. It was such a shock, seeing him hanging there like that!" She paused a few moments and breathed out, Kyle handing her a mug of tea. "I'll give a statement. Let me just have this cuppa."

"Did he leave a note, Michelle?" asked Pat, hearing a car pull up outside. "Most people leave a note or tell someone."

"No – nothing."

Sergeant Rose stepped into the kitchen with his police hat under his arm.

"I did knock. I hope it's okay, me coming in unannounced, Michelle?"

Michelle nodded her head, and Sergeant Rose followed PC Patrick up the stairs to see Baker hanging.

"Well, there's something I never thought I'd see. Good result all round. One of society's biggest wasters finally did the decent thing."

"He certainly did, Sarge. I can't believe he did it here at Michelle's. He was a horrible lowlife, but he did like his sister. I thought he could at least have had the decency to do it at his own place."

"Who cares, Pat? We're well rid. Let's wait for SoCo, and then we can move him."

"Okay, Sarge. We're going to take a statement from Michelle before going to the bail hostel."

"You and Kyle carry on, Pat. I'll sort this here. I don't want you two tied up here for hours. Don't forget: be wary with Walters. He was proper kicking off last night and, according to the staff, this morning he's expecting us to nick him."

"Nice one, Sarge. I'll say goodbye to Michelle. Have fun."

Pat walked downstairs and into the kitchen, gently placing his hand on Michelle's shoulder.

'Kyle and I are going. The Sergeant will be sorting everything out with you. For what it's worth, Michelle, I'm really sorry this has happened to you."

"He's been a pain for you lot for years, in and out of prison and that St Mary's. You must be relieved. I know they will be and the hospital. Let's face it. He was never going to change. He was addicted to drugs, alcohol and anything else he could get his hands on. I'll have to move now. There's no way I can live here anymore. I'm going to stay with some friends for a while and take it from there."

"Okay, if there's anything you need, you know how to get in touch. Take care of yourself," said Pat, who left with Kyle.

Driving off, they headed towards the bail hostel.

"You must be pleased with that result, Pat – one of the biggest scroungers out of the way?"

"I'm going to sound like a heartless old bastard, but yes I am. I'm just feeling bad for Michelle, and the fact it was us that took him there in the first place. And now she wants to sell her lovely house. Oh well, not my problem anymore."

"No, it's not. And if Carl wasn't such a waster, none of this would've happened."

"I know," Pat nodded.

The car fell silent for the five-minute journey to the bail hostel, Baker's hanging corpse lingering in Pat's mind. As they parked up, he briefed Kyle.

"Right, Kyle, you're about to meet a really nasty piece of work. He smashed the kitchen up last night, and the hostel wants to make a complaint of criminal damage. He's expecting us. He's Simon Walters – burglar, drug dealer and cop hater. He's just done three years for crimes that included assaulting police. They let him out about a month ago, and he's still on licence. He's been getting more and more argumentative. Now, he doesn't like me because I can handle him, but he'll still have a go, so be on your guard."

"Okay, this sounds like a bit of a giggle."

They got out of the car and walked up to the door to the hostel, Pat pressing the buzzer on the intercom.

"Hello?" came a female voice.

"It's the police," said Pat.

The intercom buzzing, he pushed the entry door open. He and PC Aston went into the hostel's office, where three members of staff met them. Pat knew them all well, and by name – not that surprising, given he found himself there between a handful and twenty-odd times every single week.

"Hello, officers. The lovely Simon Walters came in last night, right on his curfew time. He was drunk, he went into the kitchen, and because there was no bread to make toast, he kicked the cupboard door off its hinges. The night staff tried to calm him down but failed, and he kicked two more cupboards that have now got big holes in them.

"He went to bed, and this morning he hasn't come out of his room. I went up to speak to him, but he told me to fuck off and said if the Old Bill turns up, he'll do to them what he did to the kitchen. So, we'd like to make a complaint of damage to the kitchen, and breach of his licence for coming back drunk and wreaking havoc."

"Okay, then. Let me have a look at the kitchen before we go and have a fight ... sorry, I meant to say chat," said Pat.

Making their way to the communal kitchen, PCs Patrick and Aston saw at first-hand the damage to the cupboards – three doors with holes in them, and one of them hanging by its hinges.

"Right, what room is he in please?"

"Seven, on the first floor," said a female member of staff.

Pat led the way, shadowed by Kyle, while the staff stayed at the bottom of the stairs, keeping a safe distance. Pat knocked on the door to room seven.

"I've already told you lot to fuck off and leave me alone!" bellowed an angry voice from the other side of the door.

"Simon, it's the police. Open the door."

"You can fuck off too! I hope there's more than you, coz I'm gonna fucking kick off!"

"Well, there is more than me, so open the door, or I will." No reply from inside. PC Patrick raised his voice and tried again: "I won't say this again, Walters. Open the fucking door, or I'll open it myself."

"Well, you'd better open it, coz I ain't!"

Pat looked at Kyle. "Stand back."

Raising his right leg, Pat gave the door an almighty kick. It flew off its hinges and crashed to the floor inside Walters's room.

"You fucking dickhead! That could've hit me!" Walters shouted as he jumped off a bed to confront the two officers stood in the doorway.

Six foot two tall, Walters was a skinhead with broad shoulders, tattoos all over his arms and wild eyes that looked on the brink of popping out of his head. He raised his right fist and motioned to punch PC Patrick, but PC Aston used his right arm to block the punch. He then punched Walters to the stomach with his left fist, kicked his feet from underneath him and, while he was dazed on the floor, pulled his hands behind his back, cuffing him. All very deliberate and controlled. PC Patrick looked on in surprise, shocked that the quiet man was capable of such pugilistic excellence.

Walters screamed and swore at the top of his voice: "LET ME OUT OF THESE CUFFS, YOU WANKERS! I'LL KICK YOUR FUCKING HEADS IN, YOU PIG BASTARDS!"

"You had your chance and failed, my son, so button it," said PC Aston.

"Just so you know, Walters: you're nicked for causing criminal damage and breach of your licence."

Pat proceeded to caution Walters, but Walters maintained his hard man act and swore throughout.

"Fuck you, pig! Fuck you! Take these cuffs off, you pair of cunts!"

"Sorry about this," Pat told the staff who hovered a few metres away. "But this particular problem won't be yours any longer."

Simon was dragged to his feet, still struggling and swearing, forcibly taken down the stairs and bundled into the police car, the door to which was slammed shut.

"Very tasty, I must say. Where did you learn to fight like that?" asked Pat.

"I was in the boy scouts, Pat."

"Well, so was I, and I don't remember them showing us stuff like that. Seriously, who taught you? The military?"

"No, I just did a little martial art here and there."

"I'm impressed. Walters is a nasty piece of work, and I've had a few rumbles with him in the past. I think you shocked him. Well done, though, mate. Really."

The officers left the hostel and drove towards the custody block at the police station, with Simon still shouting and swearing in the back of the car.

"Shut the fuck up! You were beaten by the better man today, and you're now getting on my nerves. You're nicked, going back to jail and in handcuffs. Accept defeat and act like a man, instead of a whining little pussy," said PC Aston.

"Fuck off, you cockney twat! Let me out of these handcuffs, and I'll show you who the pussy is! Then I'll rape your old lady, your missus, and your little cockney bastard kids!"

Kyle leant back in his chair, caught Pat's eye, and mouthed very quietly: "I'm not taking that off him, Pat. Is there somewhere en route where we can stop, so I can have another chat with him?"

Pat winked back at him and went on a slight detour, driving down a small track that led to the back of some allotments. Not overlooked by any houses, it was a secluded spot shielded by hedges, bushes and trees. Pat stopping the car, PC Aston shot out of the passenger's seat, opened the rear door closest to where Walters was sitting and wrenched him headfirst from the vehicle. Kyle then removed Walters's handcuffs and stood back.

"Get to your feet, you piece of shit! You don't know me, my missus, my old lady or my kids. The cuffs are off, so now you can see how much of a pussy I am – c'mon, give it your best shot!"

PC Aston stood with his arms folded across his chest. Walters got to his feet in silence and brushed the dirt from his clothes, remaining silent. The cockiness of before was absent, his formerly defiant posturing displaced by uncertainty at odds with the belligerence he typically exuded and revelled in.

"Just take me to the station, so I can go back to prison," he muttered, climbing back into the car and shutting the door.

"If you say anything abusive or insulting, I'll put the cuffs back on, so sit back and enjoy your last five minutes of freedom in comfort," said Kyle, getting back in the car.

Walters stared out of the window and didn't speak again on the journey to the station. At the station, he was booked into the custody block without so much as a peep. Both officers went to the report room, where PC Aston put some paperwork on the desk, before heading to the kitchen. Sergeant Rose wasn't present, still dealing with Baker's suicide, but other members of the shift were in the room.

"You'll be pleased to know that the pretty boy from London has just impressed the hell out of me," PC Patrick told PC Arnold. "He totally demoralised Simon Walters. I've never seen him so overpowered and timid. It was pretty spectacular, to say the least."

"Tell me more, Pat. Is this the man of my dreams at last?" Kate smiled.

"He could be, but I have the feeling there's more to him than meets the eye."

Pat sat down at a desk and started to update the hostel incident on a computer. A few minutes later, Sergeant Rose walked in, sitting next to him.

"Kate, has Pat told you the fantastic news about the delightful Mr Baker? He topped himself, so no more taking from that fucking waster."

"I heard it come over the air, Sarge. Yes, it is good news. Have you just come back from the scene?"

"Yep, SoCo have done their bit. He's been taken to the morgue, and a statement has been taken from his sister. I'm just going to sort the coroner's report and that, my dear, is that." Rose patted PC Patrick on the back. "Do what you do best, Pat, and stick the kettle on to celebrate."

"Will do, Sarge, but, blimey, it's only a suicide. What's with the smiles all of a sudden?"

"No, it's not just a suicide, Pat – it's a blessing in disguise. He's off the books for good now. No more constant watches, and no more running around all over the city looking for him every couple of days. It's a great result. Now get me that cuppa so I can put my feet up and enjoy the moment."

Pat went into the kitchen to find Kyle eating some rice and chicken, and a newspaper splayed out on the table in front of him.

"Rosey's in a great mood, celebrating Baker's hanging like he's just won an Oscar. I forgot to tell him about your destruction of Walters."

"Pat, don't bother. It was no big deal. Let me just eat this, and we'll go out and have a look around."

PC Patrick made the tea and took a cup in for Sergeant Rose, sitting back down at his station.

"He told me not to say anything, Rosey, but the boy wonder really has got it in his locker."

Sergeant Rose cocked his head Pat's way. "Got a pair of hands on him, has he?"

"He's got more than that, Sarge. Not only did he put Walters on his arse, but he also shut him the fuck up too. He was so calm and just, well… you don't often see a Bobby do that. He seems to have some special skills or something. Very clean-cut, very secretive, but a really capable chap."

"Pat, you bend people up into little balls and throw them into the back of police cars, so why isn't he allowed to too?"

"It's just not what I expected. I can't put my finger on it." Pat glanced at his watch. "Oh well, time to get going. Can I leave the Baker stuff to you, Rosey?"

"Oh, yes – the pleasure's all mine."

Pat went back into the report room and rejoined the other officers, who were drinking the cups of tea he'd made. PC Aston glanced up at him.

"In the last twelve months, we've attended almost forty jobs to Baker. That's some attention he was getting. No wonder Rosey's so happy about his demise. You don't seem too happy yourself though, Pat – what's up?"

''Nothing Kyle. Just got other things on my mind. Are you ready to go out?"

At that, PC Aston got up from his desk, Pat following him out of the room. Reaching the police car, they climbed in, Pat driving off. His head buzzed with the questions he wanted to put to Kyle, but he kept schtum, waiting to see if Aston started a conversation. After driving around for a while, Kyle broke the silence.

"Pat, you might as well know. I was married. She was a cop in the Met too. She was killed, knocked over on a pedestrian crossing eighteen months ago. He was drunk … and got eight years. I sold the house and moved up here to get away from the constant reminders. She was a hell of a girl, a hell of a cop, and my best friend. I went off the rails for six months, the job ran out of patience, and I went down to half pay. So, I came back to work, and as soon as I got the chance, I moved here. I've got a sister in the area, so it was easier to come here. Now you know why Walters pushed my buttons. You know… dying and … you know, Pat."

"Jesus, sorry, mate. How you got through that, I'll never know. I don't know what I'd do without my kids."

"How old are they?" asked Kyle.

"Thirteen and fifteen-years-old. They're my pride and joy. Ever since I got divorced, I live on my own, though I still see my ex a fair bit. We get on much better these days." Pat paused, realising this probably wasn't what Kyle wanted to hear. "Where are you living, Kyle?"

"A place across town. I'm renting for a while until I find my feet. Got a bit of money put aside, so I can buy whenever."

"Nice position to be in." Pat stopped. He'd already put his foot in it but didn't want to leave it there. "What I mean is: at least you've got a few quid behind you and aren't at the mercy of a landlord any longer than you have to be." He glanced at Kyle. "As you can see, I'm not at my best with words."

"Don't worry about it," said PC Aston. "No need to tread around eggshells with me."

Their conversation was interrupted by the Controller's latest address: "Tango Alpha One from Control, you're showing as free. Can you do a little job for me please?"

"Yeah, go ahead," said Kyle.

"Outside the library on High Street. We've got a complaint from staff that two men are outside hassling people, asking for money. Their names have been given as Joe Cunningham and Larry Bell."

"Two more of our regulars, Kyle," said Pat. "Proper scroungers and horrible little bastards."

"Roger, on our way, Control," said PC Aston.

The officers pulled up outside the library, where the two men sat on its steps. Cunningham was a 51-year-old alcoholic. Scruffy, wearing tatty old clothes, with holes in shoes that were about three sizes too big, he had a huge beer belly that spilt over jeans so dirty there was barely a patch of denim to be seen; a full head of thick, unwashed, uncombed hair, black teeth and a smell that could strip paint.

His partner in grime, Bell, was 42-years-old, and another scruffy alcoholic who was also addicted to a variety of drugs. Wearing a smart red jacket he'd probably recently stolen, he had a new pair of white trainers on – another suspected rob – slicked back, greasy jet-black hair, pale skin and a frame so skinny he resembled a clothes horse.

"Alright, Pat, how are you, mate? All good, I hope?" said Bell in a sarcastic lilt. "Come to move us on, have you? Who's the new boy? Is he your secretary?" Smiling lopsidedly, he flashed Kyle his nicotine yellow teeth. "Alright, Mister Secretary, what's your name, then? Sheila? Mary? Margaret?"

"Shut up, Larry," said Cunningham. "Don't know when to call it a day, do you?"

"Move, or I'll move you both – and don't come back. And, Bell: it's PC Patrick to you. Joe: get lost and take him with you."

Cunningham pulled at Bell's jacket, as if to gesture for him to leave, then started to walk off. Bell slowly got to his feet and, as he began to walk away, looked at PC Aston to say: "See you, sweetheart, come round to mine anytime you want, and you can do my washing."

As they walked off up the High Street, PCs Aston and Patrick got back into the car.

"Cunningham can be reasonable, but Bell's a horrible, gobby scumbag and has far too much to say for himself. Lots of previous, including sex offences against children. He really is the pits."

Kyle didn't respond, sitting back in his seat and glancing out of the car window as Pat drove off.

3 pm and the shift was over. Thursday was pub day for the earlies shift, which usually involved a pint or two at the local pub, near the nick. On this occasion, the entire shift went, except PC Aston, who made his excuses and left for home.

A traditional old boozer that had yet to be 'jazzed-up' to move with the times, it bore the hallmarks of past decades, save for the absence of the plumes of cigarette smoke that had been banned years earlier. Pat often stepped back into yesteryear when drinking here, the ghosts of the past revisiting him in the form of lost colleagues, and others who'd long since moved on.

"Well, come on, Pat," asked Kate Arnold, dragging Pat back into the here and now. "Tell us about the blue-eyed boy. What do you know?"

"Not a lot. He seems very private. All he told me is he worked in the Met for five years and has family up here."

"Family? Really? What family? Does he have a lady or what? Come on, Pat. Is he married, single, separated, divorced, gay?"

"Widower, so take it easy on him, Kate, for god's sake."

"Oh, god. Poor boy." She looked genuinely remorseful for Kyle. Then swiftly changed tact. "Maybe I should console him. What do you reckon, Pat?"

Pat just gave her a look, never surprised at the shallowness and self-centredness of the human race, even among the members of it he actually liked.

A few drinks later, the shift went their separate ways. For Pat, and the overwhelming majority of his colleagues, the switch from days to nights signalled a massacre of his body clock. Never able to fully adapt, he often found himself staring at the ceiling when he should've been banking valuable sleep; and craving sleep when he was supposed to be trying to keep the streets free of crime.

Part of Pat's problem was he knew he had little to no chance of anything like quality sleep, which put him on the back foot before he so much as slipped into his pyjamas. His body was exhausted, but his mind was alert and constantly ticking over. He was in a near-permanent state of jetlag, which made his prospects of making old age pretty damn slim. And, indeed, he spent the next day in a bit of a daze, desperately trying to reset the clock in time for the evening's fun to begin all over again.

That night at ten o'clock, Sergeant Rose walked in with his usual pile of crimes to hand out during his shift briefing. Sitting down with a cup of tea, he cleared his throat and started to speak:

"Evening, everyone. To start with: some more good news. You may or may not be aware that there's been another incident of note. Last night, the one and only Laurence Bell – also known as Larry Bell – was reported dead. His body was pulled out of the canal still wearing his lovely red jacket. Initial reports are that he was high as a kite and fell in on his way home to Lime Court.

Obviously, Mr Cunningham was the last person to see him alive and is said to be in shock. Aw – bless!"

There was a cheer from some of the officers in the room. PC Patrick looked at PC Aston, who stared at his cup of tea.

"Sarge, that's now two deaths in as many days where Kyle and I have been involved with the deceased. What's going on, then?"

"Who cares, Pat? Surely you must be pleased another arsehole is off our streets and there are more taxes to go round? The other losers don't worry about it."

"I'm not worried, Sarge, I'm just saying. What do you think, Kyle?"

"I really don't care, Pat. He was a horrible little twat."

"Bloody hell, Kyle, you sound just like he does – he's clearly rubbing off on you," said PC Arnold.

"Anyway, it's Friday night," said Sergeant Rose. "Same crewing as yesterday. Keep an eye on the nightclubs, especially the Matrix. There were problems there last weekend between out-of-towners and locals. Zero tolerance please – that's come from royalty. Take your breaks when you can, and no more than two crews at a time, please. That's it – short and sweet tonight. Out you go."

While the rest of the crew busied themselves, Pat went out to check the police car, and Kyle sat at a computer.

"Kyle, have you got a minute?" shouted Sergeant Rose.

PC Aston went into the Sergeant's office and shut the door. He was still in there when PC Patrick re-entered the office.

"Where's Kyle, Kate?"

Kate pointed at the Sergeant's office. "Been in there a good five minutes, Pat. I wonder what that's all about?"

PC Patrick knocked on the Sergeant's door, then walked in to see PC Aston stood next to the Sergeant's computer. As the Sergeant looked up to see Pat, he seemed uneasy, clearing his computer screen.

"Right, Kyle," Sergeant Rose told PC Aston. "That's it. That's how you do a coroner's report."

PC Patrick sensed something wasn't right but dismissed it from his mind. "Ready to come out and play, Kyle?"

"Yes, mate," said Kyle. He turned to face Sergeant Rose. "Ahem, thanks, Sarge. Nice one for that."

Kyle followed Pat out of the office, shutting the door behind him. Reaching the back yard, they placed their kit in the police car and drove out of the station. An uneasy silence between them, Pat felt himself wanting to say something, but bit his lip and drove around the busy town centre, looking at the many revellers hurling themselves towards intoxication.

FRIDAY NIGHT AT 22.15. Short skirts, low tops and what might best be described as people in a merry mood, with men dancing in the street, lots of smiles and waves at the police cars slowly patrolling the streets. A friendliness, a calm, a politeness. It would count for nothing as more and more alcohol was consumed, and the night turned to early morning. That's when the mood changed for the worse, characterised by broken bottles, groups of men swaggering and swearing, women screaming and flirtation morphing into anger.

It was the same in every city now, as dictated by the many scourges of society: alcohol, cannabis, cocaine, uppers, downers, money worries, government cuts, riots, relationship breakdowns, job losses and the dreaded winter months on their way. Society was now so contaminated by its manifold ills that there seemed to be no way back. Friday and Saturday nights on patrol were the busiest, the most demanding and a real eye opener when it came to revealing the true face of British life.

Hospitals would be full of drunken louts with cuts and bumps and bruises, with ambulances stretched to breaking point responding to calls to assist collapsed females, teenagers and assaulted men – all because of alcohol and the abuse of soft and hard drugs. The system simply couldn't cope anymore and was on the brink of collapse. And when the goodwill of the emergency services ran out, what would happen to whatever remained of a once decent society?

As the first call of the night came in, PC Patrick shook his head in disbelief, wondering what had happened to good old-fashioned crime – the occasional stereo being lifted from a car or a vehicle being stolen; house burglaries and assaults. For tonight, he would be back at 23 Lime Court. Yes, another of the city's most demanding patrons: Marie Jones.

"Are we going to that, Pat?" PC Aston asked.

"Wait and see if there's anyone else, Kyle. I'm not in the mood for Lime Court tonight."

"Second call please: anyone to twenty-three Lime Court. Break in progress, offenders still on scene."

Silence. No unit answered the call, because they all knew who it was and the type of job it entailed – it could be a quick in and out, or a whole night, depending on Marie and the severity of whatever state she was in.

"Tango Alpha One, are you free, Pat? Can you have a look, please?"

"Fuck sake, I knew it!" Pat growled. "Where's everyone else? Why us again? This really annoys me, Kyle."

"Tango Alpha One, show us as on our way," replied PC Aston.

Pat headed off to Lime Court, briefing Kyle on the way. Upon arrival at the block, as usual, the communal door was off its hinges, and the lifts were out of order, which meant a trek up the eight flights of stairs to the fourth floor. The smell of urine and vomit became almost unbearable the higher they climbed and, as they reached the fourth floor, they heard shouting coming from a couple of familiar, dishevelled faces in a state of inebriation.

Ah, yes – Jimmy and Owen. Another pair of miscreants, these friends of humanity could be smelt from miles off; but whereas Rosey's pungent fragrance swept harmlessly through Pat's nasal glands, the stench emitted by the likes of this duo left him, and anybody else unfortunate enough to be in its wake, gagging. With alcohol and drugs their dual-headed god, they'd yet to get their shit together in their forties, which meant an entire life spent pissed, snorted and injected away – all sponsored by the state – since they'd never sort themselves out now. Both were, of course, in possession of debtor dishes – satellite dishes to most people, who didn't rely on the government to finance their descent into the sewer.

Talking of sewers, Pat had long since grasped the necessity of never asking them to remove their shoes when in custody. On the one occasion he had – in order to remove their laces, in case they decided to do society a favour, as Carl Baker had – a stench so foul it brought tears to the eyes flew up at him with such potency it felt like a smack to the face. Self-defence, courtesy of the chav community.

"Jimmy, Owen, what you are doing to Marie now?" asked Pat, who knew that both men regularly drank with Marie in her flat.

"Hello, Pat," said Jimmy, whose toothy grin revealed a tongue coated with an amber tinge. "Everything alright, mate?"

"All the better for seeing you, Jim," said Pat, who acknowledged the pair as mid-table mediocrity in the Premier League of dossers and societal drain. They'd taken from the system all their lives, but were rarely aggressive, which counted for something in his eyes, at least. "Jimmy Sullivan – the sixth of the seventh, sixty-nine – and Owen Carmichael – the third of the twelfth, seventy-four. Both local. Do me a favour, Kyle: run them both through for me. They're normally good for a wanted report or warrant."

PC Aston moved away from the men and spoke into his radio to commence the checks.

"So, come on, lads: what's been going on?" asked Pat.

"We'd been drinking with Marie, hadn't we?" Owen piped up, dragging on a roll-up. "But we ran outta booze, so me and Jim went down the offie to get some more."

"That and some baccy," sniffed Jimmy. "When we got back, there was no reply. We kept knocking and shouting, but she never came to open the door. How did you lot know we were here?"

"Might have something to do with the neighbours getting sick of your racket," said Pat.

"Right. Yeah. Hadn't thought of that," smirked Jimmy.

Knocking on the door and receiving no reply, PC Patrick shouted through the letterbox: "Marie, it's Pat! Open the door!"

Another minute or two of continuous shouting and knocking produced the same result. While Pat debated whether to kick the door in, Kyle came over and whispered in his ear that Sullivan was wanted for a non-payment of fines warrant … and, with no bail, that meant being sent straight to the cells.

PC Patrick quickly weighed up his options. It was a Friday night in a busy town, with the station's cells likely to be nearing capacity. Even if he could justify a space for Sullivan, he was smashed and would have to be on constant watch until he sobered up all of which added up to: there was no way he'd be lifted that night.

"You know what? Tonight's not the night to pull him in – we haven't got the manpower. We can nick him another time – and there'll be plenty. But we've still got the small matter of what to do with Marie Jones. If she doesn't answer, we might have to go in. It's the last thing I want to do, but well … I can't believe this … Friday night again, Jesus fucking Christ." He kicked the door, then shouted a couple of times through the letterbox. "Marie, open up! It's Pat! Come on, let us in – just to make sure you're okay."

Nothing – not a stir, not a sound. Jimmy and Owen just sat on the floor, swigging from a can of Special Brew, passing it to each other every couple of swigs. Pat put his hands on his hips, looked up and took a huge intake of breath, then a slow breath out. He knew his night was over – this one job would probably take him to the end of his shift at 7 am. Pat so wanted to walk away, but it was Marie. Anyone else, he would've walked… but it was Marie.

The anniversary of Darren and the boys' deaths were drawing ever closer. Pat barricaded his emotions inside because he didn't want Kyle to know about his moral dilemmas or his history with Marie. He looked at Kyle, took one step backwards, raised his right leg and kicked the door, which flew off its hinges.

First Pat, then Kyle stepped into the lounge. Sprawled out on a dirty single quilt lay Marie's motionless body. At first glance, it looked like she was dead – her eyes were rolled back, her lips were a faint blue, and there was vomit on the floor, around her mouth and in her hair. Pat checked her wrist to see if there was a pulse – there was; it was slight, but she was alive.

"Tango Alpha One, can we have an ambulance, please. Female unconscious, weak pulse, in her forties. Clear signs of alcohol abuse and recent vomiting. Can you get boarding up too please – we had to force the door."

The Controller acknowledged the transmission, and Pat asked Jimmy and Owen if they'd taken any drugs in addition to their drinking. They both shook their heads, and Jimmy raised the can of Special Brew as if to confirm it was just drink. The ambulance arrived quickly, Marie was taken to A&E, and Pat told the paramedics he'd pop over to the hospital once the door has been secured.

Stepping out of the flat, he saw Jimmy and Owen still sitting on the ground, clearly expecting to get back into Marie's flat to continue their alcohol binge. When Pat told them to find somewhere else to go and to be quiet as they went on their way, they staggered off down the stairs with a bag full of cheap booze, sharing a joke ... without making a single enquiry about Marie.

"Tango Alpha One, boarding up has been contacted. They've said at least an hour. Sorry, we did try to hurry them along, but that's the best they can do. So, show us as being here, until further notice."

Pat and Kyle stood in the hallway outside Marie's flat, forced out by the horrendous smell inside – filthy old clothes, stale alcohol, rotting and fresh vomit, and mouldy, putrefying food. The hallway, as bad as it was, complete with dirty floor and walls, broken doors, puddles of piss and nappies – often hurled out of windows, followed by a complaint to the local council that nobody was bothering to pick them up – was deemed the lesser of two evils. Pat occasionally pinched his nostrils to give them a break from the stench, his mind elsewhere; temporarily marooned in the moments after he walked into Rosey's office, and the awkward atmosphere he encountered.

Kyle had little to say in the hour that passed before Pat rang up to see how much longer it would be before somebody showed up to fix the door. That hour seemed to take forever to pass, as Pat grew increasingly frustrated, stuck in a fetid hallway on a Friday night with a partner who said even less as the night wore on.

"So, Rosey was showing you how to do the coroner's report earlier?" asked Pat. "Are you expecting a lot of stiffs up here, Kyle?"

"I hope not," sniggered Kyle. "It's just something else to learn, and now that's out of the way I can cross it off the list. It's so different up here, Pat. We seemed to have less paperwork in the Met and had initial responders. They never got involved in paperwork. They just take control and calm things down, then the backup crew comes along to do whatever needs doing, and we leave for the next job."

"Yeah, but there are thousands and thousands of Bobbies down there, Kyle. We parade with ten on a Friday and Saturday night –

if we're lucky. They tried that initial responder thing before, but we just never had enough staff. It lasted a week."

Kyle just nodded. Pat looked out of a window with a view into town, unconvinced by his answer, which felt vague and scripted; and with the distinct impression that there really was more to Kyle Aston from the Met. Around half an hour later, he heard a noise coming from the stairwell, followed by footsteps in the hallway as the council carpenter turned up, all heavy-lidded and messy-haired from having his night's sleep crudely interrupted.

"Alright, lads? Sorry for the delay, but it's just me tonight. The other lad's off sick. A front door needs putting back on – is that right?"

"Indeed, it is," Pat sighed wearily.

He showed the carpenter the door, and he got to work, putting it back on its hinges – fortunately, it didn't need a new door, or lock and keys. Pat went into Marie's flat, found her keys on top of the television, came back out, then tested the door to ensure it locked. Hey presto – as good as new.

"Take care, fellas. Hope it's a quiet night for you," said the carpenter as he grabbed his tools to leave.

Driving to the hospital to check on Marie and leave her keys, Pat and Kyle arrived at A&E, announcing themselves at reception. As they walked through to the cubicles, they passed about a dozen people waiting to be seen. Pat glanced at a clock on the wall. It was a few minutes to one in the morning and already very busy; by three, it would be absolutely heaving. Finding the sister in charge – a familiar face owing to years of attending A&E – she spoke as frankly and sarcastically as might be expected from a nurse with 25 years of dealing with the same rubbish, day after day.

"Just alcohol again, Pat. She's on a drip, getting some fluids. She's actually starting to recover quite quickly this week. Last week it took about ten hours to rouse her. The week before that, you may remember, she was here for two days. It's all good."

The sister smiled as she walked past the officers, leaving them in the cubicle with Marie, who was awake, staring at the ceiling. Pat stepped over to her.

"Marie, it's every week now. When's this going to stop? How much more do you think your body can take? And while I'm at it, it's Friday night. We're busy, the staff here are busy, and yet again we're all babysitting you. You've had police, ambulance, hospital and the council boarding up."

"Oh, Pat, give it a rest, will you?" sighed Marie. "Please … leave me alone. I feel ill, and I'm not in the mood for a lecture. I didn't ask for all of this. Why didn't you just leave me in the flat? I'd have been fine by the morning. I bet you kicked my door off its hinges again, didn't you? I do wish you lot would leave me be."

Pat half-heartedly threw the flat keys at Marie and walked out, muttering "Ungrateful bitch" under his breath as he left the cubicle, which drew a chuckle from Kyle.

"Don't call us when it's time to discharge her," Pat told the sister on their way out. "She can make her own way home."

The sister smiled in sympathy at his frustration before the officers left and got back into their car.

"So, Pat, on the scale of waste of oxygen, is Marie up there with the best of them?" asked Kyle. "Hospital and police every weekend, and that flat was a disgrace – I've never smelt anything so bad. How on earth do people live like that in these modern times? How long has she been like that?"

"Years. Bloody years, mate."

Pat's mind remained elsewhere as he drove, glancing at Kyle to see him staring out of the window. It was two in the morning, and they'd accomplished jack shit, other than dealing with society's wasters as usual. Heading back to the station for some food and a cup of tea, Sergeant Rose was quick to question the officers about Marie Jones:

"Well, what is it this time, chaps? The usual, I suppose – paralytic, unconscious, kicked the door in, waste of everyone's time, stuck in the hospital for hours, blah blah blah."

"Yes, Sarge, that's it in a nutshell," said Kyle. "The door has been put back on its hinges, and we dropped the keys off at the hospital. She was conscious and without a care in the world."

"Thanks, Kyle. She's one of our regulars. I'm sure you'll get to see a lot of her and her wonderful friends from Lime Court. Are you having some grub and a brew now? Well, if you are, two sugars, please. Let's see how good your tea-making skills are new boy."

Sergeant Rose went into his office, Kyle headed into the kitchen, and Pat followed him with his food bag. In the kitchen, chat was in short supply as other members of the shift ate their lunch.

"Jones again, Pat. I bet you're sick to the back teeth of her, pal," said PC Drew Williams, an older, grizzled member of the team, edging towards retirement. "Same old same old, was it?"

"Yes, Drew, same old."

Pat opened his food bag, sat down with the others, and quietly ate his lunch. A few moments later, Kyle carried a big pot of tea in, putting it on a table.

"Help yourselves to milk and sugar," he said, pouring a cup and taking it into Sergeant Rose's office.

"He seems alright, doesn't he, Pat?" asked Williams. "Having a good week with him?"

"Yeah, top lad. Capable and friendly enough, but a bit too quiet for my liking. Then again, he is finding his feet. He's had to see a lot of the shit out there so far. I'm looking forward to seeing him deal with other stuff, but so far so good, Drew."

Kyle was gone for a good fifteen minutes, by which time Pat had finished his food, making small talk with a couple of the others in the kitchen. Nothing much said, but the mutual desire for some kind of conversation, however banal, fulfilled in part. An easy-going atmosphere abruptly punctured as the radio announced a fight outside the Kaleidoscope club on High Street. Six officers ran out to the three cars in operation and sped to the club, situated about a minute away from the station.

The first to arrive, Pat and Kyle stepped into chaos – a large crowd had gathered, two men had blood on their white shirts, doorman held another group back, while women screamed and shouted, one of them holding her high heeled shoes and swinging them in the direction of one of the men with the bloodied shirts.

The other cars duly arrived, and, between them, the officers were able to regain some calm and normality.

It turned out that one of the men had bumped into his ex-girlfriend. She was with her new boyfriend, and the three of them started to fight. Others gathered and joined in, but the door staff were able to break it up before it got out of hand. Both parties refused to talk to the police, the female and her new boyfriend jumped in a taxi, and the other male walked off with his group of friends in tow.

The cars patrolled the town to keep a good visible presence, especially as it was close to kicking out time and tensions were rising; but before too long, the radio informed the officers on duty that a unit was needed to check an alarm sounding at a premises on an industrial estate on the other side of town. Tango Alpha Two obliged. Another call, relating to suspicious males checking car doors in Cherry Street – again, on the other side of town – saw Tango Alpha Three attend … which left two cars and the Sergeant patrolling the streets at kicking out time, with the other double crewed unit having their food back at the station.

Pat and Kyle were at the top end of the town, sat outside a club called Liquid, where students and younger partygoers gathered. They get out of the car to calm a group of rowdy males who'd just left the club and were starting to reach the point where they needed to be spoken to. It did the trick, the males hailed a taxi, and off they went into the night.

Pat and Kyle remained outside the club and had a chat with the door staff. Seeing the police tended to stop the lairiest pissheads kicking off and lessen some of the noise emanating from the less threatening revellers; and, while the odd one or two left the club singing, swearing and shouting, they soon calmed down when the officers had a quiet word in their ears. The radio then called for a unit to go to a missing person call: a 14-year-old girl hadn't returned home, her mobile phone was off, and her parents had no idea where she could be.

"She's fourteen-years-old, it's almost three o'clock in the morning, and now her parents decide their little princess is missing," moaned Pat. "Three o'clock, Kyle, and we have to go looking for a brat!"

"Tango Alpha Four, we're finished from our break. We'll take that one. Go again with the address."

The Controller repeated the address over the air, and the girl's name was disclosed. She was another regular who would almost certainly be shacked up with a group of teenagers, drinking and making noise somewhere near town. Parents simply had no control these days, and their kids turned into horrible little shits as soon as they reached thirteen – another waste of police time and money.

Some of the other units attended an incident involving a smashed shop window. The town centre CCTV called to identify a male with a blue and white shirt, black jeans and black shoes, who was seen running away from the area. A full bottle of beer was used to smash the window and lay spilling out inside the shop. The CCTV operator relayed that the same male was walking away from town with two others and glancing back every few seconds. With Pat and Kyle not too far away, they drove the short distance to the location. As they did, the described male clocked the police unit and started to walk with purpose. The officers pulled up in front of the group, stopped the car and climbed out.

"Alright, pal, can you stop there for me a minute," said Kyle, taking the lead, to Pat's surprise. "I just need to have a quick word."

The three men stopped but didn't speak.

"Where have you boys just come from, then?"

"Town," said one of the other two males. "Been to Liquid. Just off home."

"Have you all been together?"

"Yeah," replied the same male.

Pat spoke to the CCTV operator, who confirmed footage of the male in the blue and white shirt throwing the bottle and smashing the window, though the other two males were on the opposite side of the road and had nothing to do with it.

"Okay, chaps. Well, for one of you, it's a night in the cells." Taking hold of the male with the blue and white shirt, Kyle told him: "You are under arrest for causing criminal damage by smashing a shop window in town, and it's all caught on CCTV."

"Are you fucking mad, mate?" the guilty party protested. "It ain't me. I ain't under arrest."

As he tried to pull away from Kyle, Aston pulled his arm back, forcing him to the ground.

"You're breaking my fucking arm – get off me!" He hollered as Kyle pinned his arm behind his back.

He was told to calm down but carried on swearing and screaming to be released. Kyle applied handcuffs with ease, quite literally picked him up off the ground and tossed him into the police car, slamming the door shut. Pat just stood and watched, yet again impressed by Kyle's ability to deal with conflict.

The other two men had their details taken and were sent on their way. Kyle sat in the back of the car with the arrested man, while Pat jumped in the front and drove towards custody. The Controller watched the live CCTV feed, confirming that they'd notified the custody block that one was coming in for criminal damage, and praising Kyle for his swift, competent arrest.

The arrested man protested his innocence during the couple of minutes it took to drive to the station. When taken to the custody suite, he refused to give his name, address or date of birth – standard procedure for so many of their 'customers'. After Kyle relayed the details of the arrest to the Desk Sergeant, he was taken to a cell and left to sober up with a coffee and a blanket.

All in all, it took a couple of hours after Pat and Kyle entered the officers' room to write statements and a crime report, and to prepare a custody printout and handover package for the interviewing team the next morning. Just after 5 am, it was time for another cup of tea. Sergeant Rose and the other officers gathered round to look at the CCTV footage showing Kyle's majestic arrest, which drew compliments from the shift and comparisons to Pat.

"Well done, Kyle. Nice little arrest," smiled Sergeant Rose.

"Yeah, nice handiwork," Kate cooed, sitting beside Kyle and placing a hand on his shoulder. Having recently split from her long-term boyfriend, she had her own house near town and hadn't quite been able to disguise her disappointment when Kyle gave the shift drink a miss. "Where did you learn that stuff?"

"I was a boy scout, did a paper round, and ended up being a lifeguard."

"Yeah, whatever. You're so full of shit, mister," said Kate, who got up and walked off red-faced.

With the worst of the night's fun and frolics over, the shift's crew looked spent – eyes were heavy, and some of the officers leant back in their chairs with theirs closed. Drew snored, while some of the others tidied their paperwork and updated incidents on the computer, when not making small talk. But, true to form, the radio broke the silence:

"Any unit please: immediate response to eighty Mount Pleasant. Domestic in progress. Young child heard crying in the background."

Tango Alpha Three and Four took up the challenge, while Pat showed Kyle how to look for previous incidents on the force's computer system. When Sergeant Rose asked for another cup of tea, Pat duly obliged, heading into the kitchen as Kyle stepped into Rosey's office, leaving the door ajar.

"You wouldn't mind eavesdropping on that pair, would you?" he asked Kate.

"Why? Think they're plotting against big bad Pat?" she smirked.

"No, nothing sinister," said Pat. "I'm just a bit intrigued – like you."

"Sure, mister para – why not?"

Once he'd finished making the tea, Pat walked into the report room to start handing it out, seeing Kyle sat at his computer. Glancing at Kate, she shrugged her shoulders, which he assumed meant she hadn't heard anything.

"Nice one," said Sergeant Rose as Pat placed his mug in front of him.

He seemed relaxed enough, but was there more to this than Pat imagined? Or were his imaginings getting the better of him, unsettling him when there wasn't any need? But if he was mistaken, why were Kyle and the Sergeant speaking so much? He hadn't seen any other new recruit develop that kind of relationship so quickly, and wondered why he'd been cut out of the equation – as the senior officer, shouldn't he be Rosey's first port of call? Or was he merely giving Kyle a more robust introduction to life under his watch?

Leaving Kyle's tea beside him, Pat saw him looking at previous incidents on the computer.

"Everything okay?" he inquired.

Kyle looked at Pat, nodded his head and sipped his tea. Pat had hoped for more than a nod and, though somebody who, rightly or wrongly, wasn't afraid to speak his mind, it was 6 a.m. after a night shift, and there would be more appropriate times to try and satisfy his curiosity.

The shift ended without any further incidents, and Pat went into the locker room, gesturing to Kate to stay put. Then, once everybody else had left, he trod towards her.

"What do you think's going on with that pair? Did you hear anything when they were in there together earlier?"

"I wasn't able to hear anything. And no, I don't know what, if anything, is going on between them. Maybe it's just to do with work. With him being the new boy, he might not want to keep asking you all the time. You know how macho you boys can be."

"No, Kate, something isn't right about him. I saw his type of martial arts a few years ago when I did a course with the army. It's typical forces stuff. And take a look at him – he's immaculate. Spotless clothes, always clean shaven, apart from that pruned little goatee. He's never late for work, and he's always 'Yes, Sergeant. No, Sergeant.' I'm telling you, there's military in that man."

"Maybe, but I don't care, because he's gorgeous. He can prune my goatee any day of the week. Enjoy your time off and see you next week."

And with that, Kate disappeared, leaving Pat with yet another unwanted image in his head.

CHAPTER 5

IT ALWAYS FELT LIKE swimming against the tide, driving home at an hour when pretty much everybody else was off to work. By the time Pat pulled up outside his semidetached house, he couldn't remember the drive home, so engrossed was he with thoughts of Sergeant Rose and PC Kyle Aston.

Letting himself in to immediately feel the benefits of the central heating that made his home nice and toasty, Pat went straight up to his bedroom, throwing his clothes over a chair. After a quick wash and cleaning his teeth, he lay in bed wondering about Kyle. He'd given up very little about his past, and Pat couldn't help wondering, again, what Kyle had done before joining the police. In his mid-thirties and with no dependents, he was a quiet but clearly competent man. Round and round went the questions in his head, until he dropped off to sleep, exhausted by his reflections and the shift that went before them.

Waking when his alarm rang out at 2 pm, Pat got out of bed to freshen up in the bathroom. He doubted he'd ever get used to eating breakfast of an afternoon, but after putting away a coffee and a bowl of cereal, he drove to his local gym. These days, it took all his slowly wilting stamina to retain the shape that came so naturally when in his twenties and thirties.

His thrice-weekly Kung Fu class had been reduced to, at best, a couple, and more often than not, a class a week. It wasn't so much lack of interest than an increasingly demanding job, coupled with his body's wear and tear, that made it more challenging to stick to the kind of training regimen that had once been his staple. But in a world as dark as this, there wasn't a hope of him hanging up the black belt that had taken him a good five years to earn the right to wrap around his waist.

After his workout, Pat sat in the sauna for ten minutes or so, before showering, getting dressed and heading into town. Frittering half an hour away in his favourite café, watching the world go by when not flicking through the pages of the local rag, Pat started walking back to his car. On his way there, he glanced at some recently built apartments.

Pricey, given their close proximity to town, they were three storeys high, had private, gated parking and, Pat suspected, were designed to attract the city's younger, snotty-nosed business types. Peering through the gates, he was able to see a black Alfa Romeo Spider, number plate K7 LYE. He frowned, having seen it parked in one of the bays at the station, prompting a slew of questions, the most prominent of which were: how could a regular Bobbie afford a motor like that; assuming he wasn't visiting somebody living at the apartment block, how did Kyle manage to pay for a luxury flat; and if he had, why lie about renting?

Finding his car, Pat drove home. The next couple of days flew by, despite being unable to see his daughters, as would typically have been the case on his time off. When he was without them, Pat felt an emptiness inside him that he tried to fill with more physical training – always a little easier once his body clock had started to adjust to a more normal routine.

Access hadn't ever proved to be a problem. Relations with his ex-wife, Dianne, were good, and there hadn't been a bitter parting of the ways, as he'd witnessed on so many occasions when friends and colleagues had split. He still couldn't put his finger on why things hadn't worked out between them, figuring it was more a case of gradually growing apart than cataclysmic falling-out.

With the girls away at a party/sleepover, the place felt so quiet, Pat often switched the radio on, to hear other voices, until those voices became so insufferably irritating that silence was the better option. He missed cooking them meals and passing down his fighting skills, knowing more than most what a violent, nasty world they were growing up in.

With another two days to kill until it was time to go back to work, Pat cleaned and tidied his house, then set off for the other side of town to meet his girlfriend, Sarah, for dinner. Ten years younger than he was at thirty-five, she worked as a solicitor for a firm handling criminal law. It was through her job that they'd met twelve months earlier when Sarah represented the kind of filth that made Pat's life a misery. But with a government falling over itself to keep them in the manner to which they'd become accustomed, Pat doubted she'd ever be short on work.

They did their best to avoid talking about anything pertaining to their respective roles, but given that they accounted for so much of their time, it was virtually impossible, requiring the imposition of a half-hour time limit, after which anything work-related was off the agenda. Pat liked to keep his time with the girls and Sarah separate. They'd met on a handful of occasions, but no more – even though Becky and Sophie liked Sarah and vice-versa, Pat cherished his time with his girls and, perhaps a little selfishly, didn't want to share them with anyone else.

Working long hours, Sarah was also often on call – as she was that night – so there was every chance their meal might be cut short. Parking close to his favourite Italian, on the other side of town, Pat spotted her sitting near a window, a lit candle standing on the table in front of her. Slim and pretty, with long blonde hair and wearing a black dress, she smiled as Pat flashed her a grin through the window, before stepping inside the restaurant and walking up to her.

"Hi, sweetie," he said, kissing her on the lips.

"Hi, Pat. You okay?"

"Not too bad."

Sitting in a chair on the opposite side of the table to Sarah, the restaurant's manager came over and shook Pat's hand.

"Hi, Pat, how are you? Still keeping those streets free of crime?"

"I don't know about 'free of', Roberto, but the streets are in good hands. How are you, my old friend?"

"Less of the old! I'm still only seventy-eight years young!" He handed them a menu each. "Enjoy your evening, both of you. Anything you need, just let me know. By the way, the meatballs are freshly made today, and I know they're your favourite."

"Sounds good," smiled Pat. "Do you know what you're having yet, honey?" he asked Sarah as Roberto left the table.

"The homemade lasagne with garlic bread, so if they call me out tonight, they'll regret it!"

"Garlic breath," smiled Pat. "You wicked girl. What about me, later, if you don't get called out?"

"You always tell me you love me just the way I am."

"And I do. Even with garlic breath. So, how was work today?"

"Okay, I suppose," shrugged Sarah. "I was office-bound. I'm dreading my three days of being on-call. I so wish I could have a glass of red tonight. How's the new boy coming along? I can't wait to meet this sexy man from London who all the girls are going nuts over."

"Hands off! I think Kate has already set her sights on him. I'm still not sure about him, though. He's very sheepish about his past. Not that I've asked him too much, but people normally tell you a bit about themselves, don't they? Not him. You know the new apartments in town, by the car park for the gym – the ones with the security gates? I saw his car parked in there today. He said he lived just outside town, but they're bloody expensive, and on our wages, there's no way he can afford to live there."

"Well, maybe he was visiting someone, or has a girlfriend, and she owns one. Why don't you ask him when you go back to work?"

"Yeah, maybe I will. Let's order before you get called out."

A couple of hours later, a tacky rom-com tested their ability to keep Roberto's cuisine in their respective stomachs, their dessert a hotchpotch of the kind of late-night/early hours dross that featured far too prominently in Pat's life for his liking. A three bedroomed, modern detached house in a nice part of town, Pat often felt more comfortable at Sarah's place than his own. Maybe that had more to do with the company and, while not unfond of his own, the hours passed more pleasantly when somebody else was around.

Not that night, though – with Sarah called out at around two in the morning, Pat had her king-sized bed all to himself; as well as his restless mind, deprived of the possibility of sharing the unending procession of questions in his head, in the hope of finding some answers. He hadn't been able to find any of his own by the time Sarah returned at just gone six, sliding into bed and snuggling up to him.

"Well?"

"Well, what?"

"What delights did you have to deal with?"

"An utterly obnoxious drink driver who questioned everything. He blew a hundred-and-four and kept repeating himself. He really took the piss, Pat – I was ready to kill him. I know he's my client, but I'll be so pleased when he's banned and fined, the dickhead. Anyway, goodnight. I'm shattered, so don't wake me until at least ten o'clock."

Falling asleep in each other's arms, Pat sunk almost immediately into a deep sleep, only waking at around eight with a bladder fit to burst. Taking a piss so blissful he nearly cried, he went downstairs and made himself a coffee. Switching the television on, he watched the local news: a depressingly familiar rundown of contemporary crime that had Pat virtually frothing at the mouth with rage. And then, another reminder of his work, rather than the person he once knew:

"Jones, from Lime Court in the city, is believed to have tried to commit suicide by jumping from her fourth-floor balcony and was found late last night by a passer-by. Jones was taken to City Hospital, where her condition is described as critical, after suffering a fractured skull and a badly broken leg. Police are appealing for witnesses."

Pat sat where he was, his head dropping into his hands. He knew he had to go and see Marie, who didn't have anybody else who gave a shit. In all fairness, it was the very least he could do, considering their history.

He got dressed, left a little note for Sarah, and drove to City Hospital, where he was directed to the intensive care unit.

"Can I help you?" asked the nurse in charge – a rotund, old school matron type, if her scowl was anything to go by.

"Yes, please. I'm here about Marie Jones, and wanted to know how she is."

"Can I ask who you are? I was led to believe there's no next of kin. We've already had the local news team asking questions. If you're press, can I direct you to our press office on the second floor?"

"No, I'm not press," said Pat. "I actually heard about her on the news this morning. I'm an old friend, and she'll be pleased to see me."

"Can I ask your name, and I'll go and get the doctor, who'll be able to tell you more."

"Yes, of course, it's Patrick. Mr Patrick."

The nurse left the unit's reception and disappeared into the ward, while Pat waited at the desk. About ten minutes later, a doctor appeared. Thin and pallid-skinned, he had the appearance of somebody swimming against the tide of shift work; though when he spoke, it was as if an inner sprightliness sprang out of him, belying the expression on his face.

"Hello, Mr Patrick, I'm Doctor Orford. I'm a neurosurgeon and am treating Mrs Jones. Can I ask how you know her? We don't have a next of kin and weren't expecting any visitors. The police have been and aren't treating her as a victim of crime."

"Hello, Doctor Orford. I'm an old friend of Marie's. I saw her a few days ago in town, and we were chatting. I know her from the benefits centre at Bank Street," said Pat, telling a white lie. He didn't want to tell the truth about his association as a result of police dealings and didn't think it would be prudent to divulge his occupation – at least, not at that point, and not unless he really had to.

"Oh okay, that's fine. Would you like to come with me?"

Pat followed the doctor into a side room, where Marie, her leg elevated in a cast, lay amid the tubes and monitors helping to keep her alive, a cardiac monitor bleeping intermittently.

"She was brought in at around two in the morning after being found at the bottom of the estate she lives on. I'm reliably informed that she lives on the fourth floor. So, a suicide attempt, then. I say attempt because, despite some serious injuries, she's still alive. She's got a very strong heart and a will like I've never seen. She really should be dead."

"What are her injuries?" asked Pat. "And has she said anything yet?"

"I'm afraid not – she's in a coma. A very deep coma. She has a fractured skull and a compound fracture to her left leg. I can only assume she was found very quickly after she jumped, otherwise she'd have bled to death for sure. There's pressure on her brain, and I may have to operate to relieve it. But for now, she's stable. Her leg has been reset and stitched.

"Assuming she survives, she'll probably need a stick to assist her mobility. We had to pin it and will see how it sets over the coming weeks. Do you mind me asking – and I apologise in advance – but her blood/alcohol ratio was extremely high, and there's evidence of cannabis and heroin in her system, not to mention anti-depressants and paracetamol – lots of paracetamol. Is she an alcohol and drug abuser?"

"Yes – to all of it. Habitual – a good ten years, at least. I've tried to help, but to no avail. A lost cause, you might say."

"Well, she'll be with us for quite some time. I've no idea if or when she'll come out of the coma. This will obviously help to get the drugs and alcohol out of her system, but we'll have to keep an eye on her body's reaction to the withdrawal. This will complicate things for the next seventy-two hours. Oh, one more thing: she has a strange mark on her neck. I told the police officer, but he didn't seem very interested."

Doctor Orford pointed to a red, bruised mark about four inches long, stretching from her left ear down to her throat, and at least an inch wide. Marie's face was unmarked, Pat concluding she must have hit the back of her head. But despite swelling to her head, and the mark on her neck, she looked pretty normal; or, at least, not that much worse than when he last saw her.

"Yes, I can see it. Why is that significant, Doc? I mean, she fell from the fourth floor."

"It might be something, and it might be nothing. But to me – and I'm only guessing – it looks like an impact strike, a blow. Hitting the back of her head, and the way her leg is broken, I can't see how that mark would've got there. I appreciate it could've been as a result of falling first in her flat, or something else that happened earlier in the day; but, Mr Patrick, it's getting redder, and the bruising is starting to come out by the hour. This suggests – and again, it's only a guess – that it was a recent blow, hit or bang."

Pat listened intently, concerned about the doctor's assumption. But if the police had already investigated, there was nothing he could do to alter the fact that it was a suicide attempt.

"Doctor, if I leave my contact details and Marie's condition changes, will you be kind enough to let me know?"

"Yes, of course. Leave them with sister at the desk, and thank you for coming in. Feel free to visit anytime. A familiar voice may help to bring her round."

The doctor left the room, and Pat leant over to kiss Marie on the cheek.

"You silly sod," Pat whispered in her ear. "Why didn't you tell me you were feeling like this?"

Pat walked out of the room and found the nurse's desk, where he left his number with the sister, asking her to get somebody to call him if Marie's condition changed. Exiting the hospital and stepping towards his car, he looked at his watch and noticed the date – the 21St of October. And then it dawned on him – the tenth anniversary of Darren and the boys' deaths was on the 20th. Marie told him that she always visited their graves on this grim commemoration to tidy them up and place fresh flowers. She'd eat some food and have a drink while talking to them.

Sitting in his car, Pat took another look at his watch. With it being only 9.30 am, Sarah would still be in bed. After a little deliberation, he set off for the Trinity, a sprawling, council-owned graveyard. Around a five-mile drive, Pat pulled up outside a flower shop at its entrance, bought a £20 bouquet, then drove into the Trinity. He hadn't visited for a good ten years, remembering those who'd been laid to rest here but struggling to find their graves.

After a good fifteen-minute search, he drove down a small track, which looked familiar. Stopping his car, Pat switched its engine off, got out and walked up and down rows of graves before finding the family plot Marie visited, with the inscription, depicted in gold lettering: 'Darren, Alistair and Raymond Jones. Gone but never forgotten. Always in our thoughts, in our hearts, and forever remembered. Together as one, together in heaven, in God we trust'.

He stared at the date they were buried – the 20th of October 2003 – and the large white angel stood on a black marble block. At the foot of the gravestone were fresh flowers – red, pink and white carnations, very nicely arranged and placed inside the pot provided by Trinity. The stones enveloping the pot had been raked, there were no leaves or rubbish, and the gravestone was spotless.

Standing beside it was a white card with a picture of a golden cross on the front. Pat opened the card and read it: 'I think about you every day, Darren, my love. I miss you so much, Ally and Ray, my lovely, beautiful boys. I hope you're behaving for Daddy! And I hope you like the flowers. I'll see you all next year and remember I love you more with every breath I take'.

Pat sat down on the grass and stared at the grave, pondering. "She was here yesterday," he muttered to himself. "She was here."

'I'll see you all next year...' Was that really the kind of sentiment expressed by somebody with suicidal intentions? Pat remembered the mark on Marie's neck and what the doctor said at the hospital. His ringing phone interrupted his musing, Sarah's number appearing. Ignoring his phone, Pat stood up and walked back to his car with his mind working overtime.

Sitting in his car, he stared out of the window. It was his day off, and here he was, in the middle of a graveyard, worrying about somebody who, while beaten down by life's injustice, was an alcoholic druggie ... a waster. It was the tenth anniversary of the deaths of her entire family, which was enough to make anybody feel suicidal, let alone Marie, with all her problems. But she'd never tried or threatened suicide before, so why this time?

HALF AN HOUR LATER, Pat pulled onto Sarah's drive. Letting himself in with his key, Sarah shouted down to him from upstairs.

"How was the gym? I tried phoning you. I assume you were driving?"

"Gym was good. Yes, I saw you phoned, but didn't answer, as I was on my way here."

"Well, I'm heading into work. I need to be there for eleven. Help yourself to food. Will you be here later? I'll be home by five, but I'm on call from eight tonight."

"Yes, of course, I'll be here. I've brought my work stuff, ready for the earlies. I'll have some dinner ready for when you get back. What do you fancy?"

"Anything. The fridge and freezer are full."

Sarah came downstairs, dressed smartly, but bleary-eyed, having been up the previous night. She kissed Pat on the lips and opened the door.

"See you tonight, honey, and enjoy your day off."

"Thanks, babe. Have a good day."

Sarah left for work, and Pat made himself a cup of coffee, which he drank in the lounge watching television. But with the box and its feeble offerings unable to distract his mind from Marie, he grabbed his black jacket and baseball cap, left the house and drove to Lime Court.

Parking in the next street, not wanting the local scum to see his car, he put his jacket and baseball cap on, pulling the cap right down so that it almost covered his eyes, then made for Marie's place. The communal front door was open, its lock damaged, as usual, so he walked up the stairs, an all too familiar stench growing stronger the higher he got.

"God, I fucking hate this place," he mumbled to himself as he opened the door leading to the floor on Marie's flat.

Making sure nobody else was about, Pat leaned against the flat door, which was loose – with no sign of a new lock, it seemed obvious to him that the police had been back the previous night. Easing it open, Pat was hit by a hideous stench – a foul medley of stale vomit, urine, body odour and cigarettes. Feeling himself starting to gag, he pulled his jacket over his nose and mouth.

Finding the balcony door unlocked, he opened it and walked onto a small balcony. There were several black bags full of empty cider bottles, take away cartons and mouldy food; and silver dust on the balcony rail – evidence of the Scenes of Crime officer having been. Pat looked over the balcony. Four floors up, it seemed an awfully long drop to the bottom, which begged the question: how the hell did Marie survive?

A large pool of blood stained the ground below, Pat guessing it resulted from her leg break. Entering the lounge, he grabbed a batch of opened letters from a table strewn with overflowing ashtrays, spent cigarette packets and sweet wrappers. Pat prised a letter out of the first envelope, it was dated the 19th of October, which was just two days earlier. From a place called the Marlow Clinic, an alcohol and drug abuse rehabilitation facility, it confirmed an appointment for the 2nd of November. He looked at another of Marie's letters: correspondence from the council's housing department, responding to her request to be moved away from Lime Court. Dated the 15th of October, she had an appointment with a housing officer in Bank Street on the 14th of November.

"What the fuck's going on here?" Pat asked himself.

Rehab, a move away from a fleapit of a flat, the gravestone tendered, the card she left and the mark on her neck ... something wasn't right. Pat put the letters down and, after peeking into the hallway to ensure the coast was clear, left the flat, pulling the door to and walking hastily downstairs. Returning to his car, he drove back to Sarah's house. As soon as he set foot through the front door, he undressed and stuffed his clothes in the washing machine, then hurried upstairs to take a shower, desperate to rid himself of the stench of Lime Court and Marie's flat.

Once showered and grabbing some fresh clothes from those he kept there, Pat dressed and went downstairs to start preparing dinner for when Sarah came home from work. Tuna pasta with salad, fresh orange juice and cheesecake for dessert. Not the most sophisticated meal ever, but something he was able to throw together quickly enough. When Sarah walked through the door at 5 pm on the dot, Pat was in the kitchen, putting the final touches to their food.

"Hello, Pat! Smells good. What are we having?"

Pat hugged Sarah and kissed her on the lips.

"Ooh, you smell lovely! To what do I owe the pleasure of this sweet-smelling man in my house?"

"I thought I'd make an effort, so I showered for the first time this month. Dinner is simple tuna pasta with salad and cheesecake for afters. It was all from your fridge, of course."

"Sounds great. Listen, I need to take a quick shower to help me unwind. I've had a busy, busy day."

Sarah dropped her jacket on the floor, kicked her shoes into the corner of the hallway and started to unbutton her white blouse while heading upstairs.

"I think you might have forgotten something, honey," she shouted down at Pat. "They look lovely, by the way."

Pat didn't have a clue what she was referring to, continuing to prepare dinner. A little while later, Sarah came back downstairs. Her hair still wet from her shower, wearing a white, thick, fluffy bathrobe, she sat down at the kitchen table.

"Looks delicious, thank you. You should come here more often. I really like this dinner ready when I walk in from work thing."

They started to eat their meal, amid small talk about their respective days.

"Anyway, have I been a good girl, or have you been a naughty boy?"

"What? You've lost me."

"I hope those lovely flowers on the back seat of your car are for me and not another lady in your life."

Pat looked vacant for a couple of seconds, before the realisation hit him like a bolt of lightning: 'Shit, shit, fuck! The flowers for Marie's grave – how could I forget?' he thought to himself.

"Oh, the flowers. Yes, of course, they're for you. Sorry, I'll go and get them, so you can stick them in some water."

Popping outside to fetch them from his car, Pat carried the flowers into the house, placing them beside Sarah, who he kissed on the cheek.

"Just a little gift for the beautiful lady in my life."

"They're stunning, thank you, Pat. I'll sort them after dinner. Oh, you are a love."

A look of contentment settled on Sarah's face as she continued to eat her meal. Pat kicked himself for being so stupid, but there wasn't a hope in hell of him coming clean – if she found out what he'd been doing that day, she'd never understood. Sarah had spent five years being married to somebody who'd cheated and lied from day one and had a very unhealthy trust of men as a result. She'd told Pat that she was dating him because he felt secure to be around, and was ten years older – an age difference, she reasoned, that meant he was less likely to play the field and cheat on her. And she was right.

Sarah had been single for six years until Pat came along. No boyfriend, special friend, or even a Christmas kiss, she sunk deeper into her work as a criminal lawyer. It was a decision that had served her well – she was already a junior partner in a very respectable law firm in the city. She had no children, something that wasn't likely to change, and at 37 saw Pat as her future partner.

They'd only been seeing other for a year, but there had been talk of moving in together at some point; and Pat had no doubt that if he were going to settle down with anyone, it would be with Sarah, especially as she got on well with his girls, which was hugely important to him. Maybe their relationship worked so well because they didn't live out of each other's pockets, seeing each other once or twice a week, dependent on Pat's shifts and Sarah's on-call duties; not to mention Pat's childcare commitments.

Outside of their respective families, though, their relationship was largely a secret – given their jobs, the force would be highly critical, as would Sarah's employer. Only Kate Arnold – who spotted them out together – knew about them at the station, and as she was a good sort, Pat didn't have any concerns that she'd spill the beans. Considering Sarah lived half an hour from Pat's work, and often represented clients at the police station or in court, it was nothing short of a miracle that nobody else had found out.

Attractive, intelligent and funny, Sarah had many admirers, including some of Pat's colleagues at the nick, who every so often made degrading, smutty remarks about her. On occasion, Kate would look over at Pat and smile embarrassingly. Pat had no choice but to remain schtum and had almost missed out on dating Sarah at all, taking twelve months to ask her out.

"Bloody hell, what kept you?" she'd said at the time. "How many hints did you need?"

The conflict of interest in their relationship and respective jobs would bring didn't bear thinking about. Sarah had hopes of making senior partner within six months and, if she did, she'd be office-bound with all the other bigwigs at the law firm ... and her days of representing society's lowlifes would be over.

Once they had eaten dinner, Pat cleared the table while Sarah went upstairs to dry her hair and get dressed. When she re-emerged several minutes later, she looked lovely – no make-up, no fuss, and without a clue how attractive she was; which made her even more desirable. Taking the flowers into the kitchen, Sarah placed them in a vase and put them on show in the centre of the dining table.

"A second night together, eh? How good is this?"

"I know," smiled Pat. "How lucky are you?"

Spending most of the night snuggled up together in front of the television, and with no callouts, they went to bed at around 11 pm. When the alarm rang out at 5 am, Pat turned over to find Sarah's side of the bed empty.

"Bloody callouts," he groaned, climbing out of bed.

He hadn't heard her leave and figured he wouldn't see her before leaving for work, which started his day on a bit of a downer. Showering and shaving, Pat got dressed and went downstairs, into the kitchen, to make himself a strong filtered coffee. Touching the coffee maker, it was warm, suggesting Sarah hadn't been out of the door too long.

Back at work for 6.20 am, Pat prepared the tea so that everybody had a brew by the time their shift started. The nightshift officers were all smiles, relieved that another stretch was over, and revelling in the perverse human pleasure of watching others about to endure what they just had. Deflecting their banter with a grin and a few choice phrases, Pat sat down in the officers' report room and logged onto the computer, typing in Marie's address. Her attempted suicide was top of the incidents list, and Pat was so engrossed with the resulting report that he failed to hear Sergeant Rose greet him.

"Oi, ignoramus! I said, good morning. Wash your ears out, you old git."

"Morning, Rosey. Sorry, I was miles away."

"Well, I hope there's a teapot in your faraway land?"

"It's all done and ready in the briefing room."

"Anything exciting while we've been off, Pat?"

"No idea, I've just logged in."

"Okay. See you in the briefing room in five. I'm just doing the handover with nights."

While Rosey went into the Sergeant's office and took the handover from the Night Sergeant, Pat locked the computer and entered the briefing room. Most of the shift were there, putting their ties on, fixing their stab vests, filling in pocket notebooks and helping themselves to the tea he'd prepared.

Kate Arnold walked in and sat next to Pat, kissing him on the cheek. "Morning, Robocop. How were your rest days?"

"Morning, young lady. You smell very pleasant today. Yeah, the rest has done me good. I would've loved to see the girls, but they had a sleepover with their mates. So, no talk about boys, pop groups, pop groups and boys. It's all they seem to do. Oh, and have their heads in their mobiles for snap chat, Facebook, Twitter, email, text, WhatsApp and all the other crap. If I missed something, I apologise. Anyway, how are you? What you been up to?"

"Not a lot. Can you believe, I'm actually pleased to be here again? I hate having four days off. They dragged and bore me so much, so being here again at this unearthly hour is all I've been waiting for."

Some of the others started to wolf whistle, berate Kate and tell her to shut up.

"Get a life, you freak!" cried another shift member in jest, a big, fat smile on her face.

A few moments later, Sergeant Rose walked in with an arm full of paperwork, handover packages, crime reports and a wry smile on his face.

"Morning, team," he began. "I hope you're all well and ready to work like Trojans for the next six days. We've got loads of stuff from nights, who were shattered last night. I'll start with some very good news: you may or may not already know, but the delightful Marie Jones decided to go for a walk at two in the morning yesterday. The only problem being, she took the back door and walked off her fourth-floor balcony. She's currently at City Hospital and not likely to survive. So, another scrounger out of the way. You must be pleased to hear that, Pat? You hated that woman."

"Well, I could think of a nicer way to go," said Pat, camouflaging his real emotions. "You say she's still alive?"

"Yep, only just – broken skull, broken leg, heavy blood loss and in a coma, so not expected to survive. Marie was found at the bottom of the flats by a passer-by. Pity they called the ambulance so quickly."

Pat didn't say another word during the briefing, staring at Rosey as he mentally re-enacted visiting Marie. Snapping out of it when the Sergeant had nearly finished his address, Pat saw him handing out paperwork.

"Right, then, that's it. Off you go and don't be late for the coroner's inquest – ten am sharp, at the courthouse. No excuses."

Pat got up and went back to the computer he was logged onto. He had no idea what his duties were, who he was with, or why Kyle wasn't at work yet. He unlocked the computer, and the Lime Court incident was still there, Pat reading it from the start again.

A call from an ambulance, stating there is a woman at the bottom of Lime Court flats with head and leg injuries, unconscious, believed to have jumped from the flats. The call came from a passer-by who is still on the scene.

Tango Alpha One, Tango Alpha Two en route.

Duty Sergeant and Duty Inspector made aware.

From Duty Inspector: As soon as units can identify the female, unit to the address, gain entry and secure the premises.

Tango Alpha One and Two show us at the scene, wait for an update.

Tango Alpha One can confirm the female is Marie Jones, well known to all officers. Her address is number 23 Lime Court.

Tango Alpha Two are going to her address to secure and preserve until further notice. Jones is unconscious, serious head and leg injury. Ambulance states she is unlikely to survive. Can the Duty Sergeant and night detective make the scene, please? Can you call Scenes of Crime?

Roger Tango Alpha One. Is the informant a witness or just an innocent passer-by?

Innocent passer-by. He's local also and will go home. We have his details and will obtain a statement shortly. I'm going with the ambulance to the hospital. 1100 is going to take the witness statement. Can Tango Alpha Two enter the flat and make an initial assessment.

Tango Alpha Two to Control, there is no visible damage to the door at 23. Entry gained, the place is a mess, I have been here many times before and it is as I remember. The balcony door is open, key still in the door, lots of black bags on the balcony, no suicide note, nothing obvious at this stage.

Received, for information: Scenes of Crime en route, the night detective is also en route, ten minutes away. Will advise boarding up. They may need to attend.

Various other updates were logged on the incident and Pat continued to read on:

From the night detective at 5 am, this is believed to be an attempted suicide. No sign of forced entry, Scenes of Crime found nothing of value inside the flat or from the balcony. No witness to the actual incident, house to house conducted on the third and fourth floor. Most occupants spoken to, though anti-police, drunk or hostile, and refusing to cooperate. Original informant statement was taken and nothing of value.

Jones is a known habitual drug user and alcoholic, no next of kin, and at this stage, she is unconscious, in a critical condition at City Hospital. Severe compound leg break and fractured skull with massive blood loss. The treating neurosurgeon is not very optimistic. Can I suggest the incident is closed pending any other evidence coming to light. Can a press release please be made with my details as the requesting detective to contact with any information.

The incident was closed by the Duty Inspector as an attempted suicide, with a request for an officer to visit the hospital at midday for any update, and a press release at 7 am.

At 1 pm the incident was re-opened by officer 977:

Visited the hospital at midday. No change in Jones' condition – still critical. Hospital will phone with any update. Day shift nurse stated a friend visited today, but no details left. Please close pending any update.

When Pat read about the visiting friend, his heart thudded, feeling like it had accelerated from about sixty beats per minute to around two hundred. Locking the computer, he went to the gents' toilets and splashed cold water on his face.

"Fuck fuck fuck!" he shouted, staring at himself in the mirror, water dripping from his face onto his uniform.

Grabbing some paper towels, he dried himself off, went into the car park and took some deep, heavy breaths.

"Right, get yourself together," he told himself, staring up at the sky. "It's no big deal. They didn't get any details, so calm down."

Returning to the officers' report room with a head full of worries, Pat sat down, trying to act as normally as possible. Grabbing his phone to act as a much-needed distraction, Sergeant Rose approached.

"Well?"

"Sorry, Sarge … well, what?"

"You were in the briefing. I distinctly saw you there. Can you go to custody and deal with the prisoner, then make sure you're at the courthouse at ten for the inquest? Remember the inquest? Come on, Pat – wakey wakey."

Pat went to the custody block to deal with a prisoner arrested by the night shift who was too drunk to be interviewed at the time. He picked up the corresponding paperwork and had a read through – '…criminal damage, leaves the pub drunk and punches a shop window, causing it to smash. 50-years-old, never been in trouble with the police, doesn't want a solicitor and admitted the offence after being arrested. This should be a very easy prisoner to deal with'.

"Hello, Nige, I'm here to interview the prisoner," Pat informed the Custody Sergeant, Nigel Mortimer, who had recently conceded defeat in his battle against a receding hairline, his shaved head giving him a slight air of menace that hadn't been present with the comb-over that preceded it.

"Surely a man of your talents is better served dealing with real criminals," said Nigel. "Aren't there any probies in there who need a nice, easy prisoner to deal with?"

"I think it's because I need to be at the coroner's court at dead on ten for the Butler boys' inquest, so I'm more than happy to have an easy start to my six days at work, Sarge."

"Where's the new boy today, Pat?"

"I've no idea. He's not at work yet, but I've no idea why."

"Maybe he needs a few more days off, the way you've worn him out the last few tours," said the Custody Sergeant with a smile.

While the prisoner was collected, Pat wondered where the hell Kyle was, unable to remember him saying he wouldn't be in that day. When the jailor handed the prisoner over at the custody desk, Pat did his best to greet him warmly – not always an easy task, given the type of people he habitually dealt with.

"Morning, Mr Preston. I'm PC Patrick, and I'm here to interview you about last night. I'm led to believe you don't want a solicitor. Can I get you a hot drink?"

"Oh, yes please, that'd be nice. Can I have a coffee with one sugar please?"

The jailor overheard and said he'd get the coffee for Pat, who entered the interview room with Mr Preston. About ten minutes later, his work with Mr Preston was done. Asking him to sit down for a minute, Pat went into the Custody Sergeant's office.

"Full and frank admission, Sarge. He's offered to pay for the damage. No previous. A really nice man, good job, home life and married, kids at university etcetera."

"Why did he do it, Pat?"

"He doesn't remember, other than he met up with friends, had a bit too much to drink and didn't have any money, so started the long walk home because his wife refused to pick him up. That's it, I guess."

"Okay, he can have a caution. Give his details to the shop, and they can bill him. Make sure he pays. He has forty-eight hours."

"Thanks. Leave it with me."

Mr Preston had his fingerprints, photograph and DNA taken by the jailor. He was then taken to the custody desk and given a caution by the Sergeant, with strict instructions to pay up within 48 hours. Given a lift home by Pat, Mr Preston was very grateful, if a little twitchy, and fearful of what his wife would say.

On his way back to the station, Pat went to the shop with the smashed window and provided them with Mr Preston's details. At the station, he completed the relevant paperwork and left the resulting file in the Sergeant's tray for finalisation — tedious procedural bullshit; but bullshit that needed doing nonetheless.

At 9 am, Pat had some tea and toast, wasted a little time pottering around the station, then grabbed some car keys and headed to court for the inquest. As he arrived, he saw that the other officers were there, as was Sergeant Rose.

"Have you woken up yet? What happened to the prisoner?" asked Rosey.

"Yes, I'm wide awake. He was cautioned and will cough up. He's been dropped off home, and all the paperwork's in your tray."

"Good man. Right, you lot, this might take some time today, so grab a sandwich and a cuppa now please, just in case."

CHAPTER 7

IT WAS JUST AS well that the courthouse had a well-stocked café. As the central court for the city, there were numerous solicitors, barristers and police officers milling about, as well as members of the public, witnesses, victims and offenders. When it turned 10 am, they all made their way to the coroner's court.

Pat, Sergeant Rose, Kate Arnold and PCs going by the name of Tony Farmer and Robert Fuller entered courtroom 6, which also contained two fire officers, a doctor from City Hospital and an ambulance crew. It was all about the emergency services on this case, with no civilian witnesses due to the Butler boys having lived in a detached house on the edge of a park, with no immediate neighbours.

The Butler boys – Francis, known as Frankie, and his twin brother, Frederick, or Freddie for short – were 28-years-old, and lived in the house left to them by their grandmother, who died when they were 19. At 2-years-old, they were abandoned by their mother, who moved to the Irish Republic, never to be seen or heard from again. The twins stayed with their grandmother and were raised by her until her death.

They had no father or grandfather – the latter of whom died before they were born – and were trouble from their first day at school. They hated any form of authority, were always fighting, and had total and utter disrespect and hatred for everyone and everything, except their grandmother, who they worshipped. Neither had worked a day in their entire life, preferring drugs, alcohol, stolen goods and social handouts, which included benefits for registered disabilities, namely depression and other mental health issues.

They'd abused hospital staff, were anti-police and very violent on arrest, which had been every week without fail. They'd had numerous spells in prison, spending their first spell behind bars at just 13-years-old. They'd intimidated witnesses, were bully boys on their estate and were hated by every facet of society.

In August, at three in the morning, their house was ablaze. The first officers on the scene were Pat, Kate, Rob and Tony, with Sergeant Rose turning up minutes after. By the time the fire brigade arrived, there was nothing anyone could do, as the house was an inferno, with both men still inside, perishing as a result. A full investigation concluded that the fire was an accident, though the cause of death had yet to be determined – thus the need for an inquest.

The usher instructed everybody to sit down, among them an administrator, whose job it was to record every word said during the proceedings, and a coroner, who sat at a desk at the top end of the room. While an official court process, there was no defence or prosecution. All the facts of the case were to be relayed to the coroner, who would make a decision as to the cause of death, based on all the information at their disposal.

The coroner looked like a hybrid of a judge and a doctor, minus the daft wig, robe and jabot. Around the mid-fifties mark, with side-parted, greying hair and round spectacles, he wore a smart pinstriped suit, collar and tie, and immaculately polished shoes.

He introduced himself, thanked everyone for attending and commented that it was the first time in thirty years that he'd held an inquest without any next of kin or family representatives being present. His job that day, he explained, was to determine the cause of death for the official records. Shortly afterwards, he called PC Patrick as his first witness:

"PC Patrick, you were first on the scene at o-three o-two hours. Can you tell me what you saw and what you did on arrival?"

"Yes, sir. I pulled up at the entrance to the park, and the house was alight. Every window had blown out, and fire and smoke were billowing out of them, up and down. A couple of locals had gathered by now. I asked the Controller to call the fire brigade and for the Duty Sergeant to make the scene. The other units then arrived, namely PC Fuller and PC Farmer. Sergeant Rose turned up about two minutes later. Oh, and PC Arnold was with me at the time – we were crewed together."

"Okay, thank you. What happened next?"

"We waited for the fire brigade. I think it was about ten minutes later that they arrived and took control of the scene. The ambulance was there, but to be fair, there was nothing they could do."

"PC Patrick, did you know at the time that there was anyone in the house?"

"We didn't know for certain, because it was three am, but the car they were using and seen in earlier that evening, was parked on the grass … and they never went anywhere on foot. Also, music was blaring out at one am when we drove past the house. The lights were on, and we saw Freddie at the upstairs window, so it was an educated guess that they would've been at home."

"Thank you. Is there anything else you would like to add at this stage?"

"I don't think so. That was my only involvement because once the fire was put out, the fire investigator and the police forensic teams carried out their investigations. There was a cordon, and PC Farmer was doing the scene log. But we had to leave and attend a fight in the town, so that was it for us."

"Out of interest, when you drove by at one am, did Frederick Butler see you?"

"Yes, he did."

"How do you know that he saw you?"

"My car window was open. It was a very warm night, and I slowed right down, he looked at me and gave me the bird … you know, his middle finger … then shouted out, calling me a wanker in a pig's uniform."

Pockets of laughter from the fire officers and ambulance crew were interrupted by the coroner: "Yes, I know what the bird is, PC Patrick. Did you say anything to him about his conduct?"

"No point, sir – it would've made him worse, his brother would've got involved, and we would've ended up arresting them. It was easier to drive off and not antagonise him. I've been called a lot worse, believe me."

"Thank you, PC Patrick. That's everything I need from you." The coroner fiddled with his spectacles, staring at Pat. "I'd like to bring something to your attention: everything you say and do as officers are logged in some way. Having received a full transcript of all communications at the scene, made by all officers' present, can you bear in mind that your flippant comment could have offended relatives, had there been any here. So, the radio transmission at o-three o-nine, from you to your Controller, and I quote: 'Yes, it would appear the Butler boys are still inside. Hopefully, the fire brigade gets caught in heavy traffic.'"

Pat bowed his head, then looked up at the coroner. "I'd like to apologise to the court for being so unprofessional. That was a remark made in very bad taste, and I should've known better. It won't happen again."

The coroner scribbled something down, paused for a few moments, then fixed Pat in his gaze. "I understand these men have been problematic for years. It's clear from the reports I have in front of me that there was an immense hatred by all concerned; that the loss to society will not be mourned. But we, as professionals, must be accountable for our actions, and the public expects us to behave without reproach, prejudice or discrimination. As far as your comments are concerned, that is the end of the matter. But I will say that they were in very bad taste indeed."

"Thank you, and sorry again, sir."

His cheeks burning, Pat returned to his seat and could feel Sergeant Rose 's stare burning through his stab vest.

The coroner confirmed that PC Arnold would only provide the same evidence as PC Patrick, so didn't need to give her account; though was told to remain, should there be the need for any questions. PCs Farmer and Fuller were next to provide their evidence before Sergeant Rose gave his account – he took charge of the scene when he arrived, arranged for the forensic teams to attend, kept the area sterile, and treated it as a crime scene until all the forensics and enquiries were complete. On finishing giving his evidence, he told the coroner that he would deal with PC Patrick's unprofessional comment, and apologised on behalf of the force.

During their lunch break, the entire team went to the courthouse's canteen, where Sergeant Rose took Pat to one side.

"What the fuck, Pat? Of all the officers, that wasn't what I expected from you. I'll record this in my note book, saying I've given you strong words of advice. I'm covering my arse, this is a public hearing, and I'll be criticised if I don't do something. Thank the lord there was no next of kin for those fucking scumbags."

"I'm sorry, Sarge," said Pat. "But you can understand why I said it. They terrorised society – and us – for years. It was a blessing in disguise, but it won't happen again, I promise."

"I do agree – good fucking riddance and all that – but there's a time and a place, Pat."

Pat sat down with his lunch, joining his fellow officers. When Sergeant Rose went to the toilet, the inevitable piss-taking started.

"Pat, you insubordinate!" joked PC Farmer. "You shall not go to the ball, because you've been a very naughty boy!"

"There there there, Pat. It's okay. Mummy will make sure these nasty men don't spill your milk," Kate sarcastically added.

"I only said what everyone else was thinking, the coroner included," said Pat.

Once lunch had finished, they filed back into the courtroom. The inquest resumed, medical evidence was heard, and it was revealed that both men had significant amounts of alcohol in their system, along with traces of heroin and cannabis. They both died as a result of smoke inhalation and one hundred per cent burns. They were burned alive while in a deep sleep that was induced by the effects of alcohol and drugs.

The fire brigade was able to determine that the fire was caused in the kitchen – the frying pan was left on the cooker with the gas on, the fire started on the cooker, then spread to the rest of the house. Both men were on the settee in the front lounge, with the television switched on. The whole house was destroyed as a result, and there were no other factors involved.

The coroner suggested a thirty-minute break for him to assess the findings and make a decision. Half an hour later, they all returned to court, and he recorded a verdict of accidental death, citing that there was no other tangible evidence to state otherwise. He thanked everyone for attending, and the court emptied.

Pat and the other officers went back to the station, but by then it was 4.30 pm, and the end of their shift, so he said goodbye to the others in the locker room before driving home. Once there, he made a cup of tea and took it into the lounge, where he sat for around an hour. His head was full of unanswered questions about Marie, the coroner's inquest and, most pressingly of all, Kyle's absence from work. His stomach groaning, he thought about making himself something to eat, but that was as far as he got; sitting on the sofa until falling asleep with exhaustion, only waking when his mobile started ringing. Grabbing it to clock Sarah's number on the phone's screen, Pat answered:

"Hey, babe, I was out cold. Can I call you back in a couple of minutes?"

"Yes, of course," replied Sarah.

Pat stood up and looked at his phone. It was nearly 7 o'clock, and he'd been asleep for a good hour. He went to the kitchen, drank a glass of water and phoned Sarah back.

"Hi, sorry, it was a long day at the coroner's court. I came home late and fell asleep in front of the television. How are you?"

"I'm okay. I'm not long home myself. I take it you realised I was called out in the early hours last night? I couldn't believe it – four am, and that bloody phone went. I was hoping for a good sleep. Anyway, the wonderful Butler boys – what was the verdict?"

"Accidental death. I had a telling-off from the coroner for inappropriate comments made at the time of the incident. He only had a full transcript of all the transmissions. Typically, it's me that gets pulled up, though to be fair he was very diplomatic about it. Rosey gave me a bollocking, but he was in total agreement about the scum getting what they deserved."

"Well, I hated representing them. They were so arrogant and very sexually suggestive. I laughed it off but always felt extremely uncomfortable around them. Both were really creepy, but they didn't deserve to die that way. It must have been horrific."

"They got what they deserved, and it's no loss to society. Bloody good riddance, I say. And think of all the money we'll save as taxpayers — anyway, enough about them. Yes, I figured you were up early because the coffee was still warm when I got up at five. I'm just off to my Kung Fu class, now that I'm wide awake after my catnap. Have a good night, honey. Catch you tomorrow at some point."

"Okay, baby. Enjoy your class. Love you."

Pat hung up, collected his gym kit and wash bag, left the house and got into his car. He sat there for a minute, Kyle darting into his mind again and, in particular, his absence from work. Driving into the city, Pat made a slight detour, heading towards the new apartments to see if Kyle's car was still parked there. As he reached the street, he drove slowly past and looked through the metal gates encircling the block of flats. There, in the same parking space as before, was Kyle's car. Pat drove off in the direction of the church hall where his class was held.

Throughout the class, Pat's thoughts flitted from one thing to another – Sarah, Marie, the Butler boys, and Kyle and Rosey's secret meetings at the station. Unusually for him, he found it hard to focus on what he was there for, his mind in a state of disconnection from his body. On the receiving end of a number of blows when sparring, Pat returned them in kind, acutely aware that if he dropped the ball on the job, he could well find himself in a lot of trouble.

Avoiding his sensei's eye at the class' conclusion, Pat drove home, taking a long, hot shower. After some food and a DVD, to avoid having to suffer more shit television, he trudged upstairs. Struggling to keep his eyes open, he took advantage of a readiness to sleep, setting his alarm for 5 am, ready for his second early shift.

"Morning, Pat," said Kyle, sitting at a computer terminal the following morning, as Pat stepped into the officers' report room.

"Blimey, you're an early bird, Kyle. Where were you yesterday?"

"I had a bit of running around to do. How were your days off?"

Kyle got up from his seat to collect a report being spat out of a printer. Pat casually walked around the desk to where he'd been sitting, spying Marie's address at the top of the screen, before Kyle made a swift return, closing the page.

"Yeah, good thanks. Yourself?"

"Not too bad. How did yesterday go?"

Pat involuntarily frowned, wondering why Kyle wanted to know about the inquest. More importantly, why had he been looking at 23 Lime Court?

"Not too bad. A long day, though – we didn't finish until four-thirty."

"What was the verdict?" asked Kyle.

"Accidental death, burned alive. But they were out cold from drugs and alcohol, so they didn't feel a thing, more's the pity."

Kyle didn't look up from his computer. Pat went into the briefing room, where the other shift members had arrived. Kyle walked in about five minutes later with Sergeant Rose.

"Morning, people," Sergeant Rose began. "I hope you're all well and not too tired after yesterday. We don't have too much handed over from nights. A few jobs are outstanding on the system, so as soon as the briefing is finished, up and out please, and get on the case. Right, first things first: you may or may not know, but the coroner recorded a verdict of accidental death for the Butlers' inquest. We didn't expect anything different, to be fair.

"I would, however, like to bring to your attention what we all say on the radio at any incident, serious or not. It came out in court yesterday that some comments were made at the time of the fire, and the coroner had a full transcript of all radio comms for the incident. I won't mention who it was, but a comment was made that was unprofessional and inappropriate.

"The coroner actually brought it up in court and gave the officer words of advice. Please remember: everything we do and say is logged or recorded somewhere, and at a serious incident where two men have burned to death, they should've been mindful. I reiterate: everything we say and do is noted and can be used against us. Right, the serious stuff is over now."

"That was me," Pat piped up. "It's better I tell you now before you lot wet yourself wanting to know who the guilty party is."

"Thanks, Pat," said Sergeant Rose. "You didn't have to say that, but I've no doubt the jungle drums would be going nonstop until you all found out. Anyway, that's it – done. Let's move on. Crewing for today, please. Tango Alpha One: Pat and Kyle. Tango Alpha Two: Kate and Tony. Tango Alpha Three: Rob and Sally. The rest of you, Jenny can you go to custody – there's a prisoner from last night. Martin, can you and Nik go to the bail hostel and see them about a recall to prison. Thanks, you lot. Let's see if we can get the job list down to a more manageable level."

The briefing room emptied amid some low muttering. Pat sat at a computer terminal and logged onto the system, finding the address 23 Lime Court ... with no update on Marie's condition. Going outside to check their vehicle in advance of the day's activities and to put his kit in the boot, Pat wondered again why Kyle had checked the system for Marie's address – was it professional curiosity or something darker at play? Kicking his doubts into touch, he went back inside to get him and head out ... but there he was again, chatting to Rosey in his office. Suppressing his resurfacing suspicions, Pat called up on the radio:

"Morning, Control. Tango Alpha One, ready willing and able. Can I have the first job of the day? Break us in gently please."

"Morning, Pat. Thank you and yes, a nice easy one for you to start with. Can you attend the precinct and check the doorway to Marks and Spencer? We had a report that there was a male sleeping rough who urinated right next to the doors. The staff have just turned up and asked if he can be moved on."

"Roger, Control, leave it with us," replied Pat.

Pat locked his computer terminal, then made for the Sergeant's office. He walked straight in without knocking, Rosey and Kyle's conversation ended abruptly.

"Come on, Kyle – we've got a job."

Kyle stood up. "Thanks, Sarge. Okay, Pat, I'll meet you on the ramp. I'll just get my kit."

Pat made his way to the police car and waited on the ramp for Kyle, who walked over, stuffing his kit in the boot and settling into the passenger's seat.

"What was that all about with Rosey?"

"I was just thanking him for letting me have yesterday off."

Pat drove out of the station and headed to the precinct, his mind busily trying to compose questions that wouldn't translate as intrusive; when, of course, that's exactly what he was doing.

"Oh okay, why were you off yesterday? What were you up to, mate?"

"I had to sort some banking out," Kyle said in only a vaguely convincing tone. "I've had to do some running around, sorting stuff since I moved up here."

Pat elected against any more questions, for now, and a short while later they arrived at the precinct. Getting out of the car, they walked towards Marks and Spencer. There was nobody by the store's doors, though a rancid puddle of piss dwelt in a corner.

"Ah. How lovely." Pat glanced at Kyle. "Fresh, at least. Rather than vintage, courtesy of some other old friends."

"You should've been on my turf when the turdster was on the loose. Fucking great Richards, he dumped all over the manor.

Even made the local news. We nabbed him when some old girl caught him dropping his latest collection in her front garden."

"Good god. Outcome?"

"They got him on some kind of public indecency charge if I remember right. Apparently, the arresting officer told him: 'This is how shit goes down!', which made me chuckle."

"You and me both," laughed Pat. "Right, let's get this shit done."

He knocked on the door, a female member of staff opening up.

"I take it he's gone, my love?" asked Kyle.

"Yes, he left when we said we were calling the police. Look at that bloody puddle. Now I've got to clean it up. He wouldn't like it if I did that outside his house, would he?"

"No, he wouldn't," said Pat. "Not that I expect he's got one. Do you know who he is or where he's from?"

"No, no idea. We have never seen him before. He wore a long black coat and shoes with no laces. He's about sixty-years-old and was really scruffy."

"Okay, we'll have a look around and give him some advice if we manage to catch hold of him," said Pat. "Take care, and if he comes back, let us know."

"Will do. Thank you, officer."

The door closed, and the staff member vanished into the store. Pat and Kyle walked back to the police car.

"Tango Alpha One Control. The male has now left the scene, and a brief description has been given. A white male, sixty-years-old, long black coat, wearing shoes with no laces. Can you ask the CCTV crew to have a look around for us? There's a puddle of you know what by the doors, which will be cleaned up. You can close that job, pending any sightings by CCTV, thanks."

"Roger that, Pat. Can you take a look outside Lime Court? We had a report from a passer-by that there are needles by the bench at the side of the flats, next to the swings. The call has only just come in."

"Roger, will do," replied Pat.

THEY DROVE OFF IN the direction of Lime Court, but there was a scant exchange of words. Pat found it hard to chat with Kyle, who did not attempt conversation, making the ten-minute journey to Marie's seem longer than usual. As they arrived, Pat parked at the front of the building, not too far from where Marie had jumped a few nights ago. They got out of the car and walked to the side of the flats. There, near the bench and swings, were about ten needles, all old and spent; and which had almost certainly been thrown out of the window from one of the flats.

"Dirty bastards. Kids play here. They have no fucking shame, this lot here. A bomb in the basement would cure this," said Pat angrily.

"It's no good, that's for sure," said Kyle. "Imagine having to live here."

Pat went to the police car, put on a pair of strengthened, anti-stab gloves, picked up a yellow disposal box and went back to the needles.

"God knows what kind of viruses these scumbags are carrying. A prick of the skin from one of these," he began, holding a blood-stained syringe aloft. "And you could be in for a hell of a shock."

Dropping the needles and syringes in the safety box, they returned to the car, Pat placing the box into the boot before joining Kyle.

"They should knock this place down and rehouse the lot – hopefully in another city," said Pat, who wanted to get Kyle talking about Marie. "The number of calls we get here, day in, day out. Is it any wonder we're always overworked?"

"I can see where you're coming from," nodded Kyle.

He didn't say anything else, other than to update the Controller with the result of the job, and Pat was relieved to make it back to the station, so as not to prolong the silence between them. They went upstairs, Kyle motioning towards the toilet while Pat entered the officers' report room. No one else was about, and Rosey wasn't in his office, so he unlocked his computer terminal and searched 23 Lime Court. Again, there was no update on Marie's condition, Pat promising himself he'd pop in and see her on his way home.

Kyle stepped into the room and sat at his computer terminal. The awkward silence from the car continued, broken by the police radio:

"Any unit, please. An immediate response to One B Lifford Road. We have a report of someone on the premises. The owner is believed to be at work, and the neighbour above said she could hear noises from the flat below. Believed burglary in progress. Silent approach required. Any unit please?"

"Tango Alpha One, we'll take that en route from the station."

"Thanks, Pat. Any other unit that can back them up please?"

"Tango Alpha Three Five, show me as en route as well."

"Thanks, Sarge," replied the Controller.

Pat and Kyle ran to the basement and jumped into the car. Pat switched the blue lights on, but kept the sirens off, so as not to alert the suspected intruder. Lifford Road was only a minute away and, as they approached, he parked the car around the corner, both officers running to the first property on the edge of Lifford Road – a large, end-terraced house converted into two flats: one up/one down.

While Kyle went to the front door, Pat climbed the wooden fence at the back of the property, landing as inconspicuously as he could manage. As he crept towards the back door, he could see that it was open. With Kyle joining Pat, the upstairs window opened, and a woman gestured to them that there was definitely somebody in there. Cautiously stepping through the back door, they heard noises emanating from the lounge. Stepping into the room, they saw a man with a holdall in his hand, placing a large pile of DVDs into it. Glancing up to see Pat and Kyle, the intruder was startled, dropping the holdall.

"Oh, fuck! Of all the Old Bill, it's bloody you, Pat."

A founding member of the TAF – Thick As Fuck – brigade, Sammy Clarke was only in his twenties, yet looked a good decade older. Skinny, with broken teeth and fetid, unkempt clothes, he was a regular customer of the force's, owing to his multiple arrests.

"Sammy Clarke, you fucking waster, you are under arrest for burglary. You do not have to say anything …"

"Yeah yeah," Clarke interrupted. "Anything I do say may be given in evidence, and all that bollocks. I fucking know it better than you, you mug."

Pat took hold of Clarke's arm, and Kyle looked in the holdall, which was stuffed full of CDs, DVDs and a mobile phone with a power lead.

"One of these days, Sammy, you're going to realise that crime doesn't pay," said Pat as he whacked handcuffs on him. "How many times have you been nicked for burglary? You're clearly a shit burglar, so why don't you try another career?"

"Fuck you, Pat. I got caught today, but I've been burgling for weeks and got away with it, so it's just your lucky day. You'll get a pat on the back and told how wonderful you are. Meanwhile, I'll be back out to start all over again. I earn more in a day burgling than you muppets earn in a month!"

"How do you know how much I earn? You can't even read or write, you thick twat," spat Pat.

Sergeant Rose walked into the lounge and saw the handcuffs on Clarke. Kyle stood clutching the holdall with the stolen items inside.

"Fuck you too, Rosey," grinned Clarke. "How on earth did they make you a sergeant? What a waste of money."

"Tango Alpha One, we have one in custody for burglary," said Pat. "The delightful Sammy Clarke has been found on the premises with stolen property in his holdall. Notify custody please."

"Roger that, Pat. Well done," replied the Controller.

Pat walked Clarke to the police car, shoved him onto the back seat and slammed the door in his face, as Clarke gave him the bird.

"Right, boys, great result," said Sergeant Rose. "I'll get a statement from her upstairs and see if I can get a contact number for the owner here. CID will want this, Pat. We've been hammered for burglaries, and you can guarantee it's Clarke, the little shit."

"Yes, he was bragging about how many burglaries he's committed over the last few weeks, Sarge, so I've no doubt it's him. I thought he was given a three-year sentence for burglary last year?"

"He was, but they released him early. The judge didn't take his early guilty plea and the fact that he admitted to fifteen other burglaries, into consideration. He appealed and won, did twelve months, and here he is doing it all again. Why the fuck do we bother, Pat?"

"Don't start me off, Sarge, for fuck's sake."

"Sorry, old boy. I know how much you love the Clarkes of this world."

Pat and Kyle returned to the police car while Sergeant Rose went to the upstairs flat to take a statement and find out who owned the property downstairs. Clarke goaded the officers from the second Pat started driving to the station, but Kyle didn't speak until they arrived at the custody block:

"Shut your mouth before I shut it for you. When we book you in, if you say one word out of turn, I'll throttle you."

"Bloody hell, Pat. Where did you get this cockney twat from?"

"Sammy, I'd shut the fuck up if I were you. Now get out and keep it zipped, for once in your life."

Pat and Kyle walked Clarke into the custody area and up to the desk. The Custody Sergeant came out and saw Clarke.

"What on earth are you doing here? Shouldn't you be in prison?"

"I did twelve months, didn't I? Been out a few weeks now. Why, have you missed me?"

"Of course. What would I do without you and your kind in my life? Anyway, enough of the pleasantries, Sammy. Let me ask these fine officers why you're here."

PC Patrick removed the handcuffs from Clarke. "Sammy Clarke has been arrested for burglary dwelling. We had a call to an address in Lifford Road, and upon arrival, we entered the downstairs flat to find him inside, placing property in his holdall. There was nobody else about, and the back door had been forced open."

"Thanks, Pat. Right, Mr Clarke, you've heard what the officer has said and, based on that, I authorise your detention. Do you understand?"

"Yep," sighed Clarke. "Can I just say, Sarge, that the flat is my aunt's place. She won't make a complaint, so I'll be out of here in an hour or so." He flashed Pat a lopsided grin, then started chuckling. "The look on your face! It'll be even funnier when they let me out!"

"He's talking rubbish, Sarge," said Pat. "There's no one on this earth who'd admit to being related to him, especially someone from a nice place like that, on Lifford Road." He looked at Clarke. "Did you think this up in the back of the car? Because you didn't mention it during your arrest, so behave and listen to the Sergeant."

Clarke was booked into custody and placed into a cell, sticking to his story that his aunt owned the flat. Pat and Kyle went to the officers' report room and made a start on the associated paperwork.

"That's a good result, Kyle. He's a fucking menace, a habitual burglar, and I'm surprised he was so clumsy today. He's normally cuter than that. He's a drug user, heroin mostly, and he'd sell his Gran for a fiver to get a fix. He's never worked a day in his life, has the rent on his flat paid and, of course, the government gives him a few extra quid for his drug dependency. Oh, and he was left thirty thousand pounds when his mother passed away – he injected the lot in less than a year."

"Wow, that's a lot of heroin. I'm amazed he didn't OD."

"If only, Kyle! I'm popping up to CID. They'll want this to help clear their burglaries and get some brownie points off the gaffers. Can you start the crime report? We'll do our statements together when I come back down."

"Okay, Pat. No problem."

Pat went upstairs to the CID office to give them the good news, then returned to the report room.

"Well, I just made their day. They reckon he's responsible for over thirty burglaries this month alone and can't wait to get their hands on him."

"A good result, then," smiled Kyle.

They got their heads down to prepare the paperwork, ready to handover to CID. The package would include both officers' statements, the witness statement from the lady above, who called the police – which was being taken by Sergeant Rose – the crime report for burglary, a statement of complaint from the householder, a printout from the computer, and a stack of information from custody, including Clarke's numerous previous convictions.

Clarke had been arrested over thirty times for house burglaries, theft from shops, drug offences and car crime. He was a habitual criminal who'd been in and out of prison his entire adult life, mostly for burglary offences. All in all, three hours of police time for a waste of space who was a continual threat to others.

"I couldn't locate the house owner, but left a calling card with instructions to call you," said Sergeant Rose, handing Pat the witness statement. "I had to get the property boarded up to keep it secure for the householder. A lot of work for one little rat."

"But worth it to keep Clarke off the streets, eh, Sarge?"

The tannoy system interrupted their conversation: "PC Patrick to reception, please. PC Patrick to reception."

"For god's sake, what now?" moaned Pat.

He made his way to the reception area, where Christine, the front office clerk, greeted him.

"Hi, Pat. Mrs Chambers is here to see you. She said a calling card was left at her address, about her flat being burgled this morning."

"Oh, fantastic. Thanks, Christine."

Pat opened the door and went into the front office. In her seventies and very smartly dressed, Mrs Chambers sat in the waiting area, smiling as she saw Pat.

"Mrs Chambers, thank you for coming in. I'm PC Patrick. Please come this way."

Pat showed her to a side room, where they both sat down.

"Firstly, I'm so sorry that you've been burgled, but the good news is we've caught the person responsible. We arrested him in your flat. He was placing some of your property into his holdall, and we caught him red-handed, as we say in the trade."

"Oh, thank you, officer, that is good news. My back door is ruined, and I'll have to get the insurance company to get it sorted. There isn't anything missing, though – I've checked. He could've taken all of my jewellery that's in the bedroom – my wedding and engagement rings that were off my husband. He passed away last year. The thought of somebody being in my home is awful, officer."

"Well, Mrs Chambers, I need to get a statement from you to confirm that you want to make an official complaint to the police. We'll make sure the courts are aware of how upset you are about this horrible incident. It won't take too long, and I'll make sure you get home safely when I've finished."

"Oh, bless you, officer. That's very thoughtful of you. I don't drive anymore, but it's only down the road to my house. I can walk, but you are kind to offer."

Just as Pat was about to start writing her statement, Sergeant Rose popped his head around the door.

"Hello, my darling. Excuse me just one minute please – I just want to speak to Pat. Pat, Mrs Chambers is Sammy Clarke's aunt. Custody has just been on – he's been driving them mad, asking if he can phone her."

"Oh, yes – Sammy's my nephew," she frowned. "He's been coming to see me every day since he came out of prison. He's my sister's boy, but she died a few years back."

"Mrs Chambers, it was Sammy Clarke we arrested at your flat for the burglary, and he's responsible for the damage to your door. He said he was your nephew, but we didn't believe him for obvious reasons," said Sergeant Rose.

"Oh, dear. Oh no, Sammy shouldn't be arrested. He's allowed in my flat. He's trying to go straight, and he's promised me he doesn't burgle houses anymore and is looking for work. He's off the drugs too. He has to have a drug test every day, and he's told me they're all clear."

"But, Mrs Chambers, he is still burgling houses. He admitted he'd been well at it since he came out of prison, and was laughing about it," said Pat. "We need to keep him locked up because he's going to admit to other burglaries in the area. He damaged your door and was trying to take your belongings, to sell to buy drugs. So, I need the statement of complaint from you now for us to do our job."

"If I give you a statement, officer, will he go back to prison?"

"Absolutely, one hundred per cent, and hopefully for more than the twelve months he received last time."

Pat saw Sergeant Rose step out of the office, leaving him with Mrs Chambers.

"Oh no – he can't go back to prison. I made him a promise I'd help him get his life together. You know, for the memory of his Mum. She'd turn in her grave if I had him sent back to prison."

"Mrs Chambers, he broke into your flat, damaged your back door, and was helping himself to your belongings. What would've happened if he'd stolen the rings and sold them for drug money?"

"He wouldn't have taken the rings, officer. He knows how important they are to me, and he adored his Uncle Jack."

"Mrs Chambers, he's a burglar. He's been breaking into houses since his release from prison, and he was laughing in our faces earlier. He couldn't care less. I think you should reconsider. He's on drugs, and that's where all his money goes – into his left arm. I'm begging you to let me take this statement so that we can get him back to prison and protect the public from him."

"No, officer. And he is off drugs – his tests are all negative, as I've already told you. Now let me out of here and let him out. I'll wait at the reception, and I'm not changing my mind."

"But what about the damage to your door?"

"That's my problem. Now let me out please."

Masking his anger and frustration behind a poker face, Pat took Mrs Chambers' statement. Reading it back to her, and confirming she didn't want to make a complaint of burglary, Mrs Chambers accepted its content and duly signed it. Pat took her into the waiting area and asked her to stay put until Clarke was released. Fuelled by rage, he stomped into the officers' report room and smashed his hands against a desk.

"I can't believe that burgling scum is walking out of here today, instead of going to prison for five years! This is fucking bullshit!"

"For god's sake, Pat. What's going on?" asked Sergeant Rose, stepping out of his office.

"He's fucking walking! She won't make a complaint, and he'll gloat for the rest of my fucking career — the stupid, stubborn old hound. Well, fuck her! If he does it again, I hope I'll be the one to say: I told you so."

"Okay, Pat, that's enough. Calm down and go and see the Custody Sergeant. Get Clarke out of here, then come back and make us all a cup of tea."

Pat looked at Kyle, who just shrugged his shoulders, then bowled towards custody, clutching Mrs Chambers' statement, approaching the Custody Sergeant.

"I have a statement of no complaint from Mrs Chambers regarding Sammy Clarke. He's walking out of here today, Sarge, and I hope he gets hit by a fucking bus, the burgling scum."

"You are kidding me, Pat."

Pat handed the statement to the Sergeant, who read it, shaking his head.

"Did you tell her about the number of burglaries he's committed and will probably admit to?"

"Sarge, I tried everything. I even thought about strangling the old coot! He's walking. I tried. Honestly, I tried, but no way am I telling him. And I won't be taking him to the front office to his aunt. If he says one word to me, I'll poleaxe the lairy little bastard."

The Custody Sergeant smiled at Pat and agreed to sort Clarke. Pat was let out of the custody block and returned to the report room. There were a number of other shift members there by now, all of whom were in total disbelief that Clarke was being let out to commit even more burglaries. Pat could tell by their expressions that they thought better of speaking to him, his heavily furrowed face staring back at him as he went to check his phone. He didn't get the chance, Sergeant Rose shouting at him from his office:

"Pat, tea please! Then come and sit down with me for a minute."

After making a pot of tea for the entire shift, Pat took his and Rosey's brews into his office, shutting the door.

"Right, don't speak – just listen. I know how upset you are, but you can't go around screaming and shouting at the top of your voice. There are admin staff, cleaners and members of the public milling about and you, of all people, should know better. He'll come again – you know he will – but I don't expect my senior officer, who's held in very high regard by me and his colleagues, to lose it like that. The gaffer heard your outburst and told me to tell you to mind your language and calm down. I'm actually surprised you lost it, Pat. You're normally calmness personified, so why has this wound you up so much?"

"I'm sorry, Sarge," sighed Pat, the rage that had consumed him dissipating. "Yes, it was out of order, but you know, and I know he'll walk out of here and rob that poor woman blind … and the next time he sees me, he'll gloat. I know he'll be breaking into houses again before we know it and putting the proceeds straight into his arm. It gets me down that we try to do our job and wankers like that laugh in our faces. We spend so much time dealing with vermin like that. Every now and again, it'd be nice to get some justice."

"I agree and understand, you know I do. But, Pat, please remember where you are and don't forget the coroner's inquest and your inappropriate comments. The last thing we need is the gaffers making an example of somebody like you. Look, it's nearly home time. Go and sort the car and take your frustrations out in the dojo or something."

"Right, Sarge. Thanks, and I'm sorry."

Pat left Rosey's office and went straight to his computer terminal. Kate made her way over to him and kissed him on the head.

"Don't let it worry you, Pat. Look at Kyle: he's all chilled and not bothered by it all."

Pat smiled tamely and, as he looked at Kyle, he smiled back at him. Checking 23 Lime Court for any updates about Marie, there was still nothing – he'd pop over to City Hospital on his way home to see her. Leaving the building with Kyle, the pair removed their kit from the car.

"Sorry about my outburst, Kyle. That's not like me at all."

"No apology needed – he's filth. I might not seem bothered but, trust me, I am."

Pat tried to find a sign in his expression, his body language, to suggest otherwise … anything to help explain his suspicions and his latest colleague's detached demeanour, but there was nothing.

LOCKING HIS CAR, PAT pulled his black baseball cap down over his eyes, then made his way to City Hospital's intensive care unit, having announced himself to the sister on duty.

He entered the room in which Marie laid, motionless, plugged into the tubes and machines keeping her alive. A nasal cannula helped her breathe, and a catheter ran under the blanket neatly folded across her breastbone. The bruise on her neck was now a sore meld of blue and green, her chest lightly rising and falling as she respired. Pat picked up a chair by the window and sat next to her. As he stared at her, the events of the last few days played repeatedly in his mind, interrupted by a nurse who came into the room to check Marie's vital signs.

"Hello, love," she smiled.

"Hi, how is she?"

"The same. She's fighting, but still very poorly."

"Do you think she'll make it?" asked Pat.

"It's fifty/fifty. The surgeon was here about a half-hour ago. He thinks it'll be some time before she wakes, if at all. The damage to her brain is severe, and her leg isn't good either, I'm afraid. He's not happy with the bruising on her neck. Are you her friend?"

"Something like that. Have there been any other visitors or enquiries about her?"

"No, love. Are you the man who came in the morning after she was admitted?"

"Yes."

"Then you're the one and only. There's no next of kin, and I've been led to believe she's an alcohol and drug user. She's had a tough few years by the sounds of it. How do you know her?"

"She's a claimant at the benefits centre where I work. I've got to know her over the last couple of years. I saw her on the news, so just popped in."

"Well, that's very nice of you. I'm sure she knows you're here and can hear your voice." She gave Pat another smile, planting her hands on her hips. "Anyway, work to be done, so I'd better be off. Stay as long as you like, and just holler if you need anything."

"Thank you. That's very kind."

Pat kissed his hand, placed it on Marie's cheek, then whispered in her ear.

"The grave looks lovely. You did a beautiful job."

Pat stood up, stared at Marie for a minute, left the room and made his way off the ward. Outside, he climbed into his car and drove to what once had been home, to see his girls.

Diane was deputy head at a large comprehensive school. A well-paid job, the house she lived in with the girls was the ex-marital home: a large, four-bedroom, modern house on an affluent estate. Pat always paid maintenance for the girls on the dot and, given her generous salary, Diane had been able to buy him out of the mortgage, which in turn had given him enough to start again. Their divorce had been amicable, with no animosity on either side. Pat and Diane had put the children first, conducting themselves as respectfully as possible to avoid upsetting them ... and, more importantly, any lasting effects that may have resulted from their parting.

Pulling up on her drive, Pat figured she was still at work because space usually occupied by her car was vacant. Knocking on the front door, he waited until fifteen-year-old Becky, still wearing her school uniform, answered. A bubbly, well-mannered girl, she had long dark hair and an air of confidence that would, Pat hoped, serve her well in life.

"Hi, Pops, how's you?" asked Becky, kissing Pat on the cheek.

"I'm good, baby girl. Where's Sophie?"

"Upstairs. Give her a shout, shall I?"

"Go on, then," smiled Pat.

He walked into the house and entered the lounge, where the television was on, and school books were scattered all over the floor. Some music channel blasted a bouncy teenybopper tune out, and Pat felt glad not knowing who the quartet of pretty boys gyrating suggestively to it was.

As Pat turned the volume down to a more eardrum-friendly timbre, Becky walked to the bottom of the stairs and shouted: "Sophie, Pops is here!"

Almost immediately, Sophie came bounding down the stairs and into the lounge with a big smile on her face. Rushing over to Pat, she gave him a big hug, followed by a kiss on the cheek. Two years younger than her sister, Sophie looked much the same, albeit smaller, and had recently started experimenting with make-up, shoving herself towards young adulthood, when Pat would've preferred her to remain firmly rooted in childhood for a couple of years yet.

"Hi, Daddy! Been to work today?"

"Hi, dolly. Yes, just finished. How's school?"

"Yeah, alright, I suppose."

"How were your party and sleepover?"

"Great, except some of the older boys made fools of themselves and were sick everywhere."

"That was the best bit!" laughed Becky.

"It was quite funny," smirked Sophie. "Do you want a bagel with peanut butter? I'm having one."

"Oh, yes, that sounds nice," said Pat.

"Do you want one, Becks?"

"Yes, please."

Pat smiled at Becky as the sound of cups and plates being placed on kitchen surfaces filled the house. Sophie had a remarkable knack of making the kind of noise more commonly associated with the aviation industry whenever she went anywhere near crockery. She was loud pretty much everywhere she went, but Pat loved her even more for it – clumsy, but a lovely girl.

"How was your day at school?"

"Good. Lots of mocks coming up, so heaps of revision, but I'm on top of it," said Becky. "Has Mom spoken to you about the trip to Barcelona next April?"

"Yes. I said you could go, and I'll put half the money up."

"Oh, good – thanks, Dad! I love Barcelona, and it'll be nice to go with my school friends. Mom didn't say she'd spoken to you, though."

"She didn't – she emailed me. I only read it this morning. Four hundred and sixty quid is a good price for a week."

"It is, Dad. I knew you'd say yes!"

Becky gave Pat the cheeky smile that had so often been his undoing when it came to treating her, but he didn't mind in the least – she wasn't any trouble. Never had been, just like her sister.

"Your Mom not around, then?" he asked.

"Not yet."

"What time's she due to be home?"

"She should be here any minute. She was late last night because of some Ofsted inspection, so she promised she'd be on time today."

Sophie walked in with a tray of bagels and peanut butter.

"Ooh, lovely. Thank you, baby girl," said Pat.

"Thanks, Sophie," said Becky.

Placing three plates on the table, Sophie returned with three cups of tea. While they sat eating the bagels, the girls transfixed by the perma-dancing pretty boys, and the front door opened, Diane walking into the lounge a few moments later.

"A picnic without me – that's so unfair!"

"Hi, Mom. I'll make you one too. Go and sit down," said Sophie.

"Thanks, Sophie. Can I have soft cheese please?"

"No probs," smiled Sophie.

Sophie left for the kitchen while Diane sat next to Pat.

"Hi, Ma, how was your day?" asked Becky.

"Good. Not as long as yesterday, thankfully."

"Dad said he'd pay half towards Barcelona."

"Thanks, Pat," said Dianne, turning to face him. "I got your email. They want a deposit to hold a place, so I'll sort that. Just give me your half when you've got it."

"Will do," said Pat. "And thanks for sorting it out. I hear you had the Ofsted inspectors at school yesterday. How did it go?"

"Bloody awful! I didn't get home until nine last night. We were run ragged, to try and make it as go as smoothly as possible. They arrived at ten and didn't leave until eight."

"Oh, well, back to normal today, eh?" said Pat. "They're a pain, especially when you have to pretend everything's running smoothly. It's so false."

"Yep, but that's it for another year. I've done my bit, and everybody was on their best behaviour. Fingers crossed that means a good report."

Sophie walked in with her Mum's cup of tea and bagel.

"Thank you, darling. You are a good girl."

Diane took her first mouthful, sipped some tea, then looked at Pat.

"Did you have anything to do with the suicide attempt at Lime Court a few days ago?"

"No, the night shift dealt with it. I was off."

"Is this the same Marie Jones, whose husband and kids were killed in that crash all those years ago? The one that you went to school with? You went to their funeral, didn't you?"

"I did. And I doubt it," Pat lied, not wanting to disclose just how far she'd fallen, an odd sense of loyalty kicking in. "She wouldn't be living in Lime Court, would she?"

"No, I suppose not. It's an awful place."

Hoping in vain that Diane would channel-hop, to spare him the torture of boy band hell, Pat took a quick glimpse either side of him, remembering when this was his day-to-day life. There were lots he missed about family life, most notably the company of his daughters, but it was pointless harking back to a past that, while good for the most part, was far from the halcyon years he sometimes liked to pretend had featured more prominently than had actually been the case.

"Thanks for the bagel and tea, baby girl," said Pat, rising to leave and kissing his girls' goodbye. "Have a good day tomorrow."

"Thanks, Dad," Becky and Sophie said in unison.

"See you later, Di," said Pat.

"Bye, Pat. Catch you soon and thanks for popping in."

Driving home, Pat stopped off at the gym for a workout. At its worst a mind-numbing source of boredom, he forced himself to push past his pain barrier, the adrenaline rush that followed, when standing in the shower, numbing muscles that age was making increasingly sore. Avoiding the temptation of a quick snack from the gym's vending machine, Pat drove home. Receiving no reply when calling Sarah, he made himself some dinner and ate it while watching television with his feet up.

Assuming she must have been working late, he went to bed at ten o'clock; falling asleep almost straight away, relieved that the shriek of his alarm clock wouldn't shake him from his slumber early the next morning. Stirring naturally at nine, Pat tossed his quilt aside and slipped into his dressing gown. With plenty of time until his shift started at three that afternoon, he made himself a brew and drank it while taking in the day's sports news. Breakfast was prepared and eaten and, after another workout at the gym, Pat returned home to ready himself for another shift.

Back at work for a little after 2.30 pm, well before the team briefing, he logged onto the computer to check on 23 Lime Court. A mountain of texts and updates awaiting him, Pat wanted to read them there and then; but with the early shift still milling around, and seeing Rosey enter his office, he had a rethink, locking the computer.

He looked up, the other officers seeming to avoid his eye. Correction: they didn't risk eye contact at all, which made him wonder what had happened to their usual joviality. Was there something he didn't know about and, if so, what? As other members of the late shift arrived, Sergeant Rose appeared behind him.

"Pat, you got a minute?"

"Sure," said Pat, getting up and following Rosey into his office.

"Shut the door, please."

"Sounds serious," said Pat, shutting the door and taking a seat opposite the Sergeant.

"I need to let you know: the shit's hit the fan."

"Really? Whose shit this time?"

"Yours and Kyle's. At this stage, it's just a suspicious incident, but it has to be treated as a death in custody because he was released yesterday and was dead within twenty-four hours."

"You've lost me, Sarge," said a bewildered Pat. "Who are we talking about?"

"Sammy Clarke."

"You've got to be fucking kidding me. What happened?"

"He was released yesterday at three pm and went back to his aunt's flat in Lifford Road. We had a call in the early hours to the garages at the back of the Prince of Wales pub, and he was found there, dead. Heroin overdose. Well, suspected overdose – there was a needle nearby, and a puncture wound in his arm. The Independent Police Complaints Commission are all over it."

"Jesus Christ. But why should Kyle and I be worried? We had nothing to do with him, apart from nicking him … and that was justified. And it was his aunt who refused to make the statement, so I'm not sure why we need to be concerned."

"You should be – they've pulled the custody tapes and, apparently, you can be heard making all sorts of threats about him being hit by a bus or something. The gaffers are going apeshit, and CID are assisting the IPCC."

"I don't think me making those kinds of comments should be too much of a problem."

"It will be, especially because of your outburst over the Butler boys, and it being brought up in the coroner's court. Plus, I've put it in my pocket book to say you were warned about your future conduct."

"Oh bollocks, I forgot about that," sighed Pat, running a hand over his face.

"To add insult to injury, Mrs Chambers came back into the nick yesterday to make an official complaint to the Duty Inspector about your conduct towards her and her nephew."

"What about my fucking conduct?!" shouted Pat. "That's bullshit, Sarge, and you know it!"

"Pat, don't shoot the messenger. I don't know too much about the complaint, so chill out. We'll get the briefing out of the way and see where today takes us."

Pat and Rosey stepped into the briefing room together; a strange hush had descended upon the crew already gathered. Pat did not attempt to disguise his frustrations, his usually relaxed demeanour ceding to a tightness, an anxiety, in his body language that must've shown in his expression too as he took a seat next to Kate.

"Right, you lot: good afternoon. Not much to handover today. Earlies were busy, but managed to get rid of a fair few jobs …

though there's some news from last night. Sammy Clarke was found dead from a suspected heroin overdose."

The death of one of society's wasters would usually have elicited a cheer and the clapping of hands. But no, not this time. News had spread that there had been a 'death in custody', and everybody present knew what that could mean for Pat.

"The IPCC are here and are all over it – they're working with our CID. There are gaffers here too, so may I suggest that as soon as the briefing is over, you get out of the station and only come in if it's absolutely necessary. Kyle and Kate, can you take Tango Alpha One. Tony and Drew, Tango Alpha Two. With it being lates, the rest of you: single crewing, please. Rob, can you take Tango Alpha One Zero." He pointed at Martin and Nik. "And you two, Tango Alpha One One and Tango Alpha One Two, please. Kyle, they may need to chat with you today, but for now, it's only Pat, so be prepared to come in as and when."

Kyle flashed Pat a wry smile, but Pat remained stone-faced. The door opened and in walked the Duty Inspector. Broad-shouldered and with a near-permanent frown on his face, he exuded an air of authority that he seemed to thrive on, and was immaculately turned out, a crisp white shirt hugging a tight frame and shiny black brogues adorning his size nines.

"Afternoon, all."

"Good afternoon, sir," the team replied together.

"Rosey, when you're done here, can you come and see me please?"

"Yes, sir. One minute – we're just finishing off."

The Inspector left, and Sergeant Rose told the shift to have a good day, reminding them to stay out of the station.

"Pat, can you stay around for a minute?" he said as the other officers exited the room, lending Pat their support by patting him on the head or shoulder … as Kyle left without saying a word.

"Wait here a moment. I won't be long," said Rosey.

While Sergeant Rose went to see the Inspector in his office, Pat unlocked his computer, wondering what awaited once they'd finished their little chat. He'd already been warned against his conduct, but the Sergeant knew as well as he did that he was a bloody good cop. Would that cut the mustard now that the IPCC and CID were involved?

He'd know soon enough, staring at the computer screen to see Marie's incident still there. That it had been reopened and put back on the system meant there had been a significant update but, much as Pat wanted to read it, he clicked on the incident at Lifford Road first. Scrolling down the screen, he arrived at the point where Clarke was released from custody, then read on.

At 17.30 hours: a call from front office asking the Duty Inspector to make contact. We have a Mrs Chambers here, and she wishes to make a complaint against police.

Duty Inspector aware. Will attend in fifteen minutes. Please ask Mrs Chambers to take a seat.

At 18.45 hours, from Duty Inspector: I have received a complaint from Mrs Chambers re recent dealings with officers from this station. I have completed the complaint form and advised Mrs Chambers we will be in touch. Forms passed to professional standards as per force policy. Please close this incident.

Incident reopened at 02.16 hours. Call from a member of the public to say there is a man unconscious in the garages at the back of the Prince of Wales pub. Ambulance called. Night shift Tango Alpha Two en route.

02.24, from Tango Alpha Two at the scene: Control, there is a deceased male here, and I can identify him as Sammy Clarke, recently released from custody. Can you make the Duty Inspector and the Sergeant aware, please? Ambulance has arrived, and they have confirmed life extinct. Of note, there is a needle by the body and his arm is exposed, showing a needle mark. Treating as suspicious and starting an incident log. Can I have another unit to join us, please?

02.26: Roger Tango Alpha Two, Inspector and Sergeant are on their way. From Duty Inspector, can you make sure nobody goes in or out, and please keep the ambulance crew at the scene? Night CID are aware and will be making their way to you.

02.28: received Control. We have taped the area off, and the body is still in situ. There is CCTV at the pub. Can you make sure this is noted on the incident, please? I am aware Clarke was released from custody this afternoon and had been released into the care of his aunt. Can we get a unit over to her address and see what we can find out? The unit attending, please note she made a complaint against police this evening.

02.33: Duty Sergeant at scene.

02.36: CID and Duty Inspector at scene.

02.39: from night detective: can we have the Scenes of Crime Officer please, and can a unit be tasked to go to Clarke's address and see if there is anyone there? Do not enter for now.

02.41: Tango Alpha Three sent to Clarke's address of 115 George Street. Scenes of Crime contacted and en route. Eta: thirty minutes.

02.43: Tango Alpha One Zero tasked to attend Lifford Road and speak to Mrs Chambers. Advised re recent complaint.

02.44, from Inspector: can a unit go to the pub and see if the CCTV was switched on or working? Bear in mind the licensee is Barry Carter, well known to officers ... he may be a little frosty?

02.46, from night detective Charlie Five Zero: I know Carter very well, I will speak to him.

02.47: Roger Five Zero.

02.55, from Tango Alpha Three: I'm at George Street, it's all in darkness. Front and back are secure. Can you advise Duty Inspector?

02.56, from Duty Inspector: received that, Tango Alpha Three. There is no need to stay there, it's secure front and back, so nothing for us to do there at this time.

02.57, from Tango Alpha Three: thanks, boss. Control show me leaving George Street.

02.58: Roger that.

03.01, from Tango Alpha One Zero: attended Lifford Road and woke Mrs Chambers. She invited me in and has been told about Sammy. She has taken it reasonably well and has asked if PC Patrick was aware of Sammy's death. Not sure what that means, Control, but I am aware Pat was the arresting officer yesterday. Mrs Chambers is adamant Sammy was off drugs since his release from prison, and she can prove it by showing us his drug test results for the last month.

She last saw Sammy when she was at the nick after his release from custody. He said he was going to see some friends and go for a drink, but he didn't say where. She said he was going home first for a shower and to get changed. She gave him twenty pounds to have a few drinks but concedes he probably went mad on the drugs because he had been wrongfully arrested. No other details here at the moment. She is okay and happy for me to leave. I have told her we will be in touch in the morning for a statement.

03.07, from Scenes of Crime: please show me at the scene.

03.08: Roger that.

03.17, from night detective: Charlie Five Zero, I have spoken to Carter at the pub. The CCTV does not work, and it has been off for two days. He has no information of note. He does know Clarke and states he has not been in the pub for a couple of weeks. This line of enquiry is no longer viable. Carter was very reasonable and co-operative.

03.21: Roger that, Five Zero, and received with thanks.

03.44, from Duty Inspector: at this moment in time we have exhausted all lines of enquiry. Can officers stand down with my thanks. Night detective is to remain at the scene to assist Scenes of Crime officer. Tango Alpha Two will stay and await the recovery of the body once Scenes of Crime has finished.

03.47, from Control: thank you, sir. All units re the above, please stand down. Tango Alpha Two, acknowledge you are staying at the scene with the night detective and Scenes of Crime.

03.48, from Tango Alpha Two: message received.

05.02, from Scenes of Crime: finished at the scene. Of note, the needle has been recovered, and the deceased's body is being taken to the morgue at City Hospital. Tango Alpha Two is going with the body, and the night detective will be seizing the clothing at the morgue. Scene has been left sealed off and boarding up are here to secure the garage, should we need to visit again in the daylight hours.

05.05, from Control: received with thanks.

06.31, from night detective: Charlie Five Zero, clothing from deceased has been seized, bagged and tagged. Clothing booked into the property store under unique reference SC01-SC08 of today's date. Body tagged and at the morgue to await post-mortem.

06.40, from Control: noted with thanks.

07.02, from Duty Inspector: day shift, Independent Police Complaints Commission has been notified due to this being a death in custody. Please close the incident until further notice.

07.08, from Control: comments at 07.02 noted. Job now view rated until further noted.

PAT SAT BACK, DEEP in thought. There wasn't anything in the report that led him to believe Clarke's death had been anything other than a straightforward overdose. Pat needed that confidence boost in time to face the wrath of his bosses, and the IPCC was like a dog with a bone whenever there was anything untoward, and a police officer was involved. Remembering the update concerning Marie, he typed in 23 Lime Court as Sergeant Rose emerged from the Inspector's office.

"Pat, can we have a word?"

"On my way," said Pat, relocking the computer and following Rosey into the Inspector's office.

"Come in, Pat. Take a seat," said the Inspector.

"Thank you, sir."

"Right, Pat, you've been told about Sammy Clarke, that the IPCC is here as a result of it being a death in custody, and our CID are assisting them now. We're waiting for the results of the post-mortem but expect an overdose to be recorded – he's a habitual drug user and abuser. The IPCC has pulled the custody tapes from the time you walked in with Clarke to the time he was released and left the front office.

"Problem number one: we have an official complaint from his aunt about the way you spoke to her while trying to convince her to make a statement of complaint about the burglary. Problem number two: the tapes from custody reveal your unsavoury comments about Clarke when you advised the Custody Sergeant about the no complaint and to release him.

"Now, from my point of view, this is a straightforward investigation re Clarke and his death, but the IPCC lead investigator isn't very pleased about your conduct and unprofessionalism. Sergeant Rose has had to speak to you recently about comments you made at the inquest into the Butler boys' deaths, so as you can see, that leaves us open to criticism, especially management."

"Boss, I do understand about the Butler boys' thing," Pat reasoned. "But that was in the summer. That was six months ago – it's not as though it was two incidents in one day. I get the feeling this is being stretched a little too far."

"Maybe, Pat. But you were told a few days ago about your conduct and unprofessional approach to these types of incidents. Yes, it happened in the summer, but you were advised this week, so to me that makes it un-stretched."

"Fair enough," shrugged Pat. "I suppose I can see that from the job's perspective."

"Anyway, they want to speak to you. Obviously, at this time, it will be informal, to get a full account from you as the arresting officer. This isn't a witch hunt. It is, as you know, standard procedure for all deaths in custody. What we do have in our favour is that your actions had no way of contributing to Clarke's demise. He was found dead in the early hours, and released from custody just after you went off duty at three pm. My advice is: listen to what they have to say and answer as best you can – which I know you will. You're a fantastic police officer and very highly regarded, Pat."

"Thank you, sir. And of course, I will. It's straightforward, apart from my comments in custody. The complaint from his aunt? That's nothing. Any officer worth their salt would've tried everything to get that statement of complaint."

"I agree, but for now let's comply with their requests and get them out of the station. I don't like having them around, telling me what to do. When you're finished, come back and let me know how it went."

"Will do, boss."

Pat stood up and, straight backed, left the Inspector's office, the door closing behind him. Striding back to his computer terminal, he was about to check the Marie Jones update when CID appeared, together with two men wearing suits, clutching clipboards and discs.

"Here we go," Pat mumbled to himself.

The CID officer, he knew well – one Jonathan Cross. A highly capable, yet somewhat peculiar-looking detective, his standard coat of fake tan had deepened to afford him an orangey glow that under other circumstances would've brought a smile to Pat's face. Pat knew from their previous interactions that Cross held him in high regard, which he hoped would work in his favour when it came to repelling whatever shitstorm was heading his way.

"Pat, this is Robert Handley and Adam Yenton. They're civilian investigators from the IPCC. I believe you've been told they need to speak to you about Sammy Clarke?"

"Yes, John, I have. Good afternoon, gents."

Pat stood up and shook their hands.

"Pat, I'll leave you with them. Take them to custody and use one of the interview rooms in there. You'll need a TV and DVD player. When you're done, can you bring them back up to my office?"

"Yes, of course. See you later, pal."

"Can I get you a drink, gentlemen?" Pat asked Handley and Yenton as John walked out of the room.

"You're alright, Pat," said Handley. "We'll get on with it if you don't mind."

"Not at all. Let me show you to the interview room."

Pat led them into the interview room in the custody suite. Not much bigger than a box room, its walls were padded for soundproofing, and the carpet was so worn it was virtually threadbare, pockmarked by the occasional cigarette burn; scars from a time when smoking was permitted. A table stood in the centre of the room, around which four chairs were positioned, with a tape machine ready to record their conversation.

Handley and Yenton sat on one side of the table, and Pat directly opposite. Pat felt more than a little strange, about to find himself on the receiving end of questions, when he was used to firing them at suspects. But, like them, he was about to face a battle of wits.

"Thanks for doing this, Pat. For the benefit of the recording, I'm Robert Handley, and this is Adam Yenton. We are civilian investigators employed by the Independent Police Complaints Commission, and our role is to gather the facts as best we can. We both have considerable experience. Adam was a police officer for thirty years, and I worked for the benefit fraud department for eighteen years. Today we need to speak to you about the incident involving Sammy Clarke. If there are any issues or anything you want to say voluntarily, please feel free. We shouldn't keep you too long. Before I start, are there any questions?"

"Yes. On what basis are you recording this interview?"

"At this moment in time, it's an informal chat to get the facts about yesterday and last night. So, we'll be making notes as we go along, depending on who's asking the questions."

"Okay, fair enough."

"Let's get started, then," said Handley. "Can you tell us why you arrested Sammy Clarke yesterday for burglary dwelling?"

"I was on duty with PC Kyle Aston, and we received a call from the occupant of flat One B Lifford Road, saying there was noise coming from the flat below and that there should be no one at home. So, we treated it as an immediate response – blue lights, but not sirens because it was so close to the nick. When we entered the downstairs flat, Sammy Clarke was placing CDs and DVDs into a holdall. He's a well-known burglar, and there was damage to the back door, so I arrested him for burglary, handcuffed him and took him to the station. The facts were relayed to the Custody Sergeant, and he was detained accordingly."

"Thanks for that, PC Patrick."

"Pat. Just call me Pat."

"Okay, Pat, it is," said Handley.

"What happened next, Pat?" asked Yenton.

"We started the paperwork, and I went up to CID to let them know that we had Clarke in custody. I came back down, and we completed the paperwork package."

"Why let CID know he'd been arrested?"

"Clarke is good for burglaries in the area, and I was aware he'd been out of prison for a few weeks. The break-ins had increased, CID was trying to find out who it was, and the last time we nicked Clarke, he admitted to loads of burglaries and was sent to prison for three years. CID would've spoken to him to clear some cases."

"Pat, can I ask you what your opinion of Clarke was?"

"My opinion? Burgling, lowlife, druggie scum who's brought misery to hundreds of victims over the years. He's a liar who'd sell his grandmother for a fiver if it meant he could get his next heroin fix."

"Wow, that's very honest of you," said Handley. "He's clearly on your radar."

"Radar? What radar?"

"You know, Pat … there are always criminals who the police love to arrest and get locked up. The ones who bring misery to hundreds of people, who'd sell their grandmother for a fiver."

"I don't have a radar. If they commit a crime and I'm there, I arrest them. That's it. If you're suggesting I'd target Clarke or anyone else, I wouldn't – that's not my style."

"It was just a figure of speech, nothing more. When you arrested Clarke, was there much of a conversation between you, him and PC Aston?"

"There were the usual pleasantries from him, and I've no doubt I gave a little back, but nothing out of the ordinary."

"Would you mind recounting the conversation, as best you can, between you and him?"

"It wasn't too much, as far as I can remember. When I arrived at the flat and walked into the lounge, Clarke looked at me and said something like: 'Fuck me, it's the Old Bill.' He knows me and said my name. I took hold of him and arrested him for burglary. I started to caution him, and he recited the caution, saying he knew it better than me. I said something like: 'You're not a very good burglar. Why don't you give up and try something else?'

"He was all cocky and said he'd been burgling for weeks. Or something like that. We handcuffed him, took him to the car, and he started on Kyle, calling him a cockney twat. That's it really. Oh yes, there was mention of him coming out of prison after twelve months, having been given three years. Sergeant Rose said it was because the judge failed to reduce his sentence for clearing up so many burglaries."

"Is that it?"

"Yes, that's it."

"What about in custody? Were there any other conversations with him?"

"Not that I recall. He may have said something here and there during the booking-in procedure, but that was my recollection of it all."

"Thank you, Pat. I'll now proceed to Mrs Chambers and her refusal to make a statement of complaint. She's made a complaint about you for the way you conducted yourself. Tell me what happened, and your conversation with Mrs Chambers."

"Sorry, but if there's a complaint about me, I need to be served forms as soon as the complaint is received. If, as you say, she's complained, then my account to you about my dealings with Mrs Chambers should be conducted with a federation representative. So, for now, until I get clarification about that, I won't discuss the matter re Mrs Chambers any further."

"Okay, Pat, we'll leave that there for now, and we respect your rights re the complaint," said Yenton. "We may speak to you about this at a later date."

Handley folded his arms across his chest. "Tell me what you know about the death of Clarke and the circumstances in which he was found."

"I don't know anything about his death. I wasn't on duty last night and came in at two-thirty today to start my late shift."

"Surely you must know something about his death, though? Have you been told what happened by the early shift, or had a look on the computer while you were waiting to be spoken to by us?"

"Look, I don't like the way you're asking that question," said Pat, his defences flying up. "I've just told you I wasn't here when it happened."

Handley and Yenton looked at each other for a moment or two, then turned back to face Pat.

"When you found out there was no official complaint about the burglary, from Mrs Chambers, what did you do next?" asked Yenton.

"I took a no complaint statement and went to custody, where I showed the statement to the Custody Sergeant and advised him to release Clarke."

"What was said by you, and then by the Custody Sergeant? Try and remember as best you can please, Pat."

Pat sat back in his chair. He knew they had a recording of their conversation, which obliged him to tell them the truth.

"I asked the Sergeant to show Clarke to the front office and said that if I took him, I'd probably break his scrawny neck. I might have referred to his aunt as an old coot or something similar."

Handley and Yenton looked surprised at Pat's honesty. Pausing a while, Yenton asked the next question:

"Pat, you arrest him after being caught in the act. He makes unsavoury comments to PC Aston, admits to committing numerous burglaries, and gloats about only serving twelve months of a three-year sentence. He laughs in your face in custody, and gets to walk out of the police station because you can't convince his aunt to make a complaint."

"Yes, that's about the gist of it."

"Would I be right in saying you were angry and annoyed that another of life's wasters was beating the system? That it gets under your skin, knowing he'll burgle again, upsetting hundreds of people and injecting heroin?"

"Yes, you'd be right to say that, and more."

"It's suspected that Clarke died of a heroin overdose in the garages behind the Prince of Wales pub."

"What a surprise."

"What you may not know is that since his release from prison, and under the terms of his licence, he had to have a drugs test every day. That's every single day since his release and, to date, that's forty-one tests – all of which have been negative. Not a trace of opiates or cannabis since his release. Had there been any positive results, he'd have been back in prison to finish the remainder of his three-year sentence."

"Now, that does surprise me," said Pat with genuine disbelief.

"I'm sure it does. What we find strange is that within a few hours of being released from custody, telling his aunt he was meeting friends to go for a drink, and going home to get changed, he's found dead with a needle mark in his arm."

"Well, I don't know what to say, other than old habits die hard. Clarke's given up before and then went back on the drugs. Maybe he was celebrating getting one up on the police and had one fix too many."

"One up on the police? Or one up on you, Pat?" asked Yenton.

"It's the same thing, isn't it? After all, I am the police, and I was the one who nicked him. And let's not forget, he broke into his aunt's house, damaged the door and was helping himself to her CDs and DVDs. He was caught burgling and wormed his way out of it. And, unfortunately for him, for the last time."

"What's that supposed to mean?"

"It means exactly what I said. His burgling days are well and truly over now, so move on because I have things to do."

Pat did not attempt to hide the irritation that hadn't so much crept into his voice than shot into it, soaking it with aggression. Unprofessional? Almost certainly, but he'd had enough of the powers that be defending the perpetrators of crime, while their victims were left to pick up the pieces of their often-shattered lives. And then it came: the question, posed by Handley, that he never thought he'd hear:

"Where were you last night, PC Patrick?"

Pat looked at them both in shock, his heart racing. He clenched his fists and, for a moment, thought he was going to faint. Waiting until the feeling passed, he stood up.

"You've got to be fucking kidding me! That's it – interview over, you pair of fucking muppets! You're asking me to justify where I was last night. Well, if you want an answer to that, arrest me and get me a fucking solicitor."

Pat stormed out of the interview room and called the jailor over.

"Let me out of here!"

The jailor let Pat out of the custody block, and he ran into the back yard for some fresh air. He felt sick, his stomach churning, head thumping. Gasping for air, his mind whizzed.

"Did they just ask me that?" he murmured to himself. "Are they pointing the finger at me because I do my fucking job? Are they fucking stupid or what? Where the fuck did they drag those pair of wankers from to ask me questions like that?"

Leaving the yard, Pat went to the gents' toilets and locked himself in a cubicle. Sitting on the toilet seat, he rubbed his eyes, still in shock at what he'd heard – they couldn't honestly consider him a suspect ... could they?

"Calm down! Calm the fuck down and get yourself together!" he hollered, smacking his palm against his forehead.

Pat remained in the cubicle, his thoughts running riot in his head until the tannoy rang out:

"PC Patrick to the Inspector's office. That's PC Patrick to the Inspector's office please."

'Oh, fuck. Now I have to face him after all of the promises I made about being professional, having just stormed out of an interview,' thought Pat. 'Oh, well – fuck it. Wait until I tell the boss what they asked me'.

Leaving the cubicle, Pat stood over a basin, splashing water on his face and looking in the mirror.

"Right, head sorted – off you go," he told his rather bemused-looking reflection.

Leaving the toilet block, he made his way to the Inspector's office. Noticing that Rosey's office door was open, he flicked his eyes to one side to see him stood talking to Handley and Yenton. Clocking Pat walking past, they all stopped talking. 'Sneaky bastards,' he thought to himself as he approached the Inspector's office, hearing the door to Sergeant Rose's office slamming shut.

Pat stood at the Inspector's door, sucking down a succession of deep breaths before giving it a knock.

"Come in!" shouted the Inspector.

Pat went in and was told to sit down. The Inspector was writing in a diary and, for a good five minutes, didn't so much as look up to acknowledge Pat. Pat knew he was in the shit and had no doubt the two IPCC officers had been in and advised the Inspector about his conduct in the interview. But what did he really have to worry about? Pat held the moral high ground, aside from a few contentious, but perfectly human, comments. But would that count for anything when faced with what he was up against?

The Inspector closed his diary and looked at Pat. He sat back in his chair, knitting his hands together and placing them on his head.

"Is it a deliberate act on your behalf to piss me off today? Or can I assume it's purely coincidental that you've behaved so unprofessionally in an interview with two members of the IPCC?"

"Hold on, boss. Before you go any further, do you know what happened in there?"

"Hold on yourself, PC Patrick, and remember who you're addressing!" barked the Inspector. "And, in answer to your question: no, I don't know or care what went on in there. We're obliged to cooperate with the IPCC. They have a huge say in matters they investigate, and, for your information, this little scenario is being monitored by the Chief. When I hear you've been swearing and shown petulance during the interview – and I have to report this to the Chief – then no – I won't bloody well hold on!"

Pat kept schtum, sensing any intervention on his part, right then, would further inflame the Inspector's wrath.

"Having been made aware of your behaviour, the Chief wants you to be served forms for incivility towards members of the public. And then there's the small matter of the complaint made by Mrs Chambers regarding the way you treated her yesterday. So, all in all, I'd say you need to be very careful about how you conduct yourself from now on because if this goes public, there could be further implications."

"What implications?" asked Pat. "I don't understand."

"You seem to forget that in the last few days you've been warned about your professionalism by the coroner, a complaint was lodged by Mrs Chambers, and now forms for incivility towards two IPCC officers. Everything we do these days is scrutinised infinitely, and having an officer on a mission to upset everyone during challenging and emotional times will not bode well! The Chief isn't your biggest fan at the moment, Pat, and to be honest nor am I. What I need to do is liaise with professional standards and get the forms over for you to sign. In the meantime, I suggest you go to Rosey's office and apologise to Mr Handley and Mr Yenton."

"Gaffer, can I just make you aware of something first?"

"No, you can't. I don't want to hear another word from you unless it has 'I apologise' in it." The Inspector sniffed disapprovingly. "That's it. Go to Rosey and get that apology sorted."

Pat sat there, desperate to tell the Inspector that he'd been asked to justify his whereabouts the night before. Was about to blurt it out, when the Inspector's expression soured even more.

"Have I not made myself clear? We're finished for now! Leave my office and go and apologise right away!"

Leaving the office, his tail firmly wedged between his legs, Pat stood in the hallway. It was as if he was glued to the carpet; such was his reluctance to walk the ten paces to Sergeant Rose's office. He was still furious with Handley and Yenton but knew he had to apologise, hard as that would be to stomach.

Forcing himself forward, he inched towards Rosey's office, the door to which was shut. Pride prevented him from immediately taking those extra few steps, so instead, he poked his head into the officers' report room and saw Kate sitting at a computer terminal. Sensing his presence, she turned, smiling thinly at Pat and walking over to him.

"What's going on, Pat?"

"I'll tell you later, Kate. Where's Kyle?"

"He's taking a statement from a woman in the front office who's had her purse stolen. Are you okay? You look shell-shocked."

"No, not really. Let's just say I have to do something that goes against my values and principles. The two IPCC knobs are with Rosey, and I've got to go in, cap in hand, and beg for forgiveness."

"Why? What the hell happened? Is this to do with Sammy Clarke?"

"Yeah, but there's more to it. Has boy wonder said anything to you about yesterday?"

With the door handle to Sergeant Rose's office being turned, Kate ran back to her computer and Pat took those extra few steps, knocking on the door in a forced gesture of ostensible willingness.

"Pat, come in," said Rosey in a stern voice. "Take a seat."

Pat stepped into the office, sitting down. Handley and Yenton were still there, sat together by the side of the desk. Sergeant Rose shut the door and sat opposite Pat.

"Thanks for coming in, Pat. Have you had a chance to speak to the gaffer?"

"Yes, Sarge, I have."

"Right, then. I won't dwell on it. Pat, over to you."

Pat looked at Handley and Yenton, swallowed a gargantuan slice of humble pie that he'd sooner have spat in their faces, and started speaking.

"Gents, I apologise for my unprofessional conduct earlier on today."

"Apology accepted, PC Patrick," replied Handley.

Pat motioned to get out of his seat. "If that's it, I have work to do?"

"Pat, sit down," said Sergeant Rose. "That is not it. These gentlemen need to ask you a question – the question you refused to answer earlier."

"So, you know the question they want to ask me, Sarge?"

"Yes, I do."

"Are you really going to allow them to ask me that?"

"Yes, Pat. If that's what they need to know, then answer it. I really can't see why it's such a big deal."

"Did they ask you where you were last night, or is it only me that's a suspect?"

"Now you're being ridiculous. How does that make you a suspect?"

"Sarge, are you for real? Why else do they need to know where I was last night? Surely you can see the implications for me. Or are you siding with them, and want to know where I was?"

"Enough, backchat!" Rosey thundered. "Answer the bloody question or find yourself suspended!"

"Fine," Pat grumbled. "I was at home all night."

"How hard was that? Now, get out of here and don't leave the station until we have a chance to speak again."

Pat got up, flung open the door, stormed out of the office and strode into the report room. Several officers turned from their screens, Kate and Kyle, among them.

"Have they asked you where you were last night yet?" Pat asked Kyle.

"No, they haven't asked me anything."

"What a fucking surprise!"

"Pat, stop it. That's enough," said Kate.

Kate stood up and walked over to Pat, grabbing him by the arm and marching him into the kitchen.

"For god's sake, what's gotten into you lately?! You're so angry all the time! And having a go at Kyle … do you really think that's going to help?"

"They wanted to know where I was last night when dickhead Clarke injected himself with smack!"

"What? Are you serious? But why? I don't understand."

"You don't understand?! How do you think I feel?! Rosey made me answer the question in front of those two jokers from the IPCC, and the Chief wants me done for incivility towards them. While I'm there, I'll be getting forms for the way I spoke to Mrs Chambers, because I tried to get a complaint statement from her for burglary. So now you know why I'm so fucking happy today, Kate!"

"Shit, Pat, that's awful. I still don't understand why they wanted to know where you were last night. Are they suggesting you had something to do with Sammy Clarke's death? I mean, really? Seriously?"

"Kate, has Kyle said anything at all? Has he spoken about Clarke, the arrest or the IPCC? Have they had him in yet, or have you been doing jobs this afternoon?"

"He did mention Clarke, but only what we already know, and we haven't been back until now because Rosey wanted us to stay out of the building, what with gaffers everywhere and the IPCC lot. Kyle said you were at Lime Court picking up needles from the play area, and how bad it was, what happened to Marie Jones."

"Now, I find that strange, because when we were there he didn't say a word and there was no mention of Marie. Don't you find Kyle a little aloof? What do we know about him? He doesn't say much about anything; he never asks questions and offers very little about what he gets up to, or even what he does on his days off."

"Pat, I think you're becoming paranoid and obsessed. Kyle's just a bit quiet. Why are you so hard on him?"

"He's sneaky, and he's always in with Rosey, having little chats about Christ knows what. And when I walk in on them, it's bloody obvious they've changed the subject. What could they have to talk about that's so important and confidential?"

"Do you ever listen to yourself, Pat? Have you any idea how weird you sound right now? I think you're making far too much of this. People are just doing their jobs, and you're taking everything far too literally and seriously."

"Maybe I am, Kate, but today has been a strange fucking day, and I'd feel a whole lot better if I knew why they asked me where I was last night. I'd also like to know when Kyle gets spoken to."

"Look, have a cup of tea, calm down, and please start thinking straight, because you're way off, in my opinion. And I promise that if I hear anything or Kyle gets spoken to, I'll let you know. Maybe then you'll apologise to him for the way you spoke to him."

"Okay, yes, I'll calm down," sighed Pat, recognising some home truths in Kate's little diatribe. "And I'm sorry for venting it all on you, but I hope you understand it's been a tough afternoon."

"Good. Now get that tea made, and I'll see you there in a bit."

Kate left the kitchen and Pat made himself a cup of tea. He continued to calm as the drink wetted his throat, his chat with Kate offering some reassurance that he might be getting carried away with himself. Switching the television on, hoping for some distraction, Pat stared blankly at the screen, unable to focus on anything outside of his immediate concerns, the most prominent of which was Marie. Tipping what remained of his tea down the sink, Pat returned to his computer terminal, unlocked it and started to read the update relating to her.

Incident reopened by Control. Received a call from City Hospital and a Dr Orford. Dr states Jones is still in a coma, but breathing unaided. He has expressed concerns about bruising on her neck. Dr is of the opinion that the bruise could not have come from the fall as it is inconsistent with her other injuries. He feels it was inflicted prior to her fall and did not know how this injury could have occurred. Dr has asked that his concerns are brought to the attention of the officer dealing with Jones and asks for officer to make contact with him at intensive care unit, City Hospital.

11.04, from Control: there is no obvious officer listed as the officer in the case. Discussed with the control room Inspector and he has advised for the day turn. CID to be made aware via the Detective Sergeant at the station. CID Sergeant Davis has been asked to view and note comments from Dr Orford.

12.40, from Detective Sergeant Davis: I have noted the comments from Dr Orford and have made an appointment to see him at ITU today at 15.00.

16.02, from Detective Sergeant Davis: I am at the hospital with Dr Orford, who has shown me the bruising to Marie Jones' neck, which is fairly substantial. Dr had explained that when Jones was first brought in last week, there was only a very slight redness to this area on her neck, and as time has gone by the bruising has come out, and is now covering a large part of her neck and lower left side of her face. This would suggest the impact on this area was at or just before the fall. However, Dr states the nature of her injuries from the fall are consistent with her falling backwards, and the bruises to her neck could not have happened as a result. I am of the same opinion as the Dr, and at this time, I have asked him to carry out a full MRI scan of the neck/face area. Can I have Scenes of Crime to the hospital to take photos of the bruising to Jones' neck and face? Can this incident be left open at my request for further work and enquiries to be carried out?

16.09, from Control: noted and incident reopened showing address as 23 Lime Court.

Pat remembered the redness to Marie's neck when he first saw her in hospital, and the bruising when he was there a couple of days ago. He was intrigued by the requests of the Detective Sergeant, and correctly assumed they might be treating her fall as suspicious. He knew for sure that there wouldn't be any CCTV at the flats. It hardly ever worked and, on the rare occasions it did, the residents smashed it up, keeping big brother out of their criminal activity.

18.19, from Scenes of Crime: I've taken photos of Jones' bruising to her neck and face.

18.40, from Detective Sergeant Davis: noted with thanks. I have passed this to Detective Warren to deal with and continue with enquiries.

Pat was pleased that Marie was being considered a victim. Not many officers would be bothered to follow this up, and most would do whatever they could to drop the case. Marie was hardly a firm favourite among the police officers who'd visited her over the years and, much as he understood the source of her pain and wanted her to pull through, he could understand why.

"Pat, can I have a word?"

"Sure," said Pat, turning to face Rosey. "Be with you in a sec, Sarge."

Pat locked the computer terminal and entered the Sergeant's office. Glad to see that the two IPCC officers had gone, he shut the door and took a seat.

"Professional standards have dropped the forms off. There are two lots: incivility towards members of the public – Handley and Yenton – and the way you dealt with Mrs Chambers yesterday."

Without saying a word, Pat signed both sets of forms, retaining a copy for himself and handing the other to Sergeant Rose.

"Have you calmed down?"

"Yes, I'm calm. Do you understand why I was so angry?"

"Pat, they were doing their job. I do understand, but there are ways to carry yourself, and it's not like you to go off like that. Besides, they never at any point suggested you had anything to do with it and were only asking the questions they're expected to ask."

"I know you don't believe one word you've just said, Sarge. Clarke was a burglar, a menace, and the way they were going on was as though the only angel left on earth had died, for god's sake."

"I have the Inspector on my back, and he has the Chief breathing down his neck, so you have to understand it's not just you who's being scrutinised. You really do need to calm down and go back to be the chilled out super cop we all know and love. The last few weeks you've been very vocal about certain things, and it's not doing you any favours."

"Right, okay – I understand. Can I go home? I don't want to be here today. My head's all over the place and the last thing I need are more forms for being a naughty boy and upsetting the good people in and out of the station."

"Yes, go home. You've got plenty of hours in the book. See you tomorrow afternoon. And make sure you put a smile on your face, ready to tackle the world."

"Thanks. I appreciate it," said Pat, who got out of his seat, not ready to find room for a smile just yet.''

PAT LEFT THE OFFICE and went straight to the locker room, where he got changed. Running to the basement, he got into his car and sped off. Pulling up once he was well clear of the station, he left the engine running and called Sarah, who answered almost immediately.

"Hi, babe. I'm on my way home and wondered what you're up to this evening?"

"Lucky you! How come? I thought you were on a late?"

"I am – long story. What you up to?"

"I'm off to the cinema with Sally, and then we're going to grab a bite to eat. Sorry, but it's a girls' night tonight. Come on, tell me: why are you going home so early?"

"It's too long to explain over the phone. Have a good night, and I'll catch you soon, and tell you all the sordid details."

"Ooh sounds interesting. I can't wait. Be good and enjoy your night of freedom, whatever you get up to."

After driving home, Pat took a shower, threw on some fresh clothes and opened a bottle of red wine. Pouring himself a large glass, he swallowed a mouthful, settled down on the settee with the television on and breathed a huge sigh of relief.

"Oh, shit!" He remembered he'd forgotten to read the rest of the Marie Jones incident and log off his computer. "Oh, well, sod it – I can have a look tomorrow," he told himself.

As days went, it had been a stinker. Pat hadn't been in so much trouble in his entire career and, for the first time in ages, dreaded going back into work. Glancing down, he saw the hand not holding the glass of wine contorted by his thumb anxiously thrusting into the wrap of bone and flesh provided by his bent fingers. Unwrapping them and spraying his hand out, Pat picked up his phone and called Becky.

"Hi, Daddio, how's work?" said Becky on answering her phone.

"All good. What are you and Sophie up to?"

"I'm doing some homework about the Second World War, and Sophie is helping Mom make dinner. I'd rather be helping with the dinner, to be honest."

"I know what you mean," smirked Pat. "History was never my strongest subject, so if you need to know anything, ask your Mom – she knows everything about everything."

"Will do. The next time I'm at yours, Dad, can we go and get some new trainers? There's a perfect sale on at the moment, and it'll save you a fortune if we get them this week or early next."

"I suppose so. Is Sophie's phone still playing up?"

"Yes. I think it's died, and she doesn't have it with her anymore. Why Pops?"

"I need to know when she's home from school, and if she's out and about, to be able to contact her and find out where she is."

"Dad, she's thirteen, not three, and can use the house phone when she gets home."

"I don't like the idea of her not having her mobile until I get the chance to buy her a new one. She's got a school trip tomorrow and won't be back until late. She'll need to phone her Mom to pick her up. Can she use your phone tomorrow?"

"Dad, no way, she can't have mine – I need it! Let her have yours if it's only for one day."

"Will you put her on please, Becks?"

Pat winced as Becky shouted at the top of her voice to call Sophie on the phone: "SOPHIE! DAD WANTS TO TALK TO YOU!"

"Hi, Dad, how are you?" asked Sophie a few moments later.

"Hi, little lady. How was school today?"

"Alright, I suppose. How's work?"

"Work's work. I hear your mobile's dead. What are you going to do for a phone tomorrow on the school trip?"

"There's nothing I can do, Dad – it's busted. I've asked Becks if I can borrow hers, but there's no chance of me getting my hands on her precious phone – she might miss a call or text from her boyfriend."

"Shut up, you! It's my phone!" Becky shouted in the background.

"Never mind her, Sophie. Listen, you can borrow mine, but only for tomorrow, and then we'll get you a new one next week when you're at mine."

"Oh, wicked! Thanks, Dad! When will you bring it over?"

"I've finished work early, so I'll drop it off in about an hour."

"Cool, see you in a bit, Pops."

Sophie handed the phone back to Becky.

"You coming over, Dad?"

"Yes, see you in about an hour, baby girl."

Ending the call, Pat sent Sarah a text, letting her know that Sophie would be using his phone until the following night, and not to send any messages or try to phone. Polishing off his glass of wine, he picked his phone up, stuffed his car keys in his pocket, then left the house.

When he arrived at the girls' house, he knocked on the door, which was opened by Sophie.

"Hello, Dad," she said, kissing him on the cheek. "Come in."

Pat walked into the kitchen, where Becky and Diane were sat at the table, finishing their dinner.

"Hi, Dad!" smiled Becky.

"Hello, Becks," said Pat, digging his phone out of his pocket and passing it to Sophie. "I expect you to take care of my phone as if it was your own, Sophie."

"Dad, I promise – and thanks. I'll only need it to phone Mom to pick me up from school after the trip. When do you want it back?"

"I'll collect it from you on Friday, after school."

"Okay, Dad, thanks."

Pat said his goodbyes and drove back home. Deciding it would be a good night to put his feet up and watch a film, he did precisely that while polishing off the bottle of red. With a lie-in to look forward to, Pat's head hit the pillow at around eleven. The next thing he knew, loud banging downstairs saw him come to with a start. Looking at the alarm clock by his bed, it gave him a time of 07.34.

"Who the bloody hell's that, this time of the morning?" he moaned, his front door rattling with the force of his uninvited intruder. "If it's a delivery driver asking me to sign for a neighbour, I'm not going to be happy."

Getting up and slipping a dressing gown on, Pat peeked through his blinds. Two cars were parked on his drive: a black Ford Focus and blue Skoda Fabia. There was nobody in either vehicle, but he could see two men in suits stood near his car; while the banging continued.

"Hold on, for god's sake!" Pat shouted as he walked downstairs.

Using his key to unlock the door, Pat opened it to find Detective Dave Warren – a smart, ruggedly handsome man in his forties, whose formerly black beard sported flecks of grey – staring at him.

"Fuck me, Dave, it's a bit early for a tea stop. Come in."

Pat moved away from the door to let Dave walk in. Three other suited men followed him, Pat assuming the third had been sniffing around, out of sight, when clocking his colleagues … but why, he had no idea. One of the trios worked at the same station as he did. Called Barry Symonds, his round, ruddy-cheeked face smiled at

Pat, who nodded back. As for the other two, he didn't have a clue who they were, assuming they too were detectives.

"Alright, Baz. Come in, pal," said Pat. "And you, gents."

Shutting the door, Pat went into the kitchen to put the kettle on. Barry and Dave trailed him, while the other two men stayed in the hall.

"Pat, this isn't a social visit," said Dave. "Put the kettle down and take a seat. I need to talk to you."

"C'mon, Dave, what's this all about?" Pat wanted to know.

"This is going to be very difficult for Baz and me, but I hope you appreciate it's us and not some other detectives doing it."

"Doing what? I'm totally lost and, I have to say, a bit concerned that there's four of you and you're talking like a police officer who barely knows me."

"Pat, I don't know if you're aware, but the Marie Jones attempted suicide has been reopened, and there's a full investigation ongoing. I'm the officer in charge of the case and, as a result of recent enquiries, we've identified a possible suspect."

"Possible suspect for what, Dave? It was an attempted suicide, and I still don't know why you're here. So, forgive my tone, but will you spit it out and tell me what you want, because I'm starting to get pissed off."

"Firstly, Pat, don't do anything stupid. There's four of us here for a reason. The suspect that's been identified is you, and we're here to arrest you on suspicion of the attempted murder of Marie Jones."

Pat cackled at the absurdity of what Dave had just told him. "It's a bit early for April's Fool, mate!"

"This is no April's Fool, Pat," Dave said solemnly.

Pat looked at Barry and Dave, whose expressions confirmed that this was no joke.

"Wow, okay. I must've been a busy bee because yesterday I was a potential suspect for the murder of Sammy Clarke … and now I've got the attempted murder of Marie Jones on my CV too. I'm a serial killer, don't you know! I get bored so easily that in my spare time I go round killing. It's ever so exciting!" Standing up, Pat stepped towards the front door, opening it. "The four of you, get the fuck out of my house before I throw you out, one by one."

Pat knew that Barry and Dave were aware of his martial arts capabilities; and that they'd have worded the other two up as well. Strength in numbers and all that – precisely the reason there were four of them, as Dave had indicated.

"Pat, this isn't a joke, and you need to listen to me very carefully," said Dave, who walked towards the door, shutting it. "I am arresting you on suspicion of the attempted murder of Marie Jones. You do not have to say anything, but it may harm your defence if you do not mention when questioned something which you later rely on in court. Anything you do say may be given in evidence."

"This is a fucking joke, and you know it!" said Pat. "I can't believe you really think I'd do something like that. Seriously, and I do mean this, Dave: I am fucking innocent and have no idea why you lot think I'd have something to do with it. If you have evidence, it's fucking made up. As they say in the trade, I'm being stitched up!"

"It's not about what I believe, Pat. But remember, at this moment in time, it is only on suspicion."

"Oh, great – that's a huge comfort! This is utter bullshit! Total crap, Dave."

"Pat, we'll be conducting a search of these premises and seizing your car, computer and mobile phone. We're looking for any potential evidence that may or may not implicate you for the offence you've been arrested for."

"Dave, can I ask what you're actually looking for?"

"Sorry, Pat, but for now get dressed, wash and freshen up. Make yourself a cup of tea or whatever. These two detectives are from The Ringway police station and are here to assist Baz and me. I know you know how this all works and, as a police officer, we won't be taking you to our nick, but The Ringway across town. Hopefully, that should prevent any embarrassment associated with going to your own station."

Pat froze a poker face while a tornado of resentment rose up from within. The urge to expel some aggression was overpowering, but he kept himself in check, knowing that he had nothing to worry about. His only concern was having been to Marie's flat, and visiting her in hospital. He put the kettle on and sat with his head in his hands, watching as the other two detectives went into the lounge, and hearing them gather his computer and its connecting wires and leads.

The kettle boiled and Pat made himself a cup of coffee, all officers declining his offer to fetch them a drink. Heading into the lounge, he saw the drawers to his units being searched, his settee being moved and inspection of the back of his television. He had no idea what they were looking for but knew there was nothing incriminating in the house; or anywhere else, for that matter.

"Pat, go and get yourself dressed and washed while we finish up here," said Dave, placing the computer by the front door. "Baz will go with you while you're upstairs."

Pat nodded, uncomfortable with Barry's close scrutiny as the detective followed him upstairs. Taking some clothes out of a wardrobe, Pat motioned towards the bathroom.

"Don't lock the door, Pat," said Barry.

"For fuck sake, Baz – seriously? Have a look at the windows in here." He and Barry both looked at the tiny top opener window, out of which a child would struggle to squeeze through. "I won't be running away."

Pat closed the bathroom door and, as requested, didn't lock it. So, this was how well-respected officers were rewarded? And what really lay behind this, he wondered, as he freshened up, donning tracksuit bottoms, a jumper and slip-on pumps before re-emerging to face Barry.

"Look, Pat, for what it's worth, we don't believe for one minute that you had anything to do with Marie's incident. But the gaffer has reviewed the evidence and went to see Professional Standards, who ordered us to do this. PS are all over it, and no doubt will be monitoring us all very closely."

"What evidence, though, Baz?! I mean, there is nothing – and I mean nothing! – so Professional Standards can get fucked!"

"All I'll say is this, Pat: I'm sure there are reasons why you've done some of the things that have drawn suspicion on you. Just tell the truth, and I'm quietly confident you'll be okay."

The other three officers joined them upstairs, to search Pat's bedroom – every wardrobe and draw, under the bed … even his jackets were given the once over.

"Where's your mobile phone, Pat?" asked Dave.

Pat remembered he'd given it to Sophie, but there was no way he was going to tell them that and have them turn up at her school, demanding it from her.

"I don't have a phone at the moment."

"What do you mean: 'at the moment'? Where is it, Pat?"

"As I said, I don't have a mobile at the moment."

Dave took his phone out of his pocket and made a call. He had Pat's number, and Pat would've put everything he owned on Dave calling his phone in the hope of disproving his claim. He glanced at the clock hanging on the wall. It was almost 8.15 am, Sophie would be leaving for her school trip, and Pat could only hope and pray that she didn't answer.

"It's switched off, straight to voicemail. So where is it, Pat?"

Pat shrugged his shoulders, thinking: 'Good girl, Sophie', as Dave smiled stiffly. The search continued in the spare room, where his girls stayed over, but there was virtually nothing in there, save for a few clothes and CDs.

"Right, that's it, boys. I think we've conducted the search to a satisfactory level. Let's get our stuff and get out of here."

The four men went downstairs, followed by Pat, who opened the front door. They all went outside, and he locked the door, hoping he'd be back before too long, but with the sense that something was seriously amiss. He watched the two other detectives drive off in their car as he climbed into the back of the Ford Focus. Barry put the computer in the boot and sat next to Pat in the back. Dave got into the car and drove off, heading for The Ringway.

"Pat, we're going to have to interview you," said Barry. "We don't want you to sit in a cell for hours on end. I won't try and influence you about having a solicitor or not – that's totally up to you – but we're ready to go as soon as we get there."

"I'll see when I get there, but thanks for the heads up, Baz."

Pat stared out of the window, smiling wryly, delighted that Sophie had turned his phone off. The journey to The Ringway was around half an hour away, time that passed without any more conversation. As they arrived at the station, Dave drove into the back yard and announced himself to gain access to the police entrance. Pat knew he didn't want him to go in via the custody entrance used for public arrests out of respect for his position and, he hoped, character, which made his predicament ever so slightly less galling.

Dave parked in the back yard. They all got out of the car, entered the station and walked to the custody block. At custody, the Sergeant was already aware that a serving police officer was under arrest.

"Good morning, gentlemen," said the Custody Sergeant, a giant of a man with a shaved head and shoulders like boulders.

"Morning, Sarge," said Barry and Dave, though Pat didn't reply.

"Can you tell me why this man is here, please?"

"Yes, Sarge. There was an incident on the twenty-first of October this year at approximately two am. A woman was seriously injured as a result of falling from the fourth floor of a tower block. Initial enquiries were made, and it was agreed her injuries were as a result of a failed suicide. The woman remains in intensive care at City Hospital, in a coma.

"Due to further information received from the doctor treating the woman, concerns were raised about bruising to her neck and face. The case was reopened, and the investigation has led us to Mr Patrick, who is suspected of having involvement and being responsible for causing her injuries. We ask that he be detained for the purpose of questioning, with regard to the offence of the attempted murder of Marie Jones."

"Okay, thank you, detective. Mr Patrick, do you understand why you've been arrested?"

"No, not at all. This is ridiculous."

"As well you know, I'm not asking if you agree. I'm asking if you understand."

"Yes, I understand."

The booking-in procedure continued. Pat was given his right to have somebody informed that he was at the station, and was read the codes of practice governing being detained at a police station, and his right to free and independent advice.

"Do you want a solicitor?"

"Yes, please."

Barry and Dave shared a frustrated look, knowing full well that the wait for a solicitor, and the associated consultations and disclosure, would drag this out. Pat had seen so many scumbags use the tactic, and now he would use it to his advantage. It was his legal right, and if they wanted to play games with him, he was happy to do likewise with them.

"Which solicitor would you like?"

"The duty's okay, thanks."

CHAPTER 12

THE JAILOR MADE THE necessary phone call to the duty solicitor. Pat checked the time. At almost precisely 9 am, the duty solicitor was unlikely to be tied up with another case and shouldn't take too long to arrive.

"Within half an hour, Sarge," the jailor told the Custody Sergeant.

Pat's property was taken from him, placed in a bag and sealed. The booking-in procedure was completed, and Pat was told he would need to wait in a cell for his solicitor to arrive. A few minutes later, after voluntarily removing the drawcord from his track bottoms and handing it to the jailor, he sat on a slim, plastic mattress staring at a metal toilet. The number of prisoners he'd thrown into a cell over the years, and here he was, sat in one himself, on suspicion of attempted murder. His mind springing back into an analytical mode, tossing more questions at him than he could answer, the jailor opened the cell hatch.

"Just to let you know: your solicitor is here. She's just having disclosure with the detectives, so hopefully not too long to wait."

"Thanks," replied Pat.

He tried to ready himself by preparing answers to the kind of questions that were likely to be posed, rather than those scurrying around his head. He suspected they would have something to put him at the scene, and had no doubt the doctor at the hospital had told them he was there and had left his number. But there would have to be more than that to arrest him on suspicion of attempted murder. Pat sat and waited for what felt like hours, regurgitating the same questions and answers, and devising new ones, until the jailor unlocked the door.

"What time is it?" asked Pat.

"Five to eleven."

Pat found it strange that the disclosure between the detectives and the solicitor had taken so long to complete, but had more pressing matters to deal with, tapping the side of his face to ready himself for what would follow.

Shown to one of the interview rooms by the jailor, Pat looked on in disbelief as the door opened. Staring at Sarah, the door shut behind him. Pat bowed his head and sat in one of the four chairs in the room.

"This is the worst day of my life," said Sarah, who started to cry. "Marie Jones, Pat! Seriously, of all people – her! I mean, she's the pits from Lime Court! Do you know how many times I've represented her, and now I'm in an interview room, representing my secret boyfriend on suspicion of attempted murder. What the fuck's going on?"

"I was hoping you could tell me that, Sarah, because the last two days have left me in total shock. The last thing I was expecting this morning was to be arrested on suspicion of attempted murder, regardless of whether it's Marie Jones or Tom fucking Jones!"

"Have you any idea how it felt, reading your custody record and seeing all of your details, knowing that as the duty solicitor, and even contemplating representing you, I'll go to prison and have my practising licence revoked? I'm hoping to make partner this year and leave all of this custody shit to somebody else!"

"Oh, that's just great," said Pat. "Here I am, in the pissing cells, fighting for my life, and all you can worry about is making partner!"

"That's so unfair, Pat! Think about what would happen if they found out we've been seeing each other. This could all go horribly wrong. I shouldn't be here. I'll have to tell them there's a conflict of interest."

"Sarah, I'm begging you to stay. I'm sorry, but I've no idea why I'm here and need you to help me make sense of it all."

Pat stood up and stepped towards Sarah. He put his arms around her and tried to kiss her on the cheek, but she resisted, pulling her face away from his.

"Pat, please sit down. Somebody could walk in at any time, and then where would we be?"

Pat looked at Sarah, who hadn't stopped crying. Sitting on the opposite side of the table from her, he could see how hard this was on her too but needed her if he was going to get out of this.

"I've had a good disclosure from them and get the feeling they're looking to remand you."

"Remand me?! Are you serious? I need you to tell me what's going on and get me the fuck out of here because it's all bullshit. I had a feeling something wasn't right with the Marie Jones incident, and think Kyle's involved, but I don't know how."

"Kyle, for god's sake? How on earth did you come to that conclusion? He's only just arrived, and all you've done is question who he is and criticise his every move."

"He's a sneak, Sarah – I'm sure of it. He doesn't give much away, and how the hell can he afford one of those plush apartments by the town when they're three hundred grand-plus? He never speaks about his days off, and he doesn't talk in the car. Kyle's always in with Rosey, and he's a fully trained martial artist. It seems like a military type of self-defence. I'm not stupid. I've got this gut feeling, and it won't go away."

"Right now, Kyle is the least of your worries. And with the evidence they have against you, you've got some way to go to convince me you're innocent, because right now even I have my doubts, Pat."

Pat looked at Sarah in absolute astonishment, unable to believe his own girlfriend would even remotely believe he had anything to do with Marie taking a tumble.

"Well, instead of us two arguing, why don't you tell me what they have, evidence wise, against me?"

Sarah opened her folder and went through many bullet points detailing the evidence provided by the two detectives.

"Can we do this one by one, so I can keep them in some kind of order as they're written?"

Pat nodded.

"To start with, you're very vocal at work about scroungers and social parasites. Every opportunity you get, you mouth off to anyone who'll listen."

"Yes, I do. I hate all of them," said Pat, folding his arms across his chest. "Next?"

"They have a statement from a neighbour on the fourth floor, and it states you were seen going into the flat that's twenty-three Lime Court the morning after the incident. You stayed for about fifteen minutes, then left. You were wearing a black jacket and baseball cap. You know the ones, Pat – they're hanging up at my house," said Sarah with a hint of sarcasm.

"That'd explain why they were searching my wardrobes. Yet the jacket and cap weren't there, were they?"

"So now, not only am I breaking every rule in the legal profession, I'm in possession of clothing worn by you at the time of an attempted murder."

"I didn't do it, so stop implying it," said Pat. "Yes, I went to the flat, and yes, I was wearing those clothes. I heard about her on the news while I was at your place. I was up, and you were still in bed, so I left you the note to say I was going to the gym. I went to the hospital to see her, then to her flat because she wasn't suicidal and never has been."

"Why, though? What do you owe her? She's hated by the police and is always calling you lot out. She's a bloody parasite and social scrounger."

Pat took a deep breath, with little option, now, but to fess up. "Sarah, I've known Marie all my life. We went to school together and lived near each other, growing up. I knew her husband, Darren, and their boys. I was at their wedding, and the funeral after Darren and the boys were killed on the motorway ten years ago. Marie was beautiful, intelligent and had a great life, and Darren was a fantastic man, husband and father." There was a short pause.

"When they died, she lost the plot. We lost contact, and I had no idea she'd become so destitute until a few years ago. I was at her flat, having received a complaint from a resident that two men were trying to get in. I met with the female occupant, and by that time the pair had gone. I was about to leave, and this woman said: 'Thank you, Pat. How's Diane and the girls?' I looked and looked, then asked how she knew my family." Pat swallowed hard, and he locked eyes with Sarah, who was listening with rapt attention.

"When she told me it was her," he continued, " I nearly fainted. And I'm not ashamed to admit, I cried. Why did I cry? Marie was beautiful, funny and full of life. She had a lovely home, money in the bank and a social network that was the envy of many. So, to see her gaunt, pale, old and haggard, with lifeless eyes that used to shine like headlights, shocked me to my core. I sat and listened to her tell me how she couldn't cope with the death of her family, how lack of sleep, prescription drugs, alcohol and then hard drugs took a grip. She lost her house, her friends and her money, and then the final straw: she was made bankrupt and moved to Lime Court. Over the years, whenever I ever went to the flat with a colleague, she was always respectful, pretending not to know me, knowing full well it would cause me problems at work. I did try to advise and help, but she was too far gone. On the odd occasion, I gave her a tenner to get some food but knew it was for drugs or otherwise.''

Another pause and Pat continued. "So that's how I know Marie, and that's why I know something's going on because at no point has she ever intimated or suggested suicide. I went to the hospital because she has no next of kin or friends, and I felt obliged. I went to her flat because I couldn't accept it was suicide, and I had a mooch around. There are letters to her from the housing lot about an appointment, because she'd asked to be moved from Lime Court. And there was a letter about rehab, so I know she was trying to turn her life around."

"Thank you for being so honest," Sarah said, but she didn't look as shocked as Pat had expected. "But there's more: they have a witness who states you parked your car nearby and walked to the flats, returning about twenty minutes later. The same witness said she saw the car there in the early hours of the morning, around two am. Marie was found at the bottom of the flats at around the same time."

"Sarah, we both know that's impossible because I was at your house that night if you remember."

"Yes, I do. But I was called out at around that time if you remember, and I can hardly provide you with an alibi, can I? For one, we can't tell them we're together, and two, I was here, representing a client."

"What else do they have?"

"Fingerprints on the paperwork on the table in her flat. Mostly yours, and they have you going to the hospital and leaving your number with the doctor in case she wakes up. They see that as sinister."

"Look, you now know why I was at the hospital. And, yes, I left my number, so if Marie woke she'd see a familiar face."

"They believe you've deliberately hidden your phone because you know they'll be able to trace your movements from your mobile."

"Yes, but where is my phone, Sarah?"

"I know Sophie has it. I got your text."

"So, now do you believe me? This is nothing to do with me."

"I haven't finished yet, Pat. The bruising on her neck. She had a scan, and it reveals severe tissue and muscle damage. The doctor has stated the injury can't have occurred as a result of the fall, and he deemed it non-accidental – consistent with a blow, or a direct strike."

"I did notice her neck, and the nurse told me the doctor had concerns. When I was at work yesterday, I had a look at the system to see if there was any update from the hospital. I only managed to read a few lines before Rosey called me into his office and I was let go early. I wish I'd read it all now because I would've known all of this."

"That's another issue," sighed Sarah. "Apparently, you've looked at twenty-three Lime Court on the work computer thirteen times in less than three days. They think you're worried that if Marie wakes up, she'll disclose what happened."

"You mean that I threw her off the fourth floor?"

"Yes."

"But what about motive ... what do they think my motive is? Surely they don't believe it's because she's a scrounger and a waste of good oxygen."

"They didn't say, but from an outsider looking in, and being given all of this evidence, what would you think, Pat?"

"I know it looks bad for me, but you know I'm not into killing people – especially somebody I've tried to help and has known all my life. She even tendered the grave on the tenth anniversary of their deaths. I went to the graveyard with flowers because I didn't think she'd have been there, but she had. The grave was immaculate – fresh flowers and a lovely card – and that's why I know she wouldn't try to kill herself. Does somebody planning suicide write 'see you next year'? And, Sarah, I need to tell you this: the flowers that were in my car that I gave to you ... I bought them to leave at the grave, but forgot."

"Oh, thanks! That makes me feel a whole lot better. You didn't even buy them for me! Bloody hell, Pat, what a mess."

"Sarah, you now know as much as I do. I'm sorry about the flowers, but you weren't meant to see them, and I forgot they were in my car."

"We've still got a major problem here. I can't be your alibi. How can I be, Pat? I'll be hung, drawn and quartered, and lose everything."

"You mustn't tell them a thing," said Pat, trying to remain calm when he was anything but calm, "you'll be in deep trouble. We just have to ride it out and see what they have to say and where we go. No matter what you have to do, get me out of here. I need to be bailed, Sarah. If there's somebody out there who wants Marie dead, I need to find out why."

Pat drew breath, frowning. "And is it a coincidence that Sammy Clarke was found dead the other night, only a few hours after he was released from custody? The IPCC was all over the nick. They interviewed me and asked where I was at the time of his death ... so that's why I finished work last night ... because I lost the plot. I had to apologise, of course, but they served me forms for incivility to members of the public. Clarke's aunt made a complaint about me, and I was served forms for that too. Not a good day ... and now this! Something's wrong, and I need to find out what ... and my money's on Kyle – he's definitely hiding something."

"I struggle to see why you're blaming him again, Pat!"

"Because it's all been going wrong since he came along, and I don't trust him and his sneaky, squeaky clean image. He's hiding something, Sarah, and I intend to find out what."

"Pat, you can't be getting caught up in police politics and casting aspersions on your colleagues. You're in enough trouble, for god's sake! Don't make it any worse, or they'll throw away the key."

"Just get me out of here, and I'll do the rest," said Pat. "What about the interview?"

"You have two choices: tell the truth or go no comment."

"Well, I can't tell the truth, because that'll create all sorts of problems, implicate you and, more than likely, get you sacked."

"Okay, then, go no comment. But you might have to give up your mobile phone. At this stage, we have circumstantial evidence and no motive. You'll more than likely have to hand in your passport and sign on every day at a police station until you answer bail."

"I don't care. I can cope with that. Get them in and let's get out of here."

Sarah stood up, walked around the table and kissed Pat on the lips.

CHAPTER 13

SARAH OPENED THE DOOR and shouted: "Detectives, we're ready." She sat back down next to Pat. "I wish you'd have told me about Marie before all of this came out. You've no idea what was going on inside my head. And, for what it's worth, I do believe you."

"Thank you, honey," said Pat, trying to hide just how relieved he was to have her onside. "You know I love you, and I'm sorry you're caught up in this mess."

Before Pat could say anything else, the two detectives stepped into the interview room.

"Sorry about the delay, Pat," said Dave.

"It's okay," replied Pat. "Let's get on with it."

Barry and Dave opened some new tapes and slotted them into the recording device. The introductions were made by all present, and the caution was read out by Dave.

"Do you understand the caution, Pat?"

"Yes, I do."

"You've been arrested on suspicion of the attempted murder of Marie Jones, and we intend to ask you some questions to establish any involvement. I'm going to ask you first and foremost, Pat: did you attempt to murder Marie Jones?"

"No comment."

Dave looked at Pat and shook his head. Barry stared at Pat with the kind of expression Pat assumed he'd given numerous suspects: one of incredulity.

"Pat, are you going to answer all of the questions we put to you with a no comment reply?"

"Yes – every single question."

"That's your right, of course, but I have to advise you that the courts may draw a negative inference from your no comment replies. I respect that you've taken advice from your solicitor, but you may answer the questions, and you don't have to accept her guidance. We'll continue to ask all relevant questions, regardless of your refusal to answer, other than stating no comment."

"I understand, Dave, but that's my right, and I'll be sticking to it."

"Very well. Pat, do you know Marie Jones from twenty-three Lime Court?"

"No comment."

"On the twenty-first of October this year, were you at twenty-three Lime Court, at approximately two am?"

"No comment."

"Were you responsible for the attempted murder of Marie Jones by throwing her from her flat on the fourth floor?"

"No comment."

"Your fingerprints were found on the paperwork on her coffee table in the lounge. Why were your fingerprints on her paperwork?"

"No comment."

"What were you looking for?"

"No comment."

"We have a statement from a resident on the fourth floor that states you were at the apartment of twenty-three Lime Court the morning after, and stayed there for around twenty minutes. Why did you go back the following morning? What were you looking for?"

"No comment."

"We also have a statement from a resident that states a car matching the description of your vehicle – a black Audi A Three, three-door – was seen parked around the corner from Lime Court at around two am, and again the following morning at about nine am. Why did you park away from Lime Court on both occasions?"

"No comment."

"The doctor at City Hospital states that you were at the hospital in the morning, making enquiries. You stated you were from the benefits centre on Bank Street. Why did you lie to the doctor?"

"No comment."

"You left your mobile number, 07727 939939, and asked the hospital staff to call you if Marie woke up. Why?"

"No comment."

"In the last three days, you've logged onto your work computer and viewed the incident at twenty-three Lime Court thirteen times. What are you looking for on the incident?"

"No comment."

"Is it possible you're hoping that Marie has passed away and that you got away with her murder?"

"No comment."

"The witnesses state that on both occasions, you were wearing a black zip-up jacket and a black baseball cap. During the search of your house, we didn't find any such items, and we didn't find your mobile phone. Where are the clothes and where's your mobile phone?"

"No comment."

"For a long time at work, you've been very vocal about the scroungers of society and timewasters. You make your feelings very well-known and are often told to calm down by your Sergeant. Why do you have such feelings about the lower class members of our society?"

"No comment."

"Is that why you hate Marie Jones so much? Because you deem her a waste of time and a scourge on society, hospitals, prisons and the police?"

"No comment."

"If Marie Jones wakes from her coma and we speak to her, will she tell us that it was you that threw her over the balcony?"

"No comment."

"The bruising on Marie's neck, in the opinion of the doctor at the hospital, is consistent with a non-accidental cause. They believe that the injury to her neck is as a result of a direct strike or blow prior to the fall. The injury couldn't have been caused at the time of the fall. How did you cause the injury to Marie's neck?"

"No comment."

"Was Marie unconscious when you threw her over the balcony?"

"No comment."

"What is it about Marie Jones and you? Why her, Pat? What does she know about you that you don't want the world to know? Were you in a relationship with Marie Jones?"

Pat laughed out loud. "No comment!" He looked at Sarah, but she failed to make eye contact with him.

"Pat, I've asked you a number of questions, and there haven't been any reasonable answers given to any of them. Is there anything you'd like to say before I terminate the interview?"

"No comment."

"I am terminating this interview, and no further questions will be asked from this point onwards."

Dave switched the tape machine off, and there was silence while the tapes were sealed and signed for. Dave stood up, as did Barry.

"In my opinion, you haven't done yourself any favours this morning, Pat. I'll be making a recommendation to the Custody Sergeant that you are remanded in custody to allow us to conduct further enquiries. If you both wait here, we'll come back to you shortly."

While Barry and Dave went to talk to the Custody Sergeant, Pat and Sarah sat in silence for a couple of minutes before Pat spoke:

"Promise me you'll get me out of here?"

"I will, but they're gunning for you, Pat. It's difficult sitting here knowing you could've answered every question and walked out of here today. This might go horribly wrong for both of us."

"They've got nothing, Sarah. It's all circumstantial. The bit about the relationship made me laugh. I mean, are they serious?"

"Well, I didn't find it funny – it made me feel sick. I know there's no truth to it, but it was still horrible to hear them ask you that."

"I know, I'm sorry. But even Dave and Baz would know it has nothing to do with being in a relationship ... but they have to ask, I suppose. That was just a fact-finding exercise. They'll interview me again, that's for sure. I wasn't there at two am – that wasn't me or my car. The witness has definitely got that wrong."

Pat got up from his chair and started to pace around the room, while Sarah scribbled something down in her A4 pad. Stopping suddenly, she looked up at Pat.

"Kate knows about you and me. What if she finds out I represents you and spills the beans?"

"Don't worry about Kate," Pat tried to reassure her. "She's a great girl and very loyal to me. She'd never do or say anything to cause me problems. Stop worrying so much, honey. It'll all be okay, I promise. Just get me out of here, and we'll see who's behind this."

"Pat, I'm worried – okay?! It's surreal, not to mention soul-destroying, how all of this has come out of the blue. You should've been more honest with me and the flowers, for god's sake."

Pat didn't say anything in response. He could see that Sarah was upset ... and who could blame her? It was the kind of event that had the potential to change lives and, though he wouldn't admit it to her, his stomach was churning, and his brain was moving at such a pace that he found it hard to focus; though he had no choice but to focus – no matter what, he had to get out of the station ... and the longer the wait for Barry and Dave, the more his anxiety threatened to get the better of him.

The wait was soon over: a minute or two later, in walked Dave.

"Right, we're ready, folks," he said. "Pat, come through to the custody desk please, and we'll explain what's going to happen."

Pat and Sarah followed Dave into the custody area, standing together while Dave walked behind the high counter and stood next to the Custody Sergeant. Pat could feel his heart beating hard and fast in his chest. Even though he was innocent, he knew that if they wanted to pin this on him, his liberty would be at risk. And being a copper inside didn't bear thinking about.

"PC Patrick, I've had a good chat with the detectives, and they advised me that you went no comment in interview," said the

Custody Sergeant. "There are a number of issues that still need resolving and lines of inquiry to be bottomed out. Your unwillingness to cooperate with this serious investigation is to your detriment."

"My client has cooperated fully," said Sarah. "A no comment interview doesn't mean or suggest any element of guilt. It's a prisoner's right to go no comment in an interview, a decision that they can make themselves or with the help of a solicitor. Please don't assume a no comment interview shows my client as not cooperating."

"It's felt that PC Patrick could have provided reasonable explanations. He could've reassured the interviewing officers by providing such explanations. We, the police and the courts can make a negative inference from a no comment interview, and today we have. There are further enquiries we need to undertake, and for that reason, we're holding him in custody to allow the officers to continue with their investigation."

Struck by a faintness, Pat steadied himself by gripping the counter. He stared at the plump, bulging veins on his taut hands and took a deep breath. This was going horribly wrong, an overpowering urge to flee radiating from the pit of his stomach; his inner voice screaming at him – 'GO!'

"Sergeant, my client is a serving police officer with an impeccable record. Refusing bail is, in my opinion, a violation of natural justice, and he's not a risk to the investigation. He has cooperated despite your concerns and, as a serving police officer, is prepared to adhere to whatever bail conditions you impose, with a view to returning to the station to be re-interviewed in the future."

"I've noted your comments," said the Custody Sergeant. "I'm not prepared to reconsider bail, and I would be criticised for allowing it, with it being an attempted murder investigation. You must also bear in mind that the victim is still in a coma, and if she were to die, then a murder inquiry would ensue. This is a serious offence, and your client is our only suspect at this stage. Bail is refused, and we'll revisit the issue once the detectives have completed their further enquiries and Mr Patrick has been re-interviewed."

Pat was speechless, knowing that, as things stood, he'd be stuck there for days. Sarah continued to argue his case, not as a solicitor, but as his girlfriend. If this was anyone else, he was sure she'd have understood the bail refusal. From a legal perspective, it made perfect sense, but her loyalty towards him was a foot pump swelling his flagging spirits; reigniting the fire that these fuckers had extinguished.

He saw the jailor milling around, moving blankets from a cupboard to a large trolley, and could hear the sound of a wagon reversing outside the custody door, before grinding to a halt. The jailor opened the custody door that led to the back yard. Pat took a step back and was able to see the wagon with its tailgate down, exposing a trolley with neatly folded blankets. The jailor removed the dirty blankets while the clean ones were being delivered.

At the bottom end of the yard, there was a large roller shutter that accessed the station yard and rear entrance to the custody block. The shutter was open, ready to let the wagon back out once the deliveries had been made. Driven by instinct, Pat shot off, sprinting through the open door from custody into the open yard, and up to the shutter. He daren't look back, running as fast as he could, needing to get as far away as possible before the alarm was raised.

Having been in good shape for most of his life, Pat had no doubts about his physical capabilities; and with adrenaline pumping through his body, it helped fuel him. He knew that legging it could get him sent to prison and lose him his job, but no way was he going down without a fight. His feet starting to ache in his pumps, Pat held the waist of his track bottoms to stop them from falling down, his chest warming beneath his grey jumper.

In the distance, police sirens wailed. Pat knew a glut of CCTV cameras would be trying to locate him, so raced to the canal that ran through the entire city. As the sirens grew ever closer, Pat started to lose a little speed … but wouldn't stop until he knew he was safe. Up ahead, stood a brick-built bridge. Running down the side of the bridge and onto the canal towpath, he stopped for about thirty seconds to catch his breath, then set off again at a steadier pace, heading out of town as the sirens started to fade. Not that he was in any way safe yet – police dogs and a helicopter would be involved in the search for him, which were even bigger obstacles to overcome.

The towpath was quiet, with just a solitary, elderly dog walker out and about. Pat continued to run at a steady pace, trying to think of somebody to help, especially with no money or phone. In the near distance was an industrial estate, and a gap in the towpath fence opening onto it. Pat made his way onto the estate and slowed to a walking pace. Feeling conspicuous in a jumper and track bottoms that barely fitted, the late autumn breeze made him colder now that he moved at only a moderate pace.

The estate was huge, with giant industrial units, car parks and heavy traffic, predominantly heavy goods vehicles. Conscious of the main road running through the estate, Pat did his best to avoid it, walking with purpose towards some houses that bordered the units. Then, spotting a pushbike lying on a grass verge, he walked up to it, picked it up, jumped on it and rode off, thinking: 'Arrested today for attempted murder, escape from lawful custody, and now theft of a pushbike'.

Riding through the housing estate, occasionally glancing over his shoulder, Pat cycled as far away from the city as possible. Stopping, he jumped off the bike and wheeled it into a small park in between some houses. Sitting on a bench, the bike at his feet, Pat took a deep breath, his thoughts turning to Sarah – what on earth was going on in her mind, having witnessed his escape from custody? And then it came to him: he could make his way to her house, as that would be the last place the police would look. There was no way he could go home or to Dianne's, where they'd be swarming like flies.

How Sarah would take to him turning up at her place was anybody's guess, though. But light on options, Pat knew he had no choice but to give it a go. Sure that it was nearing briefing time at work, he tried to envisage Sergeant Rose and his colleagues as news of his arrest and escape was announced. Picking the bike up, Pat jumped back on and rode slowly out of the park, with Sarah's house in mind.

CHAPTER 14

THE BRIEFNG ROOM WAS full of officers ready for their shift to start … except there was no sign of Pat. The officers chatted among themselves, though Kyle didn't say anything, sat next to Kate. Sergeant Rose was nowhere to be seen.

"Is Pat in today, or is he having another day off after yesterday's debacle?" asked Kate.

"Not a clue, Kate," said Tony, shrugging his muscular shoulders and scratching his lightly bearded face.

Kate called Pat, but as his mobile was switched off, she sent a text: 'You off again today Mr?'

A red-faced Sergeant Rose then appeared, looking a little nervous. "Right, people, where to start? Firstly, I can only tell you what I know, so don't start firing questions at me until I've finished." He cleared his throat, took a deep breath, and spoke in an uncharacteristically quiet tone. "Pat was arrested this morning on suspicion of the attempted murder of Marie Jones."

Transitory, nervy laughter punctuated the ensuing silence. Sergeant Rose took the room in, waiting for the first person to speak.

"Marie Jones? Are you serious, Sarge? She jumped off a fourth-floor balcony last week! Why on earth would Pat have any involvement with that scumbag?" said Tony.

"I appreciate it's difficult to comprehend but listen. There's an ongoing investigation into Marie's alleged attempted murder. It was deemed suspicious as a result of injuries she sustained before the fall. CID has made enquiries and, as a result, Pat is deemed to be the only suspect and was arrested at home this morning. I've no idea what evidence they have, but on arrest, he was taken to The Ringway police station across town to avoid prying eyes from this nick. He was interviewed and, I've been told, answered no comment. Bail was refused, so Pat decided it'd be a good idea to escape from the custody block."

"Come on, Sarge!" smiled Kate. "Stop messing about."

"I'm not joking, Kate," said a stern-faced Rosey.

"Fair play to Pat – that's hilarious," smirked Tony. "In fact, I wish I'd been there to see it! As far as I'm concerned, it's total bullshit that he had anything to do with it, and I'm fucking delighted he's made a laughing stock of The Ringway and their CID."

"Tony shut it," snapped Sergeant Rose. "And it wasn't their CID. It was ours – as in Baz and Dave from upstairs."

"Do you think they let him escape on purpose, Sarge?" asked Tony. "Good, capable detectives are those two. Or at least were."

"Seriously, Tony, are you looking to piss me off today? Of course not – they wouldn't risk their jobs or reputations … even for someone like Pat."

"Sorry, Sarge, but I'm struggling with this," said Tony.

"You should know by now that, so often in life, things aren't what they seem."

"Yeah, but Pat…?"

"Tony, Pat has escaped and is on the run. This is all very recent, so there'll be more updates as and when. I can't offer anything else at this time, but I will say this: if he makes contact with any of you and you help him in any way, you'll be arrested for assisting a known offender. I don't care how innocent you think he is, tell him to hand himself in, try to find out where he is, and let me know straight away."

Tony shook his head in disbelief, while Kate wiped her cheeks free of tears.

"I mean it, folks. Don't put your careers on the line, and remember: there's no smoke without fire. Our own CID has implicated pat, and Dave is the officer on the case, so give him some credit. I know how hard this is for us all, but we've got a job to do and have to continue to provide a service to the public. Twenty-three Lime Court is now a view rated job, and only the gaffers can access it. So, don't bother trying to look at the incident. To keep things simple, can we all have the same call signs and crewing as yesterday please?"

The room fell silent again. Sergeant Rose stood up and motioned to leave, stopping before he reached the door.

"Yesterday, Pat was spoken to by the IPCC and asked about the death of Sammy Clarke. He refused to answer their question about where he was at the time of Clarke's death. You all know Pat has been a bit vocal about his sort lately, and he's mouthed off in front of us all. I'm not saying he's guilty, but his behaviour of late is cause for concern, so before you all start to defend him, please be aware of this."

Sergeant Rose left the room. The rest of the shift remained where they were, Kate turning to face Tony.

"There's no way Pat would do it. Yeah, he's vocal, but so are we. We all hate the Marie Jones' and Sammy Clarkes' of this world, and I'm actually pleased he escaped."

"I think it's fucking hilarious. If I did see Pat, I'd shake his hand, and the last person I'd be telling is Rosey," said Tony.

Kate listened to the supportive voices for Pat and the expressions of disbelief at his predicament. All except, that is, for Kyle, who kept quiet throughout. Leaving the briefing room with the rest of the shift, she picked up some car keys and told Kyle she was doing the vehicle check. While in the back yard, Kate tried to call Pat again, but his phone was still switched off. As she hung up, Kyle came out with his kit bag, placed it in the boot, and advised her that he needed to get a statement from a victim of theft from yesterday's incident.

"You didn't say much in there today," Kate began as they left the station. "What do you think?"

"I don't know Pat as well as you lot, so it was easier for me to keep my mouth shut. I agree with Rosey, though – Pat is very vocal about his hatred for the likes of Jones and Clarke. He must have some involvement, otherwise, he'd never have been arrested. And don't forget they refused his bail."

"I know ... but not Pat. He's a brilliant copper and the last person any of us would suspect."

"Kate, if he's so innocent, why did he escape from custody?"

Kate didn't like what Kyle was implying, but he did have a point.

"I've no idea, but knowing Pat, I bet there'll be a bloody good reason."

"I hope so, Kate because it's a serious offence and he'll be in big trouble when this hits the news. I don't expect he'll find it very easy to hide in this city once his mugshot is flashed across the press and news channels."

Kate bit her tongue, uncomfortable with Kyle's stance ... and wondering how close to the truth he was.

Across town, Pat arrived at Sarah's house undetected – at least, as far as he knew. Climbing over a side gate, he opened it from the other side and wheeled the bike into the back garden, hiding it in some bushes. Sitting down by her back door, Pat knew that his very existence was now entirely dependent on Sarah. He looked through the window at a clock in the kitchen. If she weren't on call or tied-up with a client, she'd be back within the hour.

Pat's thoughts switched again to Sophie. With her in possession of his phone, if CID located it she'd be in for a nasty surprise – inadvertently of his doing – and that was the last thing he wanted. His heart sank as he considered the effect publicity would have on his chances of freedom. It was only a matter of time before his arrest and escape would be all over the news … and then what? For now, there was nothing he could do but wait for Sarah.

As it started to get cold and dark, Pat hugged himself for warmth, trying to devise a plan to get himself out of the shit. His stomach groaning for sustenance, he heard the sound a car pulling up on the drive, on the other side of the house and knew from the sound of its engine that it was Sarah arriving home. Pat stood up and waited by the back door for her to enter the house.

He saw the hall light come on, and the kitchen door open. Clutching that day's post, Sarah screamed upon seeing what Pat assumed she thought was an intruder, dropping the envelopes that had been in her hand. He knocked on the door and, as Sarah switched the kitchen light on, she was able to see him. Yanking her keys from her pocket, she unlocked and opened the back door. Pat walked straight in, and Sarah took a few paces back, leaning against a worktop. Pat shut the door and pulled its curtain to prevent anyone from looking in.

"I could murder a cup of tea," said Pat, his voice loaded with irony. "I've had a hell of a day."

"Have you any idea what you've done?" asked Sarah, showing him her palms. "Do you realise the implications of your actions, you stupid, stupid man? I've been beside myself all afternoon, and then I come home, and you frighten the living fucking daylights out of me! Why have you come here, Pat?"

"Seriously, Sarah, where else can I go?"

"I'm in so much shit I'm drowning! And now I'm housing a fugitive and assisting a known offender. Well, it's prison time for me! Maybe they'll let us share a cell and live happily ever after! Pat, what was in your head to escape? You'd have been out by the morning at the latest, but now things have got a whole lot bloody worse!"

"I panicked and just went for it," said Pat. "There was no way I was staying in a cell and letting them set me up for something I didn't do. Out here, I have a chance. In there, I'm a sitting target."

"Well, you can't stay here," said Sarah. "Get cleaned up, have something to eat, then get on your bike and decide where you want to go, because as much as I love you, you've really fucked up this time!"

"Stop swearing. It's not like you."

"Pat, if I had a rope, I'd be putting it around my neck right about now, so please don't patronise me about swearing, because it's that or a rope – you decide."

"Look, I know we're both in the shit, but for now they don't know about you, and they'll never find me here – this is the last place they'll suspect or look. Let me stay here and get my head together. There are some things I need to do and do quickly before they build a head of steam. But for now, can we eat, and can I have a cuppa, because I'm starving, and I need to warm up and take a shower."

"Okay, go have a shower, and I'll sort something to eat. Then you can tell me what's in your head and let me hear this plan you've concocted."

Planting a kiss on Sarah's forehead, Pat headed upstairs for a shower. Within twenty minutes, he was back downstairs, eating the meal Sarah had rustled up and washed it down with a mug of tea.

"Right, let's hear it, then," said Sarah, sitting down after dumping his plate and mug in a bowl of soapy water.

"Well, I'm hoping for some input from you, but for now this is what I need to do. Sophie has got my phone, and they're looking for it. As soon as she turns it on, they'll know where it is and head for her school, but I don't want the girls involved."

"Pat, this will be all over the news before we know it and, don't forget, my neighbours know who you are. Once the news has it, I'm in trouble too – not just trouble; I'll be locked up for sure, so you'd better get this right."

"I know, but I think we have a few hours' grace. They'll try everything to find me, to save embarrassment to the force. If they get desperate, they'll go public, but that'll be the last resort. Sophie will only switch my phone on when she gets back to school at about nine tonight. She'll phone Diane to pick her up, and they'll go straight home. I've no doubt there'll be detectives sat up at my and Diane's houses, so we need to go to the school and get the phone from Sophie."

"How do you propose doing that?"

Pat just looked at Sarah, saying nothing.

"Oh, no – not on your life, Mr! I am not getting involved! You're serious too, aren't you?"

"Sarah, I can't go, can I? If you'd be willing to help, let Sophie phone Diane and then take the phone from her. Just say I need it for work: first thing in the morning, I've had a shift change. She'll believe that. Take the SIM card and battery out, and the last transmission will be near the school. If they turn up, there'll be nobody about, and they'll have a false lead."

Sarah blew out, shaking her head. It took a few moments. "Are you sure it's as easy as that?"

"Yes – I promise. I'll phone Diane from a phone box and try to explain as best I can what's going on. But for now, until it hits the news, I don't want the girls involved."

"I understand about the girls, Pat, but it'll be all over the news by the morning. So, is this all worth it? Just let them have the damn phone – it's not going to prove much, is it?"

"I had it on me at Marie's flat, at the graveyard and the hospital. They'll track my every move and, as innocent as I am, it'll give credibility to their case until I find out what's going on."

"Okay, fair enough. I'll go and get the phone and do that for you. Then what?"

"I need to find out what's going on at work and whether Kyle has said anything of note to Kate. So tonight, I'll head over to her place and see what she knows. I know he has something to do with this, and that's why I'm going down to London first thing in the morning. He told me a few things about why he came up here to work, and I need to find out a bit more about him. He was stationed at Islington, so I'll go there and see if I can uncover anything."

"Bloody hell, Pat, that's so risky! What if the person you're quizzing knows him and tips him off?"

"It's a chance I have to take, Sarah," said Pat. "There's no other way of looking into him. I've got a gut feeling about this, and it's no coincidence that these things have been happening since his arrival. And I can get the train for free using my warrant card."

"Pat, they have your warrant card."

"They have one of my warrant cards. The other one's in my police tunic, in the wardrobe at my place."

"Yes, at your place. And how do you propose to get it when they'll be waiting for you?"

"At the back of my house, you can walk from the road that's directly at the back. There's an alleyway that leads to the service road accessing the garages. Climb the back fence into my garden, and you know where I keep my spare key. Let yourself in and go upstairs. The blinds in my room are still closed, so you won't be seen. Put your hand in the inside pocket of my tunic, and you'll find my old warrant card. Then leave the same way you came in. And bring me some decent clothes – I need to look smart for London – and another pair of tracksuit bottoms, so I can rid of these bloody things."

"You assume so much, Pat! I'm shitting myself and can't believe you're expecting this of me! What if it goes wrong and they're round the back?"

"They won't be. You can't see my house because of the layout and conifer trees, so they'll be parked down the road, waiting to see if I turn up. Do you know the alleyway I'm on about, and how to get to it from the road behind my house?"

"I think so. I know the road at the back of your house. I take it there's only one alleyway?"

"Yes. There's a lamppost at the entrance. Park there, walk down the alley at the bottom, turn left, and my garage is about the fifth one down on the right – you know what it looks like. Climb the fence between the conifer trees. You can't be seen from there, so don't worry."

"Okay," sighed Sarah, shaking her head. "I really can't believe I agree with this. I feel like James Bond."

"Don't you mean James Blonde?"

"Ha ha, very funny. Anything else while we're at it?" asked Sarah sarcastically.

"Get the phone off Sophie first, then go to mine, get the warrant card and some clothes. Oh, and my wash bag in the bathroom." He took a breath, needing something else. "Sorry, but I have another request: can you lend me a few hundred quid? I don't want to use my cards because they'll be monitoring those too."

"I suppose so. In for a penny and all that."

"Thank you, love. I really am very grateful and know this is a huge risk for you to take."

"Don't thank me just yet. Wait and see if I return in one piece. What time should I get to the school?"

"Around eight forty-five. I'll go to the phone box down the road and call Diane in a bit."

"Okay, let's have another cup of tea before the madness begins. And can I suggest you wear your black jacket and cap? You know, the ones you wore when you tried to kill Marie Jones."

Pat looked at Sarah and shook his head. He knew it was a joke, but he was feeling the pressure and jokes of that gravity he could do without. Sarah made them another cup of tea, and they sat in the kitchen in total silence, their respective predicaments hitting home. Pat stood up, went upstairs to the wardrobe he kept some clothes in, removed his jacket, cap and a spare watch, put them on and returned to the kitchen, wishing he'd had the good sense to keep a pair of jeans or track bottoms there too.

"These bloody things are driving me mad," he said, pointing to his loose bottoms. "Have you got some change for the phone please?"

Sarah handed Pat a handful of change, kissed him on the cheek and handed him the front door key.

"Hurry back, and good luck with Diane."

Pat left the house and walked down the road with his head bowed, one hand clutching his track bottoms by the waist. Making it to the telephone box, a wave of anxiety washed over him. He knew Diane would find all of this too much to take, but he had to prepare her regardless. Slotting change into the coin receptor, he dialled her number. It rang around ten times and was answered by Becky.

"Hi, dolly, it's Dad. You okay?"

"Hi, Dad. Yes, good thanks."

"Listen, can I just have a quick chat with your Mom?"

"Hold on a minute. She's just in the bath."

Pat could hear Becky knocking on the bathroom door and telling Diane that he wanted a word with her, followed by the door unlocking. As he waited for her to come to the phone, urging her to hurry up about it, Pat glanced out of the phone box, thrumming his fingers against the glass window.

"A woman can't even have a bath these days without being pestered by her ex-husband," said Diane a minute or so later.

"Sorry, Dianne."

"Make it quick, cos I've got a towel wrapped around me and my bath is calling me."

"Sorry, but it's important."

"For god's sake, stop apologising. What is it?"

Pat went on to explain the whole story to Diane. It took him about ten minutes, without any interruption from her, and when he'd finished, she didn't say anything.

"Please don't get abusive, Di. I've had a bad couple of days."

"Abusive? Why would I be abusive? I'm in shock and really can't believe what I've just heard. Are you okay? Is there anything I can do?"

"I'm trying to come to terms with it, but for now there are a few things I need to do. Sarah is going to the school at eight forty-five to meet Sophie because I need to get my phone back as soon as Sophie phones you, she'll take the phone and bring it to me. It'll be explained that I've got a shift change tomorrow and need the phone, and Sophie will believe that. I'm expecting the news to be all over this tomorrow morning, but for tonight let's keep the girls out of it."

"Okay, fair enough. Be careful, Pat. I know you will be, but you're one of them, remember, and it can go against you. I take it you can't go home or come here? Are you staying at Sarah's?"

"Yes, until I can sort this mess out. Be mindful that they may be watching your every move … and the girls, of course. Keep an eye out for suited men in unmarked cars. There'll be two aerials on the roof of the cars. They might even knock on the door and ask if you've seen or spoken to me."

"Thanks for the tip and phone when you can. I'll keep the girls close until this is over, assuming the news channels and papers don't get to us first."

Thanking Diane and placing the phone back in its cradle, Pat was surprised at how calm and understanding she was. Walking back to the house, he let himself in and stepped into the kitchen where Sarah sat at the table.

"Well … how did it go?"

"She was really good about it all, to be fair. I was expecting a hard time, but it didn't come. She was fully supportive and will keep an eye on the girls until this hits the news, or everything's resolved."

"That's good to hear. At least Diane isn't on your back. Does she know you're here?"

"Yeah."

"Okay," nodded Sarah. "I'm going to change into some comfortable clothes if I'm going to be scaling fences and trying to avoid your mates."

While Sarah went upstairs, Pat put the television on, flicking through all of the news channels without finding anything about him on any of them. He didn't know whether to feel relieved or concerned.

"There's nothing on any of the news channels yet," he shouted up the stairs.

Receiving no reply, Pat headed upstairs and into Sarah's bedroom, where she was donning a dark blue tracksuit and black trainers.

"What happened when I escaped? I forgot to ask you."

"They panicked. Dave ran after you, but you were long gone. The Custody Sergeant contacted the Controller and made them aware you'd done a runner, then gave the jailor an almighty bollocking. After about five minutes, the Sergeant looked at me, sat on the bench, and said something like: 'He's done himself no favours whatsoever, and if you have any influence over him, may I suggest you get him to come back.' But I was still in shock and couldn't believe you'd run off. Then the Duty Inspector arrived and had his say, but I've no idea what."

Pat felt terrible for the jailor and Custody Sergeant, as well as Barry and Dave, but it was done now, and he had other things to worry about.

"It's nearly half seven, love," he said nervily. "You'd better get going."

They went downstairs together. Sarah picked up her car keys and walked to the front door, kissing Pat on the lips.

"I'll see you when I see you … if they don't get to me first."

"Listen to me, Sarah. If you change your mind about going into the house, I understand. But if you do go, take a discreet look out of the window to see if there are any unusual cars parked on my street. The ones you'll be looking for will have two aerials on the roof, and each car will have at least two people in them."

"Right, okay," breathed Sarah. "Wish me luck."

"You'll be fine," said Pat, a little uneasy at seeing her go, but realising he had little choice in the matter if he wanted to do this his way; and, crucially, clear his name and find out what the hell was going on.

Locking the door behind her, Sarah left the house. Pat went onto her computer and looked at the train times to London. The earliest one left Birmingham New Street at 05.45 and took a little over an hour and forty minutes to get into Euston.

"That's me," said Pat, another part of his plan ready to be executed.

CHAPTER 15

AS SARAH PULLED UP outside Sophie's school, she glanced around in search of her, amid the throngs of parents waiting to collect their children. Switching the radio on, she listened to music, her mind wandering to Pat and his predicament … which was now hers too. In truth, she was petrified to be on this side of the law but felt as if she had little choice if she wanted to help the man she loved. Had she stupidly chosen a man over a career? Or would everything blow over before she knew it, allowing her to get back to her standard routine, representing people she didn't like very much, if at all?

The arrival of a large coach full of kids reminded her what she was doing there, Sarah climbing out of the car to wait for them to disembark. When Sophie saw her, she waved, walking up to her.

"Hello again. Where's Dad?"

"He's still at work, sweetheart. He needs his phone for work tomorrow now that he has a shift change, so I've just come to collect it if that's okay?"

"Yeah, no worries. Let me ring my Mom to come and collect me unless you can drop me home?"

Sarah wasn't expecting that and knew she couldn't do any such thing until the phone's SIM and battery were disconnected. And if the house was being watched, the last thing she wanted was for her car to be seen there.

"Oh sorry, darling, I'm on call and need to get home and get changed."

"No problem, I understand," replied Sophie. "Let me just call Mom."

Sophie switched the phone on and called Diane, asking her to collect her. Almost as soon as she got off the phone, it started ringing again. Sophie looked at Sarah.

"I bet that's Mom calling back." Sophie answered: "Hello, Mom, is that you?"

Sarah didn't know what to do – should she grab the phone off her or wait and see who it was? And what if it was the police?

"Doctor who? Sorry, what's your name again?"

There was a brief reply from a male voice on the other end of the line, which Sarah struggled to hear.

"It's his daughter, doctor. I'm just using his phone. I'll tell him you called. Will he know who you are and what it's about?" Sophie fiddled with her sleeve while the man said something else. "Okay, doctor, I'll pass that on. Bye."

"What was that all about, Sophie?"

"A Doctor Orford, or Oxford, from City Hospital. He said to tell Dad that Marie has opened her eyes. That was it. He reckons Dad will know what it's about."

"Must be work-related," said Sarah. "I'll tell him later."

"Thanks, Sarah."

Sophie gave the phone to Sarah, kissed her goodbye and made for the school reception, joining her classmates, most of whom were chatting with their parents. Sarah got into her car, disconnected the phone's battery, removed the SIM card, and put them in the glovebox. Breathing heavily, she waited until she'd calmed a little, then drove off.

The closer she got to Pat's house, the worse the knotting in her stomach grew – did she have it in her to do this? Turning right and pulling up just before the left turn into Pat's street, she took three long, deep breaths, then slowly pulled out and turned into his street. She looked either side of herself to see if any cars stood out, but nothing looked untoward; at least, as far as she could tell in the darkness of night, thrown into only occasional focus by the splashes of light emitted by streetlamps. Driving past Pat's house, she continued for around fifty yards before taking a right, following the road round to the right and stopping by the lamppost in front of the alleyway.

Sarah turned the engine off, had a little look to make sure nobody was around, then got out of the car, locking it. Walking down the alleyway, she turned left, past some garages, and came to Pat's place, with the conifer trees to the side. Hesitating a few instants, she stepped between the trees. Glancing around again, Sarah hooked her fingers over the top of the fence and jumped, pulling her body weight up and leaning on the top of the fence with both elbows.

"Ow, shit!" she yelped, her tracksuit top catching the top of the fence as she scrambled over it.

She heard it rip as she landed on the ground, on the other side of the fence and inside the garden. Crouching down, she snuck down the garden and up to the back door. Lifting a concrete toadstool, Sarah found Pat's spare key, which she jammed into the lock on the back door, opening it.

Once inside, she poured herself a glass of water and swallowed the lot in one go. Heart pounding, she crept upstairs, easing the bedroom door open and stepping inside. Glad of the cover offered by the closed blinds, Sarah opened the wardrobe nearest to the window and rummaged through Pat's clothes until she came across his police tunic. Checking the inside pocket, she pulled out and opened a small wallet. Sure enough, his old warrant card was inside, as Pat had promised. Pocketing it, Sarah quietly shut the door and tiptoed towards the windows.

Inching towards a small gap in the blinds, she peered out. About seven houses away, facing Pat's house, a black transit van, with two aerials on its roof, was parked. Pulling sharply back, she didn't get the chance to see how many people were in the front … nor did she care – it was obvious that they were the police; and that if she made a wrong move now, it could be curtains for both her and Pat.

Opening another wardrobe, Sarah picked out some casual clothes, a pair of shoes and a smart jacket, grabbed some underwear and socks from a drawer, then went into the bathroom, found Pat's washbag and put it with his other gear. Returning to the wardrobe, she grasped a roomy sports bag and stuffed the clothes, shoes and washbag inside, zipping it shut and hooking it over her shoulder.

Slinking downstairs, she slipped out of the back door, locked it and put the key back under the toadstool. Treading as lightly as she could, she made it to the fence and crouched down for a few moments to catch her breath. Her heartbeat echoed in her eardrums and, in spite of the darkness, she was able to see her breath as it streamed out of her mouth. Then, standing up, she tossed the sports bag over the fence and threw herself at it, pulling herself up and scrambling over, dropping to the other side, between the trees.

Seizing the bag, Sarah walked at a fast pace back to her car, unlocking it. Throwing the bag on the passenger's seat, she thrust the key in the ignition and set off, driving to the top of the road. Turning the car round, Sarah headed back to the junction with Pat's road, took a left and, driving by his house, stole a glance at the van. As she passed it, she could see two men sat in the front, both wearing dark clothing. They looked at Sarah, but she turned away and drove on, checking her rear-view mirror.

With nobody on her tail, she made it back home after a journey that seemed to take forever, passing a couple of police cars en route. Each time, she remained as calm as possible, pulling onto her drive around twenty minutes later and switching the engine off. She felt terrible about lying to Sophie about the lift and hadn't enjoyed her experience one little bit, but she'd made it back.

Letting herself in, she stepped into the hallway with the bag and phone.

"Well ... how did it go?" asked Pat as he hugged and kissed Sarah.

"Get that bloody kettle on! That was the worst experience of my life! I've never been so scared, and I actually thought I was going to pass out through fear, especially when I saw the van."

Pat started to make tea. "What van?"

"A black transit type with two aerials on the roof and two men in dark clothing sat in the front, a few houses down from yours."

"That wouldn't be Old Bill. Not in transit vans. They must be there for something else."

"I'm telling you now. They were there watching your house. It was so obvious, and there weren't any other cars about with anyone in, or with aerials."

"I wonder who that was because it certainly isn't any of the police I know," said a genuinely puzzled Pat. "Unless it was detectives from another station. How strange. Anyway, I assume you got everything?"

"Yes."

"Was Sophie, okay?"

"Yes, good as gold. A lovely young lady. I disconnected the battery and SIM straight away. After calling her Mom, it rang virtually as soon as she hung up. Sophie answered, and it was a Doctor Oxford or something like that, from City Hospital. He said to tell you that Marie has opened her eyes."

"Was that it? Anything else?"

"That was it. Short and sweet."

"Shit, that's all I need. I could do with speaking to Marie before they get their claws into her."

"But surely that's a good thing? She's awake, and can tell them who it was and what happened."

"It is a good thing, but she's more likely to talk to me. And if somebody is trying to hurt her, I want to know first."

"You mean if she confirms it's Kyle?"

"That's exactly what I mean."

"But what if it isn't, and she admits she tried to commit suicide?"

"Well, either way, I'm in the shit. But I need to know."

Sarah handed the phone, SIM card and battery to Pat.

"Thank you so much for doing that. I'm going to have some fun with this tomorrow morning."

"Fun? What do you mean: fun?"

"I'm getting the first train to London. When I get there, I'll put the battery and SIM card back in for a minute. They'll get the signal, and it'll confuse the hell out of them."

"If I were you, I'd just leave it off. Don't give them any clues that you're in London. That's asking for trouble, and you're in enough of that as it is."

Sarah gave Pat three hundred pounds she withdrew from a cashpoint, prior to meeting Sophie.

"Here, take this. It's as much as I could withdraw."

"Thanks, love," said Pat, handing Sarah her tea.

"Look what I did, jumping your back fence," she said, removing her tracksuit top. "This is my favourite one too."

"Don't worry. I'll buy you a new one once this is all over." He clutched his mug of tea. "Let's go and sit down for a minute."

They went into the lounge, sitting next to each other on a sofa.

"Be careful in London, won't you," said Sarah.

"I will. But before that, I need to go to the hospital. And I could really do with going tonight and finding out what Marie knows or doesn't know. I should really try and speak to Kate too."

"Pat, if a police officer sees you, you'll get caught. And what about security at the hospital? They'll have been told not to let anyone in without permission from the police. That's assuming there aren't police guarding her room. So how do you propose getting in there to see her?"

"I'm open to suggestions." Pat stood up and started to pace up and down the lounge, desperately trying to unearth a solution. "Doctor Orford phoned just after nine tonight, so if I ring him and plead ignorance, and say I was returning his call and see what he says, he might still be on duty."

"I suppose, but you'll have to be so careful what you ask, and how. And make sure you call from near the hospital, in case they trace it."

"Yes, you're right. Okay, that's what I'll do. Have you got some more change please?"

Sarah stood up, found her purse and gave Pat another handful of coins.

"Can I use your car to get there, and go to Kate's later please?"

Sarah nodded and gave Pat her car keys. Pat put his trousers and belt on, picked up his black jacket and baseball cap, walked to the front door, with Sarah following him, then kissed her at the door.

"I'll be back soon. And don't worry about me. I'll be okay, promise."

Pat opened the door and strode towards Sarah's car, hearing her lock the door behind him. Climbing behind the wheel, he drove off in the direction of City Hospital. He tried to formulate the wording and questions he was going to ask the doctor without arousing suspicion. It wasn't inconceivable that CID had left instructions with him to call them if Pat made contact, which was a very real concern and a tangible threat to his freedom.

Around a mile away from the hospital, he turned down some side roads looking for a payphone. Finding one near to a newsagent and fish and chips shop, Pat stopped the car and entered the payphone kiosk, unfolding a piece of paper with the hospital telephone number written on it.

"Here goes," said Pat to himself as he picked up the receiver, put some money into the coin dispenser and dialled the number.

"Hello, City Hospital. How may I help you?"

"Intensive care unit, please."

"Putting you through, caller. Please hold the line."

Pat's nerves frayed a little more with every second he was kept on hold. Around thirty seconds later, a nurse answered.

"Intensive care unit," came a female voice. "Staff Nurse Collins."

"Hi, is it possible to speak to Doctor Orford please?"

"I'm sorry, he's not here. He went off duty about half an hour ago. Can I help you at all?"

"Maybe. I'm returning his call. He phoned me earlier to let me know that Marie Jones had opened her eyes."

The line went quiet, and Pat feared the worst, supposing the nurse was alerting the police.

"I've just looked at her file," said Nurse Collins. "There's nothing of note on there, but I'm just temping tonight, covering for an absence, so I'm not totally sure where to look. Oh, wait … can you hold the line for a minute?"

"Sure," said Pat, his stomach tying itself in knots, fearing she'd seen something written on Marie's records about him calling. "No problem."

"I've just liaised with my colleague," said the nurse a few moments later. "She said Marie isn't allowed visitors without permission from the doctor or the police."

"Yes, I'm aware of that. Can you put me through to the police officer who's there at the moment and I'll confirm it with them," said Pat, chancing his arm, hoping she wouldn't call his bluff.

"He left about ten minutes ago. The night shift officer will be here within the hour, according to the notes. Can I ask who you are, please?"

"Of course. I'm a friend of Marie's, and the doctor said he'd phone me if there were any change in her condition, but I was at work and missed his call. I'm on my way in to see her now, but am happy to wait for the police to arrive if you'd prefer?" said Pat, crossing his fingers, hoping he'd be able to slip in and out before the night shift officer came on duty.

"I suppose so, especially if the doctor phoned you. How long will you be?"

"I'm only five minutes away and won't stay long.'"

"Okay, see you in a bit."

The nurse ended the call. Pat couldn't believe his luck, but knew he had to move quickly if he was to stand a chance of accomplishing his mission without incident. Returning to the car, he drove close to the hospital, parking in a side street and walking in via the main entrance. With CCTV dotted about, he kept his head down, safe in the knowledge that, if the shit hit the fan, they wouldn't see Sarah's car and connect it to him. Entering the intensive care unit, Pat rang the buzzer.

"ITU, Staff Nurse Collins?"

"Hi, it's me," Pat said as chirpily as he could. "I told you I was only round the corner."

The nurse buzzing him in, and Pat walked in, removing his cap. Approaching the nurse's desk with a smile plastered to his face, he was greeted by Nurse Collins, a short, plump, middle-aged woman with rosy red cheeks.

"Blimey, yes – you were quick! Just so you know, she's asleep but has had her eyes open for a few hours this evening. She's yet to speak, and they're going to do some tests tomorrow to see what her responses are like. She's had an operation on her leg, and it's in an elevated sling, so be careful not to knock it."

"Thanks, nurse, you're a star. I won't be long," said Pat as he walked towards the room where Marie lay.

He entered the room to find Marie, a white bandage wrapped around the top of her head, asleep. Her leg was elevated in a mechanical sling, and the bruising on her neck and face was still very evident. Pat pulled up a chair and sat close to her, gently stroking her face.

"Marie, it's Pat," he whispered in her ear. "Can you hear me?"

Marie's eyelids fluttered. Turning her head away from Pat, she sighed lightly.

"Marie, it's Pat, can you hear me?" he repeated. "Open your eyes, Marie. Come on. It's me – Pat."

Marie lay there, motionless. Glancing at a clock on the wall, Pat knew that in the next few minutes a police officer would arrive on the ward. He racked his brain for something to stir her, remembering the grave and how nice it looked.

"I saw the grave, you know. The card you wrote and left with the flowers was lovely. Darren and the boys would be so proud of you. I am too. When did you go to the grave, Marie?"

Marie turned her head back towards Pat and fluttered her eyelids again.

"Marie, it's Pat. I went to the grave. It's lovely, and Darren and the boys would be so proud of you."

Marie's eyes opened, and she looked at Pat, who continued to stroke her face. Her gaze turned into a stare so intense that Pat began to feel a little unnerved.

"Marie, it's Pat. Can you hear me, sweetheart? Come on, it's me, Patty."

Marie lifted her arm and, with an open palm, touched Pat's face and blinked a couple of times.

"Marie, do you know it's me – Pat?"

Marie blinked once and took a deep breath.

"Are you blinking once to say yes, you know it's me?"

Marie nodded slightly, painstakingly lifting her hand to her badly bruised neck and grimacing in pain, tears trickling down her face.

"I know this is difficult for you, love. You're in City Hospital. You can understand me – right?"

Again, Marie nodded slightly and blinked once.

"You jumped, Marie – why? When I heard that, I didn't think it was something you'd ever do. Was it because of the hurt over Darren, the boys and the anniversary? I know you went to the grave and read your lovely card."

Marie tried to move her lips as if to talk to Pat, who put his ear right next to her mouth. He could hear something, but she was too quiet and mumbled, making it impossible to discern.

"I can't make out what you're saying. I'm sorry, but I have to go in a bit."

Marie reached for Pat's arm and blinked twice.

"I'll come back, I promise. I can't explain right now, but listen … can I ask you something about why you're here?"

Marie blinked once.

"Did you try to commit suicide by jumping from the balcony?"

Marie applied a little force to Pat's arm and blinked twice.

"No. So you didn't try to kill yourself?"

Marie tried to speak again, but couldn't, a look of agitation on her face. Squeezing Pat's arm, she blinked twice again.

"Was it someone you know who pushed you off? Was it a police officer?"

Marie nodded again, her other hand sliding across her neck as she winced in pain. She blinked once, then slowly turned her head to the side and away from Pat.

"Marie, please look at me. Was it someone I work with? A copper who's been to your flat with me?"

Marie gradually turned her head to look at Pat, nodding steadily. So now he knew for sure that Kyle was behind this. What he needed to know now was why.

"Why, Marie? Do you know why?"

Marie closed her eyes, let go of Pat's arm, and appeared to fall asleep again. Pat stood up, his body lightly trembling at her revelation. If he didn't leave now, he ran the risk of being caught, so he kissed Marie's forehead, put his cap on and, with the nurses nowhere to be seen, slipped out without saying goodbye. Pacing out of the hospital, he walked through the car park to the side road where Sarah's car was parked.

And then: a sight that would typically have brought relief and familiarity, but which now represented a threat – a police car entered the car park. Pat ducked down as if to tie his shoelace. He glanced over his shoulder, and the car slowed as it got to within twenty feet of him. Standing, Pat paced off. His heart racing, he carried on walking without looking back, the sound of the police car drawing closer; dreading hearing the very words he'd used so many times himself.

"Excuse me, sir, have you got a minute, please?" said the officer in the police car, his window wound down.

Pat didn't respond, heading for a gap where a footpath led to the side road he'd parked Sarah's car in. The police car pulled up right next to him.

"Excuse me, can you stay where you are? I need to speak to you."

Making it to the gap, Pat heard the police car draw to a halt and a door slamming shut. Walking at pace, he looked over his shoulder to see the officer jogging towards him.

"Stay where you are!"

Pat ran off, passing Sarah's car; pursued by the officer, whose voice he was still able to hear:

"Control, I have a male making off from City Hospital. Can I have all available units, including the dog and helicopter? Suspect is believed to be PC Patrick. Can a unit go to the hospital and check on Jones as a matter of urgency?"

Pat upped the pace, the officer repeating his warning:

"PC Patrick, stay where you are!"

Sprinting as fast as he could, Pat needed to find somewhere where the dogs and helicopter wouldn't be able to see him. Racing along the footpath leading to the housing estate adjacent to the hospital, he took another look over his shoulder. The officer was failing to keep up with him, running out of breath and making his next radio transmission:

"Control, suspect is still in sight, on Falstaff Road, heading towards the park on the Rushmere estate. Any luck with other units and the chopper?"

Pat put even more distance between them, knowing he had at most ten minutes before the area would be flooded with officers, with a helicopter flying above him. Turning into a park, he ran across its lawn, heading towards some houses that backed onto it. Glancing behind, Pat could no longer see the officer pursuing him. He needed to get back to Sarah's car and didn't want to go too far out of his way, not being particularly familiar with the area.

The police dogs would pick up his scent, and he needed to find something to aid his getaway. Stopping at a garden with a low, four-foot fence, a small BMX leant against a washing line. Noticing that the curtains to the house were drawn, Pat climbed the fence and crept towards the bike. Far from ideal for a man of his size, it would do for what he needed it for. Picking the bike up, he lifted it over the fence, climbed back over and mounted its saddle.

Cycling towards an alleyway that had a lamppost, Pat slowed as he reached it, peering down the alley to ensure the coast was clear. It was, so he cycled down it to see the road in front of him. Stopping just before Pat reached the end of the alleyway, he climbed off the bike and wheeled it forward. It was a little darker this end and, as he went to look left and right to make sure the coast was clear, he felt an almighty bang on his left arm and fell to the ground with the bike landing on him. Glancing up, a police officer motioned to grab his arm, a baton in his other hand.

"You're under arrest for escaping from lawful custody and theft of that bike!" yelled the officer, a lanky beanpole of a man whose face was screwed up with aggression.

Pat used his right leg to sweep the officer's legs from underneath him, causing him to fall. He tried to pick the BMX up, but the officer held onto it. Both men getting to their feet, the officer pointed his baton at Pat.

"I'll use this if I have to, and you're under arrest, so stay there!"

As the officer attempted to speak into his radio, Pat stepped forward and kicked him to the stomach. Yelping, the officer crouched down, holding his abdomen.

"I'm sorry, that's the last thing I wanted to do," said Pat. "But I have to go. This isn't your problem, and I can't come with you."

Pat grabbed the officer's radio and threw it into the nearest garden. He picked the bike up, jumped on it and rode off, looking back to see the officer bent over, still holding his stomach. Short-lived guilt on Pat's part, but he simply couldn't be arrested, his feet moving like pistons, powering the bike. It would be minutes, if not seconds, before the helicopter and other officers would be all over the area. Finding Sarah's car, he opened the boot and shoved the BMX inside. Slamming the boot shut, he jumped behind the wheel, started the engine and drove out of the side road towards the main road.

Pat looked up and, through the windscreen, saw the police helicopter flying towards the park. On the opposite side of the road, heading in the same direction as the helicopter, was a police car with its lights and sirens flashing. Looking for a man on foot, they had no idea about Sarah's car, and Pat knew he'd made it by the skin of his teeth.

He drove without bringing any attention to himself, stopping at a set of traffic lights. Across the road, facing him, a black transit van with two males on board awaited a green light. Looking straight ahead, Pat pulled away at a steady thirty miles per hour. The van went by, Pat checking his rear-view mirror to notice two aerials on its roof. He remembered what Sarah had said about the same van, parked on his road, and knew it was no coincidence that it was joining the hunt for him.

With no idea who the men could be and why they were involved, he drove back to Sarah's house, pulled up on the drive, locked the car and let himself into the house. Sarah was stood in the hall, hugging Pat as he stepped towards her.

"You were gone a while, Pat. I thought something had happened to you!"

"You won't believe what I've got to tell you, but first I need a strong coffee."

They went into the kitchen and Sarah made them a coffee. Sitting in the lounge, Pat proceeded to tell her everything that had happened. Sarah just sat and held him for a minute without saying a word.

"I did tell you about Kyle, didn't I? I just knew there was no way Marie would try to kill herself."

"You did. I'm in shock, Pat. But why would he do that to her? What possible reason could there be for him to throw her from the fourth floor? More importantly, why's he letting you take the fall for it?"

"I don't know, but I intend to find out. Maybe London might give me some answers."

"Is there any way you can speak to Rosey and let him know what's going on?"

"I will, just not right now. I need to go to London and see what I can find out down there. And I could really do with seeing Kate, to find out what she knows."

"Let's go to Kate's house now and see what's going on at work," said Sarah, standing up.

"There's no way you're getting involved in this bit of it," said Pat, shaking his head. "You've risked enough already."

Pat got up, put his empty cup on the table and walked to the front door. Then put his jacket and cap back on.

"I'm going to Kate's house. She'll be home soon, and I want to be there when she turns up."

"Okay," said Sarah. "Keep your eyes peeled and good luck."

IT TOOK PAT AROUND half an hour to get to where Kate lived. Parking a few houses down from hers, he sat, listening to the radio, while waiting for her to return home. Repeatedly checking his watch, Pat shifted uneasily in his seat. It was well past her finishing time, and even taking into account her journey back, she should've been home by now.

Another car came and went. Pat growled frustratingly – where the hell was she? If she was on a night out, he could be waiting there for hours, and that's something he wasn't prepared to risk, however much he needed to speak to her. Not only that, but he had a train to catch at 05.45, and he could have done with banking a couple of hours' sleep beforehand.

Driving past Kate's house, which had no lights on, he set off for Sarah's place when Kyle popped into his head again. Pat wanted to see if his car was parked behind the gates of his swanky new apartment, so he took a detour to check it out. Pat slowly drove past. Kyle's car was in the parking bay ... as was Kate's.

Pat's bottom lip dropped in bewilderment, a multitude of questions filling his head. For a start, why was she there? Had she followed up her interest in him, or had Kyle asked her out? Was she in danger because of her loyalty to him? Or was there a much simpler explanation, the like of which Pat wouldn't be able to locate among the less loaded of his cerebral contemplations?

Whatever the answer, Pat needed to know more. Parking the car down the road, he locked it and walked towards the apartments. Built overlooking the canal, Pat walked up to the towpath at the back of them. There were six apartments housed within the building – two on each of the three floors – with a six-foot fence separating the small rear gardens from the canal towpath.

Pat had no idea which of the apartments Kyle lived in and positioned by the corner of the fence, he gained about three inches by standing on a small post that enabled him to see the rear of all six of them. There were lights on in only two of them: a ground floor, to the left, and the top apartment on the right. The windows to the ground floor apartment had their blinds closed, but the top apartment had no blinds or curtains, and Pat could see that a television was on.

The apartments on the first and top floors each had a small balcony with black rails around them, with enough space for a small table and a couple of chairs, accessible by two French type doors leading to the lounge. Pat continued to watch and, with the light afforded by the television, could see shadows moving around in the lounge. Kyle then appeared at the doors, joined shortly afterwards by Kate, who was still in her white police shirt and black trousers, sipping what he supposed was a glass of wine.

"What the fuck is she doing here with him?" Pat asked himself.

He thought it better to leave Kate alone until he could find out more about Kyle, waiting until they moved out of sight before leaving. Driving back to Sarah's, bristling with nervous energy, Pat explained everything to her.

"Bloody hell, Pat, what a mess," said Sarah.

"Yes it is, but I need some shut-eye. I have to be up in a couple of hours to get the train to London, so come on – let's go to bed."

But, lying in bed, Pat simply couldn't sleep; and, judging by her unusual restlessness, neither could Sarah. He didn't try and instigate conversation, supposing she'd heard enough about everything that had been going on, and not wanting to risk waking her if she was on the brink of dropping off. When the alarm rang out at 04.45, Pat groaned. If he'd banked any sleep at all, it seemed like no more than a few minutes … and now he had to prepare himself for another day of hide and seek.

"Jesus. I'm sure I only just closed my eyes," he moaned.

"Be quiet and go and make a cuppa," sighed Sarah.

Pat got out of bed, went downstairs and made the tea. When he came back, he used the remote to switch the television in the bedroom on, flicking between the BBC, ITV and Sky news channels.

"Pat, what are you doing?" asked a sleepy Sarah.

"Checking the news channels out."

"Well, do it quietly, will you?"

Pat drank his tea in bed until 5 am when he rechecked the news channels, the sound on low – yet still no mention of him. "I'm going for a quick shower. Will you wake up and drink your tea?"

"In a bit, Pat," sighed Sarah. "Just another few minutes."

When Pat returned from taking a shower, Sarah was sat up in bed, flicking through the news channels.

"Still no word of me?" he asked, putting on some of the clothes she picked up from his house.

"Nothing."

"It's all very odd," said Pat. "Anyway, I've got to leave at five-thirty, so shake a leg, honey."

"I've only got to throw my tracky on, so let me know when you're ready to leave."

Pat went downstairs to load some fuel into his system. Eating a bowl of cereal and necking a glass of juice, it was 05.24 when he shouted up to Sarah that he was ready to go. Sarah came downstairs with her hair in a bun, no makeup, with her tracksuit on. Even like this, exhausted and far from her best, she looked fantastic – a woman in her prime – and Pat knew that if he lost her over this, he'd be absolutely devastated. Holding her in his arms, he kissed her passionately.

"I love you and couldn't bear not having you in my life. I need you to know how grateful I am for all the help you've given me, and for believing in me."

"I love you too, Pat, and I'll always be here for you. Just watch your back in London. Leave the phone here in bits and don't give them any clues as to where you are."

Pat took the phone, SIM card and battery from his jacket pocket and left them on the side unit, near the front door.

"At last, you're listening to me," smiled Sarah. "And you know it makes sense."

Pulling up a few hundred yards away from Birmingham New Street station, to avoid any CCTV, Sarah left the engine running while Pat readied himself to leave.

"Remember what I told you," she said.

"Will do," said Pat, kissing her on the cheek. "See you later."

As she drove off, Pat made for the station. Waiting on the platform for London, he was acutely aware that a plethora of cameras were watching his and everyone else's every move. Aside from the occasional glance around, he kept his head down until the train for London pulled into the platform. Stepping aboard, Pat found a table seat, plonking himself down. When the doors to the carriage slammed shut, he scanned those around him – a few suits heading to work were scattered about, but that was about it.

With an hour and forty-five-minute journey ahead of him, Pat had the four seats to himself, kicking his shoes off and putting his feet up. Lying back, he closed his eyes and didn't remember a thing until a male voice broke his slumber:

"Sir, excuse me. Ticket please."

Pat opened his eyes to find a conductor peering down at him. Showing him his warrant card, the conductor nodded.

"Thank you, sir."

"Where are we please?" asked Pat.

"Just passed Watford Junction. Are you down here for business or pleasure?"

"Business, I'm afraid," replied Pat.

Pat was pleasantly surprised to have so easily fallen into a deep sleep, but the previous twenty-four hours had been intense, taking more out of him than he cared to admit. Making his way to the buffet carriage, he ordered a coffee and bacon sandwich, then returned to his seat. He ate the sandwich, drank the coffee, and before he knew it, the train had pulled into Euston station.

Rather than feeling intimidated by relatively foreign territory, Pat felt some of the tension drain from him, safe in the knowledge that nobody would be looking for him here. He made his way to the Victoria Line and, using his warrant card as a travelcard, found himself in the thick of the absurdly busy morning rush, bodies seemingly multiplying by the second.

Glad to be free of the crush of human bodies as he stepped off at Highbury and Islington station, Pat walked up the high street, making his way to the police station and clocking the time – 07.50. Walking up the stairs to the station, he went to the main reception and pressed the buzzer on the top of the desk. A woman with shoulder-length dark hair appeared in a civilian style uniform.

"Morning, love, how can I help you?" she asked in a thick cockney accent.

"Morning. I'm looking for a PC Kyle Aston, please. Is he about?"

"He's not here anymore, I'm afraid. Can I get another officer for you?"

"No, it was Kyle I was hoping to speak to."

"Can I ask who you are and what you want him for?"

"Yeah, sure. I'm a Bobby from up north. I did some training with Kyle a few years ago, and I'm down here for a couple of days, so thought I'd look him up."

Pat took his warrant card out of his jacket pocket and handed it to the clerk, who looked at it and gave it back.

"I'm sorry, love, I just needed to know who you are. Kyle left a few months ago. Shame really, he was a lovely lad and a very popular officer. Did you train with him in the police or the army? He was Special Forces, apparently, wasn't he? Were you one of 'em too?"

"Sorry … left, you say?" asked Pat, taken aback by the mention of Special Forces.

"He never came back after what happened to his wife. He lost the plot, went off the rails and nobody's seen him since. He was on the sick for months, and all we know is: he's not coming back here. It was all very hush-hush, to be honest."

"Oh, okay," said Pat. "That's a shame. I was hoping to catch up with him. Do you know if he's been assigned elsewhere?"

"Couldn't tell you, love," sniffed the clerk. "Somebody told me he works for the Home Office somewhere up north, but it could be a crock of shit for all I know."

Pat hid his concerns behind a smile, wondering how Kyle could he be working for the Home Office when he was wearing a police uniform in the Midlands.

"What happened to his wife? I haven't seen him for so long. I didn't even know he was married."

"Poor girl got knocked down on a pelican crossing by a drunk driver. Killed her, he did. Julia was her name. She worked here too. Right good looker and such a good Bobby too. It hit the station hard, but not as hard as Kyle. He never recovered, so not only did we lose her, but him an' all."

"Oh, dear, that's awful," said Pat. "Did they get the driver?"

"Yeah. He's locked up now. Got a few years for death by dangerous, or something like that."

Pat had heard all he needed to know, and Kyle had a lot of questions to answer. He may have told the truth about his wife, but the rest was horse shit. Pat knew Kyle had military training by the way he used his self-defence, and if he was working for the Home Office, and not as a police officer, then Pat needed to discover why.

"Thank you very much," he said. "It's such a pity I didn't get to see him, but I appreciate your time."

"That's alright. Mind how you go."

Leaving the station even more confused than when he'd arrived, Pat walked back to Highbury and Islington station, catching a train to Euston. Making the 09.05 train back to Birmingham New Street, he spent most of the journey going through everything in his mind. If he could get into Kyle's apartment and have a look around, he might be able to find something that tied him to Marie's attempted murder, and whatever else he was involved in.

His thoughts darted around his head as he tried to find a link between Kyle, Marie, the police, the army, the black transit van, how Kyle could afford his apartment, his strange behaviour whenever he was in Rosey's office, his reluctance to communicate and, most recently, his association with Kate.

Hurrying off the train once it arrived in the station, Pat caught a taxi back to Sarah's, asking the driver to drop him at the end of her road. It took several knocks on her door before she answered, still wearing her nightie and looking half-asleep.

"I'm shattered, love," she said, making her way back upstairs. "I need to get some more sleep. You don't mind, do you?"

"No, of course not. In fact, I'm coming to join you."

Taking his clothes off, Pat slipped into bed beside Sarah, cuddling up beside her.

"What time is it, Pat?"

"Quarter past eleven."

"Wow. You've been to London and back in five and a half hours – that's some going. How did you get on?"

"I'll fill you in when we wake if that's okay."

"Sounds good to me. Sleep well, honey."

When Pat stirred, Sarah was fast asleep. Getting out of bed to use the toilet, he only noticed the time when re-entering her bedroom.

"Three o'clock? Bloody hell," he muttered.

Sarah stirred and moaned something incoherent. Pat went downstairs and made two cups of coffee, carrying them upstairs.

"Come on, love, wake up, the day's nearly over. Here's coffee here for you."

Sarah sat up, rubbed her eyes and took the coffee from Pat. She checked the time, looked at him and smiled.

"I can't believe the time! I slept like a log. God, I had some strange dreams."

"Oh, yeah? Anything fruity?"

"Yes – a threesome with Brad Pitt and Johnny Depp."

"Lucky girl. I'm envious," smiled Pat.

"Ta for the coffee. Now tell me how you got on in London."

"I was there for twenty minutes and caught the train straight home but spoke to a very helpful front office clerk at Islington. Basically, Kyle's wife was killed as a result of a drunk driver. He went off with stress and was never seen again, as far as they're concerned. He quit the police and works for the Home Office, or so I was told."

"If that's the case, how the hell is he working as a police officer up here? You have to say something, Pat, for god's sake. Go to Rosey, or even higher. Surely they must listen to you, especially with Marie likely to confirm it was Kyle."

"I need evidence, and the only way I can find it is to get into his apartment. I'll have a snoop around later tonight when he's on nights. He should leave for work about ten-ish, so I'll head over about eleven."

"Pat, just speak to someone," said Sarah, sipping her coffee. "What are you expecting to find, and how will you get into his apartment?"

"Don't worry – I'll find a way. There must be something in there that'll give me some answers. Soon as I've got my hands on it, I'll go to Rosey."

Pat picked up the remote control, switched the television on and flicked through the news channels again – still nothing about him on any of them.

"Nothing. Again. Seriously, it should be all over the news. Why isn't it?"

"It's very strange. Have you spoken to the girls or Diane?"

"No, I'll buzz her in a bit. Come on, let's get up and have some food. Then I'll give her a call."

By the time Pat and Sarah had some breakfast, showered and got dressed, it was almost four-thirty. Pat couldn't use the phone box down the road, in case Diane's phone was being monitored and the police flagged it up. He suggested that he and Sarah head out for a drive, away from town, to find another phone box, once it was dark.

Sarah agreed, and Pat sat in front of the television, obsessively channel-hopping, and even switching the radio on, to no avail – there was still no mention of him, and something was definitely amiss. Around an hour later, with darkness setting in, they put their coats on in readiness to leave, Pat donning his black cap. Driving them a few miles out of the city, Sarah parked near a pub with a public phone outside.

"Di, it's me," said Pat, once she'd picked up.

"Pat, are you okay?"

"I'm fine. Don't worry about me."

"But I am worried, and so are the kids. They told me there was a black van following them when they left the house to go swimming this morning. And I saw a black van parked up the road, with two men in the front seats. It's clearly your lot."

"Do the girls know anything?"

"No, nothing. But the van was very conspicuous and has been around a few times today."

"I'm sorry, Di. It's not my lot, and I've no idea who they are. The black van is a new one for me too. It's been seen near my house as well and driving around locally last night. I've found out some stuff and hope to get this mess cleared once and for all."

"I've been looking at the news all day and had the radio on," said Dianne. "But there's been nothing about you at all."

"So have I. It's odd – it should've been all over the TV and radio. Keep the girls at home until I sort this out."

"Okay, will do. Give me a call tomorrow if you can. Do you think they'll be listening to this call?"

"Possibly. I'll be in touch soon."

Pat hung up, returned to the car and told Sarah about the black van following the girls.

"This is scary stuff, Pat. I wonder who the black van men are?"

"I don't know, but I'm pretty sure it isn't the police. They wouldn't be so open and blatant. Whoever it is, they clearly want to find me."

BACK AT THE HOUSE, Pat rechecked the news channels, then killed time making dinner with Sarah. Watching television together until late into the evening, Pat waited until it was approaching eleven o'clock before starting to get ready to go to Kyle's apartment. He put his black jacket, cap and trainers on then picked up a torch from under the sink. Sarah handed her car keys to him and kissed him.

"Be vigilant, for God's sake, and come straight home."

"I will. Shouldn't be too long."

Reaching Kyle's apartment block, Pat drove past its gates, with no sign of his car. Parking down the road, he locked the car and made his way to the rear of the apartments via the canal towpath. Pat stood on the post: the bottom and middle ones to the left had lights on, but there were none at all on in the top two apartments. Climbing over the fence and landing on the grass facing the apartments, he crept to the right-hand corner of the garden.

The fence was almost directly underneath the balcony to the right middle apartment. Pat climbed onto it, jumped forward and, using both hands, was able to hang on the balcony. Using his upper body strength to pull himself up, he grabbed the balcony handrail, levering his body up and over the rail and onto the balcony of the middle right side apartment. Pat stood on the rail nearest the wall and jumped up again, gripping the bottom part of the balcony to Kyle's apartment. He pulled himself up and reached again with his left arm, grabbing the top of the rail and climbing onto Kyle's balcony.

Pat crouched down and regained his breath, peering through the curtainless French doors into the lounge. Had Kyle left the French doors unlocked, safe in the knowledge that it's so high up, he wasn't at risk of being burgled? Did he have the apartment alarmed? Placing his hand on the handle of one of the doors, Pat turned it. The door opened to his relief, and he stepped inside, bracing himself for an alarm that, thankfully, either hadn't been installed or set. Shutting the door behind him, he took his torch from his pocket, turned it on and had a look around the apartment.

The spacious lounge contained a white corner suite, glass coffee table and a flatscreen television attached to the wall. The floor was wooden and looked as though it had been newly fitted, with a handful of cut-offs leaning against a freshly-painted skirting board. The walls were white, and there were no pictures or mirrors on any of them.

Pat made his way out of the lounge and into the kitchen, which looked untouched, save for a box of cornflakes, some tea bags and a pyramid of washed dishes, pots and saucepan lying on a draining board. He took in the rest of the room: brand spanking new cooker, microwave, shiny white cupboards, a silver dishwasher, fridge and washing machine. He opened some of the cupboards, which were empty aside from a few cups, plates and glasses. The hallway leading to the bedrooms had wooden floors, with a pile of floor cuttings stacked against the wall. It had all been recently done, clearly cost a lot of money, and Kyle couldn't have been there very long.

Pat opened a door leading to one of the bedrooms, the floor of which had black bags, suitcases and boxes sprawled across it. Closing the door, he opened another that led to a larger bedroom that was plainly Kyle's, containing a low-level king-size bed with a cream and black quilt cover, two bedside tables that had expensive-looking lamps standing on them, fitted wardrobes and another flatscreen television fixed to the wall at the end of the bed. The door to an ensuite bathroom was ajar, and inside it stood a miscellany of aftershaves, skin creams, hair gels and waxes, and various other metrosexual essentials.

Pat opened the wardrobes to find Kyle's clothes hanging neatly and in colour order. Beneath the clothes were racks of trainers and well-polished shoes. Beneath the racks, a brown box had been pushed back as far as possible, with two pairs of trainers placed in front of it, to hide it from view. Pat removed the box. Heavy, he lifted it onto the bed and sat down, removing the lid. A copy of The Sun had been placed on top of a number of cream coloured files.

Pat took the newspaper out and noticed the date: Thursday, April the 21St 2011. He flicked through its pages, not knowing what he was looking for or why it was there, but nothing leapt out at him as being unusual. Putting it down, he removed the top file, which featured a photograph of Sammy Clarke on its front.

"Why the fuck has he got a photo of Sammy in his apartment?" Pat said aloud.

He turned to the next page of the file, which had a full breakdown of Clarke's nominals, including his full name, date of birth and address; and his current status: alcoholic, drug user and non-worker on full benefits. The next page contained a full breakdown of his benefits and how much the state was paying to keep him in prison and hospital and to cover his use of emergency services.

For the 12 month period prior to recent prison stay, Mr Sammy Clarke: MONTH   YEAR

Unemployment   benefit............£260   per   month £260   £3120

Housing   benefit....................... £320   per   month £320   £3840

Disability   benefit..................... £160   per   month £160   £1920

Council   tax   exemption.............. £80   per   month £80   £800

Free   prescriptions.................... £15.70   per   month £15.70   £188

Prison sentence 12 months.......£2800 per month x 12 £2800 £33600

Hospital visits per visit..............£360 x 16 visits in 12 months prior to prison £360 £4320

Ambulance use/callout..............£180 x 9 callouts prior to prison £180 £1620

Police station visit/arrest..........£400 x 19 prior to prison £400 £7600

Legal aid at police station...........£180 x 19 arrests £180 £3420

GP appointments/attendance... £90 x 14 appointments £90 £1260

Total cost to the country and tax payer............... £4,845.70 £61,688

£61,688 saved per year.

Pat was so shocked, and he had to stop reading. Making for the kitchen, he ran the cold tap and drank water from his cupped hands, splashed some on his face and stared at his reflection in the kitchen window. What had he been looking at, and what did it mean? It was the last line on the page that concerned him the most: £61,688 saved per year.

Remembering the newspaper, he ran back to the bedroom, picked up the copy of The Sun and turned the page to find the headline: 21,000 addicts on sick for ten years. Boozers and junkies cost taxpayer £1bn.

He reread the headline and realised what he was looking at: Kyle was saving the taxpayer money by killing Sammy Clarke and had tried to do the same to Marie. Pat removed the second file from the box, and it was no surprise to find a photo of Marie Jones on the opening page. He stood up and paced around the bedroom.

"Fuck, fuck, fuck. This can't be real! He's fucking killing them off, and I'm getting the blame!"

Picking the newspaper up, Pat read the article.

'An astonishing 21,000 junkies and alcoholics have been claiming sickness benefits for more than 10 YEARS. And taxpayers have been left to pick up the £1BILLION bill. The scandal is revealed today as ministers vow to overhaul the discredited incapacity system. A total of 2.1 million people are on IB, with many getting the maximum £91.40 a week. They include about 80,000 who are paid because they are addicted to booze or drugs. Astonishingly, 12,880 alcoholics and 9,220 junkies have been getting IB for more than a decade. Each one gets up to £4,700 a year ...

'Work and Pensions minister Chris Grayling said the revelations underline why the system had to change. He said: "It's not fair on anyone for this to continue. The benefits system has trapped thousands in a cycle of addiction and welfare dependency ..." ... The figures show 902,300 people have been getting the benefit for more than ten years ...'

It seemed evident that the article and files were linked. Kyle had been sent to save the government money, and the recession had taken a new, highly sinister twist. Flicking through Marie's file, Pat saw that her cost to the country was £49,366 a year which, combined with the money saved from Sammy's death, gave a figure of over £100,000 a year that the government wouldn't have to pay out; though in Marie's case if she lived, her additional care would probably exceed what she'd been awarded prior to her attempted murder. Did that mean Kyle would be back to finish her off?

About to look at the other files in the box, Pat was alerted to a torchlight shining through the bedroom window. He ducked down and made his way to the lounge window that overlooked the road and had open blinds. Pat slunk into a corner and peeked out of the window to see where the light was coming from.

Stood at the gates were two men in suits, one of whom was holding a torch and pointing it at Kyle's apartment. Pat could see a dark blue van parked opposite the gates and, while sure that these were the same men who'd been hanging around, the other van, as described by Sarah and Diane, was black … which meant they had to be police – possibly the Special Ops, or sneaky beaky squad, as they were known in the force – from another station.

Pat panicked, returning to the bedroom, placing the files and newspaper in the box and putting it back in the wardrobe, placing both pairs of trainers in front of it. He took another look out of the window, the van was still there, but there was no sign of the two men. Pat opened the French doors and stood on the balcony, closing them behind him. He leant over the balcony and lowered himself down to the middle apartment balcony, then repeated the procedure, putting his feet on top of the six-foot fence. Jumping down and landing on the grass, he made his way to the corner of the garden, pulled himself up and over the fence, and fell back on the canal towpath.

He stayed crouched down for a minute to catch his breath and gather himself before returning to Sarah's car. He knew the suited men would be hanging around and didn't want to arouse their suspicion. Standing up and walking away from the apartments, he headed down the towpath to the gap where he could return to the street. But as he stepped forward, one of the men stood in his way. Six-foot-tall and clean-shaven, with short dark hair, and wearing a black suit with a white shirt and dark tie, Pat's heart skipped a beat. He took a step backwards as the man walked towards him.

"A little late for a stroll along the canal," said the man.

"I couldn't sleep, so why not?" replied Pat, who tried to work out his next move; wondering where the other guy was.

The man lunged at Pat, who used his right arm to side block his advance. Using both of his hands to shove the man back, he stumbled and lost his footing, landing on his backside; though not for long – he leapt straight back up and threw a right at Pat's face. Pat moved to his right and, with his left hand, blocked the strike, sending a right of his own into the man's stomach; following up with a knee to the face, knocking him out after a momentary yelp. Pat leant over him and started to rummage through his pockets, looking for some form of identification. When he opened his jacket, there was a small handgun in a holster.

"What the fuck, who are they?" he said, continuing to check the man's pockets, which were empty, aside from the gun. Removing the weapon from the holster, he threw it into the canal, the water's surface gulping as it sucked it down. But as he started to make his way through the gap in the fence, the second man ran towards him.

"Stay right there! Don't fucking move!"

Pat stood with his back to the canal, facing the second man – a virtual clone of the first, who was still sprawled out on the ground in front of him.

"Don't worry, he's not dead, just having a little nap. So, who the fuck are you guys?"

"Never mind who we are, PC Patrick. You need to come with us."

"Oh, so you know who I am?"

"Yes, we know who you are alright."

"Why don't you tell me who you are?"

"Who we are isn't important, but you're coming with us."

The man opened his jacket and pulled out a gun that looked to be the same model as the one Pat lobbed in the canal.

"There's no need for that," said Pat. "I won't cause you any trouble, so stop pointing it at me."

The man stepped forward and took hold of Pat's right arm, while still pointing the gun at his chest. Taking a small step back, his heels touching the edge of the path, Pat took hold of the man's left arm, moved to the side, kicked the gun from his hand with his left foot and, in the same sweeping move, pulled him forward and launched him into the canal. The gun landing on the path, Pat picked it up, tossing into the water.

Charging through the gap in the fence, he could hear the man splashing around in the canal behind him. At the end of the path, Pat ran up to the van parked opposite the gates, looked through the driver's side window, then checked the doors, which were locked. Inside the van, there was nothing but empty coffee cups and sandwich wrappers strewn around, so Pat took off again, sprinting down the road, climbing into Sarah's car and driving away.

During the journey back, Pat tried to make sense of everything he'd seen and heard over the last few days. Who the hell were the men in the vans? Were there one or two vans, and were they government agents, happy to point guns in people's faces? What was Kyle into, and how many more of society's lowlifes had he murdered or tried to?

Pat pulled onto Sarah's drive, climbed out of the car and let himself in. Sarah was still awake, sat on the sofa with the television on low and a laptop resting on her legs.

"It's Kyle, Sarah – just like I said. He's murdering them and tried to kill Marie to save the government money. I've seen the files in his apartment, and the men in the vans have guns and tried to kill me by the canal. Kate's in danger. I need to get to her to tell her, and I've got to see Rosey so that he can put a stop to this."

"Pat, please stop! You're ranting, and you're scaring me! What are you on about – guns and murder?"

Pat paced around the room, shaking his head. Sarah stood up and took his hand in hers.

"Pat, this is getting out of hand! What happened at the canal?"

"I was able to climb the balconies and get into Kyle's apartment. In his bedroom, hidden behind some shoes, was a brown box containing files. There was one in there on Marie, and another on Sammy Clarke. It has a full breakdown of every benefit and cost of all the services they use in a year – prison costs, police station arrests, dole money, incapacity benefit – and a total at the bottom, showing how much the government has saved by eliminating them. Between Marie and Sammy, it's over a hundred grand a year.

"There was a newspaper from a few years ago, with an article showing how drunks and druggies are receiving all sorts of benefits and handouts that cost the taxpayer billions. So Kyle's killing them off to save the taxpayer billions of pounds a year. Then the suits in the dark blue van turned up ... not a black van, so I think there's more than two of them. I put the files back and left the apartment, but when I got to the canal towpath, one of the suits confronted me, and we had a fight. I knocked him to the floor, and he had a gun inside his jacket, so I threw it in the canal.

"The other suit took hold of me and pointed a gun at my chest, saying I needed to go with him, but wouldn't say who he was or worked for. He and his gun ended up in the canal too. My guess is that the suits are working with Kyle to try and find me, set me up or, even worse, do away with me if they think I've found out about their little scheme. How far does it go, Sarah? If it's the government, they have everything at their disposal, and that'll include getting to my children. I need to get Diane and the girls somewhere safe. Also, honey, there's nothing on the news ... what's going on?"

"Pat, you need some help with this," said Sarah, who had started to cry. "Who can you go to, though? What if the police chiefs are involved?"

"I don't know, but I need to sort the girls first. Then I'll worry about who to speak to and how to put a stop to Kyle and his chums. I can't believe it was him who put the needle in Clarke's arm and threw Marie from the balcony."

"Why didn't you look at the other files when you had the chance?" asked Sarah. "More importantly, why didn't you bring them with you for evidence?"

"I couldn't," said Pat. "The suits were outside, shining torches into Kyle's place, so I had to get the hell out of there. I might try and go back and take them with me next time."

"Pat, come on! He'll know you were there once the suits have dried themselves off, and they tell him you were sniffing around."

"Possibly, but they don't know I was in the apartment – they only saw me on the canal. I'll worry about that later. For now, I need to phone Diane's mobile from the phone box."

"You can't make any more calls, Pat. They'll be listening, especially if it's the government. They'll have every gadget at their disposal."

"You're right, but I have no choice. I have to go to the house and speak to Diane."

"Pat, it's one o'clock in the morning! Wait until tomorrow and, besides, how on earth do you expect to get there without being seen, if the suits are waiting for you to turn up?"

"I can go round the back. I know how to get into the back garden without being seen. Would you mind taking me there now?"

Sarah hesitated for a few seconds, looking at Pat. "No, I don't mind. Just make sure you don't get caught. This isn't a game anymore – your life is at risk."

"I know, but I need to get my family to safety, so come on – let's go."

PAT ONLY SPOKE TO direct Sarah towards Diane's house. Sarah barely breathed a word either, an uncharacteristic silence passing between them. With Diane's home situated on a new estate, Sarah could park at the back of the common land it overlooked, and Pat would be able to walk through the wooded area that led to her back fence. He guessed the suits would be parked at the front of the house, affording them a vantage point that would've been lost at the back of the house. Parking the car by the common land, Sarah turned the lights and engine off.

"Stay here and keep the doors locked," said Pat. "If anyone comes, drive off, and don't worry about me. If it gets too scary or you have to go for whatever reason, I'll meet you back at yours, even if I have to walk. I should only be twenty minutes."

"Okay," said Sarah. "Just hurry back, safe and sound."

Pat kissed Sarah and got out of the car. He heard her lock the car doors and made his way through the woods and onto the common land. From there, Pat could see the back of the houses on the estate and walked in the pitch black to the rear fence of Diane's house. As he reached a wooden panelled fence, he trod on tiptoe to peer over it. There was a light on in the lounge, and he could see the flickering of the television, which spelt good news – he didn't want to start banging on doors and windows at this time of night.

Climbing the fence and landing in the garden, Pat lightly trod up to the window. Through a small gap between the curtains, he could see Diane sat on the sofa watching television. Gently tapping the window, Diane jumped, stood up and started to bite her nails. Tapping again, he saw her go upstairs, Pat stepping back to gaze up at the rear bedroom window. As Diane peeped through the side of the curtains, he waved his arms and gestured for her to come back down and let him. A minute or so later, the back door was unlocked, and Diane ushered Pat inside.

"You scared the living daylights out of me! What the hell, Pat?! It's nearly two in the morning!"

"I'm so sorry, but it's important," he said. "Where are the girls?"

"Both in bed a good while now."

"Right, listen: things have got a whole lot worse. You and the girls need to go away for a few days until this has all blown over."

Pat proceeded to tell Diane what happened earlier and the events at the canal with the suits.

"Jesus, Pat! Please tell me you're joking!"

"I wish I was, but no. So, this is what I need you to do: tomorrow morning, pack three bags. All of you wear your tracksuits as if you're going to the gym or swimming. Pack enough clothes for three days, head towards the leisure centre and see if the suits are following you in the van. If you are – and they probably will tail you – go to the leisure centre and make out you're swimming or using the gym. Go out the back onto the running track and use the far side gate. Make your way into town, across the park, then onto the train station.

"Go to your brother's in Nottingham. There's plenty of room there, and he'll keep you all safe. But please remember – and this is very important – no phones, as they'll be monitoring them, so leave yours and Becky's here. Sophie still has her old Nokia, so take that with you, and when you're in Nottingham buy a pay as you go SIM card. I'll phone Paul's house at some point tomorrow to make sure you arrived safe and sound. Oh, and – again – very important: no bank cards, cash only. So, at some point en route to the gym, go to the cashpoint and withdraw a few hundred pounds. Hopefully, by the time they realise you're not coming back to your car, you'll be in Nottingham with Paul."

"Okay, but what do I tell the girls, Pat? They're already asking questions, and the black van is still up the road. They're not stupid and reckon it's something to do with your work."

"Tell them the truth, but wait until you get to Paul's, when you can explain it all in one go."

"Why hasn't this been on the news?" asked Diane.

"Because, I suspect, they want to get hold of me, and publicity will only hinder their search."

"Pat, I'm not afraid to say that I'm terrified. What if they get hold of us, and try to hurt us to get to you?"

"I'm scared too, Di," said Pat. "That's why you need to do exactly as I say, and you'll all be okay. They won't find you in Nottingham, and it'll give me time to sort this out, knowing you lot are safe. Give me Paul's number and write it down for me. Can I go upstairs and see if the van is still there?"

"Yes, but quietly. Don't wake the girls."

Pat went upstairs and into Diane's bedroom. Leaving the light off, he peeked through the curtains to see a dark coloured van parked further up the road.

"Fucking bastards," he muttered to himself before going back downstairs.

"Here's Paul's number," said Diane, handing Pat a scrap of paper.

"Thanks. Remember to make sure Becky doesn't bring her phone and that Sophie takes the old Nokia – and the charger, of course. Right, I'm off. Sarah's waiting at the common for me. Good luck and I'll speak to you tomorrow."

Pat hugged Diane and let himself out of the back door, looking back to see her lock it and draw the curtains. Clambering over the fence, Pat ran to the woods, stopping as the forest of trees came to an end. Seeing that Sarah was still sat there with the engine running, he sprinted up to the passenger's side and climbed in.

"Thank god you're back," said Sarah. "I was shitting myself, sat here. It's so bloody creepy, and the noises from those woods freaked me out. How did it go?"

"Yeah, good. It's all sorted. Let's get out of here and go home."

Sarah drove off while Pat explained the plan for Diane and the girls. Once they were safely back home, Sarah made them both a cup of tea, and they sat in the lounge.

"I need to go back to Kyle's and get those files, Sarah."

Sarah shook her head. "No way. That'd be suicide, and you know it. What if they're there waiting for you and use the guns this time?"

"They had their chance and, for some reason, wanted me to go with them. Where I haven't a clue, but they want me alive."

"Who cares? This isn't a game, Pat! If what you're telling me is true, and they're here to kill, to save money, then you're dispensable, and a thorn they need to get rid of. Wait until tomorrow, when you know Diane and the girls are safe, then go and see Rosey. Tell him everything and put a stop to Kyle before he kills again."

"You're right, but I need evidence. Right now, the fingers are pointing in my direction, and I'm an escaped prisoner who's on the run, accused of trying to kill and probably still in the frame for the Sammy Clarke murder. God knows how many suits and vans are out there looking for me. Sarah, I don't know who to trust. Kyle was very cosy with Rosey, and a little sneaky too. I don't have the answers, but I know that whoever I do go to, I need some form of evidence. I can't walk in there making outrageous allegations with my thumb up my ass."

"There's no need to be rude," frowned Sarah. "You know what I'm saying, and remember: I've just as much to lose if they find out I've been harbouring an escaped prisoner, assisting you and perverting the course of justice. I'll do some serious prison time, not to mention losing my job, my home and my reputation."

Pat hugged Sarah and kissed her on the forehead. "I'm sorry. I know you've put yourself in a very precarious position for me. And you know I can't do this without you. I love you, but you're doing this because you know I'm innocent. In your profession, knowing a man is innocent is a fundamental facet, and you'd defend him to the ends of the earth. I'm trying to sort this out, and if I come across as unappreciative, I'm sorry. But I'm worried for me, you and my girls. I need evidence, Sarah."

"Okay, I know. But it's such a huge risk going there again. What if they've alerted Kyle and he went home, knew you were in his apartment, moved the files and locked the doors?"

"I could always try and have a look. The suits aren't exactly inconspicuous and are quite happy to be seen, so it can't hurt for me to try again. And they certainly wouldn't expect me to be at Kyle's flat, after what happened earlier. It's been bothering me about them shining their torches into his apartment windows. Why would they do that?"

"Maybe they had a tip-off, or Kyle asked them to keep an eye on his place, and it was a coincidence that they were there when you were."

"Maybe. It'd help if I could speak to Kate, but I can't be sure Kyle hasn't turned her. I don't believe for one minute that she'd go against me, but she's on nights and won't be home until after seven o'clock. That's assuming she goes home and not back to Kyle's place."

"I'd leave Kate out of it if I were you. You don't know what they've been told. They could've portrayed you as a monster, and she goes and calls the police or even tries to arrest you herself."

"I can't see it, Sarah. She might pay lip service, but she must know it's not me. I might try her house later, but I do need to get the files."

"It's up to you, Pat. Once you've made your mind up, I can't change it. But if the suits are there, drive away, for god's sake."

"I hear you. I take it you won't be going to bed until I get back?"

"You honestly think I'm going to be able to sleep until you do?"

Pat stood up and took the car keys from a table. He kissed Sarah on the lips and donned his black jacket and cap.

"It's like that's your sneaking around uniform, that bloody jacket and cap. Every time you put them on, I know you're out and about like a secret agent."

Pat sniggered at her unintentional gallows humour.

"I'm not pissing about, Pat! This is serious."

"I know. I'll be back before you know it."

His foot resting lightly on the accelerator, Pat felt a flutter of nerves as he neared Kyle's apartment. Would the suits be there and, if they were and they managed to get hold of him, where would they take him and what would they do? The answer that came back at him made him feel even worse, so he banished it from his mind and tried to bring himself back down to earth – he needed evidence, and soon because his luck could run out at any moment.

It was 4 am and cold, with a slight mist in the air. Glancing at the deserted streets, Pat switched the radio on in time to catch the hourly news. Again, no word of his escape ... nor did he expect there to be now. Years of experience had taught him that whenever a fugitive was on the run from the police, the media were notified within hours, advising the public not to approach, and to call the police straight away ... so why not him? Amid his confusion, Pat felt a sense of relief – if there were media involvement, he would've been spotted long before now.

His thoughts turned to Sarah and the risks she was taking – a lengthy prison sentence and the loss of her job, reputation and home – which made him all the more determined to clear his name. As he passed Kyle's apartment block, seeing that his car wasn't parked in its space, Pat drove around the surrounding streets for a few minutes to see if the suits were around. There wasn't any sign of them, so he parked in the same side street as before.

Pacing to the back of the apartments, he stepped on the small post and stared ahead – no lights in any of them. Pat pulled himself up onto the fence and jumped over, landing in the rear garden. Creeping to the wall between the two ground floor apartments, he climbed onto the wooden fence, pulled himself up and grabbed the bottom of the middle floor apartment's balcony ... but as he tried to pull himself up, he could feel his hands slipping.

The mist in the air supported dampness that made it harder to maintain his grip, and his hands slipped, causing him to fall the ten feet or so onto the grass in the garden below. He landed with a thud and screeched as his back hit the ground. Winded by the fall, he looked up to see if any lights came on in the apartments – nothing. After a few seconds lying there, he gradually rose to his feet and hid in the corner to avoid being seen, covering his mouth to try and divert the steam from his breath into his jacket. Crouching down, he felt a sharp pain in his back, massaging it to warm it up.

Pulling his hands down to his waist, Pat reached the fence, pulled himself up and reached for the balcony. Ignoring the sting in his lower back, he used all of his strength to grab hold of the balcony rail and pull himself onto the middle floor's balcony. Standing on the rail in the corner, Pat reached up and jumped, grabbing the bottom of the balcony to Kyle's apartment, pulling himself up. With all of his might, he grabbed the rail to the balcony, briefly looking down and hoping his hands and back wouldn't give way. Pat dragged himself over the rail and landed on Kyle's balcony.

Remaining there for a minute or so to catch his breath, Pat stood up and tried the handle to the French doors. To his surprise, they opened, and in he snuck in. Pat Tiptoed around the apartment, and it was clear that nobody had been there since his last visit. From that, Pat deduced that the suits couldn't have known he'd been inside and told Kyle, otherwise the doors would've been locked. Entering the bedroom, he took the brown box from the wardrobe, placing it on the bed. Removing the lid, he saw that everything from before was still there.

He couldn't decide whether it would be best to leave via the front door or the French doors, the latter of which he'd sooner avoid, inviting injury and damaging the box and its contents. He walked to the front door, which had a Yale type and a Mortice lock. Looking at a gap between the door and its frame, he saw that the Mortice wasn't locked. An odd juxtaposition: Kyle had been in the Special Forces, and must have known a thing or two about security … and yet his residence was as easy to negotiate entry into as a public toilet. Which, considering the box he had in his apartment, was pretty damn stupid.

Pat turned the Yale lock, and the door opened. Collecting the box from the bedroom, he left the apartment, placed it into the hallway and gently pulled the door closed, its latch clicking into position. Picking the box up, he walked downstairs. At the bottom of the stairs, on the ground floor, the front door led to the car park and the electric gates; and a back door opened out onto the garden and canal towpath.

Leaving the building, Pat walked to the fence at the top of the garden and placed the box on a corner, where it joined another part of the fence at a ninety-degree angle. Relief washed over him: with the box's contents in his possession, he could back his claims up with proof. Now Pat had to put it into the right hands so that they could do something about it. Pulling himself up, he jumped onto the towpath, lifted the box off the fence, found his way to the gap in the fence and out onto the side road where Sarah's car was parked. Unlocking the car, Pat placed the box in the boot and opened the driver's door when a voice startled him.

"Hello, Pat," said Kyle, who stood facing the car.

Pat took a step back and looked at Kyle, who wore his police uniform. "Hello, Kyle. Bit of a piss-take, you wearing that uniform, don't you think?"

"Really? Why's that, then?"

"Don't treat me like a fucking fool. I know your game, and I've got evidence too. You're a fake, you fucking prick, using the queen's uniform to do your dirty work."

Kyle edged towards Pat, who took a transitory glance around to check for the suits.

"Dirty work? It's not dirty work! And that's rich, coming from you, the escaped fugitive and burglar!"

"Fuck you! Burglary, my arse – it's evidence, and I'm taking it with me."

"I don't think so, Pat. You've no idea what you're doing. I need those files back, so get them from the boot and hand them over. Then you're coming with me, and we can talk about this."

"No, sorry – it's not happening like that. Where are your mates tonight?"

"Mates? What mates?"

"Come on, Kyle. Stop treating me like a fucking idiot!"

"Pat, you don't know what's really going on. Give me the files back, and we can sort this out."

Kyle shot forward, taking him to the driver's door. Pat moved equally as quickly, towards the boot, Kyle removing his baton from its holder, closing in on him.

"Pat, the last thing I want to do is use this, but I need those files and can't let you take them with you. I promise I'll tell you everything. I'm not here to arrest you, and I know you're innocent."

"I bet you do, you bastard. I know it's you! I've seen the files, and I know why you're here, so get fucked – I'm taking the files, and you won't be stopping me."

Kyle lunged at Pat, who kicked his leg, causing him to buckle and go down on one knee. Standing back up, Kyle raised the baton above his head and went to strike Pat, who blocked the baton and punched Kyle in the face with his right fist. Kyle fell to the ground, and Pat kicked him in the stomach, Kyle folding into the foetal position.

"Pat, you're making a huge mistake!" he gasped.

Pat shaped to kick Kyle again, but Kyle grabbed Pat's left foot, sweeping his legs from under him, causing Pat to fall to the ground. Blood streaming from his nose and mouth, Kyle sprang to his feet and repeatedly hit Pat across the back with the baton. Groaning with pain, Pat tried to get up as Kyle wiped the blood from his face and opened the boot, reaching for the box. Before he could take it, Pat leapt forward, slamming his fists into Kyle's kidney, Kyle returning fire with a hard right to Pat's face, followed immediately by a baton strike to his arm.

Blood dripped from Pat's mouth, and he breathed heavily. He threw two punches out, but Kyle blocked them, countering by throwing a combination at Pat, who made him miss. With both men bleeding and out of breath, Kyle motioned to strike Pat on the head with the baton, but Pat blocked his arm, and the baton fell to the ground, by his feet. As Pat grabbed the baton, Kyle rugby tackled him, both of them landing in a heap by the open boot. Before Kyle could launch another strike, Pat cracked him over the head with the baton; then another couple of times to keep him down.

A fresh laceration on his head leaking blood, Kyle lay on the ground with his arms out and his eyes closed. Standing, Pat looked at his lifeless body, tossing the baton aside. Slamming the boot shut, he used his sleeve to mop blood from his mouth. Dragging Kyle away from the car, Pat dumped himself down behind the wheel. He cared not a jot for Kyle, who'd been murdering people, self-preservation his mainspring.

Speeding off, he saw a black transit van in the distance. Slowing down, Pat pulled his cap over his forehead. The vehicles passed in opposite directions, and Pat drove on, putting his foot down when turning into an adjoining road.

CHAPTER 19

THE BOX LODGED BETWEEN his underarm and bicep, and Pat let himself into Sarah's house. Locking the door and placing the box in the hall, he stepped into the lounge to find Sarah asleep on the sofa with the television on. Leaving her be, he went upstairs to change into a dressing gown.

Standing in front of a mirror, he glanced at his reflection. His face was cut, bruised and a touch bloated, with a fat lip, and his hands wore a medley of grazes and nicks. Putting his muddy, bloodied clothes into a plastic bag, he took them into the kitchen, stuffing them in the washing machine. Making himself a cup of tea, he sat down and took a sip.

"Jesus, Pat!" said Sarah, walking in. "What the hell happened to you?"

She sat down next to Pat, putting her arms around him.

"Kyle's dead."

For a few seconds, Sarah just stared at him, unable to find the words. "What? I mean … when? Who killed him? For god's sake, Pat, what happened?"

"I killed him, Sarah. I murdered him outside the apartments. He caught me red-handed with the files. He wouldn't let me take them, so a fight broke out. He hit me with his baton, but after a while, I took hold of it and used it on him. Hit him a few times on the head, and now he's dead. There was blood everywhere and, as I left, the suits were on their way. I saw them drive past me."

Pat dabbed his mouth with a tissue, looking at Sarah, who raked her hands through her hair.

"Pat, we have to end this now! We need to go to Rosey, and he needs to see the files. Tell him what happened to Kyle. It could've been you tonight. It has to stop now! I can't take this anymore! We have to go to them, Pat!"

"I need to take a bath and get some sleep, Sarah," said an exhausted Pat, planting a hand on his sore back. "I fell about ten foot from the balcony trying to get into Kyle's. My back's in bits, I need to sleep for a few hours, and then we'll go to Rosey – he'll know what to do." He shifted a little in his chair, straightening his back. "What's worrying me is that with Kyle dead, they'll be a huge police operation. But I can't do anything about that for now – I'm busted. We need to get some sleep, and I need to phone Diane at some point tomorrow to make sure they're okay at Paul's. Shit, what a mess. But thank god I've got the files."

"Alright," said Sarah, kissing Pat. "I'll run a bath, then let's get some sleep. I need to try and forget about all of this for a few hours."

Pat got up and went into the hall, kneeling down to take the lid off the box. Picking out Marie Jones' file, he handed it to Sarah.

"I never thought our government could stoop so low. I know there's a major recession, but this is barbaric. If anyone finds out, it'll bring the government down, and whoever else is involved."

Sarah passed the file to Pat, who put it back in the box, replacing the lid and carrying it upstairs, placing it on the bedroom floor. He sat on the bed for a few minutes, the events of the past few days replaying continuously in his head, however hard he tried to find a distraction.

"Pat, come on. Your bath's ready."

Heading into the bathroom, Pat lightly moaned as he eased his aching body into hot, foamy water that stung his lacerations. Sarah rubbed his shoulders and cleaned the dried blood from his neck and ears.

"Is this your blood I'm washing away, or Kyle's?"

"Probably both."

"Will we go to Rosey's house or are you going to wait until he's at work?"

"What's with this, we thing? You can't be involved now, Sarah. They mustn't know you've been helping me and that we have any kind of association beyond what goes on in the station."

"I think it's a little late for that, don't you? Kyle is dead, and you need all the help you can get right now. I'm your alibi, remember."

"I know. But we need to make sure this is all over before there's any mention of you and me being together. I won't tell

Rosey until I know this is dealt with, so for now, please let me sort it out."

"No, I'm in this until the end, and I'm a witness to the suits. I just hope Marie can tell them what happened. Assuming he doesn't get to her and shut her up."

"The police will be guarding her twenty-four-seven now, since my little security breach. And it's not our nick. It's The Ringway looking after her, so she should be safe."

Once he'd bathed and changed, they sat in bed, Pat unable to take his eyes off the box on the floor.

"Leave it and get some sleep," said Sarah.

"I just want to have a look at the other files and see who else he's murdered for our wonderful government."

"Pat, you need sleep, and your body's a mess, so lie down and do it later."

"It's no good, I can't stop thinking about it," said Pat. He got out of bed and lifted the box onto the bed. Finding Sammy Clarke's file, he gave it to Sarah.

"Bloody hell, Clarke was an expensive British commodity," she said in a sarcastic lilt.

"Now look at this," said Pat, putting the newspaper in front of her and turning to the second page.

"I still don't believe this is real, Pat. How long has this been going on? How many people are involved? And how many have they murdered?"

"I've no idea," said Pat. "And I doubt we'll ever know."

He took another file from the box. Carl Baker's, it revealed an even greater abuse of funds than either of his predecessors.

"Fuck me. I thought Sammy Clarke was expensive but look at Baker: eighty-one thousand pounds saved for the good old British taxpayer. Clever twat, Kyle. I wonder how he managed that. We were together when the call came in."

"How could he have done it if you were there with him?"

"After Baker threatened suicide, we took him to his sister's house. She was on nights, and when we were called there the next morning, he was hanging from the loft. Which means Kyle must've gone back at night while she was working and did it then. There was no sign of a struggle, just a stool near to where he was hanging."

"Pat let's get some sleep. Put them down please."

"I will. Just one more first."

Pat took the next file from the box and found another name he was highly familiar with: Laurence Bell.

"This is getting a bit spooky now," he said. "I had dealings with Bell the day he died, and it was Kyle and me together. He drowned apparently and was high on drugs. So, Kyle must've been looking for potential victims on the jobs we were sent to, using his cover as a police officer to get to them."

"You make it sound as though he's smart, but he's a murderer. Kyle's dead, but you're still alive, and they can just as easily point the finger at you. You were there, remember."

"I know. It's clear now that Kyle was covering his tracks, the sneaky bastard, and that I was going to take the rap if they were rumbled. Sod them. We have the evidence right here and, with Kyle dead, the suits will be trying their upmost to get it back, so I need to get it to Rosey sooner rather than later. Anyway, Bell had a seventy-three thousand pounds bounty on his head. Still not in Carl Baker's league, but impressive nonetheless."

"Right, that's it. Put the files down and get some sleep," said Sarah, taking the files from Pat and, together with the newspaper, putting them back in the box and replacing the lid.

Pat and Sarah laid down, Sarah switching the bedside lamp off. Pat lay there, wide-eyed, unable to break his habit of replaying recent events in his mind. He focused on Kyle, justifying his death quite matter-of-factly – what goes around comes around and all that. But what were the implications for him if he wasn't able to clear his name? He was now a murderer – would that sit as easily on his shoulders as the years went by, presuming whoever hired Kyle didn't do away with him?

Eventually falling asleep, the early morning silence was broken by the sound of banging on the front door. Pat sat up in bed and rubbed Sarah's arm.

"Sarah, wake up! Someone's banging on the door."

"Oh, god," she groaned, coming to in panic. "What is it now?"

"I don't know. Look out of the window, but don't go down."

Sarah got out of bed and put her dressing gown on, while Pat looked at the clock: it was only 05.43, roughly half an hour after they hit the sack. Sarah stepped towards the bedroom window and, looking through the curtains, saw a black transit van parked at the front of her drive. Then, as she glanced down towards the front door, two men in suits peered up at her.

"Oh fuck, it's them, Pat – they're fucking here!"

"Stay calm," said Pat, feeling anything but calm. "Ignore them and see what they do."

"They've seen me looking – how can I ignore them?! What shall I do?!"

"Just open the window and go from there."

Pat got out of bed and crouched down by Sarah as she opened the window. One of the suited men shone a torch into Sarah's face, while the other spoke.

"Can you come down, please? We need to have a quick word with you."

"I was in bed and am on my own, so don't really want to open the door. Who are you, and what do you want?"

"We're looking for someone. Is this your car?" he asked, pointing to a Saab 9-3 Convertible.

"Yes, it's mine. Why? What about it?"

"We need to speak to you about this car. Can you come down please?"

"I've already told you: I'm on my own and I'm not coming down. Say what you have to say from there, and tell me who you are please."

The man speaking to her produced a small wallet from his jacket pocket, flipping it open and raising it aloft for Sarah to see. It was a badge of sorts with a photo, very similar to a police warrant card.

"So, you're police? Is that a warrant card?"

"We're a type of police. We work for an agency. Come to the door. We need to talk to you."

Sarah didn't say anything in response.

"Either you open the door and talk to us, or we'll open it. Do you understand?"

Sarah shut the window and crouched down with Pat. "Agency? What agency could it be, Pat?" she whispered.

"I've no idea. Maybe MI Five or Six. Go down and see what they have to say. They must've seen me driving away from Kyle's place in your car. Tell them it was you, that you were working. Let them ask the questions first. Don't offer any information, wait for the question. You'll be fine. Have a good look at their ID and see who they are. I'll try and get the registration number from the van when they drive away. Let me come down and hide in the cupboard under the stairs, just in case."

The banging continued, so Pat ran downstairs and hid in the cupboard. Sarah slowly made her way down to the front door, which she opened. The two suited men pushed past her and stood in the hall.

"Excuse me! Don't just force your way into my house. Show me your ID and tell me what you want, then leave, or I'll call the police."

"Calm down. We're only here to ask you a few questions," said the man she'd already spoken to, his dark brown eyes glaring at her.

As he reproduced the ID from his jacket pocket, Sarah saw a gun in a shoulder holster. She looked at the ID, which gave the name A. Campbell and a photo of the man in front of her. She was able to discern a coat of arms made from a silver metal before the man snapped the wallet shut, placing it back in his jacket pocket.

"So, Mr Campbell, who do you work for and what do you want at this time of the morning?" she asked, clocking out of her peripheral vision, the other man snooping around.

"We work for the government, we're looking for someone, and you may know who he is. Can I ask if you've been out tonight?"

"Yes, I have."

"Where did you go?"

"To work."

"Work in the early hours of a Sunday morning? What do you do?"

"I'm an on-call solicitor, so I work all sorts of hours, as you can imagine."

"I take it that's your car on the drive?"

"Yes, it is," said Sarah. "Why?"

"It was seen across town around an hour or so ago, and we're looking for someone, so just following up all potential leads."

"Well, that was me. I've been on call with a client, and was on my way home, so that's why I was out tonight."

"Who was your client, and where were you?"

"That, I'm afraid, is privileged information, but he's in police custody not too far from town. That's all I'm prepared to say. Now, if that's all you want, I could really do with going to bed, as I'm on call all weekend. You said you were looking for someone. Can I assume it's PC Patrick?"

"You assume correctly," said Campbell. "We know you're his legal representative. Has he been in touch at all?"

"So, you know who I am and what I do," said Sarah. "That's a little shifty, don't you think?"

"Just making sure you tell us the truth. I'm sure you understand that more than most."

"I suppose, but there's no way he'll be contacting me. I'm no longer representing him after he pulled that stunt at The Ringway. I've never been so embarrassed in all my life. He really made me look stupid, and the amount of grief I've had over him has been relentless. So no, he hasn't been in touch. And if he does, I'll tell him what I think of him and where to go."

"Can we make another suggestion? If your former client does contact you and divulges where he is, can you play along and let us know so that we can go and pick him up?"

"With pleasure. How do I get hold of you?"

Campbell removed a small white card from his wallet. All it had on it was a phone number and the name A. Campbell.

"It's monitored twenty-four-seven, and it's imperative we catch up with him. Can I ask what he told you while you were representing him?"

"Sorry, I can't divulge due to privileged information. Can I ask you a question?"

"Yes, you can."

"Why are you looking for him, and not the real police?"

"The real police have much more important things to do with their time."

"It seems like a lot of fuss for such an incident. Surely you lot deal with serious stuff like terrorists, military coups and spies?"

"We do whatever we're told to. And for now, we need to find him, so we could do with your help if, at some point, he decides to make contact. Do you understand?"

"Absolutely," said Sarah, who masked surprise at his menacing tone. "Now can you leave me to go back to bed? It's been a long night."

The two men left the house, Sarah shut and locked the door, and Pat emerged from the cupboard, ran upstairs and peeped through the curtains. He couldn't see the van's registration number because it was too dark, and on driving away, it had no lights on. Pat went back downstairs as Sarah gulped water down.

"You were brilliant," said Pat, embracing her. "That was so believable and very cool, I must say."

"Are you kidding me? I was shitting myself! I've never been so scared in all my life! Thank god that's over. Do you think they believed me?"

"Yes, of course – they believed you. I can't believe the men confirmed that they're government agents. They must work for MI Five or Six, and that explains why it's not on the news. The local police aren't even involved – it's just them lot."

"Only one of them spoke, while the other was looking around. I saw a gun in a holster when he showed me his ID. It must be the same two you confronted at the canal."

"No, it wasn't," said Pat. "I didn't recognise his voice at all. It must be the other pair who are driving around looking for me. Strange they never mentioned Kyle, though." He scratched an itch, yawned. "Well done, you. Now let's go back to bed for a couple of hours."

While Sarah dozed off pretty much straight away, Pat's overactive mind reminded him of another concern: that the suits knew about her car. But, rather than going over and over it, he must've joined Sarah in a deep sleep, for the next thing he knew it was 9 am, and the alarm had woken him. With Sarah still dead to the world, Pat got up, took a piss, then went downstairs to make two cups of coffee. Placing Sarah's on a bedside table, he peeped through the curtains to see if the suits were hanging around – no sign of them.

"There's a coffee for you, honey," he said as Sarah came to. "We need to get a move on. Time is against us, they're closing in on us, and we need to get to Rosey. And I need to phone Paul later on. I hope the girls got away okay."

"Just give me five more minutes," groaned Sarah.

After another check on the news channels, Pat drank his coffee and went to the bathroom, taking a quick shower before waking Sarah, who'd dozed off again.

"Wakey wakey, love," he said, stroking her hair.

"Oh, god. Is it time already?"

"Over time. I'll be downstairs."

Pat went into the kitchen to make some toast, Sarah joining him once she'd showered and put her tracksuit on.

"They know my car now, so how can we get to Rosey's?" she asked.

"You drive, and I'll lie down on the back seats. There's no other way."

"Hopefully they'll leave me alone, now they know who I am."

"Yes, hopefully. But we can't get complacent. Just remember: they're not stupid and might be watching your every move, so can I suggest you go for a little recky first to see if they're hanging around? Then come back for me."

CHAPTER 20

ACROSS TOWN, DIANE WAS up and getting ready to go to Nottingham. She woke the girls early and asked them to come downstairs, which didn't go down well, what with it being 9 am on a Sunday morning. A bleary-eyed Becky was the first to appear, closely followed by Sophie, who was a little sprightlier.

"Right, both of you: sit down, have some breakfast and listen very carefully to what I have to say."

"Oh no, Mom, please don't tell me you've got a boyfriend," said Becky.

"No, nothing as exciting as that. Just listen to me and don't interrupt. I need you both to get some clothes together. Enough for about three days, but it has to go in your sports bags, and I need you both to dress in your tracksuits. Becky, you have to leave your mobile phone here. Sophie, will you bring your old Nokia with the charger, and make sure they go in your bag. We're going to Uncle Paul's in Nottingham for a few days, on the train."

"Mom, what's going on?" asked Becky. "Is this to do with Dad, by any chance?"

"It is, but what made you ask?"

"I know he was here in the early hours yesterday. I heard you both talking and saw him leaving and climbing the fence to go over the common. It's to do with the men in the van that we keep seeing around, isn't it?"

"You don't miss a trick, do you, young lady? Yes, it's to do with your Dad. And yes, it's to do with the men in the van. They're looking for him. He's had a bit of trouble at work and has decided to stay away for a while to let things calm down, but they want to talk to him now."

"It must be serious if we're running to Uncle Paul's, Mom," said Sophie.

"Yes, it is. I'll explain more when we get there because Paul will need to know what's going on. But, for now, all you need to do is get your stuff together. Sophie, make sure you bring the Nokia, and Becky, leave your phone here. We need to make it look like we're going to the gym to swim.

"The men in the van are still parked up the road and will most likely follow us, so don't keep looking back and draw attention to us. I'll need to stop on the way to get some cash. I'll park at the leisure centre, and we'll walk through to the running track, then out of the gate into the park, and make our way to the train station.

Hopefully, they'll stay in their van in the car park and, by the time they come looking for us, we'll be long gone."

"Is Dad in trouble, though?" asked Sophie. "What's he done wrong, Mom?"

"Dad's fine, and he'll sort this out, but he wants us out of the way, just in case they try to use us to get to him. This is all his idea, and he sends his love to you both. Now eat up, then get your stuff together. I want us to leave in the next ten minutes."

Becky and Sophie didn't ask any more questions, finishing their breakfast and starting to pack. All three were ready in less than fifteen minutes, standing nervously at the front door.

"Remember: don't look at them, girls," said Diane as they stepped onto the drive.

Locking up, Diane followed the girls into the car after they'd put their bags in the boot. Reversing off the drive, she headed out of the estate, clocking the van trailing them. Stopping at a petrol station, Diane withdrew three hundred pounds from a cashpoint, ostensibly unmoved as the van drove past.

Climbing back into the car, she pulled off the forecourt, turned left and, as she passed the first road on the right, saw the van pull out of a side road to follow from a distance. Diane didn't say anything to the girls, who were busy chatting about boys and music. Fifteen minutes later, they arrived at the leisure centre, Diane parking in a bay not too far from its main doors. Turning the engine off, she spoke to the girls without looking back.

"Act natural and walk casually to the entrance. They've parked a fair bit away but can see us from where they are. Grab your bags and don't look back."

They got out of the car and took their respective bags out of the boot. Diane locking the vehicle, they walked casually to the entrance and through its automatic double doors, standing in the reception area.

"Three to swim please," Diane told the receptionist, a pretty young woman in her twenties.

"No problem, madam. Have you got a membership card?"

"Yes," said Diane, raiding her purse and handing it to the receptionist.

Settling, Diane led the girls through the centre and out towards the running track. Nobody spoke as they strolled into a café. Overlooking the car park, it had windows that could be seen out of, but not into.

"Wait here a minute, girls. I won't be long," said Diane, heading upstairs to look at the car park and see if the suits were still there. The van was in the car park, but there was nobody in its front seats.

"Shit, where are they?" she asked herself, making her way back down to the girls, whose expressions belied their seemingly calm exterior. "Right, they aren't in the van, so we can't leave just yet. Let's go to the changing rooms. They might be checking we're here, so remember to keep calm and act as naturally as you can."

As they were about to enter the communal changing rooms, they saw the back of a man in a black suit walking towards the shower area. Diane grabbed the girls and pushed them into a cubicle.

"Stand on the bench and don't say a word," she whispered.

Standing there, wordless, too scared to move, they heard two pairs of footsteps close by.

"I saw them a few moments ago," said one of the suits.

"Maybe they're already in the water," said the other suit. "You check the pool. I'll have a look around the centre, and see what else is going on in here today."

Diane put her finger to her lips as the girls looked at her. Hearing the men leave, she grabbed the girls, the trio leaving the changing rooms. Stepping calmly out of the automatic doors, they ran back to the car with their bags in tow. Reaching the car, Diane unlocked the doors.

"C'mon – let's get out of here!"

They all jumped into the car, and Diane started the engine, putting the car into reverse and, in a panic, making it wheel spin. She slammed the gear into first, and the wheels continued to spin, making a loud screeching sound as she steered them out of the car park. Checking the rear-view mirror, Diane saw the suits running out of the leisure centre after them.

"Shit – they've seen us!"

Becky and Sophie kept looking behind to see if the van was chasing them down. Diane took a left, going through the gears so that they were doing 60MPH in a 30 zone. The Sunday morning drivers were out in force and, as Diane drove even closer to the vehicle in front, she hit her horn, flashing her lights to get the slower cars out of her way. It didn't do any good, the traffic ahead moving at no more than a leisurely pace.

Seeing an opportunity to overtake, Diane pulled out; but as she drew level with the car in front, a gas-guzzler reversed from a driveway and into her path. She slammed on the breaks, and smoke engulfed the car, the girls screaming as it jolted forward. Avoiding a full-on collision by a whisker, Diane ignored the driver of the other vehicle as he yelled and gestured at her, speeding off, the girls crying.

Diane rechecked the rear-view mirror; there was no sign of the van. Driving out of town, within ten minutes they'd reached the motorway, and were on their way to Nottingham. Stopping at the first service station, Diane turned the engine off and as good as collapsed in her seat.

"I'm so sorry!" she cried. Clambering out of the car, she saw, through watery eyes, Becky and Sophie rush up to and embrace her. "That was awful! I'm so, so sorry, girlies!"

The girls clung to Diane, who sucked air down, her heartbeat returning to something like normal. They would have to be on the move again soon, especially with the suits having her registration number; but for a few moments, all she wanted to do was hold her children close.

CHAPTER 21

NEARLY READY TO LEAVE, Pat asked Sarah to take the car for a quick spin, to see if the suits were around. Looping the estate on which she lived, and driving along the main road, Sarah returned not having seen them. Hearing her pull up on the drive, Pat locked up and darted in the back, lying down as Sarah drove off towards town.

"Do me a favour. Will you take a slight detour and head towards Kyle's?" asked Pat.

"No way! Are you mad? What if there's a roadblock? Seriously, Pat, are you determined to get caught? It's only been a few hours. There'll be cops everywhere."

"Look, I know it seems like a bad idea, but there was still nothing on the news about Kyle or me. I want to see what's going on over there."

"Pat, this is a horrible idea, and I think you need to reconsider. Honestly, it's suicide, if you ask me."

"The main road will be open. It happened on the side road, near the canal towpath, so they wouldn't be interested in the main road. We can drive by, see if there's a crime scene and take it from there. And if there is a roadblock, we'll be able to turn off before the cops stop us."

"And what if there's a substantial block? It's a police officer in uniform, on duty, so they'll be all over it like a rash."

"Sarah, trust me on this. If it were going to be splashed across the news, it would've happened by now."

"I've got to admit, that is unusual."

"Does that mean you'll drive by?"

"Okay, Pat, but on your head, be it."

Pat directed her towards Kyle's apartment block. As Pat suspected, there was no roadblock and, several minutes later, they approached the side road.

"I think it's okay for you to sit up," said Sarah. "There's virtually nobody about."

Pat sat up in time to see them as good as reaching their destination. "Slow down, it's just up there," he said.

Sarah slowed to a virtual standstill, and they both looked towards the side road, which had no police bunting, no police officers and no Scenes of Crime tent.

"Nothing at all," said Pat. "How strange. Drive to the top of the road, come back down, and let me out of the car. I need to take a closer look."

Sarah did as he asked, Pat, finding the spot where he and Kyle fought. Marked by a couple of sprays of blood, he ran up to the fence and checked the towpath, which was clear. Nobody was around, so he made his way back to where Sarah had parked, climbing into the back of the car and lying down.

"Let's get out of here."

Sarah drove off, heading for the opposite side of town and towards Rosey's house. "Well, what did you find?"

"Nothing, apart from a few splashes of blood."

"So, what does that mean?"

"I've no idea, but someone has taken Kyle, and my guess is it's his suited friends. Why and where, God only knows, but one thing's for sure: it's all being kept very quiet, so they must have friends in high places."

It didn't take a genius to work out that the government agents had the authority, manpower and connections to make a dead police officer in uniform disappear and keep it from the public eye. They were clearly involved in a highly sinister plot to commit murder, and Pat knew that just one mistake could see him, and Sarah become their next victims. If he had to go, he had to go; but neither his lover nor family should've been put at risk.

"Shit, we've got company," said Sarah, breaking his train of thought. "The men in the van have just overtaken the vehicle behind me, so stay down."

"Okay, keep calm, stay at the speed limit and stop talking to me," said Pat. "Or if you do, don't move your lips."

"They're keeping well back. I think they've done this deliberately, letting me know they're following me to see where I'm going."

"Will there be anyone in your office at this time on a Sunday morning?"

"No."

"Head over there. It's actually en route, so that should get the men off your tail. Have you got your office keys with you?"

"Yes, in my handbag."

"Good. Do what I said, and we'll see how they react when you arrive."

Sarah drove towards her place of work, keeping an intermittent eye on the van, which followed them the entire way, maintaining a reasonable distance behind. Arriving at the firm's underground parking, Sarah pulled up at the barrier guarding it, entering the code to gain entry. As the barrier lifted, she could see the van parked across the road, and that its occupants were the same pair she spoke to earlier.

"It's them again, Pat. They're parking across the road," she said, driving into the parking lot.

"Go over to them and ask what they want. Tell them you're catching up with your work from the weekend, then come back and go into your office."

"Jesus, Pat!" she cried. "I'm not cut out for all of this!"

"You're doing great," said Pat. "And it's important that they know you're on the ball."

"Okay," sighed Sarah, climbing out of the car.

Crouching under the barrier, she walked towards the men, one of whom lowered his window.

"Don't you two ever sleep?" she asked, her voice carrying traces of anger that overrode the fear underpinning it.

"When the job's done, yes," said Campbell. "What is this place anyway?"

"The offices where I work. I've got some paperwork to catch up with over the weekend."

"We'll leave you to it, then."

"Are you going to keep following me until PC Patrick has been arrested?"

"We'll be keeping all avenues open for now, so you'll see us around occasionally."

"I have to go," said Sarah. "Good luck with your hunt."

Inside her office, Sarah watched from her window as the van drove off shortly after she switched on the light. A few minutes later, Pat joined her.

"They've gone," said Sarah.

"I know, but I used the basement entrance, just in case." He took a look around the office. "Wow, this is nice. Must've cost a bomb, but I'm not surprised, the amount of money you solicitors make. Anyway, what did they have to say for themselves?"

"Not a lot. The men admitted they'll be hanging around until they find you. They were checking what I was doing here on a Sunday morning."

"The bastards. They don't exactly keep a low profile, do they?"

"No, they do not. It's as though the men want me to know they're watching me. I wonder why?"

"To see if you slip up. Knowing that they're watching you will make you more nervous, more likely to do something stupid or make a mistake. We do it all the time with some of our crims."

"Well, thanks for that, Sherlock. So, how long do we wait here?"

"Give it ten minutes, and we'll go to Rosey's, and get this nightmare over and done with."

After drinking a coffee each, Sarah made her way to the top floor, to take another look out of the window. The suits were nowhere to be seen, so she returned to her office and told Pat the coast was clear. They locked the office and returned to the car using the basement door, Pat climbing into the back and lying down as Sarah drove out of the barrier and back across town.

"When we get to Rosey's, I want you to drop me off. Park near to the entrance, by the kids' park, and don't go anywhere or do anything until you see me. If I'm not back in half an hour, go back home and wait for me, no matter what you see or hear."

"What do you mean: see or hear?"

"I'm just ultra-cautious, making sure I can trust him one hundred per cent."

"You're not telling me he might be caught up in this too?"

"I doubt it, but right about now, I don't know quite what to think. He'll have been to bed, having finished a night shift, so it might take me a few minutes to get him up. Stay by the entrance to the park, where you can see everything coming and going, and if something does happen, you can drive down the hill to safety, and still be able to see his house from there."

"And what if something does happen? Who am I supposed to turn to for help?"

"You won't need to, I promise. I'm just thinking aloud. Just keep an eye on his house, and after thirty minutes I want you gone. Promise me, Sarah."

"I promise."

As she hadn't visited before, Pat did his best to guide Sarah towards Rosey's house, while trying to remain out of view in the back of the car. As they reached the road on which he lived, Pat pointed his house out, then showed Sarah the children's park. Stopping the car so that it faced downwards, towards the hill, she switched the engine off. Pat leaned into the front of the car, kissing her.

"I love you. Hopefully, this nightmare can now be over." He looked at the car's digital clock. "It's coming up to half-ten. If I'm not back by eleven on the dot, I want you to go home."

"Okay, I will. Please be careful, and I love you too."

Closing the car door, Pat made for Rosey's front drive. Once there, he wanted to check she could see him, so gave her a quick wave, Sarah waving back. Taking a deep breath, Pat rang the doorbell. No reply, he glanced at the boss' black Audi A3 on the drive, then tried again. Nothing. Glancing up, Pat saw that the curtains were drawn in the front bedroom.

Divorced, with his children living at his ex-wife's, it was a pretty safe bet that, if in, Rosey was alone. Figuring he'd just come off a night shift, Pat took to banging the front door and ringing the bell at the same time. Lo and behold, after five or six attempts, he saw the curtains to the bedroom window twitch, followed by Rosey's face gazing down at him. Gesturing for him to come to the door, a few seconds later it opened to reveal Rosey wearing a vest and boxer shorts.

"Pat, what are you doing here? Shit, come in for god's sake."

As Pat stepped inside, he noticed Rosey looking up and down the road, which struck him as a little odd. Putting it to one side, he went into the lounge and sat on a sofa. Rosey glared at Pat.

"Pat, what the fuck? Jesus, man, have you any idea how much shit you're in? Why have you come here? Where have you been for the last few days?"

"I'll explain it all to you, and then maybe you can give me some answers. I'm desperate, and you're my only hope of helping me sort this fucking mess out."

"Pat, you've got a fucking nerve, putting me in this position. By rights, I should be arresting you and handing you in, so this had better be good. Do you want a cup of tea or coffee?"

"Yes, coffee, please."

While the kettle boiled, Rosey went upstairs, put his dressing gown on and came back down. The coffees were made, and he returned to the lounge, sitting down.

"Right, let me hear it, then," he sighed.

"It's hard to know where to start, but here goes. I was spoken to about the attempted murder of Marie Jones. Yes, I was there. Yes, I went to the hospital, and yes, I left my number for the doctor to call me should her condition improve. My prints were on her letters in the flat because when I heard about her on the news, I went there to have a look around for myself, feeling she was never suicidal. The witness did see my car parked around the corner, the morning after she jumped, but I wasn't there when she actually jumped. That, I can assure you, wasn't me – they must've been mistaken. The truth is: I've known Marie all my life. We grew up together, went to school together, and I knew her husband and kids when they were alive."

"You know Marie Jones, and you kept it a secret all this time? She never said a word to any other officer. Why, Pat?"

"Out of loyalty to me. Marie knew that if you lot had any idea we knew each other, it would've made my life a living hell, so she kept it to herself."

"Fucking hell, Pat. So, when you went to the hospital to see her, and had the run-in with the officer from The Ringway, what actually happened? Why did you hurt him? What did he see or what did he know?"

"I didn't want to get caught, knowing what I'd just found out."

"What do you mean: found out?"

"From Marie."

"But she's a mess in a coma, and barely able to talk. She has a brain injury, an alcoholic and a druggie. What the hell could she have told you when she can't even converse with the doctors or the police?"

"She was able to tell me that she didn't try to kill herself. She was thrown off the balcony by one of my mates."

"Mate? What mate's that, then?"

"Kyle."

Rosey laughed hard. "Kyle?! Are you serious? She told you that, and you believe her?"

"Yes, I do, and there's much more evidence. Kyle's not what or who you think he is. And incidentally, where is Kyle?" asked Pat, knowing he was dead, but intrigued by what Rosey's answer would be.

"He was off last night, so I assume he's at home. Why do you ask?"

"Because he's dead."

Rosey looked at Pat and smiled. "Pat, what the fuck are you going on about? He's not dead. He had the night off. A family emergency, he said. And how do you know he's dead? Dead is a serious revelation. How the hell have you come to that conclusion?"

"Because I killed him in the early hours and left him by the side road, near to his apartment."

"Of course, you did! Do you really expect me to believe all of this shit? You killed Kyle, and Marie Jones told you he tried to kill her, while everybody's looking at you for her attempted murder? Then there's Sammy Clarke, and you're being implicated in the murder of a few others too. Maybe you're running scared and trying to blame Kyle when it's clear you're the one who's responsible."

"Hold on a fucking minute," said Pat, raising his voice. "What others, and who's implicated me? Where has this crap come from?"

"Keep your voice down – I've got neighbours! And don't treat me like a fucking idiot, Pat. The evidence all points to you, and you're blaming Kyle, who can't defend himself, because he's dead, according to you."

"Sarge, I came here to get your help. I need your help and, before you start listening to your own bullshit, maybe if you let me finish and actually listen to what I have to say, you won't be so fucking judgemental."

"Okay, speak, and I won't interrupt. But remember, I've been at work and had to listen to all of the allegations against you, and saw the evidence for myself, so don't assume I don't know anything. You're the one on the run, and you're the one telling me you killed Kyle."

"Fair point but hear me out for five minutes. Then judge for yourself."

"Okay, Pat – fire away."

Pat looked at a clock on a mantelpiece. It was 10.40, which gave him twenty minutes before Sarah left without him.

"Carl Baker: I went to that job with Kyle, and he knew he was staying at his sister's and that she was on nights. So, he had the opportunity to go there while she was at work, and killed him – probably with the help of his friends."

"Friends?" asked Rosey.

"Men in suits in dark transit vans – I'll explain that bit in a minute. Laurence Bell: Kyle was with me when we went to that job. The next day he's dead, drowned. Sammy Clarke: Kyle was with me for that job too, and within hours of his release from custody, he's dead from an overdose. Clarke had been drug-free since he got out of prison. All of his tests had been clear.

"Kyle was with me for the Marie Jones job when we were on nights. Then, within a couple of days, she's bouncing off the concrete at Lime Court. They all have one thing in common: drugs and alcohol abuse, don't work, abuse all services, go to prison, waste our time, the hospitals' and doctors' time, get benefits and cost the government and taxpayer billions, according to the files."

"Files?"

"Yes – files. There's a box full of them, with all of this information on each of them."

"How do you know?"

"Because I've got them."

"So, you have the files, and you've read them?"

"Yes, to both."

"Where are they now, Pat?

"In a very safe place. There's more, though. I knew there was something wrong with Kyle. He was sneaky, and he didn't sit well with me, so I took a trip to London. I went to his old station and was told that he quit the force and is now working for the Home Office. So, how is it he's now in a uniform working with us?''

"He was a squaddie too, Special Forces, so he knows how to do this undercover stuff, and kill, and get away with it. Where did he get the money to buy that apartment? That's three hundred grand on a copper's wage. I don't think so somehow. Somebody's paying him some serious money, and now we know who."

"Do we really? So … who is it, Pat?"

"The government. He's working for them, killing off the lowlifes – the wasters of society … you know the ones I'm always bleating on about. He's sent in, locates them, then kills them with the help of these suited men in transit vans who've been hanging around. I had a face-off with them. They've got guns and are everywhere I go. They're looking for me because Kyle knew I was onto him, and we had a fight when I was at his apartment and took the files. Kyle wanted them back, we fought, it became nasty, and I hit him over the head a few times with his baton, killing him."

"So, the files were at Kyle's apartment all this time?"

"Yeah, loads of them. All of his victims all were showing how much each dead person saved the taxpayer."

"How many files have you read, Pat?"

"Baker, Clarke, Bell and Jones. There are others, but I haven't had a chance to look at them yet. Kyle's body has gone. I imagine the suits have picked him up because when we drove past a few minutes ago, there was no crime scene. And now I know he had the night off. That's why you lot weren't missing him. He had his uniform on, so was no doubt looking for his next victim when he realised I had the files and caught me with them."

"This is quite a revelation, Pat," said Rosey, running a hand over his mouth. "Does anyone else know about this? And where have you been staying the last few days?"

"No, it's only me, and I've been staying in a hotel just outside of town."

"But you said: when we were driving around. Who is we, and what have you been driving, because your car was seized?"

"I meant me," said Pat, pissed off with himself for dropping the ball with a slip of the vernacular. "And I take a taxi so as not to draw any attention to myself."

"Can you prove any of this, Pat?"

"All of it. I have the files, as well as an alibi on the night Marie was thrown off the balcony … plus all of the evidence against Kyle, and finding the files in his apartment. The suits have been hanging around my house, following my ex-wife and kids too.

And then there's Marie – she can confirm it was Kyle who threw her off the balcony."

"Okay, get me the files, and we can go from there. Where are they, Pat?"

"I've already told you: they're in a safe place for now, and I need to know that you'll protect me and do the right thing."

"I'll have to hand you in, but if I have the files, we can go from there and build your case. Just out of interest, have you got any of the registration numbers to these vans?"

"No. All I can tell you is that they're black and dark blue Transits. And the men wear black suits and go round in twos."

Pat checked the time. It was 10.55 – almost time to go.

"Look, I need to go," he said. "I've got to meet somebody."

"Are you serious?" frowned Rosey. "You come here and make these incredible accusations, and need my help. You're on the run for murder, and I'm just supposed to let you out of my sight?"

"I need to go, Sarge. I promise I'll be back soon, and we can formulate a plan for all of this. But I have to go now."

Pat stood up and walked towards the front door, Rosey joining him.

"Just wait a minute," said Rosey. "I need the loo."

"As I said: I'm in a hurry, boss."

"One minute. There's something I need to tell you, but you woke me up before I could take a leak."

"Okay, but be quick," said Pat.

Rosey went upstairs. Pat was sure he could hear him whispering to someone before flushing the toilet. A woman he wanted to hide? Or was it a male voice and, if so, what did that mean? Pat inched towards the stairs, pulling back when Rosey came downstairs and stood next to him.

"Give me a few more minutes, Pat. There are so many questions I need to ask that I need answers to so that I can start to put things in motion to get you out of this fucking mess."

"Sarge, I have to go. I need to get out of here and meet someone, but I promise I'll be back in a few hours. I need to make sure Diane and the girls are safe. I heard you whispering to someone up there – who is it?"

"I was muttering to myself in disbelief. You mentioned Di and the girls. Where are they?"

"Somewhere safe. That's all I'm prepared to say for now."

As Pat opened the front door, Rosey put his foot in the way.

"What are you doing, Sarge? I told you I need to go."

Pat nudged Rosey out of the way, opened the door and walked out. Rosey followed him, standing on the drive.

"I need to make sure you're coming back, Pat. And I have to be honest: I'm reluctant to let you leave."

"With all due respect, Sarge, you won't stop me. I'm leaving, and that's that. I told you I'll be back, and I mean it."

Pat walked off in the direction of the main road, hearing Rosey close his door. He could see Sarah at the top of the road, by the park, and looked at his watch – 11.00 am on the dot. He carried on walking and stopped when he was out of Rosey's view. When Sarah saw Pat, she started the car; but as Pat stood by the side of the road, a dark transit van screeched to a halt next to him. The side door to the back of the van opened, and a man in a suit pointed a gun at Pat.

"Get in – now," he demanded.

Pat looked up the road and knew Sarah could see what was going on … but had no choice but to comply. He climbed into the van, and the side door was slammed shut. The van turned around and headed away from Rosey's house … and Sarah. Pat sat down. The suited man continued to point the gun at him. It wasn't the same men he fought with on the canal towpath, so assumed it was the pair who visited Sarah that morning.

"So, are you two the A team or the B team?" asked Pat.

"Shut the fuck up and enjoy the ride," said the man with the gun.

"Why, are we going anywhere nice?"

The man leant over, raised his right arm and hit Pat on the top of his head with the butt of the gun. Pat fell down and grabbed his head, yelping with pain.

"You fucking coward," he said, blood running down the side of his face. "Put the gun down and try that again."

"I told you to shut the fuck up. We won't be as soft as the other crew, ending up in the fucking canal. So sit there, or you'll get another, and another, until you aren't able to speak."

Pat knew instinctively that this was serious, and that playing the smartarse, right now, would only get him into more trouble. He clutched his aching head, then looked at the blood staining his hand. The van was being driven erratically, and he could hear the driver on his mobile phone.

"We've got him. He's in the back of the van, and we'll be there in about fifteen minutes."

Fifteen minutes equated to a destination that wasn't very far away. There was nothing at all in the back of the van, aside from the side panels and a strong smell of body odour that must've been generated by the suits over the last couple of days. Pat sat up and tried to look out of the front window, to see where they were going, but the seats blocked his view.

The man with the gun spoke to the driver, but Pat struggled to make out what was being said amid the racket created by the van's engine. Then the van stopped at what seemed to be traffic lights. Shuffling towards the side door, Pat pulled the handle to open it, but the man dived on top of him.

"For fuck's sake!" shouted the driver.

Punching the man twice in the face, he fell backwards, Pat pulling the door handle, the door flying open. But before he could jump out, the man grabbed Pat, and they both fell by the door. As the van raced forward, Pat took a hit to the ribs, causing him to lose his grip. Pat's head was hanging out of the door, and the man had both of his hands around his neck, squeezing tightly.

Pat could see that the van was travelling at speed, with traffic ahead. Pummelling the man in the ribs, he refused to loosen his grip on Pat's throat. Looking to his left, Pat saw a queue of traffic, the driver accelerating again to overtake. If he didn't act immediately, he risked decapitation, so using his left leg, he lifted the man up and pulled his arms down at the same time. Pushing with both feet, Pat threw the man over him and into the street; then launched himself at the driver, firmly planting his hands around his neck.

"Stop this fucking van now, or I'll snap your fucking neck!"

The van veering left, and right, it narrowly avoided a collision with the cars in the queue ahead. Its wheels clipping a kerb, the van came to a stop. Pat continued to squeeze the driver's neck and could feel him becoming weaker, the hand drifting towards his inner pocket stalling. And then, as he was about to finish him off, he felt a mighty blow to the back of his head, causing him to release the driver.

The other man had caught up with the van, jumped in and belted Pat across the head with the butt of his gun; as the driver restarted the van, speeding off, onlookers staring in disbelief. The second man produced some cable ties, rolled Pat onto his stomach, took his hands, placing them behind his back, then applied the ties to his wrists in the back-to-back position.

"Is he still alive?" asked the driver.

"Who gives a fuck? But yeah, he's still with us," replied the man in the back with Pat.

Around ten minutes later, they arrived at a disused warehouse just outside of town on an old industrial estate. The van pulled up round the back, and the two men carried Pat's limp body into the warehouse, throwing him into a room with a table and three chairs, crisp and chocolate wrappers, and lots of paper coffee cups, with computer equipment and other gadgets set up in the main warehouse space.

Pat was dragged towards and dumped in a chair. His body was still limp, his head falling backwards and blood from his fresh wounds dripping onto the ground. The suits made themselves a cup of coffee and appeared to be updating something on the computers. One of them made a call from a phone sitting on the desk next to the computer.

"He's here, and unconscious. We had a bit of an incident on the way, but he's here now." On the other end of the line, a male voice spoke. "Okay, leave it with us, and we'll get back to you."

The other man went to the kitchen area and filled a bucket of cold water, carrying it back and hurling it over Pat's head. He immediately came to, his head jolting forward.

"Wakey wakey, sunshine. We need to have a little chat."

Pat's wide eyes stared at the suited men sat in front of him in chairs. One of them wiped Pat's face with a towel.

"Fuck you!" said Pat, his bottom lip quivering with cold.

"Now now, there's no need for that, is there? At this point, the odds are clearly not in your favour, and you need to be nice, so sit the fuck back, calm down and be sensible. We need to talk to you, and hopefully, you'll give us the answers we need so that we can go home ... and you, my friend, can go to prison!"

"Ask away, but I've no idea what you want," replied a still-jaded Pat.

"Oh, you will – trust me. And don't be so negative. You'll be surprised how much you can help us. Anyway, enough small talk. Where are the files?"

Pat laughed, shaking his head.

"You seem nervous, PC Patrick. Where are the files?"

"These bloody files ... everyone seems to be really interested in them. I wonder why that is? Maybe you two can tell me all about them, and why you need them so desperately?"

One of the men stood up and smashed his fist into Pat's face. Pat's head flew back and forwards again, blood oozing from his nose.

"Fuck you!" he yelled.

"You don't seem to understand that the more you fuck us around, the more pain you'll feel. We'll keep going until we find out where the files are. Now let me try again."

Just as he was about to ask another question, Pat heard a vehicle grind to a halt somewhere outside. A few seconds later, two doors slammed, and a pair of footsteps drew closer. Pat couldn't see who it was at first, but he certainly recognised their voices.

"Not so cocky now, is he? And there's no water around for us to return the favour."

Pat saw the man he'd fought with, sporting a black eye, standing next to the one he threw into the canal.

"Hello, boys, nice to see you again. How was your swim?" he asked smirking.

The man with the black eye slapped Pat across the face using the back of his hand. Pat couldn't help but groan at the force of the blow, his head bowing and blood dripping onto his lap.

"You seem to forget that, right now, you're fucked. And that was for throwing me into the canal."

There were now four suited men looking like they wanted to go to town on him. Pat knew he was going to get seriously hurt, but no way would he tell them where the files were. He would protect Sarah at all costs, even if it cost him his life.

"Let's try again, shall we? Where are the files?" asked the man who'd been posing the questions.

"What files? I've no idea what you're on about."

"Listen, Pat, I'll only ask you one more time, and then this will be getting a whole lot more exciting. Now, where are the files you took from Kyle's apartment?"

"Oh, Kyle. Where is he, I wonder?"

Pat was struck by another backhand blow across the face, growling in pain and spitting blood on the ground. His head wounds reopening, blood slalomed down his face, joining the small puddle collecting beneath him.

"You know Kyle. Your buddy, the fake copper who was doing all of your dirty work. Have you lost him?"

"Okay, Pat, we tried to play this nicely. But it seems to me that we need to make this a little more interesting. Your ex-wife and two little daughters went on a jolly this morning to the leisure centre, didn't they?"

Pat glared at them all, wondering how much they knew about where they were. "Not against the law, is it?"

"No. But when your family go into the leisure centre with their big bags and pretend to go swimming, only to try and do a runner, then it does become a problem … but only a problem for you, Pat, as I'm sure you wouldn't want them to come to any harm. So, tell us where the files are, we'll reunite you, and you can be one big, happy family again."

Pat thought again. If they had Di and the girls, surely they'd be here as an incentive to speak. But what if they were being held elsewhere?

"You don't have them," Pat dared. "You're bluffing. If you had them, they'd be here, and you'd be torturing them to get me to tell you where the files are. So, if you do have them, let me see them, and I'll tell you where they are. If not, get fucked."

"Do you really think we're that stupid? That we'd put all of our eggs in one basket? They're in their tracksuits, and the car is a Black Volkswagen Passat estate. It's in a safe place, and we'll let them go once we have the files."

Pat's brain raced, trying to devise a plan to test what he'd just been told. "Okay, I'll tell you where the files are, but on one condition: you let me phone my eldest daughter on her mobile phone. If I hear her voice and she confirm you have them, I'll get you the files."

The four men walked off and started to talk among themselves. Pat had no choice but to take a chance and hoped beyond all hope that Becky left her phone at home. They'd be able to trace it, but with nobody at home and the phone not switched on or answered, Pat would know that they were safe, and at Paul's, as agreed.

"Okay, you can call her," said one of the men, as they walked up to him. "What's her number?"

Pat gave him the number which he dialled. It kept ringing out, while another of the men sat at one of the computers to, Pat suspected, trace the call. He immediately became emboldened, sure that Diane and the girls were out of harm's way.

"No reply," said the man who'd tried Becky's phone. "But we've traced her number to her home address, so thanks for the tip-off. We'll have a little waiting game while my colleagues go to the house to pick them up. Thanks for making that so easy for us."

Pat didn't say a word as two of the men left for Diane's house. The other pair ate sandwiches and drank coffee while messing around with the computers. It was only a matter of time before the departed duo returned – hopefully empty-handed – and Pat knew he'd be even in even deeper shit. Shivering, he sat slumped in the chair, his head throbbing with pain and blood continuing to drip on the ground.

He struggled to see a way out of this. If they wanted him dead, nobody would know ... and what would happen to Diane and the girls? To Sarah? All manner of ramifications tormented him in the time that passed so agonisingly slowly before the two men returned. They walked over to the other pair and whispered among themselves. Then one of them marched over to Pat, pulled his gun from the holster inside his jacket and put it in his mouth.

"Tell me where the files are, or I'll blow your fucking head off!"

Pat didn't speak. The suit's reaction meant there was nobody at the house. He wasn't going to tell them where the files were, which might well be as good as a death sentence … but at least his family were safe … for now, at least. The gun was pushed further into Pat's mouth, rattling against his teeth.

"Tell me where the fucking files are, or die right here and now, you piece of shit!"

The gun was removed from Pat's mouth, and his head rolled forward. The suit pulled his head back and punched him in the stomach, forcing him to pull his knees to his chest and cry out in pain. Becoming colder by the minute, Pat gasped for breath and was struck again and again, until passing out. His body slumped in the chair, blood streamed from his mouth, head, and now his wrists, where the cable ties were digging in and getting tighter.

CHAPTER 23

AS PAT STARTED TO stir, he heard one of the men on a phone call, updating whoever they were speaking to. He kept his eyes shut, feigning continued unconsciousness, wanting as much as possible to keep track of what was being said. But instead he heard the sound of another vehicle pulling up outside, and more footsteps.

"He's not talking. We've tried everything. He knows where the files are, but he's point-blank refusing to tell us."

"Well, wake him up and see what he says this time."

Pat recognised the voice straight away. Another cold bucket of water was thrown over him and, hearing footsteps behind him, he opened his eyes.

"No! Oh, no! Please tell me it's not true! You can't be one of them!" said Pat as Rosey sat down in front of him.

"Hello again, Pat. I'm sorry it had to be like this, but we need the files, and I'll get them with or without your help."

"Rosey, you bastard! How could you? Of all people, I never thought it'd be you. Go and rot in hell! I'd rather die than tell you where the files are, so fuck you! Fuck all of you!"

Pat shuffled in the chair, trying to get to Rosey, but his bound hands, hooked behind his back and over the rear of the chair, kept him firmly in place. As Rosey lifted Pat's head by his hair, Pat spat in his face. One of the men hit Pat in the stomach, forcing him to double up again. Pulling a tissue out of his pocket, Rosey used it to wipe his face.

"I need ... "

"Fuck you, Rosey – you'll never find them! Your little secret is out, and I've left instructions with someone that if I don't return, to go to the newspapers. Do your worst, you piece of shit," glowered Pat.

"Clean him up a bit, and give him something to eat and drink," said Rosey, pulling his gaze away from Pat and strolling off.

A couple of the suits carelessly wiped blood from Pat's face. They then fed him a sandwich and held a bottle of water to his lips for him to drink, placing a blanket around him. Once they'd finished, Rosey sat back down opposite Pat.

"I know you're in shock, Pat, but hear me out, and then maybe you might have a change of heart. It's not as bad as you think." Rosey looked at Pat, then drew a breath. "I listened to what you had to say at my house this morning and, to be fair, you know some of the stories. There's a heck of a lot you don't know, though, and some of it you've got totally wrong. So, I'll tell you the whole story and fill in the blanks for you. Firstly, I'm a police officer and always have been but, like you – although I was never as vocal – I was fed up with all the time wasters and alcoholics, druggies, scroungers and society's wasters.

"Do you know how much this lot cost the country, and how much time and resources they use and abuse every single day? Billions every year, and it's you and me who pay for it. We work so that scum can drink and take drugs, and live on benefits, and they never pay a fucking penny or contribute in any way. So, I was getting disillusioned, just like you. While I was in London a couple of years ago, I was approached by some people who work for the government.

"They were fed up too – so much so that they offered me a financial package that was too good to turn down, and a guarantee that my safety and liberty would remain intact should this ever get out. Times are hard for everyone, Pat, and money needed to be saved, so for the taxpayer to be paying scumbags like Baker and Clarke tens of thousands of pounds a year … well, it was wrong, and it needed to stop. The recession is wiping us out, and drastic action had to be taken. At first, I was dead against their plans, but it was going to happen with or without me … so in for a penny, in for a pound.

"I was given very strict guidelines to work under and, after a few months, I had a list of people who were, in our opinion, deserving targets for … how can I put it … elimination. The Clarkes and Bakers of this world are of no use to man nor beast, and we were doing society a favour, not to mention saving the good old taxpayer a shedload of money. It was easy, and it was working well for a good twelve months. We've saved millions, Pat."

"What do you mean: twelve months? I thought it started with Carl Baker and Marie Jones a few weeks ago?"

"Oh no, long before them, but I'll get to that in a minute. Be patient, my good man, all will be revealed." Rosey folded one leg over the other. "So, I drew up a list and sent it to London for approval. They were in touch within a week, and of the thirty-eight names I provided, twenty-nine were given the go-ahead. As time has gone on, with the help of my learned friends behind me, we started to work from the list and eliminated them when the opportunity presented itself.

"The beauty of being in the police, and being financed by the government, is that you can get things done very quickly and efficiently – and, most importantly, we can cover our tracks. The first two or three were a little sloppy, but we soon got the hang of it and, to date, of the twenty-nine on our list, we've managed to eradicate twenty-three, with only six remaining until we submit another list of potentials."

"You're fucking deluded," said Pat, shaking his head. "And you make it sound so normal. You're kidding yourself if you think you'll be spared if it all comes out – and it will … trust me, and it will. Do you really think the government will let something like this be linked to them?"

"Pat, stop interrupting me and let me finish, so you have a full understanding of whom and what you're dealing with here. Now, where was I? Oh yes, the list … we've managed to eliminate some of the wasters and save a tonne of money to help the British taxpayer through a very long and difficult recession. But we've had to change our tactics recently, because of your little fuck-ups.

You see, you've unknowingly got involved along the way, and the fucking IPCC have stuck their noses in.

"You being arrested, and the fact Marie Jones survived, caused us all sorts of problems ... and then the files disappeared. You went on the run, and we were going to pin the Clarke and Jones murders on you. We had all the pieces of the puzzle, but you became a real fucking thorn in our side. So here we are, back in control, but we need the files. You said you saw four of the files. You should've read the rest because you'd have seen just how much money we saved the Treasury."

"While you're baring your soul, how did you kill them?" asked Pat.

"Take Carl Baker. You and Kyle dropped him at his sister's house. You may remember, I told you not to arrest him. Arrested and in prison? He was on our list, so we needed him out. I read the job, spoke to you, saw his sister was on nights, and the rest was easy. We went round in the early hours. I knocked on the door in uniform, he opened it, and the boys followed me in.

"We took him to the loft, fixed the rope and tied the noose around his neck. He hung while we were holding his legs and mouth to stop any screams, and when he was dead, we placed the stool on the floor to make it look like a suicide. You asked me to attend the next day, so I finished the paperwork, looked after the Scenes of Crime Officer, and wrote the coroner's report. It was so fucking easy."

"What about Marie Jones? She's still alive."

"Yes – a big mistake, and that's probably where we were sloppy and have brought this on ourselves. Everyone knows

Marie's front door is easy to break into, so we went in the early hours. I parked around the corner and met the other two lads by the side of the flats. We went up the stairs, and I made my way into her flat. It's a shitpit, the smell was awful, and she was out cold on the settee, pissed or high as a kite. We picked her up and went to the balcony. But as we lifted her up, she woke up and it startled us. We dropped her, and she hit her neck and face on the balcony rail, which knocked her out again, so we dropped her over the balcony and left the flat.

"We never thought in a million years that she'd survive but hoped her injuries would eventually kill her. The last thing we were prepared for was her knowing you and telling you it was one of your mates." Rosey smiled smugly. "Well, you certainly read that wrong, didn't you, Pat? It wasn't Kyle she saw when waking up – it was me.

"CID got involved because the doctor was convinced the bruising on her neck was inflicted before the fall. They started the investigation, your name came up, and you were arrested. The doctor was told to phone you. It was a trap but wasn't planned very well, because it was The Ringway Bobbies who were on changeover, and you managed to slip in and out without getting caught.

"So, the finger was pointed at you. You were getting angry about Clarke, and you upset his aunt, you were loud and mouthing off. It was easy for them to believe it was you who killed Clarke, and that you tried to do the same to Marie. Then the way you behaved afterwards, together with your escape, made them even more convinced. We needed you to get caught and sent to jail, to take any attention away from us. We'd let the dust settle and carry on where we left off. I even had the added bonus of the coroner at the Butler boys' inquest giving you a bollocking for your comments over the radio, so of course that all went against you as well."

"The Butler boys – was that you too?" asked Pat in disbelief.

"Oh yes, of course – two birds with one stone. That one was easy. You came in and said they gave you the bird, and while you were on your break with Kate, I made a quick phone call. They never lock their back door, which leads to the park. They fell asleep on the sofa, pissed up, and all we did was put the pan on the hob with the gas on full and walk out. The house went up like a bonfire, and they were no more. You were first on the scene with Kate, and you called up and asked me to join you … and I did. The funny thing is, I hadn't long left their house. But you have to admit, of all the scum we deal with, those two were the absolute pits, and you must be glad they're gone. They gave you a torrid time and abused you at every opportunity."

"What about Larry Bell and Sammy Clarke?"

"Larry Bell? He was easy too, Pat – drunk and high as a kite, just like the rest of them. He was on his way home after leaving Cunningham, so we took him by the arms, frogmarched him to the canal and threw him in. He was so pissed and loaded on heroin, and there was no way he could swim – especially with that big, stupid red jacket filling up with water and weighing him down. Cunningham is on the list too, and in time will be eliminated.

"Now, the delightful Mr Clarke. I had no idea he was drug-free. We picked him up at his house, he answered the door to me, I was in uniform of course, and he was cocky and full of his own self-importance. He thought I was there about the complaint against you! How ironic is that?! So, after an initial barrage of abuse, I let my team in, and we held him down. We injected him with a high dose of seriously potent heroin, threw him unconscious into the van, and dropped him at the garages at the rear of the pub. The dose was so high, and he would've been dead in about two minutes. In and out in less than twenty minutes, and with all the commotion you caused with his lovely aunt and your comments in custody – all caught on camera – it was going to be easy to blame you ... or at least put the suspicion at your door."

Pat's thoughts turned to Kyle. How was he involved? Who was he working for, and how did he end up with the files in his apartment? And, most pertinently of all: where was his body? Pat wasn't sure whether to ask, even though Rosey was telling all ... which begged an even more pressing question: why was he spilling the beans so freely, and what did that mean for Pat? He expected to be executed by these arseholes or framed for the murder of Sammy Clarke, and the attempted murder of Marie Jones. But Marie was alive and would be able to identify Rosey, so she was a risk and, almost certainly, still a target.

While Rosey sat at one of the computers, the other four men checked files. Pat wondered, with dread, what their next move would be. He knew Diane and the girls were safe for now, and that Sarah would have gone back home; but that she'd seen him get bundled into the van at gunpoint.

He started to recall some of the things Rosey had disclosed and, in particular, the witness who put Pat around the corner from Lime Court on the night Marie was hurt; and the following morning, saying it was the same car on both occasions. Pat now knew that Rosey accounted for the first, wholly sinister visit. They both drove a Black Audi A3, and that's what the witness saw … not that it mattered right now.

Rosey returned to Pat, sat in front of him and sipped from a cup of coffee. "What do you think about everything you've heard, Pat?"

"Of all the people it could've been, you were the last I would've suspected. What gets me the most is how nonchalant you were when telling me how and who you murdered. Do you really believe you've done the country a great service and saved the poor old taxpayer millions?"

"Not murder, Pat – it's elimination, and saving the taxpayer money. There's a difference, and they all deserved it."

"No, you're wrong," said Pat, shaking his head. "Marie didn't deserve it. She was booking herself into rehab and trying to move away from Lime Court – that's why my prints were on her letters in the flat. She knew she needed to make changes to her life, and now she'll never walk properly again and will more than likely have brain damage, thanks to you. So, forgive me if I don't subscribe to your way of thinking."

"You're such a fucking hypocrite, Pat," smirked Rosey. "You were the world's worst moaner, and sick to death of her and Lime Court. The hours you spent there, because of her, on Friday and Saturday nights – going to the hospital, waiting for boarding up, and the calls she made to us … every fucking shift we were at her door! So, forgive me if I don't shed a tear for you and your new best friend. Seriously, listen to yourself, for fuck's sake! We've done the world a huge favour, and you know it. And I'll tell you something else: deep down, you must agree with what we're doing."

"Don't kid yourself," said Pat. "I've no allegiance to you and your cause, you fucking Hitler wannabee."

Rosey laughed, standing up and sauntering over to the computer he'd been working at and Pat grimaced as he tried to move his hands, which had become numb, thanks to the cable wires being tied so tightly. Looking down at the pool of blood between his legs, it became painfully clear that if something wasn't done to alleviate the bleeding, he wouldn't be around for very much longer.

"Are you going to let me bleed to death? And my fucking hands are numb. Can you remove these cable ties before my hands fall off? I can't feel them, Rosey."

Rosey looked over at Pat, then addressed two of the men: "You, point a gun at him in case he tries something. And you, cut the cable wires."

The pair doing as Rosey asked, Pat, felt the cable wires being cut. Edging his hands onto his lap, he saw that they'd turned blue and felt the blood rushing back into them. His head felt light and, before he knew it, a faintness engulfed him, sending him crashing forward, knocking him out. Rosey and one of the men carried Pat to the room where the table and chairs were and laid him on the table. Rosey got some bandage from a small first aid box and wrapped it around his head to try and stop the bleeding. With Pat's clothes wet and soaked in blood, Rosey covered him with blankets and left one of the men in the room to guard him with a gun.

Rosey looked at Pat. Even in his current state, Rosey knew that he was an extremely capable individual. He needed the files and, while he had to up the ante to get him talking, he couldn't let him die ... yet. He let Pat sleep for a while to recuperate, puzzled by how he'd managed to move around the city unnoticed. Pat had told him he'd been staying in a hotel and getting about via taxi, but Rosey had his doubts.

Checking Pat's pockets, he had nothing on him – no money, no keys ... nothing. Rosey wondered where his hotel room key was, and why he didn't have any cash on him, supposing he must've been getting help from somewhere. Going through all of the evidence presented to him, he came across the registration of a car seen leaving the area close to Kyle's apartment ... a car that belonged to the woman who'd represented him before he fled. Maybe Pat reached out to her and she was protecting her client. Rosey already had her address, and two of his team had already been to her house, so he called them over.

"When you went to Sarah Flemming's house, did she seem genuine?" he asked Campbell.

"Yes. Why do you ask?"

"She must be Pat's solicitor. Her car was seen leaving the area close to Kyle's apartment, so maybe he's been using her car to move around. We need to look at her again."

Rosey decided Pat had been out for long enough and shrugged him awake, ready to hurl the mug of tea he was holding over his face if he tried anything, while the man guarding him held his gun at the ready.

"Time to wake up, Pat," said Rosey.

Pat's eyes slowly opened. With consciousness came a sudden burst of pain, Pat instinctively placing his palm on the nastier of his wounds, wincing.

"A big, strong man like you moaning about a little bump to the head. You surprise me, Pat."

"Get fucked," growled Pat.

"Bring him to the chairs," Rosey told the man guarding him.

Pat considered trying to make a run for it, but the gun pressed against the back of his cranium forced a rethink. Made to sit in the same chair as before, he looked at the now dry pool of blood on the ground; then glanced up at Rosey, who claimed the seat in front of him, while the other three men joined them.

"I hope you had a good sleep, and that your mind's a little clearer because there have been some developments while you've been snoozing."

"Sounds interesting," said Pat. "Let me guess: the lovely Peter Sutcliffe has joined your little gang? Or maybe that should be Bin Laden?"

"Oh, no," grinned Rosey. "We can do much better than that … Sarah."

Pat did his best to camouflage the flagrant panic coursing through his body, his teeth grinding together.

"That's right – the lovely Sarah. She's going to get another visit, and this time we'll be a little more assertive. Maybe she can tell us where you put the files? What do you think, Pat?"

"You're barking up the wrong tree. Sarah's got nothing to do with it and is the last person I'd go to after making her look stupid, being her client and an escaped fugitive."

"I don't believe you, and your reaction would suggest you're telling lies." Rosey left a pregnant pause, then stared at Pat. "So, we'll have to see, won't we?" He turned his attention to two of the men. "You two, go back and see her. Make sure you get in and have a good look around. If she gives you any shit, bring her here too. And if she's not there, break in."

The two men grabbed a set of keys and made for the exit.

"If you hurt her, I'll fucking kill you!" Pat shouted at them before they disappeared.

"Tut tut, Pat … a little touchy, aren't we? I thought you didn't get her involved. Or maybe she is, and I've touched a nerve?"

"If any harm comes to her …!"

"Yes, Pat, I know," said Rosey. "Start making arrangements for my funeral, shall I?"

Laughing, Rosey returned to his computer. Pat stared at the goon pointing a gun at him, wondering how on earth he could get out of this mess. If they brought Sarah along too and got hold of the files, it was game over – for both of them. He thought of Kyle again, but couldn't figure out why Rosey hadn't probed a little more about him. He'd had the files in his flat, after all, so what was going on?

"Where's Kyle, Rosey?"

Rosey looked up from the computer but ignored the question. "He had the files in the first place, so where did he get them? I bet you were gutted when you found out he'd betrayed you. Where were they originally – at work or in your house?"

"Well, according to you, he's dead, so who gives a shit?"

"I thought he was working with the suits. He never really said much, he was always in your office and acted sneakily around the computer. What was all of that about? Have you two got a secret you'd like to share?"

"Pat, shut up. You've no idea what you're talking about, just to put your mind at rest – not that it's any of your business – I was helping him sort out his new apartment."

"Oh, I get it," Pat smirked sourly. "You wouldn't happen to own it, would you? Financed by that nice little package you couldn't refuse?"

"Bingo! You are catching on, brainbox. That apartment has already gone up by forty grand in the last month. The new boy was looking for somewhere to rent, and I knew the perfect place, but he didn't know it was mine – it belongs to a friend of a friend as far as he's concerned."

Pat found it hard to believe his suspicions had arisen from Rosey renting his apartment to Kyle. He looked at the man he'd once so admired, a surge of anger consuming him as Pat considered how he'd profited from deception. And what of Kate? Did she have anything to do with this, given she'd been drinking wine with Kyle at the apartment? He was even more confused now, but there was nothing he could do about it, staring at a gun.

PULLING UP ON SARAH'S drive, the two men got out of the van and approached her house. While one of them tried to peer inside via a curtain, Campbell looked through the letterbox. Nothing could be seen or heard, so the door was given a good knock. Upstairs in the bedroom, Sarah teased a curtain aside to see the men and their van.

"Oh no, please not again!" she cried, petrified.

The men knocked on the door even harder and longer. Sarah froze for a few seconds, then went downstairs to open it, feeling that if she didn't, they might put it through. Desperately worried about Pat, would her assistance help him? But what if they had sinister intentions? Surely they wouldn't risk creating a scene in a residential area like hers?

Unlocking the door and cautiously opening it, the two men barged in, knocking her to the floor. With both of them in her hallway, she scrambled backwards until her spine hit the first step on the stairs. Campbell grabbed her by her hair, pulling her to her feet.

"Get the fuck off me!" she screamed. "What do you want?!"

Dragged into the lounge, one of the men threw her onto the settee. One sat next to her, while Campbell stood over her.

"No more fucking around!" snarled Campbell, jabbing a finger in her face. "We have your client with us, and he told us you know where the files are ... so where are they, Sarah?"

"I've no idea what you're talking about," she gasped, her eyes welling up. "PC Patrick is not my client anymore, and I don't know anything about any files."

"Well, he seems to think you're still representing him, so for now let's keep it simple. We believe you have some files that belong to us, and we want them back. He told us to come here and that you'll be able to take us to them, so stop fucking us around and do as we ask."

"I don't know what you mean," said Sarah, knowing Pat would never betray her.

"Take a look around," Campbell told his colleague.

Sarah stayed where she was, Campbell staring at her while his partner rooted through her belongings. Beginning with the lounge, he opened cupboard doors and threw items on the floor, before proceeding to the kitchen and repeating the process. A few moments later, he stepped back into the lounge holding a mobile phone, charger and SIM card.

"Who's is this?"

"It's my old phone," said Sarah.

"What make is it and which mobile provider is on the SIM card?" he asked.

"HTC is the manufacturer, but I don't know about the SIM card. I'm useless with tech."

"We'll keep this and see what it tells us a little later on."

He went to the downstairs cupboard and had a rummage around, moving onto the bedroom.

"It's up here!" he shouted from upstairs.

Sarah's stomach knotted. She knew what that meant and, several seconds later, he re-entered the lounge, showing Campbell the box.

"Right, you lying bitch – you're coming with us."

Sarah tried to resist, but they were far too strong for her, marching her out of the house.

"Help me, please!" she screamed at the top of her voice. "Somebody call the police!"

As Campbell covered her mouth with his hand, the other man opened the van, put the files inside, then threw Sarah in the back, where Campbell joined her. Sarah daren't look at him, staring at her feet as the van sped off. She remained in that position for the duration of the journey, barely able to breathe with nerves.

When they arrived at the disused warehouse, Sarah was frogmarched inside. Resisting the urge to cover her mouth and suppress the nauseating medley of blood, sweat and other bodily fluids, she saw Pat sat on a chair, blood saturating his clothes and the bandage on his head.

Pat's heart sank upon seeing Sarah being brought in and the man carrying the brown box – he'd been desperate to protect her, but her life was in the hands of thugs devoid of conscience; and despite his internal protestations to the contrary, who might, quite literally, get away with murder. Breaking free of Campbell, Sarah ran to Pat, hugged him and broke down.

"Are you okay?" she whimpered. "What have they done to you?"

"I've been better," said Pat, holding her close to him, in spite of his aching limbs. "Did they hurt you?"

"They dragged me around a bit, but I'm okay. I'm so sorry. The men forced their way into my house."

"It's okay," said Pat, finding a smile for her. "Don't worry."

"Well well well," said Rosey, picking the box up and stepping towards them. "What have we got here? Crossed the line between the professional and personal? Tut tut tut." He turned to the men who'd just returned. "Where were they?"

"In her bedroom, just sat on the floor."

"Well done. Any problems?"

"She screamed as we left the house. One of her neighbours might've seen and heard something."

"They certainly won't find us here, so not a problem," said Rosey.

"We also found this in one of the drawers. She couldn't tell us where it came from or who it belongs to, but I think it might be Pat's. Weren't they looking for his mobile phone?"

"Yes, they were," smiled Rosey. "Could be interesting."

Pat looked at Rosey, holding his phone. He also had the files and had arranged for Sarah to be kidnapped. And with Pat in a bad way, he had to question how he could've done things differently, where he slipped up ... and what would become of the woman he loved.

"So how long have you two been an item?" asked Rosey, gazing at Sarah. "I assume your boss doesn't know that you're seeing Pat?" Sarah said nothing. Rosey smiled. "No, of course, they don't. Imagine the fallout from that – talk about conflict of interest! Every case the two of you were involved in would have to be reviewed. It'd probably finish your employer ... but as for you, Miss Flemming: assisting a known offender and perverting the course of natural justice ... now, that's some serious prison time."

Sarah clung to Pat, not responding.

"What's the matter? Cat got our tongue?"

"Leave her the fuck alone," snarled Pat.

"Now now, Pat, play nicely. By the way, is this your mobile phone?"

Pat said nothing, staring at Rosey.

"Not keen to talk? Shame. Let's turn it on and see, shall we? Because if it is, we'll have all the pieces of the jigsaw. We can hand you in, you'll be done for the murder of Sammy Clarke, and I'm pretty sure we can pin a few of the others on you too. As for your pretty lady, perhaps I can bend the ear of whichever judge dishes her sentence out. None of us wants to see her in the kind of jail where inmates have the screws under their thumb." He found a particularly sickly smile. "What might happen then?"

"You'll never get away with it," Pat grimaced. "We've got evidence against you and your fucking monkeys. And there's Marie Jones and what she can say. You're crazy. Do you know that? Totally fucking crazy."

"Jones is fucked with brain damage and an alcoholic druggie," sneered Rosey. "Who will they believe – her or us? I mean, seriously, Pat – come on!"

The gun still pointing at Pat, Rosey pulled Sarah from his lap and sat her next to him in a separate chair. Then placed the SIM card and battery into the phone and switched it on.

"Let's see if this is your phone, shall we, Pat? I'm sure it is, and then we'll be able to put you at the scene of Marie's incident. It'll show you at or near Sarah's house, helping to get her sent down. She might even be accused of helping you escape. Now, wouldn't that be cool?"

Pat heard his phone start-up and saw Rosey pressing various keys. A minute or so later:

"Oh, how sweet! A text to Sarah with a kiss next to her name! So little Sophie had your phone. Interesting."

Pat looked at Sarah. It was impossible to deny that his phone was another nail in his coffin, providing evidence to CID and the IPCC, placing him at the hospital and Marie's flat. But with Rosey's talk of jail time, surely that meant he and Sarah wouldn't be murdered by the scumbags who'd humiliated him? Sarah leant over and tried to whisper something to Pat, but was pulled back by the man guarding them.

"Sit still and keep quiet," said Rosey.

He called two of the men over. The trio talked among themselves, Pat unable to hear what they were saying until Rosey raised his voice.

"I don't care! Find him and bring him here. Check the hospitals and go back to his apartment. He can't have just disappeared into thin air."

The two men grabbed some keys and exited the warehouse. It was obvious to Pat that they were discussing Kyle, and he too wanted to know what had happened to his body.

"I need to take a piss," he told Rosey.

Rosey gestured at the man holding the gun, who frogmarched him to an ancient toilet with a cracked, stained seat. From where he stood, Pat could hear Rosey speaking to Sarah:

"Did you read the files?"

"You're a very sick man."

"I didn't ask for your opinion. I asked if you read the files, so just answer the fucking question."

"What difference does it make if I did or didn't?"

"Typical solicitor with a smart mouth, and never a straight answer."

Pat heard a slap echo around the large warehouse, coupled with a scream and the sound of Sarah crying.

"Yes, I read a couple of them, you fucking prick!" shouted Sarah.

"See how easy it is when you put your mind to it? So … what do you think of it all? The money the government's saving you, the taxpayer, by getting rid of all of this scum." He laughed. "Some of whom are your clients – how ironic is that? So, in a way, you're actually losing out on business and, for that, I'm truly sorry. Though I've no doubt it won't be missed, the thousands of scummy wankers still out there, and the amount of money you lot earn."

"I think you need help. This is a slaughter, and you're a murderer, no matter how you try to justify yourself. You must know this will catch up with you and the government eventually. You can't keep something like this a secret. Do you think you're indispensable? Because when it all goes wrong, they'll deny all knowledge of you and throw you to the lions. So do your worst, because you'll get what's coming to you."

Flushing the toilet, Pat felt the gun press against his back as he was walked back into the main body of the warehouse. Sarah was clearly very distressed, her cheek red from the slap; with Rosey stood over her.

"What the fuck are you doing?!" he hollered. "Leave her alone, or I swear I'll snap your neck like a twig!"

"Will you now?" smiled Rosey. "And how do you propose doing that, with a gun pointing at you?"

"I'm okay," said Sarah, placing a hand on her cheek. "Just leave it. He's not worth it."

"No touching," said the suit aiming the gun at Pat, after he wiped Sarah's tears away.

Wanting to ask what exactly had happened to her after he was taken, Pat batted the urge away, glaring at the suit. For the next couple of hours, another of the suits guarded them, Sarah was taken to the toilet, and they were given some food and drink. Pat watched as Rosey and the other man started packing some of the equipment into boxes and crates. Phone calls were made to Rosey, though Pat was unable to hear what was going on. The only thing that seemed to be certain was that they were leaving the location and, most likely, moving their operation to other premises ... with him and Sarah unlikely to join them.

Assuming he was right to think Rosey would indeed hand them in and be hailed as a hero, what would become of Sarah? Was he going to arrest her too and bring her world crumbling down? However, Rosey played it, there would be serious ramifications for her. Of course, this was all guesswork on Pat's part, and he hadn't a clue whether Rosey was playing mind games, with a different agenda to the one he laid out regarding their rather grim futures behind bars. Before he sunk even deeper into his dark musings, the return of the van outside refocused him, the sound of slamming doors and the other pair's footsteps dumping him firmly back in reality.

"Well?" asked Rosey.

"Nothing. His apartment's empty and there have been no admissions at City Hospital or University Hospital across town," came the reply.

"Was his car there?"

"No."

"Oh well, there's nothing we can do for now. Let's get this stuff moved and worry about him later. Load those boxes onto the van and put these two into the other one. Keep an eye on Pat – I want him guarded, and don't get complacent. In fact, put cable ties on them both."

Campbell picked up the ties. "Hands behind your backs," he ordered, Pat and Sarah complying.

He secured their hands while the other suits went about loading the equipment onto the van, the brown box remaining by Rosey's side.

"So … what's the plan now?" asked Pat glowering at Rosey.

"You'll learn your fate soon enough, and that's all you need to know for now. So, sit there and keep quiet while we get this lot together."

Pat and Sarah did just that, watching the warehouse empty, apart from the chairs they were tied to; and the box of files. Rosey picked the box up and walked to the van, placing it on the front seat. He returned to take hold of Sarah, while the man with the gun walked Pat to the van, as the equipment was loaded onto the second van by the other two suits. Forced into the back of the van, the side door was slammed shut, and Pat and Sarah sat down, a gun still pointed at them. Rosey sat as the front seat passenger, Campbell was the driver, and the suit with the gun guarded Pat and Sarah. Rosey gave the thumbs up to the driver of the second van, who pulled away, pausing to speak to Campbell:

"You know what to do."

The van drove off, heading out of the estate towards town. Pat recognised a couple of buildings as he looked through the front side windows. They weren't travelling towards the station; instead, they were heading in the opposite direction. Around fifteen minutes later, nobody had spoken; a silence broken by Campbell:

"We're almost there. Make the call."

Pat watched as Rosey removed a mobile phone from his jacket pocket and dialled a number. The beeps suggested only three numbers were pressed – confirmed when Rosey spoke:

"Police please." Silence for around ten seconds. Then: "My name is Sergeant Rose, I'm currently off-duty and have been told of the whereabouts of a wanted police officer who's on the run."

Pat couldn't hear the reply from the Controller. Rosey continued speaking:

"Yes, that's him ... yes, I've been told he's currently at his girlfriend's house. Her name is Sarah Flemming, and she lives at twenty-four Rowan Drive ... Can you tell the attending officers that I'll meet them there? How far away are the cars? ... Five minutes. Thank you."

A minute or two later, they arrived at Sarah's house, pulling up on her drive. Rosey got out of the van, opened the side door and walked Pat and Sarah to the front door.

"I need your keys."

Sarah handing Rosey her keys, he opened the door and marched them into the lounge, the man with the gun followed. Through the window, Pat could see Campbell drive the van away and park up several houses away. Rosey cut the cable ties from Pat and Sarah.

"Sit down," he told them.

Rosey went into the kitchen and unlocked the back door. Returning to the lounge, he looked at the man holding the gun.

"As soon as they knock on the front door, leave via the back. Climb over the fence and Campbell will be waiting at the top of the road."

The man nodded and stood holding the gun at Pat and Sarah. Almost immediately, there was a knock on the front door.

"Bloody hell, that was quick. Right, off you go – get out of here," said Rosey.

The suit went into the kitchen, opened the back door, shut it behind him, climbed the fence, and was gone. Rosey left the room to answer the door, leaving Pat and Sarah sat on the sofa to await their fate. Rosey opened the door to an officer in uniform; then, as quickly as he'd opened it, tried to slam it shut.

"Open the door, Rosey!" shouted the officer.

Rosey used all of his bodyweight to try and close the door. Hearing the commotion, Pat ran into the hall and threw himself at Rosey, taking him down with a rugby tackle. The front door flew open and in came the officer in uniform, who joined Pat in taking control of Rosey.

To Pat's staggered amazement, Kyle was assisting him. Pat took hold of Rosey's left arm, and Kyle his right, and together they dragged him to the lounge.

"You fucking bastard!" cried Sarah, who booted Rosey in the ribs.

"I thought you were dead!" Pat told Kyle.

"Dead? What the hell, Pat? It was a smack to the head – it takes more than that."

Rosey curled up in a ball, holding his stomach. Sarah went to kick him again but was withheld by Pat, who ushered her away.

"Sarah, no. Just calm down. We're safe now."

He crouched close to Rosey, who had Kyle leaning over him.

"Now what?" asked Pat, looking at Kyle.

"FREEZE! DON'T FUCKING MOVE!"

The suited man appeared at the lounge door. Gun firmly directed their way.

"Campbell saw what happened and called," he told Rosey, who wriggled away from Pat and Kyle.

"Get over there and sit down!" He waved the gun to gesture where they were to sit. "If you move, I'll put a fucking bullet in your head!"

Rosey stood up, clutching his stomach. "Well done. Impeccable timing, I must say. The police will be here any second. Keep an eye on them while I deal with the officers. Then get the cable ties – we'll have to bring them with us."

Rosey strode out of the house and onto the driveway. Giving Campbell the thumbs-up, he gestured at him to stay where he was — waited for a minute or so until a pair of patrol cars showed up, a quartet of officers emerging from them. Rosey produced his warrant card and greeted them at the bottom of the driveway.

"It was me who called it in. I'm Sergeant Rose, and I'm afraid it's a false alarm. My apologies. It was a call with good intent – I was acting on information received. He's not here, but she is and hasn't heard from him since his escape. Sorry for the wasted journey."

Pat listened intently as he and the officers exchanged a few words, but their voices became less clear as Rosey walked them further away from the house. The officers got back into their cars and drove off. Once they were out of sight, Rosey gestured for Campbell to join him. Rosey entered the van and collected some cable ties, re-entering the lounge. With the suit guarding them, Rosey tied Pat, Sarah and Kyle's hands behind their backs.

"Put them in the van," he told the suit. "We'll go back to the warehouse and regroup."

"This will come back on you," Kyle told Rosey. "And bring you down."

"Shut the fuck up. You've caused me unnecessary stress, and stealing my files was a big mistake. It's a pity Pat didn't kill you – it would've saved me from having to do it. Now get up, all of you."

The three of them were marched to the van and thrown in the back, joined by the man with the gun. In the front, Rosey sat with Campbell.

"Back to the warehouse," said Rosey.

"What happened in there?" asked Campbell.

"Pat took me down, Kyle turned up, and they messed me up a bit, while missy back there kicked me in the ribs; though thankfully, Ed came back."

"I saw something was up, so I phoned him to get back in there."

"Well done. That was too close for comfort. Let's get back to the warehouse, and we'll have a rethink, now that boy wonder is back in the equation."

As they travelled back to the warehouse, Kyle kept trying to strike up a conversation with Rosey, but Ed punched him in the stomach every time he opened his mouth, his gun hovering menacingly close to his head. Pat observed wordlessly, Sarah leaning into him. Kyle's appearance seemed to have changed things for them. There was no more talk of handing them in, with a far more sinister fate seemingly awaiting them; summed-up by a phone call made by Rosey:

"Make your way back to the warehouse. There's been an unexpected development. We'll be there in about ten minutes."

And what fun those ten minutes were, all three of them silently locked into inner worlds of fear. When they arrived at the warehouse, Rosey and Campbell got out of the van, opened the side door and let Ed out.

"You three: up you get," said Rosey, as Ed and Campbell as good as threw Pat, Sarah and Kyle out of the van, pushing them into the warehouse.

Ordered to sit in chairs, they did as they were told. Rosey and the two men motioned off towards a small office; far enough away for Pat to attempt conversation with Kyle.

"What the fuck's going on?" he whispered. "What happened after we fought? Where the hell have you been, who are you, and who the fuck do you work for? Because one thing I know for sure is you're no longer a copper."

"I can't have been out long, but when I came to, covered in blood, I went to the hospital, where they glued the cut. I knew there was no point going back to the apartment because they'd be sniffing around, so once I was finished at the hospital, I phoned somebody to come and pick me up."

"Let me guess – Kate," said Pat.

"Yes, Kate. She took me back to hers and cleaned me up."

"I bet she did."

"It's not like that, Pat – don't be so presumptuous. And I am a copper, but I work for the government. I was contacted after my wife's accident, and they recruited me as my six months' sick leave was coming to an end. As far as work was concerned, I'd quit the force, but I moved to the Midlands, and now I'm here."

"But if you work for the government, and they work for the government, what the hell's going on? Who do we trust? I must've screwed-up badly, because I thought you were the bad guy all along ... and still could be, for all I know."

"If I was a wrong 'un, what would I be doing here with you? The Home Office was alerted to the goings-on with Rosey and his crew. I was sent in to infiltrate his team and call in the cavalry when I had the evidence. They do appear to be working for someone in power in the government but, as of now, I don't know who that is."

"How did you get the files?" asked Pat.

"I needed somewhere to live. I was going to stay with my sister for a while, but thought better of it – we're tight, but I didn't want to risk any friction between us. I mentioned it to Rosey when I first met him the week before I started. He told me he had a friend who owns a couple of apartments near to town that he was looking to rent out, so I had a look, loved the gaffs, and agreed to rent one for six months. The floors in the apartment needed to be finished off, and I had to pick up a couple of packs of flooring from Rosey's house.

"He gave me his house keys when we were on nights, and I had a good look around. He probably expected me to go into the garage, but I went into the house and had free reign. After a few minutes, I found the files in the spare room he uses as an office. They were hidden under a pile of books and DVDs. I had a look and couldn't believe what I'd found. I took them to my apartment, and then it all kicked off with you and Marie Jones. It's been mayhem ever since, but he had no idea I took the files."

"Not true, I'm afraid. I told Rosey I found the files in your apartment, though he did seem genuinely surprised. It all makes so much sense now." Pat coughed up a globule of blood that he spat on the ground. "So, when we were down the road, near the canal, and you told me you'd explain everything, you were actually genuine? I thought you just wanted the files for you and the suits."

"Yes, Pat, I was going to tell you everything, because I knew you could be trusted, but it went horribly wrong."

"Shit, Kyle, I'm so sorry. But how was I to know? I mean, Rosey of all people." He shook his head. "How did you find us at Sarah's house?"

"Kate ran the car registration through, and it came back as Sarah's. She also told me that you two are an item."

"Did she now?" said Pat. "I have to ask ... your martial arts skills ... I've seen them before. I used to run some courses, and you look as if the military taught you – am I right?"

"Yeah. I was a Royal Marine for seven years, then moved to a different department for seven years. I'd had enough by then and joined the police."

"SAS?" asked Pat.

Kyle nodded.

"I knew it." Pat turned to Sarah, who stared at her lap. "I said he was military, didn't I?"

"Sure – you told me. But we've got a more pressing problem. Namely: what's going to happen to us? There's no way we're leaving here in one piece. Not now that Kyle's here. If it's a choice between going to prison and becoming another of Rosey's statistics, I'd rather be put inside."

Pat looked at Rosey and the two men, who chatted amongst themselves. "Any ideas, Kyle?"

"We need to get hold of one of the guns. I can get out of these ties, but it'll take time, and you'll have to follow my lead. I appreciate you're a bit of a mess, but between us, if we get this right, we might be able to get out of here. Are you okay? You look like death warmed up."

"Fuck you very much," smiled Pat. "Yeah, I'm okay."

He looked at Kyle, who rolled his shoulders as he rubbed the ties against the wooden chair. Pat watched as Kyle continued his odd little dance, then felt a sickeningly familiar sense of dread:

the other van pulled up outside. The other pair of suits entered the warehouse, joining Rosey, Campbell and Ed. Within seconds, an argument broke out among them, though Pat was unable to decipher its contents.

"If we get out of here, who are you going to call? Will your lot come and do the necessary here?" he asked.

"Yeah, they'll come. But we need the files more than ever, and if Rosey gets away with them, there's no tangible evidence, and we're in big trouble."

"Tell me something I don't know," said Sarah, her voice drenched in irony.

"How long has this been going on?" asked Pat. "He admitted that they murdered the Butler brothers, which was in July – four months ago."

"No idea, but one thing's for sure: they're going to kill a lot more if we don't stop him and his hench mob."

"Are you still employed by the police, or are you a government employee? Who pays your wages?"

"Pat, for god's sake, leave him alone! Let him try and get the ties off," said Sarah.

"Sorry, but I need to know."

"Well, wait. There'll be plenty of time for all of that later, so stop talking," said Sarah, giving Pat a look, as Kyle gained momentum, furiously rubbing his wrists against the back of the chair.

"Right, you lot: time to go," said Rosey as he walked over to them.

"Where to this time?" asked Pat.

"No more questions," snapped Rosey. "I'm sick of the sight of you and her ... and boy wonder, of course. We've made a decision, and that's all you need to know. Ed, come over here and keep an eye on this lot."

Ed walked over, holding the gun. Rosey paced up to the other three suits, the four of them leaving the warehouse for the rear yard, where both vans were parked.

"Listen, Ed, these ties are cutting off my blood supply," asked Kyle. "I can't feel my fingers, and one of them's cutting into my bone. Can you at least readjust them for me?"

Ed strode up to Kyle. Stooping to his haunches to look at the ties, Kyle broke free, spun quickly around and hit him with an uppercut that moved with such pace and power that it sent him flying. Front kicking him to the stomach, Ed dropped the gun; but as Kyle moved to grab it, Ed took hold of Kyle's leg, pulling him back. Ed got to his feet and punched Kyle hard on the side of the face, Pat and Sarah looking on hopelessly as the two men fought for the gun.

Kyle lunged at Ed, hitting him in the stomach, but Ed seized Kyle and threw him over his shoulder with a Judo-style move, Kyle landing with a thud that prompted a shriek. Ed went to pick the gun up, but Kyle swept both of his feet from under him, Ed landing on top of him, the pair rolling around, momentarily outdoing the other.

Pat stretched out his leg to try and reach the gun, but it edged out of reach as Kyle and Ed flung each other around. Grabbing Kyle in a headlock, Ed yelled as Kyle sent fierce hooks crashing into his ribs. Releasing Kyle, Ed threw a punch at his face.

Blocking it, Kyle threw Ed over his hip, letting him fall to the ground. Rushing over to the gun, Kyle grasped it, pointing it at Ed.

"Get down on your knees, you motherfucker!" said an out of breath Kyle.

"Don't do anything stupid," said Pat. "We need him."

Ed sunk to his knees, gulping air down in deep, voluminous breaths.

"Move, and I'll blow that fucked-up brain of yours apart," Kyle warned as Ed lay on the floor, exhausted.

Kyle rushed to Pat and, using the end of the gun, broke the ties, then freed Sarah, who virtually collapsed in Pat's arms. Gripping Ed's ankles, Kyle dragged him towards the warehouse entrance and left him there.

"Don't move," he told Ed.

Standing near the door that led to the car park, Kyle saw Rosey and the other three men transferring equipment from one van to the other.

"ROSEY!" Ed shouted at the top of his voice.

Kyle turned swiftly around, flooring a rising Ed by striking him to the side of his head with the butt of the gun, putting him out. Rosey and the other three stopped what they were doing, treading towards the warehouse door and producing weapons from their jackets.

"They're coming, go back inside," whispered Kyle to Pat and Sarah. "In here."

Pointing at the office near the entrance, the trio darted inside. Rosey was first to re-enter the warehouse, finding the chairs empty and Ed sprawled out on the ground in front of him. As the other three appeared, Kyle pointed the gun at one of them, shooting him in the shoulder. He fell to the ground, shouting, clutching his shoulder, Rosey and the other two suits opening fire. Down on one knee, Kyle fired at Campbell, hitting him in the leg. Campbell fell but kept on firing at Kyle; as Rosey backed off.

The other two moved forward firing their guns, missing Kyle, who sent a bullet tearing into Campbell's chest, his dead body thumping to the ground. Rolling away from his position, Kyle fired again, and his precision shot flying through the other man's head, blood fountaining from the wound. Spying Rosey running towards the rear entrance, Kyle span round, hearing the suit with the injured shoulder shuffling around behind him, gun in hand. Before he had the chance to use it, Kyle shot him between the eyes. Pat and Sarah emerged from the office as Rosey escaped via the back entrance.

"Rosey's had it on his toes," said Kyle. "Come on!"

They ran out of the warehouse as the black van shot out of sight. Sprinting towards the blue one, which still had its keys in the ignition, Pat jumped into the driver's seat and started the engine, speeding off in pursuit after Kyle leapt into the passenger's seat, with Sarah in the back.

"We have to stop him and get those files!" Kyle bellowed.

Pat accelerated, reaching the end of the estate. Looking either side of him, he saw the black van disappearing into the distance.

"There he is!" shouted Kyle.

Swinging a right, Pat hit the accelerator and followed Rosey, who was a couple of hundred yards ahead. Hitting close to eighty miles per hour, Pat weaved in and out of traffic amid a flurry of horns. Some fifty yards ahead, Rosey clipped a parked vehicle overtaking a slower car. The traffic lights a few metres forward changed to red, but Rosey sped through them, causing vehicles to skid and stop. Two cars crashed together in a head-on collision. Pat hit the brakes to avoid joining them, cranking up the speed as he manoeuvred around the one blocking his path. Sarah screamed, and Kyle held onto his seatbelt.

"Sorry," Pat apologised. "Hold on tight!"

He kept his foot on the accelerator and sped towards Rosey, who swerved left and right as Pat tried to get alongside him.

"Kyle, shoot at his tyres! We need to stop him before somebody gets killed!" Pat yelled.

"I've only got one bullet left, and we might need that if we stop him," Kyle shouted. "He's still got a gun remember."

"Shit! That's all we need."

Joining a dual carriageway, Rosey floored the van, flashing his headlights and sounding his horn. With Pat right behind, they continued to weave in and out of traffic; and, as the road narrowed to one lane, Rosey flew forward, scraping other vehicles as he overtook at pace.

"Pat, don't lose him!" Kyle screamed. "We need those fucking files!"

"I know, but I can't get close to him!"

He glanced in the rear-view mirror to see Sarah in bits. The road was widening again, so Pat speedily overtook the vehicles blocking his path. Rosey tried to make a third lane, Pat trailing in his slipstream, hitting ninety miles per hour. Entering a built-up area, Rosey went even faster, pedestrians leaping out of the way as he hurtled past. Pat looked in his side mirror and saw flashing blue lights, their sirens wailing.

"Shit, that's all we need – we've got company."

"Just keep going!" Kyle thundered.

Pat increased his speed in a bid to match Rosey's, but Rosey spun around to drive into oncoming traffic. Drivers furiously sounded their horns, pulling over to let him pass, while Pat dropped back a little. A helicopter chugged overhead, and Pat knew that there was no way out of this. The smell of the burning clutch filled the van, Pat reckoning they had a few minutes at most before it gave way.

The road ahead opening up into the countryside, Rosey accelerated again; but as the road bent to the right, the van sped off-road, Pat slamming on the brakes. Grinding to a halt in a cloud of smoke, he reversed, driving around the police car behind, despite it trying to block him off.

Swerving past another pair of police cars, accidentally clipping one of them, Pat stopped at the bend, plumes of smoke coming from the field. He, Kyle and Sarah shot out of the van and ran towards the van Rosey had been driving. Its front end embedded in a tree, flames started to take hold.

"Get the files before it goes up in flames!" screeched Pat.

With Kyle and Sarah pulling at the back doors to the van, Pat ran to the front. Blood gushing from his mouth, Rosey was slumped over the steering wheel, and the engine block had almost entered the cabin, which looked to have created a tomb for him. Pat tried to pull the driver's door open to get Rosey out, but it was too badly damaged. Picking up a rock, Pat smashed the window and tried to pull Rosey from the wreck, but his legs were trapped, and the steering wheel was crushing his chest. A pair of officers joined Pat in trying to pull the door open.

"Hold on!" Pat shouted, the heat emanating from the van almost too much to bear.

"I'm going nowhere, Pat," Rosey sputtered, struggling to breathe. "It's over for me."

The other officers sprayed fire extinguishers, grabbed from the boots of their cars, to try and douse the flames that spewed from the front of the van.

"Why do it, Rosey?" asked Pat, reaching for his hand. "Was it worth it?"

Rosey looked at Pat and smiled. He took a shallow breath, then spoke: "Getting that scum off the streets was worth every penny we saved. And it's not over yet."

The spent fire extinguishers lying on the ground, the officers restrained Pat, pulling him back from the van.

"What do you mean, it's not over?" cried Pat, who glanced to his side to see Kyle holding Sarah back, the box of files at their feet and the van's back doors gaping open, belching smoke. Looking back at Rosey, he was all but obscured by the increasingly ferocious blaze.

"There are forty-three police forces in England and Wales," he smirked. "You work it out! We're everywhere, but you fucked it up, and now I'm a dead man."

A chilling scream filled the ether as flames started consuming Rosey's trapped, crumpled body. Pat took a step back as Sarah shrieked at him:

"GET AWAY – IT'S GOING TO EXPLODE!"

But as Pat turned, he was unable to see the gun in the Sergeant's hand, and barely felt the bullets Rosey fired as they entered his body, which hit the ground. There was no pain or panic. To the contrary, he was filled with serenity as the officers dragged him away from the van.

Pat felt himself floating, the officers' words muting as they hauled him further away from the van, which exploded into a fireball.

"Oh, God – no!" cried Sarah. "PAT – NO!"

Sarah was crying uncontrollably as she cradled Pat's head in her lap. As Pat's eyes closed, Kyle looked on helplessly while holding the box of files.

ABOUT THE AUTHOR

Born and bred in Birmingham, where Elimination is set, Mark Sexton
spent fifteen years serving as a police officer before retiring with
PTSD, aged 45, due to the horrendous events he witnessed while in
the job. Prior to joining the police force, he was a county court
certificated bailiff for eight years. Now aged 52, and the father of two
daughters, Mark spends part of each year in Thailand, where his
girlfriend lives.

Lightning Source UK Ltd.
Milton Keynes UK
UKHW020850130721
387083UK00007B/84

9 781913 142124